The Sleighriders

Other Books
by Jude Thompson

Fiction

The Mouse and the Microlight

The Stowaways

Non-Fiction

A Red Waterproof Jacket

Jude Thompson

The Sleighriders

Publisher

Jude Thompson

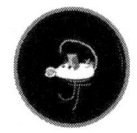

Copyright * Jude Thompson 2017

The right of Jude Thompson to be identified as the author of the work has been asserted by her in accordance with the Copyright, Designs and Patents Act 1988

This book is sold subject to the condition that it shall not,by way of trade or otherwise, be lent, resold, hired out, or otherwise circulated without the publishers' prior consent in any form of binding or cover other than that which it is published and without a similar condition, including this condition, being imposed upon the subsequent purchaser.

Jacket design by Jude Thompson

Fortune favours the brave

Virgil

I
Christmas Castle

Petal let out a small sigh of exasperation and shoved a strand of dark hair back behind an elvish ear.

'What's up?' asked Zeb, coming over to sit on the hay bale next to her. She was frowning with intense concentration and scraping determinedly at the bottom of a small round tin with the corner of a rag. A red leather reindeer harness, adorned with silver bells, lay across her lap. She didn't look up when he spoke.

'Run out of polish, and I only had two more of Ru's bells to do,' she said, frowning and digging insistently in the bottom of the tin.

'No more in the cupboard?'

'No, this was the last one.'

'Never mind, there's no rush. You can pop up to the metal-work shop and ask Fynn for some more. Old 'Shiny-Nose's harness isn't desperate anyway. The weather report is excellent so he won't be flying this year.'

Zeb was pleased at the way Petal took her work so

seriously, far more intensely in fact than the elf-lads. Everything had to be perfect. And she showed an amazing sense of responsibility for a thirteen year old. He had been stable manager at Christmas Castle for years and in all that time he had never ever had an elf-girl wanting to work in the stable. He had to admit he'd been doubtful at first, it wasn't ... well ... traditional. But she had just about nagged him to death, and in the end he had agreed to give her a trial. He had told her he couldn't make exceptions. She would have to do everything the lads did, which included lugging bales and shovelling muck. He wouldn't forget her reply: 'Anything they can do I can do ... just as well.' He'd had a sneaky feeling that she'd wanted to finish that sentence with *better* and suddenly changed her mind. No matter, she had without doubt proved herself a worthy stable-hand in her first year as a young trainee.

'Yes, but if the weather did change,' she was saying, 'I couldn't have Ru going off leading the sleigh with half his bells tarnished. And it's always good to have a clean harness as a spare, isn't it?' She looked up at Zeb earnestly with those huge violet eyes. She was going to be a beautiful young elf woman in a few years time, although looks seemed very low on her list of priorities at the moment. As usual she was in her old, over-sized, red plaid stable jacket, somebody's cast-off, with sleeves that were too long, grubby jeans, and muck-caked work boots. All the elves had gradually converted to modern clothes. Petal pushed back more strands of dark hair that had escaped from her ponytail, and rubbed absent-mindedly at an itch on her nose. Her fingers left a small trail of dark polish. 'I'll go get some more right now,' she said, jumping up off the bale and waving the empty tin at Zeb. He smiled at her enthusiasm as she dashed off.

Petal sprinted across the courtyard, as fast as it was possible to sprint in the deep snow. Winter was wearing her softest coat of sparkling white under a speedwell-blue sky. It was December the twenty-third, and Zeb was right, the weather was going to be great for the Christmas delivery. Inside, the castle was a hive of activity as everyone prepared for tomorrow night, the biggest night of the year, and the climax of a years work. Wonderful aromas were wafting from the kitchen and mingling with the sweet scent of the pine and cedar boughs, which adorned beams and framed windows. Petal loved the warm festive atmosphere.

She ran lightly up the stairs and along the passageways to the metalwork shop, and pushed open the door. Inside it was noisy with the sound of machines and other tools as elves worked on various projects. Fynn, the workshop manager, was nowhere to be seen. She knew where the polish was kept, maybe she should just go and get some? As she stood in the doorway, undecided, a young elf a couple of years older than her came out of a store-room. He saw her and immediately came across.

'Hi Petal,' he said, with a smile, 'Can I help?'

Her heart quickened ever such a little. 'Oh ... Hi Aleron ... um, yes, I need some more silver polish.' She showed him the empty tin.

'No problem, I'll get you some.' He went back to the store-room and returned a few minutes later. He handed her the new one. 'There you go. So how's it going with the stable job then?'

Petal eyed him cautiously. Was he really interested? Or, like all the others, was he just winding her up ready to crack some stupid joke? She wasn't sure.

'I love it,' she said, a little defensively, 'I've never wanted to do anything else.' She knew a lot of the elves thought she was odd, wanting to do an elf-guy's job. She had taken enough teasing over the past year. The guys cracked jokes and the girls whispered and giggled when they thought she wasn't looking.

'Hard work though?' said Aleron.

He was way taller than she was. She had to look up to him. She loved the old denim jacket he was wearing. And the way he wore his dark hair, long and tied back with that green scarf. The trend with most of the guys these days was to have short hairstyles.

'Bales are a bit heavy sometimes,' she said, 'but if I can't lift them I can roll them. Where there's a will there's a way.' It was said with the slightest tilt of her chin. Aleron decided she must have a lot of will because she was only about five feet two inches tall and the bales were pretty darned big. He had suddenly come to notice her more in the last year. Maybe because of her un-elf-girl appearance. In fact she dressed more like an elf-guy, forever in those baggy stable clothes, which somehow didn't fit with such a strikingly pretty face. A face that today had a dark smudge of polish on its nose.

'It's great when you're learning, and working with stuff you enjoy,' he said, wondering if she knew about her nose, 'I always wanted to work in here with all the different metals. Fynn's a great teacher.'

Petal understood his enthusiasm. 'Yes, I had to nag poor old Zeb something wicked to give me a trial. He kept on about it not being a suitable job for girls. I don't see why not, if that's what they want to do - as long as they're able to do it. Actually I think he's quite pleased with me.'

'Good for you,' Aleron grinned. He thought it took guts to do what she'd done.

'Well thanks for the polish. I must get back and clean the rest of Rudolph's harness. See you later.'

'Don't work too hard,' he called. He got a quick grin and a wave as she hurried off down the corridor.

The snow sparkled, and squeaked under her boots as she made her way back to the stables. The tin of polish felt warm in her hand. She thought about Aleron, and how serious, and intense he was ... and cute! Like her, he was full of enthusiasm about his work. A movement near the castle gate broke her train of thought. A white rabbit. A snowbun, and a tired looking one at that, making heavy weather of the small drifts. She changed direction and went to meet it.

'Frisk!' She recognised him as soon as he got closer. He was one of the snowbuns from the warren on the edge of Pine Copse, a few miles away, on the far hill. 'Are you okay? What's happened?'

'Oh Petal, I'm sorry to be a nuisance, but it's not for me, I've come for Moonbeam. She's not very well. She has a cough and it just won't go away. I wondered if Elestyal may be able to give me a little something for her ... one of his potions?'

'I'm certain he will,' said Petal. 'We'll go and see him at once. But how are your babies?'

'Good, they're all good, and growing fast. And a bit too full of energy for Moonbeam's liking at the moment, especially Iceace! He's wanting out of the burrow already. It's such a worry when they're so young.'

'You have four don't you?'

'Yes, but of course Crystal, Leaf, and Lickety, being girls, are far less boisterous and far more patient.'

'Boys are definitely a pain!' laughed Petal, 'Come on, we'll go and see what Elestyal can find among his wizard's potions. And then I'll see if I can give you a lift home. You look tired.'

Petal took Frisk through the castle kitchen and down the back stairs to Elestyal's room. Unusually, the door was shut. Petal knocked.

'Just a minute!' The voice sounded somewhat out of breath. Then after a few seconds, 'Okay, you can come in now.'

Petal opened the door. They were greeted by a fat, red-suited, white-bearded figure who was breathing heavily and sweating. Frisk stopped in his tracks and gaped at the vision in red.

'Ah, sorry to keep you. I was having a bit of a tussle with the suit. Had to try it on. It's a bit tight. Must get Bizz to let it out a couple of inches. Now, Miss Petal, and my dear friend Frisk, what can I do for you?'

Frisk just kept staring. It was a few seconds before Elestyal suddenly twigged.

'Oh my goodness. You've never seen me like this before have you? It is me underneath this lot.'

'Your voice is the same,' said Frisk cautiously, waggling one long ear.

Petal was giggling, 'It really is him Frisk. Honestly.'

Elestyal pointed at himself, 'I have to wear this outfit every Christmas Eve when we do our delivery. It's part of the tradition when I carry out my duties as St Nicholas.' He raised his hands and then patted the protruding girth, 'What do you think?'

'I think you've been eating a lot since I saw you last,' said Frisk.

Elestyal started to laugh. 'Petal, kindly give me a hand with these boots would you. I can't sit around like this for the rest of the day.' He flopped backwards onto the bed and Petal, with much tugging, managed to pull the boots off. A few minutes later after a deal of huffing and puffing the red suit, complete with fat belly, was back on its hanger beside the one-piece hat and white beard combo.

'Now I know you!' said Frisk, looking up at the wiry old wizard with the grey beard. Underneath his suit Elestyal had been wearing his normal faded green dungarees and a patched pink shirt. 'I must say that 'outfit' as you call it ... well, it's quite astonishing. You were very well hidden.'

'Yes,' said Elestyal, 'And to be honest I'm glad I only have to wear it once a year. It's what you might call ... cumbersome!' He dabbed at his brow with his handkerchief, still sweating slightly from the exertion. 'Well, now that I'm back to normal, how can I help you?'

Petal spoke first, 'Frisk has come for a little medicine for Moonbeam. She has a cough that won't go away. I said I was sure you could help.'

Elestyal looked at Frisk, 'How long has she had it?'

'Two weeks maybe, and she gets very tired too, although I suppose that's natural with four young ones.'

'Let's see what we can find.' He went to a tall cupboard and lifted a box off the top shelf. It was full of little bottles and boxes and jars, of all shapes and sizes, each one containing some sort of remedy, powder or potion. He looked through them for a few minutes and picked out two small bags of herbs. 'Here, this should do the trick. It should have the cough cleared up in no time. And this is a little tonic for tiredness. Tell Moonbeam to take some of each every day.' He handed the two small cloth bags to Petal, at the same time thinking Frisk didn't look a hundred percent himself. 'You have a little of that tonic too,' he added, 'And maybe one of our kind young elves could find time to give you a lift home.'

'I'll take him,' said Petal quickly. 'I'll just check with Zeb first.'

Frisk thanked Elestyal and he and Petal went off to the barn. Zeb was nowhere to be found.

'No matter,' said Petal, 'I'm sure he won't mind if I take you home.' Besides, she loved the idea of riding Smooch, her favourite reindeer, over to Pine Copse on such a brilliant day. She would finish her work when she returned. She threw the colourful blanket over Smooch's back and then saddled him while he nuzzled her lovingly.

'Come on Smoochy,' she said. The three of them walked out into the yard where she lifted Frisk up first and set him on the front of the saddle. He teetered nervously while Petal prepared to mount. She swung herself up keeping him in front of her, holding him safe with one hand, her reins in the other.

'I've forgotten something!' said Frisk, suddenly skewing around and looking up at her, 'I meant to tell Elestyal that we have heard rumours just recently!'

'Rumours? What sort of rumours?'

'Well it sounds crazy, but word has passed down, whispers from our cousins up north, they say *trolls* have been seen!'

Petal frowned, 'Gosh! I thought those creatures were supposed to have left these lands years ago, and moved to foreign parts across the water.'

'I thought so too,' said Frisk.

'I'll make sure to tell Elestyal when I get back.'

Frisk looked concerned. 'Don't forget.'

It was windy as they crossed the open plain, quite bitter. Petal was glad she was bundled up in her warmest clothes. She pulled her old woolly hat down over her ears and held tight to Frisk who was rather undecided about this alien way of getting from A to B. Smooch made light of the snow as they cantered on, weaving through the drifts that the wind had carved, his long legs eating up the ground.

Eventually they arrived at Pine Copse. The warren was in a bank at the edge of the trees. Petal dismounted and

Frisk jumped lightly to the ground.

'Thank you Petal. I must admit I was very tired at the castle.'

'It was no trouble,' said Petal. She took the two small bags of medicine out of her pocket and handed them to him. There was an understanding between the elves and all the wild creatures, and always had been. 'I hope Moonbeam is better soon, and do give her our best wishes,' she said as she mounted Smooch again. Frisk bade her farewell and watched her ride away. What wonderful folk the elves were, he thought. Then he headed down into the warren to his family.

Frisk heard Moonbeam before he saw her. Iceace was obviously causing trouble again judging by the conversation drifting along the run.

Moonbeam: 'Side-kicks are *not* meant for *in* the burrow. Save them for when you go up to the outside. I've had enough of it Iceace. That's the third time you've kicked one of your sisters!'

Iceace: 'Sorry Ma, (not sounding sorry at all), but when *can* I go up there then?'

Moonbeam: 'I've already told you! When Pa is ready to take you, and not before. Jolly well be patient till then.'

Iceace: 'Why can't *you* take me *now*?'

Moonbeam: 'Will you stop pestering! Haven't I told you already about the dangers up there? Do you want to end up in rabbit-heaven, before you've lived? Don't you care about the thought of being eaten up by a fang-toothed weasel, or a lynx? Or foxes? Or great birds that drop out of the sky? Not to mention a gulo-gulo!'

'A *goolio what*?'

'A gulo-gulo ... a wolverine. Gulo-gulo is the ancient name. It's the most savage predator in the forest.' Moonbeam started coughing a little rasping cough.

Iceace: 'But *please* Ma, can't we just go up for a minute?'

Frisk had heard enough. He hopped into the den and frowned at Iceace who went suddenly quiet.

'Enough Iceace! You're wearing us all out with your impatience. Your Ma isn't well ... although I doubt you've noticed. You're too busy thinking of yourself, and what you want. If I hear any more from you about wanting to go up to the outside I shall box your ears and keep you down here even longer. Is that understood?'

'Yes Pa,' said the young snowbun sulkily.

'It's only for your own good that you haven't been allowed to go up yet.' Frisk drew a breath. 'You are a rabbit,' he said sternly, 'A Snowbun, and always be proud of it. Our greatest attribute is our speed and agility, but you're still a bit young. You must be ready to run very fast before you go up to the outside.'

'But I *can* run fast Pa,' whined Iceace. Then, seeing the look on Frisk's face he turned around and loped quickly away down the burrow, muttering something about boring.

'Boring but safe,' called Moonbeam to his departing tail.

Frisk gave her Elestyal's potions. 'This is for your cough, and this is something to perk up your energy.'

'It's that little perisher that tires me out,' she sighed, 'Maybe he is ready to go up to the outside. He's amazingly strong for his age. I don't think we've ever had such a strong and determined kit ever. But it's not just about strength ... I worry about how he wants to rush into everything. He needs to learn to think, and look before he leaps.'

'I'll take him up in a couple of days,' said Frisk, 'and run some of his pent-up energy off him. Give you a break. You go and lie down now and rest. And take that medicine.

Petal rode back towards the castle. It looked so pretty in the distance with the sun on it. All sparkly ice-blue with its tall frosted turrets like pointy wizard's hats. A raven called loudly somewhere behind her. Smooch faltered, stopped, and swung his head. His ears were pricked and his gaze intense, as though he had caught wind of something behind them. Petal turned in the saddle and looked back towards Pine Copse, suddenly recalling what Frisk had told her about the whisperings in the wild. The thought of trolls gave her a little chill. But then lots of rumours reached the ears of the elves. She felt sure this must be just that - a rumour. There was nothing to be seen near the copse. It all looked normal. 'Just a silly old raven, Smoochy,' she said, pulling her jacket more closely about her. 'Come on, let's get home.' She clucked her tongue and the reindeer picked up his pace. Her stomach was telling her she was late for lunch.

By the time Petal got back it was well after lunch. She quickly put Smooch in his stable and fed him, then hurried into the castle to find some food. Skyler, the chief kitchen elf, raised a disapproving eyebrow at her grubby appearance as she slid into a chair at the table. She noticed the look.

'I'm re-ally sorry Skyler,' she wheedled, 'I had to ride all the way to Pine Copse this morning to take Frisk back. He came to get medicine from Elestyal, for Moonbeam, she has a cough. And he didn't seem too well either. I've only just got back.' She proceeded to flash him her sweetest smile.

Skyler's disapproval evaporated like the steam from one of his saucepans. 'What would you like?' he asked, shaking his head in feigned resignation. 'How about soup and a sandwich?'

'Ooh Yes!'

As she ate, she watched Skyler and Perks making mince pies. Perks, who was head-gardener in the summer, and kitchen helper amongst other things in the winter, was the oldest elf in the castle. He had been keeping a very interested beady eye on Petal for a while now. He liked her style, and the way that the criticism of her taking an elf-guy's job hadn't deterred her at all. Now he watched with amusement as she downed her soup and started devouring her sandwich in the most unladylike bites. He couldn't help grinning.

'Hungry then?'

Petal loved Perks. He was like the Dad she had never had.

'Mm!' she mumbled, through cheese and tomato.

'Helps if you chew it.'

'Mm ... starving ... guess what ... '

'You've decided you want to be a sleighrider as well as a stable-hand?'

'No ... but hey! ... *that's* not a bad idea at all!'

Perks groaned, 'It is a very *bad* idea. And I never suggested it!' He didn't like the way her eyes had suddenly lit up.

'Well actually, what I was going to say was that Frisk told me about a rumour this morning and I have to tell Elestyal.'

Perks and Skyler both looked at her expectantly.

Both of her cheeks were now doing hamster impressions following another huge bite of sandwich. They waited. She swallowed.

'Frisk said there are whisperings of *trolls* up north.'

'Humph,' grunted Skyler, 'I know the snowbuns message network is pretty good, but trolls? ... that's crazy.'

Perks scratched his head. 'Does seem like a most unlikely story. Every single band of them headed for foreign lands a hundred years ago.'

'I read about them in school once, and they looked pretty scary,' said Petal.

'Scary is an understatement,' muttered Perks, 'They're just meanness on legs. Murdering savages. Nothing more.'

Petal swallowed the last bite of sandwich, 'I'll go and give Elestyal Frisk's message anyway. I promised him I wouldn't forget.' She got up and put her dishes away. 'See you later for a mince pie.'

'If I save one for you Miss cheeky!' called Skyler.

Perks chuckled, 'That one's going to be trouble,' he said as Petal disappeared. Then his expression took on a more serious tone. The mention of trolls, however unlikely any truth in the rumour, had unsettled him.

2
The Sleighriders' Draw

It was twelve noon and there was a tremendous buzz of nervous excitement in the great hall. Everyone awaited Elestyal who was due to start the annual Christmas Eve meeting. The progress meeting was always held at the same time each year. With only twelve hours to go to the Christmas delivery it was important to make sure that all departments were on schedule. The nervous anticipation however had nothing at all to do with the state of progress.

At last Elestyal arrived, greeting them with a big wave as he hurried up onto the makeshift stage. Under his arm he carried a wooden chest which he set down carefully on the table. It was made from rich, dark wood, a beautifully crafted piece, hand-carved with moons and stars, owls and bats, and other creatures of the night. In the top was a wide slot. He started fishing around in his dungarees pockets, of which there were many, for the key. To everyone's relief he eventually found it in the very last one. After inserting it into the lock he turned to face his audience, adjusted his old denim cap, embroidered with leeks, and bowed ceremoniously. An enormous cheer went up.

'Good day! Good day!' he called, casting sparkly blue eyes full of energy around the great hall. 'Thank you all for coming. First of all I would like to check on progress, and then we'll get on to what I know you're all waiting for.' Excited chatter broke out immediately. Elestyal held up his hand. 'First the reports.' He pulled a piece of paper from a pocket and unfolded it, then started to pat other pockets for his glasses. Elves groaned in frustration. 'Ah! Here we are.' He balanced the spectacles on the end of his nose and peered at the first name on the list. 'Gift wrapping ... Jem?'

Jem raised his hand. 'Right on schedule,' he called, 'Everything in so far is finished and wrapped in our finest paper, with ribbons and bows and tinsel too.'

'Thanks Jem. Good work. What about Christmas lists? Peppi?'

Peppi was standing just down at the edge of the stage. 'All checked off Elestyal. Everything was in stock and all lists were passed to stores some time ago for order filling.' Peppi looked pleased with himself.

'Excellent work. What about stores? How are you doing Lanri?'

'We're holding our own,' called Lanri looking tired. He

had the biggest job of all, in charge of filling Christmas lists, which seemed to get longer every year. 'We could do with a few extra pairs of hands this afternoon.'

'Done,' said Elestyal. There was a pause as he started to check his list again.

'You'll be needing some reindeer I suspect!' called a voice.

'And a sleigh maybe!' called another.

Laughter rippled around the room.

'Yes, yes! Okay you two! Take pity on a wizard who's getting on in years. I assume we have some reindeer ... and a sleigh ... and that they're ready?'

Cries of 'Of course!' greeted him.

There were a number of other items on the list which took a little while to check. Eventually, to everyone's relief, he came to the last name.

'Okay, last but not least, I've just remembered my suit.' He sought out a chubby female elf called Bizz.

'I think you could do with a new one,' she called.

'What? Surely not? I tried it on and it was fine, just needs the waist letting out a bit.'

'Begging your pardon Mr Elestyal, but you've had this one for the last thirty years. The velvet is going threadbare. I've had to repair the pockets, change the fur, which was very grey, put a new set of buttons on, and add a few pounds of stuffing.'

'Stuffing?' enquired Elestyal curiously.

'Yes,' said Bizz, 'Your belly had got quite flat. We have to keep up appearances, can't have you looking like you've been on a diet. What if someone spots you? You're supposed to fat and jolly. Oh yes, and I've washed your beard.'

'*Washed* my beard?'

'It was full of last year's mince-pie crumbs and stained with sherry and hot chocolate.' Bizz raised an eyebrow.

'There have to be some perks to the job,' said the old wizard looking suitably guilty.

'As long as the perks go *in* your mouth!'

'Point taken Bizz. I shall be more careful tonight.'

With reports finished Elestyal folded his list and returned it to his pocket. Then he bent down and unlocked the wooden chest. He turned back to the waiting elves.

'I suppose you're all waiting to have this draw?' he called.

A tremendous cheer erupted throughout the great hall, followed by cries of 'Today not tomorrow!' and 'Put us out of our misery!'

'You're all so impatient,' said the wizard, feigning disapproval and shaking his head. 'Okay, let's get started. First, for the benefit of any newcomers I will quickly go over the rules. As most of you know there are only ten places on the sleigh, and every year there are many, many more of you wanting to go than there are places. The only fair way to choose the riders is to put your names in a draw. If you've been lucky in the past, and you've had the honour of being a rider then you cannot enter your name again. You only get to go once. So, all those who wanted to try their luck have posted their names in here, in the riders' box.' He patted the wooden chest beside him. 'As usual, the honour of drawing the names will be given to two young trainees who have worked particularly hard, and excelled in their jobs in the last year.' He paused and glanced quickly around the packed hall. 'This year those two are ... Master Aleron, and ... Miss Petal!'

Petal could hardly believe her ears. She looked around in amazement, wondering if maybe Elestyal had made a mistake.

Elestyal spotted her and smiled at her confusion. 'I did mean you Petal,' he called.

Aleron was already on the stage. Petal joined him with a huge grin, while the waiting elves gave them a round of applause. Elestyal asked them if they would like to say a few words.

'Just thank you to Fynn for all his help this year. And it's a real honour to pull these names!' said Aleron. Everyone clapped.

Elestyal looked at Petal.

Petal looked at the audience. 'I um ... ' she started nervously, 'I want to thank Zeb so much for allowing me to try a job in the stable. I had to bug him for weeks before he gave in.' A ripple of chuckles ran through the crowd. Petal continued. 'It's hard work but I love it. And, now that a girl has proved her worth in the stable, I think ... well ... I definitely think they should also be considered as sleighriders.'

For a few seconds you could have heard a pin drop in the old hall. Then the crowd erupted into incredulous laughter. She was obviously joking. A thirteen year old elf-chick, bold as brass, thinking *females* should be allowed on *the* most prestigious job? It was unthinkable, unimaginable. Cries of 'Never!', 'It's a guy's job!', and, 'Elf-Chicks aren't allowed - stick to sewing!' came back to her along with cat-calls and whistles.

'Okay, Okay!' cried Elestyal, raising his hands for quiet, 'Petal was only having a little joke.' Then he caught sight of her expression. Annoyance and indignation flaring from those big violet eyes, and her mouth set in a determined line. Good lord the girl had been serious. Whatever next! What was happening to tradition around here? He quickly suggested they started drawing the names. He didn't notice Perks standing at the edge of the stage trying to keep a straight face.

Aleron drew the first name out of the box, but instead of reading it he handed it to Petal who was trying to control her temper. Her cheeks were flushed a dull red and she looked ready to explode. He thought she looked even more attractive when she was mad.

'Here, you read the first one.'

The little gesture surprised her so much it took her mind off her anger and embarrassment at not being taken seriously. She took the slip of paper and gave him the vestige of a smile. At least he wasn't making fun of her.

'Thanks.' She unfolded it and looked at the name, then she looked around at the little sea of faces, all waiting with bated breath. Her gaze fell on Perks standing at the edge of the stage, and a mischievous grin started to spread from ear to ear. He read her expression and his mouth dropped open. He started to mouth the word *impossible*. Still holding his gaze she cried, 'The first rider is ... *Perks!*

The old gardener was still speechless. He had long ago given up hope of ever being one of the lucky ones. His face, creased with age and laughter lines, was suddenly starting to beam with pure delight. He leapt onto the stage and hugged Petal.

'Think an old-timer like you can hang on to that sleigh?' called someone.

'I'll take your place! I'm younger!' called another voice.

'Be off with all of you!' he cried, 'I've waited a hundred years for this!'

Petal reached into the chest, swirled her hand among the little papers and plucked one out. She handed it to Aleron.

'Your turn.'

There was dead silence as he unfolded it.

'And the next rider is ... Skyler!'

'Oh boy I can't believe it!' yelled Skyler. He was on the stage in seconds, grabbing Perks and hugging the life out of him. The two started a celebratory jig around the stage.

Someone yelled something about 'Not another Grandpa!' and 'There should be an age limit!'

Aleron handed Petal another paper and they continued the draw until all ten riders were up on stage, crazy with excitement and slapping one another on the back.

Elestyal read out the final list: 'Perks, Skyler, Jake, Chip, Wingo, Hugo, Archy, Sid, Perry and Hip. We congratulate all of you. It is a great honour and privilege to ride the sleigh. You will travel at speeds you have never even imagined. It's not for the faint-hearted. Enjoy every minute! Now quickly, down to the sewing room all of you and Bizz will sort out your suits.' He turned to address everyone in the hall. 'Supper will be at seven in the parlour. Tomorrow evening of course the Christmas feast will be in here.'

There was much clapping and cheering and excited discussion as folk dispersed back to their jobs. Among them the disappointed faces of many who had so badly wanted to ride the delivery. They would have to try their luck again next year. Elestyal closed the box and turned to Aleron and Petal.

'I do love seeing their faces when their name is called out.'

Petal agreed. 'Perks was so funny. He really didn't believe it at first.' She ran her hand over the lid of the chest and stared curiously at the intricate carvings. Elestyal followed her gaze.

'The creatures of the night,' he said.

'It's beautiful.' She traced the outline of the moon, an owl, and a fox, and then her fingers came to rest on a small bird depicted singing on top of a bush. She puzzled over it. 'What's this? Why is there a song bird here? Birds don't sing at night.'

'Oh that one does,' said the wizard. 'It's called a nightingale, and it sings so sweetly that you'd think it was magic. But it's not a native of these parts. It lives in the south, in warmer climes.'

Petal thought about southern climates. The only way an elf usually went south was on the delivery. She felt her earlier annoyance returning, and a defiance crept into her voice. 'Maybe *I'll* get to go south one day and hear a nightingale … when the rule is changed and girls *are* allowed to be sleighriders.'

Elestyal said nothing for a few seconds.

Aleron frowned and looked sideways at Petal.

'Well why not?' said Petal, reading the disapproval in their silence.

'Miss Petal,' said Elestyal, with a firm note in his voice. 'Just because you have mastered, amazingly well I must say, a job not normally done by females, it does not mean you can change *every* elvish tradition. Working in the stable is one thing, but female sleighriders are completely out of the question. It's far too dangerous for girls. I think it best if we left it at that … don't you?'

It wasn't a question. She was being told to drop the subject. She nodded and said nothing.

'Right then,' said Elestyal briskly, 'back to work. And I must go and see Bizz about letting out the waist in my suit.'

After he'd gone Aleron and Petal stood by the sleighrider box. Petal let out a sigh. 'It's just so unfair,' she said, sounding totally cheesed off.

'What ... that girls aren't allowed to be sleighriders?'

'Yes. I mean if I'm capable of working in the stable like a guy then why can't I have the opportunity of riding the sleigh like a guy?'

'It's always been that way,' said Aleron with a little shrug.

'You mean it's *always* been unfair?'

'Well, no, I mean it's tradition, isn't it? It's always been something that just the elf-guys do.'

'But just because something has always been done a certain way doesn't mean it can't change ... especially if there's no good reason not to change it.'

'It's just not traditional. And it's too dangerous.'

'*Who* said it's too dangerous? Maybe the same person that said girls couldn't work in the stables. Well he got that wrong didn't he.'

Aleron sighed. Petal had fight written all over her face. She obviously wasn't going to give up on this latest notion, and he liked her too much to argue with her.

'Maybe they'll come around to the idea one day,' he said patiently.

'Humph!' snorted Petal. Then she turned and looked up at him and her expression softened. 'Thank you at least for not laughing at me. I think you and Perks are the only ones who don't think I'm quite mad.'

'Of course I don't think you're mad. There's nothing wrong with having a dream.' He looked so earnest that Petal couldn't possibly disbelieve him.

'It will come true one day, I know it will.'

Aleron smiled. He loved her passion. It had taken guts to speak her mind on the stage. And she had taken the crowd's reaction on the chin.

'Meet me at supper,' he said suddenly, 'I've got something to tell you.'

Petal made her way back to the stable with mixed emotions. Half of her was pleased to bits that she had been chosen as one of the two who had excelled in their jobs. It was a real feather in her cap and a huge step forward for female elves, even if no other females wanted to work in the stable. Another part of her was still smarting from the comments and laughter hurled at her suggestion of female sleighriders. Damn their stupid tradition she thought, they should jolly well move on, like they had in the human world, which she had read a considerable amount about. Lastly she thought about Aleron with his serious brown eyes. How he hadn't criticised her. How he allowed her her dream. She wondered what he wanted to tell her at supper.

3
Zorils at Pine Copse

In the snowbun's deep burrow Iceace woke suddenly. His sisters were snuggled against his mother, all of them sound asleep. Pa was dreaming peacefully in the den.

As carefully and quietly as he could he slipped out of the nursery and headed up the main run towards the great outside. He would have a peek at this big scary place that had so far been denied to him and then come back. No one would ever know. He just couldn't wait any longer. He followed the main run up and up until he eventually saw a faint light. This must be it! His heart beat a little faster as he made his way cautiously to the burrow entrance. Then he took his first exploratory hop into the outside world.

It was cold. Bitter. He looked around in wonder at the frozen waste with its deep blue shadows and heavy pale grey mists to the east. To the west of the burrow, set on top of a high icy prominence was Christmas Castle. He observed the shapely towers and turrets rising high in the evening sky, glistening with encrusted ice as the last delicate rays of pale sun enveloped them. He thought it all looked wonderful out here. What was his mother so worried about? Curiosity tugged at him and he ventured another few feet along the snowy path away from the burrow. The snow was big and soft and fluffy. He tried a big hop and felt so exhilarated that he did two or three sidekicks as well. Then he tore around in circles leaping for sheer delight in the powdery snow. He came to rest a short distance from the burrow entrance, knowing he should go back down before he was missed, but he wanted to see more, learn more. He found tundra plants growing nearby, clumps of fluffy-headed cotton grass, pale grey lichens on the rocks, and spongy silver-green reindeer moss. He nuzzled and nibbled them all, intrigued by the differing tastes and textures.

He was just about to turn around and go back when suddenly the sharp north wind picked up. It tugged at the fur across his back, and on that wind something else was carried, something that even at his tender age sent a basic instinctual warning. He turned, heart beating fast, and peered northwards towards the bad feeling. Sounds were reaching him, guttural sounds in the mists, low throaty grunts and snarls and a rhythmic dull thudding, as though a number of large animals were marching. He heard screeching too, that of large birds, a raucous weird call. The noises drew closer. Iceace watched with wide fearful eyes, his long sensitive ears filtering every sound, while his mother's words rang in his brain *'Other animals that will kill and eat you!'* He sensed the danger but didn't know why, and froze as whatever it was approached, his white fur perfectly camouflaged in the snow. Now he flattened his ears along his back and became motionless but for the rapid twitching of his tiny pink nose.

The sounds drew closer and closer. And then he saw them as they emerged from the mists. Not clear at first, but as they moved closer he saw they were two-legged creatures, stocky and powerful with broad shoulders and hunched backs. They were coming his way. He shrank deeper into the snow, terrified. The creatures came on, muttering and growling, about fifty of them, if he could have counted. They stopped a short distance away by a fallen tree and started arguing. He could see them clearly now, their large heads with wild matted hair, small mean yellow eyes set under solid jutting brows, noses broad and flat, under which crawled a thin line of a mouth. When the lips were drawn back they showed the teeth of a meat-eater. They were clad in the furs of other animals, all but their feet, which were bare, save for their own growth of course matted hair.

One of them, who looked bigger and stronger than the rest and seemed to be the leader, had perched himself on a rock. He was brandishing a heavy axe, the head, a wedge of sharpened stone, the handle made from the bone of some large animal. He had a net thrown over one shoulder. For extra warmth around his neck he had draped the skins of dead rabbits.

Iceace stared at the skins in fascination, and at the coarse hairy hand that gripped the axe. The fingers were short and thick, the nails long and yellowed. It was a primitive hand. The other animals were the same and all carried similar objects. A sudden change in the wind brought their scent to him. He wrinkled his nose in distaste at the foul odour. All his senses told him not to move, not one whisker. He must not catch their attention. His stomach turned as once again he noticed the white rabbit skins swinging in the wind when the leader turned to speak to the others.

'Bring the tall one here!' he commanded loudly.

Iceace's eyes grew wide as he saw a new and different type of creature come into view through the mist. It was bound with ropes around the neck and waist and was being pushed and pulled along by its captors. It was much taller than they were, but thinner, stooped and ponderous. He wanted to see its face but the foul creatures had covered its head with a sack.

'Down!' snarled the leader, as the new creature was shoved in front of him. It sank to its knees unsteadily, reaching out quickly with bound hands to stop itself from falling.

'Get the sack off!'

The lackeys undid the twine and pulled it off. The creature immediately dropped its head and covered its face with its hands, but not before Iceace saw blood for the first time in his life. He shivered. The leader slid off his rock and grabbed the rope attached to its neck. He yanked on it.

'Who owns the castle?' he shouted in a hoarse growl, 'The one over there!'

There was a whimpering sound as the creature pawed at its neck.

'Speak!' The leader kicked out and caught it in the ribs with a filthy foot. It jumped and gasped, looking up and around quickly, keeping its hands in front of its face in self-protection.

'Who *owns* it?'

Silence.

'You want some of my axe? I'll chop off your toes one by one!'

'Please ... ' The cry was pitiful and hoarse, just a rasping whisper as the poor creature tried to draw its rag-wrapped feet underneath it.

'Well?' hissed the captor, his yellow slit-eyes narrowing further. 'Time is running *out!*'

'I'm ... I'm ... not ... sure ... ' There was a sob in its voice.

'Not sure? But you are one of the Erudite people! Your clan knows everything. Your people are legendary for their knowledge. Maybe you are *unwilling* rather than unable to answer my question? In which case I'll just feed you to the gulo! He's been starved for three days ... death will be quick, I assure you.' He pulled on the rope so hard that the tall creature fell sideways onto the snow. 'Bring the beast!' he yelled.

There was yelling and jeering as the crowd started to part. Then they started to chant: 'Gulo-gulo ... gulo-gulo!' Iceace felt his blood run cold at the sound of the name. The very name his mother had warned him about only yesterday. He saw how the gang members were keeping well back and giving it a wide berth. It was taking the strength of four of the creatures to hold on to the chained beast. The young snowbun watched, wide-eyed as this prisoner of a very different ilk was brought forth. The wolverine.

The animal slavered and strained at its chains, and

howled as its captors tried to hold it back. It sensed live prey, and it was ravenous. Iceace quivered in blind terror and stared transfixed at the beast, a hundred times his size. Its small red-eyes seemed to gleam like fire-coals in its ferrety face. Its lips were contorted, drawn back in a snarl over lethal yellowed fangs. The body was muscular, the stomach bloated, the hair a course and spiky yellow-brown mix. It waggled its stubby tail in anticipation.

'Last chance! Who lives in the castle?' The leader put a matted foot on the tall one's back and hauled up on the rope. Now Iceace had a clear view of the captive's face. It was pale and hairless, except for the chin where a bushy red beard sprouted. The eyes were large and sad, one of them bruised dark blue-black, no doubt a gift from one of its gaolers. He stared at the face knowing instinctively that it belonged to a good soul. A tear oozed from one of the creature's eyes and roll down his cheek. It fell into the snow. The young rabbit felt an immense sadness clutch at his heart.

'I *will* give you to the gulo if you do not speak.' This time the leader's words were slow and soft, but full of menace. The hungry beast tried to scrabble closer, pulling its handlers with it. It gave a low gurgling growl. The tall creature glanced sideways at it and then up at his captor.

His words were barely audible.

'Saint ... Nicholas ... ' he whispered.

'What? Who? Speak up!'

'Saint ... Nicholas.' The voice was strangled and beaten.

'Who is this *Nicholas?*' snarled the leader loosening the rope slightly.

'He delivers the toys ... ' The tall one started to cough.

'Cut the noise! What are these *toys*? *Who* does he deliver to?'

The wolverine howled and strained at its chains.

'Toys are ... gifts. He delivers them to the human children ... all over the world ... at Christmas ... with the help of elves.'

'You speak in riddles! I have never heard of this 'Christmas',' barked the leader.

'It is every year, on December 25th. A religious festival in the human calendar ... a feast, similar to your Walpurgis night.

'What's the date today?'

'It is December the twenty-fourth.' The tall creature's head slumped forward as if in defeat.

'What of this delivery they make? How can one man deliver all around the world in one night? You must be lying!' He growled and tugged on the rope, making his prisoner wince.

'Saint Nicholas is not a man ... he is a retired wizard. It is said that it's the magic of Christmas itself that gives him and the elves the power to deliver gifts to all human children in one night.'

The leader was thoughtful. Then he smiled. One old retired wizard and a bunch of elves posed little problem for fifty trolls, especially if they were caught napping early in the morning, still in their beds. And since tonight was the very night of their delivery, the night they would have worked all night, they would surely be sleeping late. The leader and his gang needed a new residence and the castle looked like a fine place to set up home.

'We'll stay the night here,' he shouted.

There was some dissension in the ranks. It was cold and they wanted proper shelter now. The leader heard the muttering.

'Build fires! We wait for the morning and the time of least resistance. Surprise is a splendid weapon. We'll take the castle at dawn. Tie the prisoner to a tree.' Then as an afterthought he turned to the tall one. 'What's your name?'

'Hibu,' whispered the prisoner.

The lackeys yanked the gulo back. It screamed in fury, denied its expected supper. They hauled on it from either side, trying to keep the chains taut.

'Get it back!' cursed the leader.

The animal was in a frenzy, straining and fighting the chains, leaping and contorting. Even the loathsome creatures themselves were in fear of it. It snapped and drooled and Iceace thought he'd faint with fear. And then if that wasn't enough another sound came to him. A hollow screeching *quark* from above. The same noise he'd heard when the creatures first arrived. He peeped up fearfully and saw great white birds circling and dipping back and forth over the group. They seemed intrigued by the beast, one of them even dipping down and flying quickly over its head.

The bird landed and sidled closer. *Quark!* it went, *quark-quark!* It stretched out its long neck and eye-balled the gulo. Iceace saw how the dirty-white feathers finished half way up its neck. From there to the top of its ugly head it was almost completely bald, save for a few sparse tufts sprouting around a curved and razor-sharp bill. The gulo growled deep in its throat as the bald-headed bird stared it down with an impudent green eye. More birds landed and sidled up behind the first one. They all *quarked* with outstretched necks until the animal was beside itself. The leader had had enough. 'Scram! Gluttons!' He picked up a rock and heaved it in the direction of the birds, catching one on the leg. It squawked violently and glared at him. He picked up a second rock and the motley crowd took off in a hurry and started to circle once more.

Iceace peeped skywards in terror. Would they see him? He was riveted to the spot. He wanted to turn and bolt back into the warren, but his legs wouldn't work. *'Great birds that drop out of the sky'* came his mother's warning words from yesterday. The birds were directly overhead now, screeching and excited. They must have seen him! He didn't dare look up again. He shut his eyes tight. Why oh why had he come up here? Why hadn't he listened to Ma? And then it happened. His breath was suddenly knocked clean out of him as something heavy landed on his back. He tried to scream but nothing came out. His neck was in a vice-like grip. Why hadn't he stayed in the warren like he'd been told to? Why had he not listened? He was limp with fear, his bones all turned to water. He hoped the end would be quick, and saw in his mind the sharp curved beak and gleaming green eye of the giant bird. Then everything went black.

4
Iceace Makes a Decision

Iceace's world was black and swirling. He had escaped the clutches of the great bird and was running across the frozen waste, running for his life. But he was getting nowhere. The birds were closing in again. He felt a draft of air as something brushed his ears. He felt the light touch of a feather on his head and a wing tip caressing the length of his back. He squealed in terror.

'Iceace ... ?' came a voice.

'How did they know his name?

'Iceace ... ?'

The birds were suddenly gone and he noticed he felt warm.

Of course! He must be in rabbit heaven and an angel was speaking to him, and death hadn't been painful at all. He breathed a small sigh of relief and opened one eye. The angel was watching him. It appeared she was also the wing-tip that had been stroking his back. In fact there were four angels all staring at him - *his mother and three sisters!* He closed the eye. His mind scrambled to understand. If he was in heaven, then so must his family be as well, which could only mean one thing, they were all dead too! They must have come to save him and all been killed, and it was all his fault for going exploring. He started to whimper.

'Iceace ... ?' His mother again.

He tried to rouse himself. 'I'm sorry Ma,' he whimpered.

'Sorry?'

'For getting you all killed ... '

'What *are* you talking about?'

Iceace opened both eyes. He was lying in the middle of the parlour floor. His sisters were looking at him with great curiosity. He scrabbled into a sitting position as images of evil creatures flooded back.

'What happened?' he whispered.

'Your father found you outside and brought you back. When he grabbed you, you fainted.' His mother looked severe, 'I told you not to go up there alone.'

'Where's Pa?' Iceace was looking panicky.

'Rushed back up to the outside for some reason,' said his mother, 'I really don't know what's going on.'

'I saw it!' breathed Iceace.

'What?' His mother looked bewildered. 'You saw what?'

'I saw it Ma ... just like you said ... and it was terrible ... terrible! I should have listened to you!' He was stumbling over his words as Frisk came dashing back into the parlour.

'What's he seen? What was up there? A fox ... an owl ... ?' Moonbeam looked at him. His whiskers were trembling. His eyes were wide and his nose was twitching rapidly.

'Pa, what's up there?' she whispered nervously.

'We must try to block the entrance. Bring the moss and sticks from the nursery. Hurry!'

'Not until you tell me what's up there.'

'No time! *Hurry!* He bolted to the nursery and started grabbing moss and twigs and rolling it under his chin. Moonbeam followed, confused and worried as they ran with the bundles up towards the entrance.

'Here!' said Frisk. They had stopped a few feet from the burrow opening. 'It's narrowest here between the rocks. We'll use earth as well from the side-walls.' He dug and scraped, then mixed the moss and small sticks with the earth. He pushed the mound forwards and gradually the light disappeared.

'More moss Ma,' he whispered. 'As much as you can bring.' She brought more and more and he scraped earth and mixed the moss and tamped it into place. After a while he looked satisfied. 'It's the best we can do.'

'Now will you tell me what has scared the whiskers off Iceace and yourself, and why we're blocking the run?' pleaded Moonbeam, barely wanting to know.

Frisk, who was a little puffed from all the digging, sat back on his haunches and proceeded to wash his face, as though maybe the washing would wipe away the picture in his head.

'What *is* it?' she insisted.

He put his paws down then, looked at her for a few seconds, breathed deeply and said 'Trolls!'

'Trolls?' She looked astounded. 'Are you sure? Are you positive? I know there was a rumour. But you've never even seen a troll. How do you know? Maybe it's something else?' she added hopefully.

'They are trolls,' said Frisk slowly and heavily. He dropped his head. 'The descriptions in the stories passed down over the years, they fit perfectly.'

Moonbeam shrank into herself, and paled beneath her fur. 'What are we to do?'

'Nothing. We wait them out. They must be looking for shelter. They'll move on. At least we had time to block the burrow, so we're safe if they've brought weasels. In the old lore it was said they used to use them for hunting, sent them down the burrows to flush us out.'

'Ma? ... Pa? ... ' Iceace's voice called from below.

'You go down,' said Frisk. 'I shall stay here for a while.'

Ma gently nuzzled his face, 'Come and talk to Iceace in a minute.' She left him deep in thought and returned below.

Iceace was waiting, seemingly quite recovered from his fright and eager to tell more of his tale. He started up as soon as his mother appeared.

'Where's Pa? What's he doing?'

'He's up at the entrance. Don't worry, we've built a strong barrier so nothing bad can get in.' She started to wash his face but he pulled away.

'Ma ... those animals ... they were very bad. I don't know how I knew, but I did. I could feel their badness before I saw them. It came on the wind.'

'That was your instinct talking to you Iceace. It serves you well already, and you should always listen to it.'

'What are they Ma? Those bad animals ... what *are* they?'

'They're trolls,' said his mother quietly, 'Evil and terrible creatures, a thousand times worse than any bear or fox.'

'They had that creature with them ... the one you called the goolio!'

'You mean the gulo? The wolverine?'

'Yes, and they were going to let it eat the tied-up animal ... if it didn't tell them who lived in the castle!'

'What do you mean? What tied up animal?' asked his mother quickly. She suddenly looked even more worried.

'It was *very* tall, a lot taller than them, but thin. Its face was pale. And it looked very sad.'

His mother looked distraught. 'It sounds as though they've captured one of the tall people!'

'Tall people?'

'Yes, known as the Erudites. They're gentle folk who live in the northern forests. Wise people.'

'I heard the trolls speaking,' said Iceace, 'and I understood. The biggest troll kept asking the tall one who lived in the castle. And the tall one didn't answer, so the big troll hurt him and then they got the goolio. It howled, and it howled! And it smelled bad and it showed its teeth, big teeth, and ... and it was dribbling, and trying to jump on the tall one, but they pulled it back!' Iceace was jabbering so fast that his mother could barely understand him.

'We need to help the tall one get free,' said Iceace with sudden great determination.

'Don't be silly Iceace. We are mere snowbuns. We couldn't possibly help.'

The mention of snowbuns brought back a vivid picture of the rabbit skins draped around the troll's neck. He shuddered. 'I saw dead rabbits on the troll,' he whispered, 'White ones like us!'

'Yes,' said his mother gently, 'And we don't want to end up the same way.'

They were both silent until Frisk appeared.

'I think we maybe okay,' he said, 'There's no movement near the burrow, that I can hear. We must sit tight and wait.'

Iceace started up again. 'Pa we have to *do* something. We have to try and help the tall one.'

'What do you mean? What tall one?'

Moonbeam broke in. 'It appears the trolls have a prisoner, probably an Erudite. Iceace saw him. They were trying to get him to tell them who lived at the castle. When he refused they brought a wolverine and threatened him with it.'

'Oh the Great Rabbit Spirit! This is surely a bad day! I only saw the trolls when I went up and grabbed Iceace.' Then a new and far greater fear flooded through him as his thoughts turned to the mention of the castle. 'Elestyal!' he whispered. 'The Elves, what if ... ?' His voice rose and then stopped, the horror of his thoughts unbearable.

Iceace broke in, sounding more determined by the minute. 'We *have* to warn the castle folk. They're our friends. You've told me how wonderful they are and how much they've helped us. The trolls are going there, first thing in the morning while the elves are still asleep! Pa! *They'll all be killed!*

Frisk was silent for a few minutes, then he shook his head. 'There's nothing we can do,' he whispered.

'We can warn them,' insisted Iceace, 'I will run there and tell them.'

'*You?* You're barely out of the nest! You're not going anywhere young bun. You've already had the fright of your life. We dare not leave the burrow. The trolls, or their friendly vultures would spot us instantly. They're only yards away. We would die for nothing. It's impossible.'

'Is there no other way out of here?'

Frisk shook his head, 'No.'

'In my Great Grandfather's day there was supposedly an old escape run somewhere down in the depths,' recalled Moonbeam thoughtfully.

'If it ever actually existed it's probably fallen in years ago,' muttered Frisk. 'Besides, I heard it was a one-way run ... whatever that was supposed to mean. And if it did exist who can say where it might lead? Maybe into the middle of the troll camp! No, we are trapped, until the beasts move on.'

'Let's go and look for it!' cried Iceace eagerly, 'It might come out on the other side of the copse. I could maybe help the tall one ... chew through his ropes and free him. And then I could run to the castle. Please Pa?'

'Stop it Iceace! Just stop right now!' His mother was as angry as he'd ever seen her. 'You're staying here, and so is your father. Do you want to end up an empty skin around the neck of a filthy troll? And if your father is caught and killed who will look after us?'

A sombre silence filled the burrow.

Iceace hung his head. He felt split in two. He didn't for the world want his mother and sisters left to fend for themselves, nor did he want to end up a lifeless rabbit skin. He didn't want to face danger and fear again, not for anything. But the face of the tall one called to him. It wouldn't leave his mind. He saw the blood, and the tears falling into the snow, and it tore at his heart. He thought of the innocent castle folk, peacefully sleeping, while the beasts crept in with their axes. Without saying any more he hopped away and sat in a corner.

'Don't worry Iceace, we'll be okay,' said Moonbeam. But it wasn't himself and his family he was worried about.

'I shall sleep up the top,' said Frisk, 'and keep an ear for any movement.'

Moonbeam cuddled together with Iceace's sisters. 'Come on Iceace, come and join us.' But Iceace seemed to have gone to sleep already. 'He must be worn out,' said Ma.

But Iceace wasn't sleeping. He was forming a vague plan. He would search for the old escape run as soon as everyone was asleep. When he found it, and being a rabbit of great optimism he had little doubt that he would, he would try to reach the tall one and help him get free. Then he would run for his life to the castle and warn the wizard and the elves. The white birds would probably be asleep at night, and so would the gulo, which he knew was tied up anyway.

An hour later Frisk was still up top, dozing by the blocked entrance. Iceace's mother and sisters were sound asleep in a knot of fluffy white fur, limbs entangled, safe and secure. He looked at them for a few minutes. 'Sorry Ma,' he whispered, 'but my heart tells me I have to do this. I hope I'll see you again soon. If not, Pa will be here to look after you all ... goodbye.'

5
The Watchers in the Loft

The supper bell, tolled by Skyler, the 'soon to be a sleigh-rider' elf, jangled at ten minutes to seven. Elves from all over the castle made for the parlour, the big dining area off the kitchen. They were soon huddled on stools and benches around the two enormous oak tables where red and green candles glowed and flickered in chunky wooden candlesticks. Branches of holly and pine hung from the ancient beams, blending their fragrance with rich cooking smells. Against the high and narrow slit windows snowflakes landed softly, melted, transformed into droplets and darted down the thick panes. Steam rose as bowls of hot stew and dumplings were passed around, followed by hunks of crusty home-made bread still warm from the oven.

Aleron and Petal sat together dunking bread in rich gravy and enjoying the hearty food after a hard day's work. Once in a while Aleron would take a sneaky sideways peek at his supper partner and chuckle inwardly at her obviously healthy appetite. Thanks to winning their respective achievements they had been rather thrown together today. He didn't mind. It was nice to get to know her better, even though she disturbed him a little with her fiery nature.

'Tomorrow night we eat in the great hall,' she said, scooping a mushroom out of her bowl with her spoon, 'I love it, it's such a feast, and it always looks so beautiful with all the decorations and candles.'

'The best thing is the silver.'

'The silver?'

'Yes. All the wonderful platters and cutlery and candlesticks, all gleaming in the candlelight. Silver is such a beautiful soft metal.'

'Soft?' The word conjured up reindeer fur in Petal's head, not dishes and spoons.

'Yes, it's good for making spoons and forks and platters, and decorative things. Different metals are used for different purposes. Tough metals, like steel for instance, are good for making swords. We've learned all about it in the workshop.'

'Oh.' Petal wasn't sure if she was interested in the qualities of metal. She preferred working with living creatures. She loved caring for them, feeding and watering and cleaning and grooming. She loved the way Ru nuzzled her cheek with his velvet nose when she was brushing his chest. 'There's just one problem with silver,' she said.

'What's that?'

'Every darned bell on the reindeer harness is made of it, and I have to clean them all!'

Aleron laughed, 'I know, I can tell by the way the polish stock has gone down!'

'So where are your parents?' She was suddenly curious to know more about him.

He was quiet for some seconds. 'They're gone.' There was the slightest catch in his voice, 'They were travelling overseas, on their way to visit my Grandfather. He was nearing his time and they wanted to see him before he passed. They had to travel through a dense forest somewhere and ... there were trolls, a band of them, horrible vicious creatures ... ' He drew a breath and swallowed, 'The trolls surprised them, jumping down from the trees over their path in the night. My parents had no chance.'

'How terrible,' whispered Petal letting her spoon sink into her bowl. 'I'm sorry, I shouldn't have asked.' She stared solemnly at Aleron's pensive face.

'It's okay. I guess I don't normally think about it too much.'

'Where were you when it happened?'

'I was here, I was just a babe. They left me with a nursemaid, thinking it safer with such a long journey ahead. One day, when I was older Elestyal told me what had happened.'

'It's a terrible story.' Petal had a tight feeling in the back of her throat. She was quiet for a while.

'What about your family?'

'Humph,' A snort of disgust. 'I was born in one of the southern countries. My mother was a Forest Elf. She ran off with some Irish elf that was part leprechaun or something, and I don't have a clue about my father. My Aunt brought me here when I was small, then she left. Just like you, Elestyal told me what happened when I was older.' Judging by her voice tone her past was a prickly subject.

'It must be where you get your looks from.'

'My looks? How do you mean?' She looked defensive.

'That touch of Leprechaun in you, maybe it's ... well, maybe it's ... ' he found himself spluttering and going red. She was going to think he was a complete idiot. 'Maybe it's that ... that makes you very pretty,' he finished in a rush.

Petal noticed the flush in his cheeks. He was serious! She couldn't believe it. Every time she looked in the mirror it was with immense criticism. Her violet eyes were too big, her chin too stubborn, her nose too tilted and her hair usually an unruly mop.

'You think I'm pretty?' She frowned.

'Yes,' said Aleron, who had suddenly become overly interested in a dumpling in his supper bowl.

'You need to get some glasses.'

'My eyesight is perfect.'

'Is that what you wanted to tell me about tonight?'

'Oh ... well actually, no. I was going to ask ... ' He leaned close to her and lowered his voice to a conspiratorial whisper. 'How would you like to come and watch them load the sleigh tonight?'

Petal looked amazed, 'But only the sleighriders are allowed at the loading.'

'I know, but I'm going anyway. There's a great place to hide in the loft, and a rather convenient knot-hole in the floor right above the sleigh!'

'What if we get caught?'

'Life is full of risks.' Aleron's face broke into a sly grin, 'Maybe, if you ever want to be a sleigh-rider, you'll have to take some. But of course if you'd rather not ...?'

'What time?' she hissed.

'Eleven-twenty sharp, behind the barrels at the back of the barn.'

'I'll be there.'

Pudding had arrived in the form of an enormous dish of hot, sugar-dusted mince pies accompanied by a jug of fresh thick cream. Elestyal stood up then and called for quiet.

'Thank you all once again,' he said, 'Everyone has worked incredibly hard. All is now ready for the loading of the sleigh, and the magic is building fast! I'm sure you can all feel it.'

There were nods of agreement from around the room. And almost as soon as the wizard's words were out, as though some greater force had been listening, a wisp of purple and silver light swirled and shimmered and sped through the old parlour. It was followed seconds later by another, and then more, as though they played and danced a magic dance together.

Elestyal continued, 'So, at eleven-thirty, sleighriders! You should be at the barn.'

He was greeted by cries of 'Absolutely!' and 'We'll be there!' Perks was already wearing his green sleigh hat.

Petal leaned towards Aleron. 'One day *I'll* wear one of those.'

'It wouldn't surprise me,' said Aleron. She was like a dog with a bone when she got an idea in her head. He slid off his stool. 'See you tonight ... don't be late.'

'I won't.'

Elves gradually left the table. Elestyal made his way downstairs to his room below the kitchen. He stretched out on the simple wooden bed and closed his eyes. Another Christmas night. He loved it. Loved the sense of comradeship and the way everyone pulled together to make the delivery happen. He himself still got excited, knowing the joy they would bring to children around the world. He heard a hum and a slight whoosh above his head as he was dozing. He didn't need to look, he knew the sound of Christmas energy from old. World energy it was, a power created by millions around the globe. Created by love and positive thought, and belief.

At eleven o'clock exactly Elestyal woke up. He stretched and yawned. Ah! Bizz had been by. There was a plate of mince pies, a hunk of bread with a wedge of good sharp cheese, and a mug of hot chocolate on his desk. He smiled. This was a hint that he should have a snack before he left, rather than eating en-route. His suit was hanging on the back of the door. Purple-silver streaks of light shimmered close to it. Time to get dressed. As usual he would wear it over his dungarees, it got a bit nippy on the sleigh.

It took a while to get his suit on, then it was just a quick comb of the moustache which was tickling his nose. He patted around his tunic pockets and drew out a soft, red leather case creased with age. Inside was a small round silver-backed mirror and a silver-edged comb. He turned the mirror fondly in his hands and read the words inscribed around the border: *'Presented to Elestyal on the twenty-fifth day of August nineteen-hundred and three, on which day he assumed the duties of St Nicholas, the bringer of gifts'.* That was the day he had taken over from his great friend, the wizard Panglossian, now fully retired. He gently buffed the back of the mirror with a corner of his tunic. It was smooth, polished to a mirror finish by Bizz. The small handle was a filigree of suns and moons, fairies and elves, all intertwined.

Elestyal gave the moustache a quick tweak and combed the stray white beard hairs into position. Then he slipped the red case back into his pocket. It was nearly eleven-thirty. No time for his snack now, besides he'd no doubt have a few goodies during the trip. He popped the food and the mug of chocolate into the corner cupboard. Time to go and meet the sleighriders.

Aleron and Petal were already in the barn. They had got in around the back, by way of a rickety ladder leading up to a weathered door, used for loading and unloading hay. Then they had crept through the bales and the sacks of grain like mice, to lie beside the 'spy-hole', which until the previous week had been a large knot in one of the old floor boards. Aleron, with the aid of some of his metalwork tools, had removed it. Shafts of sparkling purple-silver light swirled around them in the darkness, playing among the sacks and circling the dusty beams. All was quiet. Petal watched in fascination. It was as though the tiny pinpoints of light were alive, like infinitesimal shooting stars. Suddenly she put her hand on Aleron's arm.

'I can hear it!' she whispered.

Aleron held his breath and listened. 'Yes! I hear it too! The magic's really building up. I love the way it sounds like it's singing!'

Petal listened in wonder to the faint but unmistakeable sound. It was as though a thousand tiny chimes had arrived on the wind, rising and falling as they joined the dance of the light. Strengthening and then fading; an ethereal fairy choir. Rapt in the magic she was suddenly brought back to earth by excited voices down below.

'Ouch!' said Aleron as they banged heads, both trying to look through the hole at once.

'You go first,' whispered Petal.

'Thanks!' said Aleron. After all it was his spy-hole.

The riders were all coming in with Elestyal. Someone lit the lamps and gradually the barn grew light.

Aleron was impressed. 'Wow! Look at that!' The sleigh, in all its glory stood in the centre of the barn, bedecked with silver bells, red ribbons, pine posies and tinsel. The runners and metalwork, polished until they gleamed, reflected the red velvet of the cushioned seats, the sleighriders' seats. The riders gathered around talking excitedly, running gentle fingers over the sleigh while purple-silver magic crackled and played around them. Perks adjusted his hat for the thousandth time. Jake bent and buffed the buckles on his boots and smoothed the front of his green jacket. All ten were in the traditional uniform, and proud of it.

'Okay,' called Elestyal, 'We'll start straight away.'

'Let me see!' Petal was jabbing Aleron in the ribs with her small elbow, 'You're hogging the hole.' Aleron reluctantly relinquished his position and she peered below. 'Fantastic!' she whispered.

Elestyal moved over to a large round door inset a few feet up in the barn wall. A sign on the front said *'Stores Chute'*. He opened the door to expose a wide and shiny metal tube disappearing upwards; a direct link to the huge storeroom on the third floor in the main building.

'Now,' he said, 'I want you to very carefully push the sleigh this way so it's just under the chute, but be careful, it's absorbing the magic rapidly. You'll need barely a touch.' He was right. Perks reckoned they could have blown on it and it would have moved. 'Okay, we're in position. Sid, would you ring the bell and let Lanri know we're ready.'

'Yes Sir!' Sid ran over to a small brass handle inset in the wall next to the chute. He gave it a pull, and in stores the elves went into action.

'Hey! Let me have a look!' Aleron was giving Petal a gentle shove. She gave in reluctantly and moved over. Aleron put his eye to the hole. 'I've always wanted to watch them do this,' he whispered. 'It's when Elestyal does his magic!'

'I wish you'd made two holes,' grumbled Petal, frustrated at no longer being able to watch.

'There was only one knot in the plank,' muttered

Aleron.

Purple light was intensifying in the barn. It crackled and popped and arced around the sleigh. The energy was electric. Everyone felt it. A shower of purple sparks made Perks jump. He was used to Christmas energy, but he'd never seen it so close up and powerful before. He adjusted his hat nervously.

'It won't hurt you,' chuckled Elestyal, 'Remember, it's created by the power of good thoughts, by the universal energy of Christmas. By midnight, when we leave, it will be the most amazing power you will ever see in your life.'

From far up at the top of the chute came a sound like distant thunder.

'They're on their way!' cried Elestyal. He stretched out both arms and pointed at the chute. 'Now! A little bit of wizardry in order to get everything in this old jalopy. He closed his eyes. His face was a mask of concentration. And then he started to speak. The elves hardly ever heard the language of the wizard. Elestyal was retired and rarely used magic, other than on the odd occasion for medicinal purposes and healing. They listened in fascination as the words flowed, strange and sing-song. Powerful and mysterious.

'Dezu-Dezu!
j'emco sait-mal
lant zainon
Cal ze on altal!
Dezu-Dezu!
a-dizpa-eer
zee'l s'im onge
Mai s'il elwair.'

He finished with a flourish, as the rumbling got closer and closer, and the gift-wrapped boxes and packages tore down the big metal tube from the stores. Then they were there, pouring from the chute in a brilliant swirling cloud of white and purple light, tumbling over one another into the sleigh. Large ones, small ones, square ones, flat ones, squishy ones and round ones, every shape and size possible wrapped in every colour imaginable. The whole barn was lit with sparkling magic light. The sleighriders stood in silent awe.

'Let me see! Let me see!' Petal was digging Aleron in the ribs furiously again. 'I'm missing it all!'

'Hang on,' hissed Aleron.

'Hole-hogger,' muttered Petal.

'*This* is incredible!'

Great! I wish I could *see* it.'

'Just a second ... !'

Groan.

He gave in and let her look.

'There's zillions of parcels going in but it's not filling up!'

'Magic!' whispered Aleron.

Perks, who was now holding his hat against his chest in sheer amazement, turned to Skyler with a look of wonder. 'I wouldn't have missed this for the world.'

'Stupendous!' exclaimed Skyler, shaking his head.

The presents kept coming and coming, and then at last they trickled to a stop. The sleigh still looked empty.

'Can't have it looking like that,' said Elestyal. He stood back and waved his hand with a flourish. There was a loud crackle and a cloud of multicoloured smoke engulfed everyone. It cleared slowly.

'How on earth do you do it?' asked Perks, peering through the fine, shimmering mist as the sleigh came back into view, this time beautifully laden.

'Practise,' said the wizard, 'Lots of practise.' A second later the old clock over the barn door chimed a quarter to midnight. Fifteen minutes to departure. 'Ready for our reindeer then!'

Archy, Wingo and Chip were off in a second, returning a few minutes later leading the eight deer, already fitted out in their red leather harness. They stood proudly, sometimes gently nuzzling an elf as he did up a buckle. The harness jingled softly now and then with the sound of silver bells.

'Don't they look beautiful,' breathed Petal.

'What?'

'The reindeer of course. And all those bells I spent hours polishing!'

'I'd tell you, if only I could see them.'

Petal moved her head and grinned at him, 'Can you make two holes in this board next year?'

Aleron took her place and feigned a sigh, 'I suppose I'm going to have to.' He eyed the scene below. 'Ah, you're right, those old moth-bags brush up quite well don't they.'

There was a squeak of indignation beside him.

'Ouch!' he grunted, as a small but pointed elbow connected with his ribs.

'*Moth-bags?* How *dare* you!'

Then she noticed his shoulders were shaking with laughter, for which he incurred another swift jab. He sat up in a hurry, ignoring his bruised ribs.

'Let's go,' he whispered.

'What? ... Why?'

'Because it's nearly time, and we have to see them take off! Come on!'

Petal followed him, picking her way over bales and sacks, scrambling down the ladder, and slipping through the shadows along under the wall. Aleron stopped at the corner of the barn and peered around. Petal pulled up right behind him. Minutes ticked by. The night sky was a deep star-spangled blue. Then they heard it, the first deep chime of the barn clock as it struck midnight and released the full magic power of Christmas. It was like flipping a switch. The old barn doors were blown open and reindeer and sleigh rocketed out and up into the heavens. Elves in woodland green whooped, silver bells jingled, and in the distance a faint *'Ho-Ho-Ho!'* floated back to them just before the sleigh disappeared into the night.

'Wow!' said Petal in a dazed voice.

Aleron was just staring. 'I *have* to be on there one day.'

'So do I!'

'They'll never change the rule Petal. They're *never* going to let girls go on *that*.' He was still staring, somewhat mesmerised, into the distance. Petal suddenly realised she'd been leaning against him as they watched the sleigh. She stepped back.

'Then I'll have to make them,' she said stubbornly, 'Come on, let's get back before we're caught.'

Aleron dragged his eyes back from that spot in the sky where the sleigh had disappeared. He didn't notice the glow of a few small camp fires on the distant hill under Pine Copse.

6
A Dangerous Mission

Iceace headed down into the warren with deep feelings of both excitement and sadness. Somewhere in his gut he knew it would be a long time before he saw his family again. He reached the lower parlour and sat for a minute. Three big runs ran off from here. It was as far as he had ever been.

He decided to work from left to right, and set off down the first run, very quickly coming to another small den which was a dead-end. He hopped back to the parlour again and set off down the second run. This one was longer. He followed it to a disused nursery, and then it forked. He followed both runs to dead ends, then returned to the lower parlour. If the old escape run existed it had to be down here somewhere. He set off for the third time, getting more and more anxious.

This time the run ran steeper into the earth, after a while levelling out and continuing for a little way before coming to a large parlour. From here five runs dispersed in different directions. Iceace heaved a sigh and set off down the first one. An hour later he had examined four. It wasn't easy; each run split and split again and after long forays he had found nothing but dead-ends. This final run, slightly smaller than the others, was his last hope.

It ran steeply for a long way before curving east. Then it divided. Iceace groaned and made a choice, only to end up in an ancient musty nursery filled with old rabbit fur and bits of dead moss. Disappointment and annoyance closed in on him and he took an angry kick at the bedding in frustration. The bedding flew in all directions. Then he noticed the hole. It wasn't a dead-end. Someone had just dumped bedding here and hidden the run. His heart thumped in anticipation as he ducked into the run and set off.

Tree roots started to appear, a thick and fibrous network, some blocking the way. He dug down underneath them to make enough room to squeeze through. It was a long time since any rabbit had been along here. The run continued, running deep. More and more roots slowing his progress. He must be on the edge of the copse of pines. The trolls were camped by the trees. He sent up a quiet prayer to the Great Rabbit Spirit to not let him pop up in the middle of them.

A short while later once again the run ran out and a

solid wall of earth greeted Iceace. His heart sank. It couldn't be. It couldn't just end here in the middle of nowhere. He scratched at the earth in front of him; it was solid. He dug harder, shoving the earth behind him with his big back feet. The earth in front became wood. The wood was a huge tree root. He tried digging under it but the run didn't continue there. He gave up, panting with frustration. If it didn't go under then what about over? He scratched at the earth above the root. It wasn't as hard packed as it was below, and after a short time it loosened and started to fall into the run. Suddenly Iceace smelled fresh air. His heart beat faster. He scraped gently and more loose soil fell down mixed with rotting wood and leaves, leaving a hole large enough for him to crawl through. Strange, he thought, why couldn't he see any sky? He slipped up through the hole. He couldn't believe it. No wonder he couldn't see sky, he was inside a hollow tree! The big old pine had died, and rotted away on the inside making it a haven for many small creatures. The soft and spongy inner wood had been eaten away by insects, and a kind of natural spiral of steps had formed over the years.

Iceace crept up and up, eventually arriving on a ledge where fresh snow was blowing in through a large hole. He hopped cautiously to the edge and peered out through fronds of creeping ivy. He was miles off the ground! What sort of rabbits made an escape route like this. Then he remembered his father's words, *'I heard it was a one-way run, whatever that's supposed to mean.'* Now he could tell him exactly what it meant. Foxes and weasels and other unwelcome critters couldn't possibly get in. But there was no return for those who left. He checked out the situation of his tree. It was a short distance from where the trolls had set up camp. He could smell them and see them lying around their fire. And he could hear them snoring. He couldn't see the tall one anywhere.

So this is it he thought as he perched on the ledge like a baby bird ready to take its first flight. If I take this jump that's it, I can't go home. The burrow entrance is blocked and I can't get back up this tree. What will happen to me? He felt if he thought too long about the answer he might lose courage. Down below the snow lay in a thin blanket where it had blown in under the trees. But a few feet from the trunk of the old pine it had swept into a nice fat drift. Good for a soft landing thought the snowbun as he gathered himself. His heart was pounding as he clung to the edge. Jump! he said to himself. Jump for the elves, and the wizard, and the tall person! His words gave him courage, and he leapt.

The sudden descent took his breath away. He landed exactly in the centre of the drift, expecting to sink into it, but instead it felt spongy and weird and he didn't sink at all. Beneath his feet it felt strangely ... warm! He cautiously wiggled a toe. A foul stench was permeating up his nostrils. His eyes widened. Instinct kicked in and his heart rate rocketed. And then the drift growled. It was a deep, bloodthirsty gurgle that turned the young bun's blood to ice-water. He had little doubt as to what he was sitting on. The stink of the beast still haunted him from earlier that day. His heart pitched into his stomach. He sat stock still, as if turned to stone, not even breathing, his eyes wide with horror. And then in its semi-dream state the wolverine rolled over, irritated by the sudden extra weight of what it thought to be snow fallen from a laden branch above. Iceace was toppled off and landed a few feet away. In a panic he did an Olympic sized jump and ended up many yards away beside another tree. He glanced quickly back over his shoulder expecting to find the monster straining at the end of its chain, slavering and howling and waking all the trolls. But all was quiet. 'Thank you Oh Great Rabbit Spirit!' he whispered.

'Not so loud young snowbun or you'll wake the trolls!' The words, whispered from the shadows, nearly made him faint with shock all over again.

He turned quickly. Sitting in the gloom with its back to the trunk of the tree was the tall one.

'It's you!' breathed Iceace.

'You know me?' The voice sounded surprised.

'I saw you earlier today when the trolls arrived, not far from our burrow.' Iceace moved across and joined him in the shadows.

'Ah yes, at that time I thought I was to be supper for our sleeping friend over there.'

'I just *jumped* on it!' Iceace was still trembling with fright.

'I saw you.'

'You did?'

'Yes, I sensed movement and when I looked around I caught sight of you poised in that tree. An unusual sight, a rabbit in a tree. I could see you were trying to decide whether to jump and I wanted to warn you about the gulo. The snow had blown in and covered him. I didn't dare call out. Thankfully he must have been sleeping heavily.'

'Thank the Great Rabbit Spirit for that.' Iceace nervously rubbed snow from his whiskers and eyed the lumpy white form across from them.

'Whatever are you doing anyway?' The tall one spoke

with great urgency, 'You should be in your burrow. There are many trolls here, it's dangerous.'

'I'm going to the castle,' whispered Iceace, 'I have to warn the elves and the wizard ... and I must chew through your ropes.'

'It's too late for that.'

'What do you mean?'

The tall one lifted his arms and metal glinted in the moonlight. 'Chains,' he said, 'They changed the ropes for chains.'

Iceace was mortified. There was nothing he could do. His whole being sagged with disappointment.

The tall one spoke, his voice grave and urgent. 'Don't worry about me young snowbun. Far more important are the folk at the castle. If you are brave enough to try and reach them I will be forever in your debt.' He waved a hand towards the camp fire where the trolls slept. 'They forced me to tell ... ' his voice broke with emotion. 'I fear the blood of Elestyal and the elves will now be on my hands.'

'You had no choice,' whispered Iceace, 'I saw what happened. They would have thrown you to that animal ... and no doubt would still have gone to the castle.'

The tall one hung his head. In the shadowy light Iceace saw the wound still fresh on his cheek, his eye swollen. He suddenly looked up. 'I think you are wise beyond your years. What is your name?'

'Iceace.'

'You are a snowbun of great courage Iceace. My name is Hibu. I am an Erudite from the forest of Frelon in the north. We are sometimes called the tall people. The foul beasts captured me a week ago.'

An owl called. The sound echoed around the small copse. Iceace looked up nervously.

'I must go,' he whispered.

Hibu spoke quickly, 'When you get to the castle tell Elestyal there are about fifty trolls in the pack. They are Zorils. They are led by one called Cacodyl. He's clever and powerful, a lot more intelligent than your average troll. He has a second in command called Lirtob who is equally canny.'

'What about the white birds?'

'They're snow-vultures. Garbage and carrion eaters, but also look-outs for the trolls. You must hurry now, it's a long way to the castle, and they intend to attack early in the morning.' He looked at Iceace, so young and eager and determined. 'Are you sure about this? It's a long way and you are barely out of the nest.'

'I have no choice,' said Iceace stoutly, 'I can no longer

get back into the burrow. Pa has blocked the entrance for fear of weasels. And the old escape run, well, you can see why I can't return that way.'

Hibu eyed the hole, half way up the trunk of the old pine, 'Your father must be very proud of you.'

'My father doesn't know,' said Iceace, 'I told him I wanted to try and rescue you and warn the elves but he said it was impossible. And my mother forbade me to go.'

'Where there is a will as strong as yours there will always be a way,' said Hibu smiling, 'And why were you bent on rescuing this old Erudite?'

'I saw the blood on your face and your tears fall into the snow, and your sadness was great. I had to help.'

'You will never know how much I owe you for this.' Hibu leaned forward and gently took one of Iceace's front paws in his huge rag-wrapped hand. 'I only hope we meet again.'

Iceace didn't want to think about Hibu's fate. He felt wildly disappointed that he couldn't free him. Now he could only try to help the folk at the castle.

'Go now,' said Hibu, 'Run for your life and stop for nothing. And may your Great Rabbit Spirit protect you.'

'I won't forget you Hibu.'

'Nor me you. Now run like the wind. Skirt the wood

that way, on the north side, and then keep low, stay in the shadows, and *hurry*. A lot of folk depend on you this night.'

Iceace looked up at his new friend. Hibu's expression was grave. 'Goodbye,' he whispered.

Not Goodbye young Iceace, farewell. We will surely meet again. And good luck!'

Iceace ran. First softly and carefully past where the wolverine slept, past the Zoril trolls snoring by the camp fire, and then out of the wood and west across the snowy waste towards the castle. He was made for running. His young legs were already strong from all his exercises in the burrow. He ate up the ground, streaking over the soft powder, leaping through drifts, his heart strong as he raced on and on. After some miles he felt himself tiring. The bitter cold was eating up his strength and the castle seemed as far away as it had a few miles back. Distances were deceptive in this white land. He had to keep going he told himself, he dare not rest, everything depended on him and him alone. On and on he ran, eyes watering in the bitter wind, tiredness pulling at him as he fought the doubt that slid insidiously into his mind. Maybe he had been stupid to think he could undertake such a task? Maybe he wasn't as strong as he thought he was? Maybe his father had been right? He slowed a little. He couldn't keep up this pace. The burrow was now some miles behind, the castle a little closer. He dropped his head, flattened his ears along his back, and faced the wind.

Some time later Iceace lay on his side in the snow, the wind rippling across his back. He was exhausted. He had run as far as he could. He wanted to sleep now, to just drift and forget his mission, and the trolls, and the loathsome goolio and the tall one. Hibu! How could he forget his new friend? Hibu's battered face swam in front of him. *'Iceace! You must get up! Iceace! You must carry on!'* it said. But his legs were weak and he lay still, listening to the wind whining across the drifts'.

He closed his eyes. It was so peaceful. He felt himself slipping away, drifting. He wandered in a strange land where the hills were green and the grass was lush. There were strange flowers and insects and other rabbits, dozens of them, small and grey, all nibbling a crop of sweet and tender leaves. Surely the Great Spirit must live in this peaceful land? He would stay here and rest. But the stillness was suddenly broken by a jingling noise, a gentle jangle that got closer and closer. The grey rabbits stopped eating and sat stock still, ears and noses twitching, alerted to danger.

'*Bell! Bell!*' cried a rabbit who had been sitting near Iceace.

'*Run! Run!*' cried others.

And suddenly they were gone, running for their lives, bolting down holes and leaving Iceace alone. The jingling noise drew closer, it was coming from behind him. He turned. An animal was charging straight at him. It was a strange version of the gulo with a pink tongue lolling from its mouth. 'WOOF!' it said, WOOF-WOOF! The creature was nearly upon him. *Jingle-jangle-jingle* it went. The snowbun was confused. What was this noise? And then he saw that it came from a bell hanging around the creature's neck. At the last second he leaped sideways and the animal flew past. Iceace woke with a start, heart thumping. How long had he slept? And what a ghastly dream. But was it a dream? He could still hear the jingling! The beast must have followed him. He dragged himself to his feet just as something whooshed overhead. He cowered and glanced up. What in the name of the Great Rabbit Spirit ... ? A new apparition had been sent to test him. It was enormous. All silver and red and green with strange horned creatures seemingly pulling it along and strange creatures riding on it!

'Ho! Ho! Ho!' called one of them.

'Dirty bunny-bumbles!' squeaked Iceace, thinking instantly how his mother would disapprove of his words. 'What is it?' Fear galvanized him into action. Suddenly his legs were moving again, first at a stiff hop and then a few seconds later he was running full tilt, running for his life. The apparition had passed straight over, trailing purple-silver light and making the air crackle. It was going towards the castle, and it was flying faster than any bird. It wasn't chasing him. Relief. He slowed a little, his lungs burning from the sudden sprint, but he didn't stop. He didn't dare, lest tiredness overtake him again.

7
A Hasty Exit

Iceace sat breathing heavily looking up at the enormous front gate. *Christmas Castle* it said on the old wooden sign. And on a smaller sign underneath, *Please ring the bell.* But Iceace couldn't read so he squeezed underneath. He had to find someone quickly. Too soon the trolls would be waking and readying themselves to march on the castle. All was quiet. He dashed across the courtyard and up the steps to a door where a red-ribboned holly wreath hung from a nail. But the door was shut. Iceace was beside himself. 'I've come all this way,' he cried, 'and now I can't get in to tell anyone, and the trolls will come and my mission will have been for nothing!' He looked around the courtyard. Was he imagining things or could he see light coming from a barn across the way? He scampered over to the building. Yes! There was a light inside and he could hear noises. And, thank the Great Rabbit Spirit, the door was open. Without further ado he hopped inside.

Iceace stopped dead. In front of him was the red and

green and silver apparition that had flown over him while he was lying in the snow. And standing around it were the strange horned beasts that had been pulling it.

'Hello,' said one of them. It was chewing hay contemplatively and staring at him with big brown eyes, 'You're up early.'

A relief, it was friendly. 'Y-yes ... er ... are you an elf?'

The reindeer laughed. 'You must be just out of the nest. Never seen a reindeer before eh? Well my name is Dancer, and I'm a reindeer.'

'Who are you talking to Dancer?' A creature with a pale face, dressed all in green came into view. It had a similar look to Hibu but was much shorter. It seemed cheerful and inquisitive and very friendly.

'Are *you* an elf?' asked Iceace quickly.

'I am indeed an elf!' said the elf laughing, and you are ...?'

'I'm Iceace, I'm a snowbun from the warren by Pine Copse, and I have an urgent message for Elestral!'

'You mean Elestyal?'

'Yes! Yes! Elestrial! Is he here?'

'He most certainly is,' said a different figure appearing from a doorway with a reindeer harness over his arm.

Iceace stared up in wonder at the fat, white-bearded

figure bedecked in red. He swallowed. So this was a wizard! This was who Ma and Pa spoke of ... who gave them medicine, and sometimes food, and cared for all wild creatures. What an amazing looking being. For a few seconds he was so stunned he nearly forgot why he was there. Then he remembered and started to babble so fast that Elestyal could barely keep up. He ended in a rush with, 'And Hibu says to tell you there are about fifty of them and the leader is called Crocodil, and they're coming early this morning!'

By the time Iceace had finished Elestyal's smile had vanished. His face was dark with shock and disbelief. 'Are you sure of this?' he whispered, 'Tell me this is no prank!'

'No, no, it's true Mr Lestrial, please, you *must* believe me!'

'You risked your life to warn us?' Elestyal looked at him harder, 'You're barely grown. This was a very brave undertaking indeed.'

'Yes, and my Ma and Pa don't know and now I can't go home cus the burrow is blocked!'

The elves who had all been listening gathered around, their faces drawn with worry. Elestyal paced up and down, tugging at his beard. Lord, the snowbun rumour had been true! It was unbelievable. All these years the savages had stayed away over the water, and now they were back, bringing a reign of terror, as had always been their want.

'Fifty Zoril trolls! ... Fifty Zoril trolls!' cried Elestyal, his voice rising in disbelief as his mind searched for some solution. The Zoril was the worst kind. Large and vicious. Mean and merciless. There was only one solution. They must flee. At least they would get away with their lives. 'We have no hope of fighting them,' he said quietly. 'We must leave ... get everyone out.'

'We could go to Panglossian, at Castle Iffi, he's closest,' said Perks.

'I was thinking the same thing,' Elestyal nodded quickly.

'You must go soon,' broke in Iceace, 'They will be coming, with the gulo, and those birds!'

'What of Hibu? How was he?' The wizard had known the Erudites for years. They were a gentle people.

'He had chains on his arms and legs,' said Iceace, 'And bad places on his face where they hit him, and blood.'

'Hells' teeth! And we cannot help him! What evil has driven Cacodyl and his scum-bullions back here!' He continued to pace the floor shaking his head, then suddenly he walked swiftly out of the barn.

The elves followed and stood beside him, following his

gaze towards the pine copse on the distant hills where a tiny flicker of flame could be seen. A camp fire. As they watched, the flame suddenly went out.

'They've doused their fire. They're on the move. We don't have much time!' Elestyal turned to face the sleighriders. 'Awaken everyone! Get them up and get the elflings dressed. Gather only necessities. We meet in the great hall in ten minutes!'

'Can I come too?' said a small voice. Iceace was looking up at the wizard. 'I cannot go home.'

'We owe you a huge debt,' said Elestyal. 'You will forever have our protection.'

'Come on Iceace, stick with me,' said Perks, wondering how on earth Frisk and Moonbeam were going to feel when they discovered Iceace was missing.

Within a short time everyone had been woken. Yawning elflings had been plucked from their beds while worried elves scurried about gathering warm clothes and necessities. Soon everyone was gathered in the candlelight of the great hall. There was a low murmur of concerned voices. What was happening? Why had they been woken? It must be very serious. Elestyal addressed them, his expression grave. He had taken off his Santa hat and beard and now looked odd in the remains of his suit.

'My friends! A brave and resourceful messenger has come into our midst tonight with fearsome news. We suddenly find ourselves in great danger. A large band of Zoril trolls are on their way here as we speak, with the intention of taking this castle for their own.' Gasps of fear and anger filled the hall. Elestyal continued, 'We have to leave, and leave quickly. This castle has been our home for many years, and it will be difficult, but what is coming here is too great for us to fight. We have little time. We go to my old and dear friend, Panglossian, in the south-west. He will give us shelter.'

The sleighriders were gathered beside him. He spoke to them quietly, 'You know of the round-room?' They nodded, they had all heard of it. 'Do any of you know the way down there?'

Skyler and Jake were the only ones.

'It's a long time ago since I went down there,' said Skyler quickly, 'But I haven't forgotten the way.'

'Me too. We'll find it,' said Jake firmly.

'You remember where the keys are hidden?'

They did.

'Good. You must lead everyone down and take them to the end of the passage. Now I need three of you to help Zeb with the reindeer.'

'I'll go,' said Sneepy quickly. Archy and Wingo nodded too.

Elestyal called for Zeb, the stable manager.

'Zeb, I want you to take all the reindeer and the sleigh around to the big pine in Tall Pine Wood. Use the old sleigh as well. Prepare all the reindeer for riders. There is still much magic and all the deer can still fly. We will leave no tracks. When everyone has arrived in the wood get them mounted up. The elderly and the elflings must go in the sleighs. Can you find your way to Panglossian's castle?'

Zeb nodded quickly, 'It's on the south side of Bearban forest, beside Loon Lake. You follow the river over Kokanee Crags.'

'Yes, good! Tell Panglossian that I will follow as soon as I can. Skylor, when everyone is safely in the wood I want you, Perks, Sid, Jake, Chip, Perry and Hugo to return to the round-room. I will meet you there.' Elestyal turned to look at the elves and their families waiting in the hall. He couldn't believe they were having to do this. It was unthinkable to have to abandon Christmas Castle.

'Have courage!' he cried to everyone, 'We have a long journey ahead of us. Now everyone ... *hurry!*

They started to file swiftly and silently out of the door

behind Skyler and Jake. The mood was grim. They were in shock. Christmas Castle had been the only home that some of them had ever known and to lose it seemed unthinkable. But they were stout-hearted folk and they trusted Elestyal. They would do what needed to be done. The candlelit procession wound its way through the festive castle kitchen and down the stairs, past Elestyal's room and through the big old door into the honeycomb of deep passages under the castle. Deeper and deeper they went, down and down.

Petal was deep in thought, hands stuffed in the pockets of her stable jacket. In the rush to leave she had just remembered she'd left her pictures under her mattress where it kept them nice and flat. They were only pictures of the reindeer which she had drawn and painted since she was small. No great value, but she was fond of them. It didn't really matter, she could draw some more. Her mind slid to the trolls. She hadn't believed the rumour. Now this! Had they been advancing towards Pine Copse when she took Frisk home? She thought about the bird call, and the creepy feeling she'd had as she was leaving and she shuddered.

'I've been trying to catch up with you!' said a voice at her shoulder.

'Aleron.'

'This is dreadful isn't it.'

'I can't believe it. Trolls coming back after all these years. It's horrible. Where are we going?'

'Dungeons, I guess.' Aleron raised his candle and peered up at the grey stone of the low arched ceiling where cobwebs dangled. A muffled, eerie quietness engulfed them. The only noise, the light tap of elfin feet on dusty stone.

'Someone said something about a round-room,' whispered Petal.

'I heard that too. No idea where it is though.'

They carried on, deep into the maze of passages until Skyler suddenly called a halt.

'I'm sure this is it,' he said to Jake. 'Stay here, 'I'll check.' He slipped off down a narrow passage to his right that could easily have been missed if a person hadn't been looking for it. His candle flickered as he crept further along, eventually coming to a solid wall. A dead-end. He held the candle as high as he could and then carefully walked backwards, keeping his eyes on the ceiling. Suddenly he smiled. Above him, inscribed on the rock was a strange symbol; an elvish sign. He knelt down directly below it and started to brush the thick dust off the old flags, paying particular attention to one which had a thin circular crack about six inches across, running around the centre. Gently, he pressed down on one side of the circle. As he did so the other side flipped up. He removed the piece of stone and looked at the key hidden in a perfect recess underneath, then he eased it out of its form and turned it over in his hands. It was smooth and heavy. The letters *RR* were etched on one side and *CC* on the other.

Skyler got up and took three measured steps forward from where the key had been inset. Again he stopped, knelt down and brushed away dust, pulling the candle closer and peering hard at the floor. He smiled and nodded. His memory had served him well. Ingeniously hidden in the cross where four thin flags met was a keyhole. He gently inserted the key and turned it. There was a *clunk* as the lock was thrown. Then he turned the key another half turn and used it as a handle. The cleverly disguised trap door pulled up easily.

Jake, waiting with the elves at the junction of the passages heard a low whistle from Skyler. 'Come on,' he called to the crowd behind him, 'He's found it.' They started to move along the passage.

'Stay here and I'll check down below,' said Skyler as Jake arrived. Jake watched him descend down the spiral staircase, holding his candle aloft. A voice soon came echoing up,

'Stairs are good ... come on!'

Jake started helping elves down through the trap door, while Skyler, now at the bottom of the stairs, looked up and around him in wonder. This place always had had a strange presence about it. He watched his breath, misty in the ice-cold atmosphere, and wondered why someone had wanted to build such a cavernous chamber down here in the bowels of the castle. He knew it had some ancient history but he had never asked about it. Once every five years or so a couple of them came down and checked that the passage, the doors, and the keys were all in working order, in case of an emergency Elestyal said. But none of them had seriously believed it would ever be necessary. The walls were a construction of massive hand-hewn rock. The central staircase carved from ancient oak corkscrewed up to the trap door in the domed ceiling, where the elves were starting their descent.

Across from the staircase was an arched door. Skyler went over to it and tested the handle. As expected it was locked. This time the key was secreted under the bottom step of the stairs. He felt around and pulled it out, then he unlocked the door and returned the key to its hiding place. Another key, hidden on the other side of the door would lock up behind them. It was the same with the trap door, hidden keys on both sides, allowing access from either direction at all times.

Half way down the stairs Petal stopped and peered over the handrail, fascinated by the grotesque shadows playing around the walls.

'This must be it ... the round-room!' she whispered to Aleron.

'I know,' said Aleron, 'Keep moving.'

Petal continued, 'What a place ... Wow! ... Is this ever exciting!'

Aleron didn't think it exciting in the slightest. His mind was glued to his anger at the beasts coming to take his home. The only home he had ever known. The home he loved. Everyone around him was upset to be leaving, and nervous of the dungeons, except Petal it seemed. She appeared immune to both. Her attitude both amazed and annoyed him.

'It's not very exciting to have to flee our home and hand it over to a bunch of stinking trolls,' he whispered, anger flaring in his voice.

The sharp retort stung. 'Then we'll just have to get it back, won't we!' she replied smartly.

'Oh yes! And how do *we* intend to do that?'

'We'll have to *think* of something.'

'Tell me when you do.'

'I will.' Petal fell silent.

'Move along down there,' called a quiet voice from above.

Petal reached the bottom and walked towards the door, stopping for a minute to turn and look back up at the staircase. Eerie and beautiful, she thought, as the elves with their candles gently circled down. She shivered a little. Was it the cold ... or was there some strange feeling in here?

'Hurry up,' urged Aleron irritably, nearly bumping into her.

Petal ran quickly to catch up with the others and stepped through the doorway. Narrow stone steps swept up and around. A cobweb tickled her hair and she swept it away. Lights in elfin hands danced along the walls as they ascended. At last, after climbing for ten minutes or so the stairs levelled out into a narrow passage. It seemed to go on forever; musty and dark and low-ceilinged. Petal thought it would never end. Bored with walking, and hurt by Aleron's attitude, she slipped past the others and squeezed up to the front behind Skyler who had finally reached the end of the passage. They had arrived at a small oval door.

'The key,' muttered Skyler. He knew it was on the right hand side of the door behind a loose stone, but the ivy had grown in thickly over the cracks. He pulled more and more away and squinted at the wall, then he looked around. 'Bring your candle,' he whispered to Petal. Petal was glad to help, and with more light Skyler suddenly saw what he was looking for, a large stone, slightly pink in colour. He eased it out and retrieved the key from behind it. The lock still worked well but the door was snagged with creeper. He started pulling at the tendrils and fibrous roots of ivy and other climbing plants which had crept in over the years. Petal helped him. It was a few minutes before the door would yield. When it did fresh cold air hit their faces and snow tumbled into the passage. Skyler called in a low voice for the elves to douse their candles.

The door to the passageway was set back under a small ridge dotted with pines. In summer a riot of ferns, wild flowers, and mosses camouflaged it. Now it was hidden by snow, with more falling. A few yards away was a clearing, and across the clearing under a particularly enormous old pine were Zeb, Sneepy, Archy and Wingo with the two sleighs and the entire herd of Christmas Castle reindeer.

'Hurry!' called Skyler softly to the waiting elves, 'Skirt round the edge of the clearing and mount up.'

They slipped between the trees. Skyler followed and headed straight to Zeb. 'We need you to leave some deer for us,' he said, 'Elestyal wants seven of us to go back to the round-room and meet him.'

Zeb looked up at the tumbling white flakes, 'Looks like this storm arrived just in time,' he said quickly, 'I'll leave you our best flyers.' He picked certain reindeer and told them to wait. They understood. Zeb rubbed their ears and scratched under their chins. They'd do anything for their master. 'You'll catch us up soon,' he whispered.

Perks took Iceace over to one of the sleighs. 'Hop in,' he said.

'Are we going up in the air?' asked Iceace, round-eyed.

'You bet! You'll be fine, just don't look down!'

'Ma and Pa will never believe this!' squeaked Iceace. Then his heart sank as he wondered if he'd ever get the chance to tell them. He jumped into the sleigh and Bizz took him under her ample wing.

'I'll keep an eye on you,' she said, puffed from the long walk, and glad to be sitting down. 'Come on young snowbun.'

Petal, who had been first over to the deer, was astride Smooch. She watched the others mount up, barely able to contain herself at the idea that they were going to fly, albeit slowly, according to Zeb. Aleron appeared beside her.

'You okay?' he felt bad about getting angry with her

earlier.

'I can't *believe* we're going to fly!' she whispered, her face all lit up with excitement.

He stared at her for a minute, his expression stunned disbelief. Brown eyes almost black with emotion. 'Yes, we're flying. Flying away from everything I love.' He ground out the words and rode off. Petal sighed. What could she do? She couldn't help it if she saw this as an adventure. She stroked Smooch's soft neck and watched the elves mount up and fill the sleighs. She noticed that seven had broken away and were running back in the direction of the secret passage. She wondered why, but before she could wonder too long Zeb called softly for them to get ready. Seconds later they were up and away. It was amazing! She squinted down through swirling snowflakes at Christmas Castle, her hair whipping into her eyes. And then they banked and headed south towards the mountains. A thrill filled her like nothing ever had before. This is what it would be like to be a sleigh-rider! Only a hundred times faster!

8
A Spell is Cast

Elestyal looked around the great hall with a heavy heart. For hundreds of years this castle had been home to St Nicholas and the elves. Now it appeared it was to be taken over by a pack of barbarous savages. The lowest of the low. And there was nothing he could do about it. He couldn't fight fifty Zorils by himself and the elves were not trained in the skills of battle as they had been a hundred years ago. He would not risk their lives by trying to make a stand. All he could do was give thanks to one small brave snowbun for having the courage to come and warn them, at the risk of his own life. If he hadn't ... Elestyal didn't dare imagine that other outcome.

He scanned the hall. Tonight they would have had the Christmas Feast in here, the banquet table laid with their beautiful silver platters and candlesticks, and pretty decorations. It was the way they celebrated the hard work of the year, culminating in the Christmas delivery. He chided himself for even thinking of the silver. As part of tradition as it was it was still only material possessions. He had to give thanks that they were escaping with their lives.

His attention was drawn back to the banquet table dominating the centre of the hall. He had needed a plan, had been waiting for something to land in his mind. Now something was forming and growing rapidly. The silver. It was as though it had spoken to him. He went quickly to one of the drawers in the carved oak sideboard and opened it. Candlelight fell on the contents. He picked out a small spoon and held it up. It shimmered in the pale light. Yes! Cacodyl would covet this! He would gloat over these spoils, this horde of elfin treasure. The wizard knew the nature of the beast from long ago, before the days of Santa Claus. If he was lucky he could turn the plunderer's avarice to his own advantage. He must get going, the elves would be waiting for him. Hurrying to the door his eye fell on the sleighriders box, left on the table after the draw. Damned if he'd leave that for them! He scooped it up and popped the silver spoon inside, then he sped off down towards the deep passages and the round-room.

Arriving at the trap door which Skyler had left open for him, Elestyal put the box and his candle carefully on the floor. The key was still in the lock. He took it out and replaced it in its hiding place under the piece of flagstone, then he eyed the black hole that he had to squeeze down through. He wasn't going to fit through it in his suit, the extra girth wouldn't allow it. He shook his head. 'Have to take it off,' he sighed. He was glad he had his dungarees on underneath. He bundled the jacket and trousers together with the beard and hat and put them in a pile. He couldn't carry the candle, the box, and the suit. He would make two trips. He slipped down onto the steps and pulled the bundle in after him. It was dark and the clothing was cumbersome, it snagged on the top of the handrail. Elestyal cursed and lifted it higher to release it. There was a sound from below. A little knocking sound. He stopped dead. The sleighriders must be back!

'Hello!' he called softly. But no one answered. He was sure he'd heard something ... 'Hello?' he called again. Nothing. He told himself he must be imagining things.

Clutching the bulky bundle to his chest he wound his way down the stairs. It was inky black at the bottom, and a little creepy even for a wizard. He quickly dumped the suit to one side and started back up to collect the box and the candle and to lock the door. He pulled the trap shut easily and held the candle up to look for the second key. Ah yes! It was hanging on its hook under one of the beams close-by.

He locked up and replaced it. He was nearly at the bottom of the stairs when he heard light running feet and muffled whispering. The sleighriders were back.

Elestyal greeted them quickly. 'Did all go well?' he asked.

'Yes. Everyone was fine. They're on their way to Panglossian,' said Skyler.

'Good, good! Well done my friends! Now we have one last task before we leave. A task with which I need your help.' They gathered closer. 'This room is a most powerful room. Hundreds of years ago it was used for making magic ... good magic. In those days the castle belonged to a wizard called Luscinia Megarhynchos, or in normal tongue, The Nightingale. He was known simply as Megar. This room was the sorcerer's room, his room. There's no time to tell you more now. All I will tell you is that with the help of Megar, whose energy still lives in these walls, we are going to cast a spell.'

The seven elves could hardly believe what they were hearing.

'What we do here tonight *must* stay between us,' said Elestyal, looking around at each of them. 'Keep what you see and hear utterly secret. It is imperative that no word reaches the Zorils. Tell no one!' The sleighriders nodded, a solemn expression on each face.

'Bring your candles,' said Elestyal. He walked a few steps away and knelt down, then he started to blow gently at the floor. The thick dust parted and swirled. He blew harder. It enveloped them all in a candlelit cloud of sparkling, pale grey particles. Perks coughed. Dust settled, and seconds later they found themselves staring at a large and curious stone set in the round-room floor.

'This is the Hawk's Eye stone,' said Elestyal, 'The stone of the wizard. The stone of vision and insight.' He dragged the candle closer, took out his handkerchief and gently buffed the surface. With the dust removed its hidden beauty shone forth. The elves stared in wonder. It was the deep blue of a midnight sky, swirled with bands of pale luminous grey, and here and there a dash of soft green. Etched in the centre was a silver bird. 'See the bird?' said the wizard, 'It's the nightingale.' Seven heads craned forward. The bird was depicted singing on the topmost branch of a thorn-bush, under the full moon. 'This is the bird Megar was named after,' said Elestyal. 'This is his stone which still has powerful magic. It will help us tonight.' He got up and walked over to the sleighriders box, opened it, and took out the silver spoon. He laid it across the stone. 'We must all stand and join hands. Place your candles in a circle around the bird. We are eight. It's a powerful number and the symbol of great sorcery. This is why I asked for seven of you to return and help me.

The seven elves moved forward and placed their candles on the floor, then they stepped back and linked hands with the wizard in a silent circle. The flickering lights rose up and lit each face. Hand in hand they waited, in awe of what they were about to be part of. Then Elestyal's voice became filled with a gravity and power they had never heard before, and the seven thought of nothing, and heard nothing but his voice. His words echoed clearly and darkly in the hollowness of the great room.

See the bird. Look at the bird. Believe in the magic with all your hearts.'

He paused.

'Now ... slowly ... slowly ... close your eyes ...'

Skyler felt his eyelids suddenly become heavy. He saw the nightingale start to spin in the circle. Faster and faster it whirled. In its beak it now carried the silver spoon. His eyes finally closed. The nightingale continued to spin. How strange, he thought. My eyes are closed yet I still see the bird. He felt light, as though he was floating, looking down on the round-room from above. And then he was surrounded by Elestyal's words as they rose and fell and whispered around the ancient walls. Wizard's tongue. A language known only to sorcerers ...

'Mee-gar ... Meee-gar ...
Carme eh ens nowd!
Arjone fin eh Arjone Arl
Arjone var eh Arjone caul
Sorb ere par o'wizze ere
Eh-gra, expa, eh starz se ner
Arri-trenty-sero a-carm
Rarelesc zer par eh duh zer ar'hm
Sond e Arvile 'ons t'eehl
Arjone! Arjone! De zerelm shahneel
Dispar'o-le arvile frae onome
Coom'no-bey-joine arayus sowme
Coom'no ary m'ch l'ee-alyt
Serrge Maygar! Avio-frete
Arjone bey arczu-shnay na'cee
Deezparton zeem'a oh-oh'Kinze
Arjone! Ab-naz'orm Ny!
Arjone! Ab-naz'orm Ny!

A sudden heavy silence fell as Elestyal finished. They stood as in a dream in the stillness, in the cold and the candlelight. Then his voice, deep and calm, came again,

'Awake now ... awake my friends!'

The seven had barely started to open their eyes when something like a small explosion rocked the old room. They were jolted back to reality as a force so strong that it nearly unbalanced them, passed through the room. Perks could have sworn he felt warm breath on his ear. And at the same moment a strange fleeting voice breathed a barely perceptible word ... *'Sassilvashakalim!'*

'What on earth was that?' he whispered, noting the equally wide-eyed glances of the others.

Elestyal smiled knowingly, 'That was Megar! The spell is good!' He picked up the silver spoon and slipped it into the pocket of his dungarees. 'Remember what I've told you. What took place here tonight stays in this room. Talk of it to no one.' They nodded in grave agreement. 'Now we must go quickly and pray that the trolls have not discovered our reindeer in the wood. Come, help me carry these things. Bizz will kill me if I leave my suit.' They gathered up the clothes and the wooden box.

'I'll lock the door,' said Skyler. He did so and placed the key quickly behind the loose rock kept for the purpose. Then they headed as fast as they could up the narrow stairs and along the passage, all arriving somewhat out of breath at the oval door. Elestyal pushed it open and peered out. It was still half-light, snowing more heavily. Across the clearing he could just make out the reindeer standing under the tall pine.

'Go!' he whispered to the elves, 'Leave your candles here. I'll lock up.'

They ran, threading their way through the trees at the edge of the clearing, nimble even in the deep snow. Perks, who was carrying Elestyal's bulky suit didn't find it quite as easy. He arrived last, nearly tripping on the bundle.

'They must have been short of deer,' called Jake in hushed tones, 'They've only left us seven.'

'I'll double-up with Elestyal,' said Perks, 'You guys mount up. Those dam Zorils could be close!'

Elestyal was just about to place the door-key behind the pink stone, then thought better of it. Time was precious. The Zorils could be upon them at any moment. He'd use the passage key normally hidden on the inside to lock up, and then he'd take it with him. The key hidden on the outside, a short distance away, could stay in its hiding place. Snow fell on snow, thick and fast. It would cover their tracks. But just to be sure he picked up a pine bough and swept away his footprints until he was well away from the door. Then he ran to the waiting party. Perks had thrown the Santa suit over their mount's back like a rug.

'Good thinking,' he whispered as Perks gave him a leg up. 'Easier than trying to carry it.'

'Better hang on to this!' Perks handed up the all in one hat and beard and Elestyal pulled it over his head.

'Listen!' hissed Skyler suddenly.

Grunts and growls were coming from the far side of the wood. There was heavy movement and the sound of low snarls as something crashed towards them through the trees.

'They're here!' cried Elestyal. 'Fly! Fly now!' Perks grabbed the wizard's outstretched hand and swung up behind him and in seconds the reindeer were airborne. They soared up through the driving snow, the Christmas energy still powerful enough to give them their wings. Up and over the woods they flew cutting swiftly away from Christmas Castle and heading south.

Below them the first Zoril trolls arrived in the clearing. They looked in puzzlement at the tracks of many reindeer which had been standing by a tall pine. The tracks went nowhere ... but the deer were gone. They snarled, confused and angry at missing their prey.

'That was close!' shouted Perks through the wind, as he hung on to the back of Elestyal's dungarees and tried to get the wizard's wind-whipped Santa-beard out of his face.

'Too close!' cried Elestyal.

Perks tightened his grip on the reindeer's smooth flanks. 'I think I'll hang on to my hat!'

9
Hibu

The door to Christmas Castle kitchen burst open and the two trolls who were dragging Hibu by his chain almost fell down the steps as their prisoner lagged back.

'Get in here!' bellowed the one called Codweb, who was seriously overweight and waddled in an upright fashion as he walked.

'Or you'll get another beating!' cursed the other, known as Emlock. He was the reverse of his mate, skinny and slightly hunch-backed, with a constantly runny nose.

Hibu stumbled painfully down the steps, his feet cut and bleeding. The rags he had wrapped around them had done little to protect them from the ice and snow. His gaolers had relieved him of his boots some days ago and fought over them. Codweb had won and now clumped about in them proudly. They were two sizes too big and his belly prevented him from reaching the laces, but he didn't care.

'We needs to find somewhere to lock 'im up,' said the

owner of the boots, who seemed to think his new footwear gave him some sort of elevated status over his mate. 'We'll try down 'ere.' He clumped over to the stairs hauling on Hibu's chain, 'You get behind 'im and give 'im a push if 'e gets difficult!'

Emlock glared at Codweb and at the coveted boots. One day, when Codweb was sleeping deeply enough, he'd have them off him. That would stop him being so full of himself. For now he just glared and stepped back behind the prisoner. The trio made slow progress down the steps and arrived at the door to what had been Elestyal's room.

'This'll do,' snarled Codweb. He threw open the door and the two bundled Hibu into the small room, forcing him to duck quickly under the low jamb. 'Get 'is chains off!'

Emlock narrowed his eyes and curled his lip. 'Do it yerself!' he barked. He threw the key to Hibu's chains on the floor, wheeled out of the room and hurried back up to the kitchen. Codweb cursed, scrabbled for the key and removed the chains. He dragged them into the hall, slammed and locked the door, and was off up the stairs as fast as he could, stumbling over his laces and swearing. He was hungry. They had planned to raid the kitchen before the rest of the clan got there. Damned if the skinny, snivelling Emlock was going to snaffle the best grub.

Hibu sank onto Elestyal's bed, closed his eyes, and put his head in his hands. A tear rolled down his cheek. He brushed it away, annoyed with himself for giving in to his despair. He was cold and hungry, tired, and hopeless. What was going to happen to him? He thought it best he didn't dwell on that train of thought. He must do whatever he could to help himself. He must keep strong, and then if the chance came he would escape. First he had to see to his feet.

He stood up stiffly and shuffled around the room. It was very basic, but neat and tidy. There was a solid-looking table and chair in one corner, a tall cupboard against the far wall, some shelves with books on and a small corner cupboard behind the door. On the back of the door were four wooden pegs from which hung a few clothes, mostly shirts and dungarees. Hibu studied the dungarees. He vaguely recalled seeing Elestyal in a pair, many years ago when he had visited here. His mind started working. He shuffled across to the shelves and looked at the books. They appeared to all be about gardening. *'Get the Best out of your vegetables', 'The Kitchen Gardener', 'When to Plant', 'Know your Onions', 'For Lovers of Leeks', 'Worrisome Weevils And Other Garden Pests'*, and many more in the same vein. At the far end of the shelf there was a much older and heavier volume, bound in leather with no title on the spine. Hibu eased it out and opened it. *Wizardopaedia* it said on the front page, and underneath *Spells and Medicines for Life*. This book definitely belonged to Elestyal. This room must be Elestyal's! A sort of warm gladness crept over Hibu and almost at once he felt better, more hopeful. He went to the tall cupboard and opened up the doors. Sitting on the shelf in front of him was a large bowl of water, some soap, a cloth and a small towel. Obviously everyone had left in a hurry. This thought brought another thought, that of young Iceace. He had made it! Yes, he had made it in time and warned Elestyal and the elves. A slow smile spread across his previously sad face. That snowbun was something very special.

His attention returned to the contents of the cupboard. On the shelf above the bowl was a wooden chest. He took it down and placed it on the desk. When he opened the lid his smile became even bigger. Elestyal's medicines! Jars and bottles of creams and potions for every possible illness or injury. Hibu lifted out a jar with a label that said *'Essence of Chamomile – For Cuts and Abrasions'*. He could have cried at this find. It was a shame there were no bandages. He quickly took the bowl of water over to the bed and placed it on the floor, then he sat down and unwrapped the rags from his feet. He placed one foot gingerly in the water. Ahhh! It felt wonderful. He dabbed and cleaned the cuts gently with the cloth, dried his foot carefully and applied the ointment. It felt wonderful, warm and soothing. He did the other foot and then he lay back and put them both up on the bed. After a short rest he tiptoed to the door and unhooked one of the old cotton shirts. The material was thin, but it smelled fresh and clean and would easily tear up for bandages. He mentally apologised to Elestyal as he tore long strips from the sleeves and carefully bound both feet. Then he hunted for socks. Surely Elestyal wore them? In the bottom drawer of the old cupboard he found plenty. A pair of Elestyal's longest ones were just big enough to come up to his ankles. He padded around for a few minutes amazed at how the pain in his feet had subsided. Then he nodded knowingly. Wizard's medicine, of course it would work!

With his feet back in working order Hibu quickly got to work. First he put the medicine chest and the books on the very top of the tall cupboard. There was a shallow recess behind the carved cornice, where they would be well hidden. He assumed the Zorils would keep him locked in here until they decided what to do with him. He hoped so.

He wanted access to the medicines and to Elestyal's *Wizardopaedia*. He didn't think they'd care much about the bowl and the soap. Trolls weren't generally prone towards cleanliness. He went to the desk and opened the drawer. Lots of pens and paper. Again of no interest to uneducated cave-dwellers. They would probably burn them, so he hid them behind the books and went back and sat on the bed. He yawned, suddenly realising how deeply tired he was from all the shock and fear of the last few days. It was catching up with him. He must try to rest and regain some strength. He lay down and covered himself with Elestyal's warm woollen blanket, but sleep evaded him. His stomach was empty and it growled and rumbled in discontent.

After a while he gave up, dragged himself back into a sitting position and found himself staring at the corner cupboard. He'd forgotten to check it. He'd better do it now before his friendly gaolers reappeared. He slid off the bed feeling weary as sin and padded across the room. When he opened the cupboard door he could barely believe his eyes. A dish with six little pies, a hunk of bread with a wedge of cheese, and a mug with some sort of drink in it greeted him. His mouth watered. He took it all quickly to the bed and sat down. He mustn't eat it all. He'd have some now and hide the rest. There was no telling when his captors would decide to feed him. The bread was delicious, a generous hunk of wholemeal with sunflower seeds, pumpkin seeds, and walnuts. Full of energy. The cheese was sharp and firm with a nutty flavour. He tried hard to eat slowly, savouring every mouthful. He ate half the bread and cheese and carefully wrapped the remains in a piece of cloth from the shirt he had cut up for bandages. He tried the drink. It was new to him ... sweet ... satisfying ... comforting. He sipped tiny sips, letting the liquid pool on his tongue for a few seconds, playing with the flavour before he swallowed. He drank half the mug and decided to test one of the pies. He bit into it and found that it too was sweet. Inside the outer layer of pastry were dried fruits with rich spices. Heavenly! Hibu closed his eyes and chewed in ecstasy. He ate two of the pies as slowly as he could and then wrapped the other four up with the bread and cheese. Then he sipped the drink until it was gone and stowed the mug and the food on the top of the cupboard with the rest of his hidden treasures. With food in his stomach he felt like a different person. He lay back down on the bed and sighed. A curious twist of fate had had his gaolers put him in this room, a room where there was everything he needed most. And with that thought he fell asleep.

About an hour later Hibu was woken suddenly by the loud screech of a troll and the rattling of a key in the door. He sat up quickly, heart thumping. Someone kicked the door open. It appeared his gaolers had been told to feed him. The scrawny troll appeared first, plunking down a bucket of water, then the fat one threw two apples and a hunk of bread onto the bed. Their leader stepped in behind them, the beefy Cacodyl. He looked down at Hibu, noticed the freshly bandaged feet, and glared at his minions.

'What was in here? Codweb? Did you search the room before you put him in here?'

'Sure boss,' lied Codweb. He gave Hibu a stare as good as to say '*Tell him any different and you'll be sorry.*'

Cacodyl walked over to the desk and opened the drawer: nothing. He shut it with a bang, then walked to the tall cupboard and threw open the doors; again nothing. He narrowed his eyes and fixed Hibu with a penetrating gaze.

'Was there anything in this room? Did you find something?'

'Well ... yes,' said Hibu, pausing to see the effect his answer had on his lying gaolers, and hoping Codweb was shaking in his - Hibu's - boots. Cacodyl would be livid if he knew what they had missed, and he had managed to hide away. Elestyal's *Wizardopaedia* would have been highly prized, even though Cacodyl couldn't read. He savoured the minute, eyeing the two trolls and enjoying the fear in their eyes. Their punishment would be heavy for being so lazy and lax. They had been too eager to raid the kitchen.

'Well?' shouted Cacodyl, 'Where is it, whatever it is?'

'Behind the door.' Hibu pointed.

Emlock and Codweb backed up in such a panic that Codweb tripped over his boot laces. He overbalanced, catching Emlock in the ribs with an elbow. Emlock screeched. Cacodyl marched to the door and threw it back. Elestyal's dungarees and old shirts swung innocently on the pegs. He snorted with disgust. 'Is that it?'

'Yes,' said Hibu shrugging, all innocence and bowing his head in feigned respect while he chuckled inside. 'That's it ... oh ... and the soap and water.' He pointed to the bowl by the bed with the torn up shirt beside it. 'I used it to do some repairs to my feet.'

Cacodyl glowered at the pair of quaking trolls. '*Watch your step!*' he said softly, 'And look after the prisoner, he may be useful. Feed him twice a day.' He looked Codweb up and down, his eyes coming to rest on the boots. 'If you don't, then he gets his shoes back.'

Humble nods from the lackeys. Cacodyl swung out of the room and headed upstairs. Codweb immediately gave

Emlock a shove.

'You should 'ave checked the room Emlock!' he hissed.

Emlock snarled. Yellow fangs showed under the curled lip. 'Think you're special 'cus you got the boots ... but we'll see about that!' He sidled up nose to nose with Codweb. 'You 'ave to sleep sometime!' And with that he shoved Codweb hard in his podgy belly and bolted for the kitchen. Codweb, caught off-balance, stood on his laces again and went down in a heap in front of Hibu. He flailed frantically for some seconds trying to right himself. A good impression of a beetle on its back, thought Hibu as he sat on the bed and smirked at the furious fat troll.

'I'll kill 'im!' squealed Codweb, eventually hoisting himself to his feet. And with a mighty roar he flung himself out of the room, slammed the door and tore off in hot pursuit.

Hibu was sure he hadn't heard the turn of a key. He crept to the door and tried it. Open! 'That's the trouble with trolls,' he muttered, shaking his head, 'Impulsive and hot-headed.' In his fury his incensed gaoler had completely forgotten it. But it was a useless opportunity. There was no hope of escape with the castle full of trolls, and besides his poor feet wouldn't get him very far. It was best he waited, bided his time. If Cacodyl had intended to kill him he would have done it already. He had told the gaolers to feed him twice a day so he must be intending to make use of him in some way. Hibu knew his best chance to stay alive was to be what the trolls wanted, a submissive servant, to all intents and purposes defeated and humble. Maybe even grateful for being allowed to live. He stood at the door thinking for a few seconds, then he opened it and left it ajar. He would play them. His act would be good. If bowing and scraping and tugging his forelock bought him time then so be it. He collected the bread and the apples off the bed and stowed them on top of the cupboard. He was full up at the moment. He would save them for later. He wondered which of his gaolers would come back first. He hoped it would be the un-booted one. If it was he had a plan.

In the castle kitchen there was mayhem. More trolls had arrived and were manically turning out cupboards in search of food. Fighting started. Two trolls having a tug-of-war with a loaf fell over a chair when the bread separated. Violent screeching filled the room when one of the contestants saw that he had come off worst and had a quarter of what the other had. Two more joined the fray and went for the big portion, knocking plates off the table as they did so. The dishes smashed on the flagstones.

'Enough!' Cacodyl stood in the doorway. He had found a large and well-honed axe in the stables and was swinging it gently but menacingly as he surveyed the mêlée in the kitchen. Respect for the leader, especially a leader with a particularly lethal looking axe, brought almost instant order. Another troll appeared beside Cacodyl. Cacodyl turned to him, 'Lirtob, get this rabble in order. Put two in charge of the kitchen and make sure the food is divided.'

Lirtob grunted assent and ambled down the steps. He was the second largest troll in the clan, standing a couple of inches shorter than the leader. He, like Cacodyl had a bearing that demanded not to be messed with. He had been with this band of Zorils for many years, always second in command, always waiting his chance to grab leadership. But there was little hope of toppling the chief. Cacodyl was not only physically powerful but he was also smart for a troll, and the group accepted him. The hierarchy was unlikely to change unless Cacodyl met with an accident, preferably a mysterious one which would not bring suspicion on Lirtob. The opportunity had never come ... yet.

'Okay you thieving rabble!' he yelled, 'Clean up the mess and put all the food on the table. Then we'll divide it.' He watched them as they reluctantly gave up what they had found. Two were still furtively squabbling over an orange.

'Give it up!' he thundered. 'Codweb and Emlock! For your trouble, you two can work in the kitchen from now on.'

The two trolls hissed and growled, but avoided eye-contact with the second in command. Emlock banged the orange down on the table. 'We already got a job,' he whined, wiping his nose with the back of his arm. 'We 'ave to look after the prisoner downstairs.'

'Yeah and feed the oaf too,' muttered Codweb.

Lirtob took three strides across the kitchen and grabbed Emlock by the left ear, raising him off the ground as he did so. The skinny troll squealed in fright.

'Arguing has painful results,' shouted Lirtob into the trapped ear.

Emlock cringed, 'Yes boss!' he wailed.

'So now you can take the fruit to the prisoner.'

'But ... '

'No *buts*!' growled Lirtob.

Emlock desperately wanted to say that the prisoner had already been fed, but he didn't dare argue further. Lirtob let go of the ear and dropped him. He scooped up the orange and scampered off down to Hibu's room feeling furious. It was Cobweb's fault. Emlock had found the orange first. He'd had enough of stinking Codweb and his bossy attitude. Arriving in front of Hibu's door he broke out in a cold sweat. It was ajar! Open! Codweb hadn't locked it! The stupid fool of a troll. Now they were both dead. He pushed the door wide, panic filling his belly, and was greeted by Hibu. The prisoner was stretched out on the bed, relaxed, staring at him. Emlock couldn't get his head around it. Open door should equal escaped prisoner. Why was he still here? He began to stutter.

'Wha ... wha ... what's going on?'

'Nothing,' said Hibu, pretending to look confused, 'I was just trying to sleep.'

'The door!' Emlock was whispering now, 'The door's unlocked!'

'I know,' Hibu looked conspiratorially at Emlock, 'It was that fat troll ... the one you call Codweb. He didn't lock it. He ran after you and forgot. Very bad news for him if your chief finds out ... not that I would say anything. I wouldn't want to cause any trouble.'

Emlock's brain was trying to cope with the subtlety of Hibu's words. He was still befuddled as to why Hibu hadn't legged it when he could. Hibu could see him struggling with his thoughts. He was going to have to spell it out. 'No point in me trying to escape,' he said in lowered tones. Emlock drew closer so he could hear better. 'My feet are wrecked, I couldn't walk a mile.' He pointed to the bandages. 'I would very much like my boots back.' He paused for a minute while Emlock wiped his nose on a grubby arm. 'Now,' he said as pointedly as he could, 'If Cacodyl was to find out that your mate had left the door unlocked then he'd be very angry and he'd take away his boots, and give them back to me. And you would get the troll of the year award for saving the day ... and we'd both be happy!'

'Saving the day?' whispered Emlock, confused.

'Yes. You could say that I must have nodded off without noticing that the door wasn't shut. Then, just as you arrived I woke up and was about to escape! But it was too late. You managed to lock the door just in time and stop me. Cacodyl will be very pleased with you. He might even put you in charge over that sloppy mate of yours.'

The lights had come on. Somebody was suddenly at home in Emlock's head. He started to smirk, showing the rotten stubs of two broken teeth. His face creased up in a ghoulish troll grin.

'Yeah,' he sneered, 'I can really drop the fat slime-bucket in it!' He suddenly looked suspiciously at Hibu, 'Why are you helping me?'

'Boots,' said Hibu pointing to his bandages, 'My feet hurt. I don't have feet like a troll. They are so very cold without my boots.' This was true, but Hibu also wanted an ally, albeit a scrawny, rotten-toothed, runny-nosed little troll. If he could win Emlock over he might be useful in the future.

Emlock nodded, 'Okay, I'll try to get yer boots. If Cacodyl asks, you say you'd just noticed the open door when I turned up ... and I stopped you from coming out.'

'Deal,' whispered Hibu.

Emlock could barely contain himself. He threw Hibu the orange and headed out of the door. He had wanted the boots for himself, but more than that he wanted the wrath of Cacodyl to come down on Codweb.

'Don't forget to lock up!' called Hibu softly.

The door shut, and then there was a loud click as the lock turned. Half an hour later Hibu had his boots back and Emlock had been elevated to the lofty position of kitchen boss.

10

Strange Friendships

Cacodyl was puffed with pride at the acquisition of the castle. Until now he had never owned anything more fancy than a large cave. He and Lirtob strode around the dining hall, admiring the enormous polished oak table. Cacodyl opened the sideboard and smiled at the stacks of silver platters and serving dishes. He had always wanted to be a troll of means. He'd had enough of cave-life, being looked down on by all and sundry and considered the lowest of the low. He wanted respect and now he would have it, demand it. He ran his fingers over a brilliant silver soup tureen. Quality! The best for the Zorils from now on, and the world had better take note. He puffed out his chest and wandered back to the door just as a dozen gang members arrived.

'This room's off limits!' he barked, 'Special occasions only. We shall keep it for feasting.' They looked disappointed. 'Anyone caught in here will wish he hadn't been.' The group grumbled and moved on to see what other spoils they could find. 'Keep an eye on them Lirtob.'

Lirtob nodded. 'I'll keep it locked,' he said.

And so the Zorils took up residence in Christmas Castle and within a few weeks they were seriously settled in. Hunting was good in the surrounding woods. Iceace's family moved away one night, taking their three children many miles to the south. They had waited five days for Iceace. It was too dangerous to wait any longer. They feared the worst, assumed that he had carried out his plan to help the elves and had been caught by the trolls. His mother could hardly bear it and wanted to wait longer, but then trolls had come hunting, digging at the warren entrance. Reluctantly she had to agree that protecting their three other children was their most important duty. And so with heavy hearts they had left.

A week after arriving at the castle Hibu had been put to work in the kitchen. He was to work for Emlock, who was alternately grateful to, and suspicious of him. His work was mostly cleaning and doing dishes. Cacodyl seemed determined to domesticate and educate his motley crew, but it was hard going. They preferred not to use plates and bowls and still threw bones all over the floor. It was worse when they got into the potato wine, which, thankfully, thought Hibu, was fast running out. Emlock however, who was particularly partial to the foul concoction, had set about brewing a new batch. He had discovered a bath in a small room above the kitchen; an entirely redundant item as far as a troll was concerned. He ordered Hibu to peel a small mountain of potatoes, and bring them upstairs by the bucketful. Slowly the bath filled up. Emlock added sugar, and various other ingredients.

'Good stuff this!' he chortled happily as he took the last bucket from Hibu and stirred it in, unsuccessfully trying to capture a large nose-dribble before it escaped into the tub, 'But first it needs a few weeks to ripen.'

Hibu eyed the greyish soup and swallowed, 'Ferment,' he said.

'What?' Emlock frowned at him.

'It needs to ferment. That's what the process is called.'

'Ah yes ... ferment ... ferment!' Emlock liked the new word. He would repeat it to Cacodyl if he got the chance, and impress him. 'I might let you 'ave some when it's done.'

'Thank you kindly,' said Hibu, trying to sound enthusiastic. 'I shall look forward to it.'

One of Hibu's jobs was to feed the gulo. Every morning

he took all the meat scraps, bones and anything else he could find, along with a bucket of fresh water, out to the stable where the animal was chained. The first time he had appeared it had thrown itself at him, come to the end of its chain and been brought up short. Then it had fallen back and howled. It was a big animal, a large male weighing over seventy pounds, the biggest Hibu had ever seen. A voracious glutton of the weasel family. Normally it would have roamed the forest, an awesome predator able to kill sizeable animals such as wolves and caribou. Now it chafed against chains, its coat dull and matted and its eyes full of pain and fear. A great empathy filled Hibu. They were both prisoners. He was just a little more able to deal with the loss of freedom.

'Be calm,' he had said softly, 'I am not here to hurt you.'

Surprised, the animal had growled deep in its throat, suspicion and hunger gnawing in its stomach. How did this creature know its language? He backed up a few feet, shaking his head, the chain clanging to and fro on the cobbled floor. Normally he was greeted by two trolls, one with a pitch-fork and one with his food. The pitch-fork was used to keep him back while the food and water were dumped on the dirty floor. The trolls then made a hasty exit. Hibu read the suspicion in the animal's eyes.

'My name is Hibu,' he said softly, 'I too am a prisoner. I was captured in the forest of Frelon, taken from my people and beaten. We are both slaves to the foul Zoril. I and my people understand the language of all animals. Please let me put your food and water down, and then I will try to find you some clean straw to lie on.' Surprised by Hibu's gentle words the creature moved further back and stood stiffly, still suspicious of every movement. Hibu moved forward and put the water and food on the ground, then he went to find clean straw. When he came back the food was gone and the gulo was chewing on a bone.

'I have straw to keep you warm,' said Hibu, 'May I put it down?' There was a low growl of assent. Hibu took the wedges of straw and shook them out. 'If you will allow me, tomorrow I will clean away the old straw.' The animal just eyed him. Hibu went to the door, then turned, 'What is your name?'

'Grrr ... rreole!'

Hibu hadn't expected a reply. He wasn't even sure what the creature had said. It sounded like a growl with maybe the hint of a name mixed in. 'Greole' maybe? It would do for now. 'I shall call you Greole then,' he said, 'I'll see you tomorrow.' Greole stared at the door for some minutes after Hibu left, then he took the bone and curled up in the clean straw.

During the following weeks Hibu was given more and more freedom in and around the castle. The gates were constantly guarded by two meaty Zorils, and the walls were far too high to climb. Escape was impossible, and his captors had obviously decided he was more use helping to feed them than locked in a room needing one of them to feed him. He went about his daily chores and kept his head down, appearing to be ever the meek slave.

One day when he was returning from the stables Cacodyl appeared and in an overly friendly fashion started to quiz him for information on the local area. The chief troll was still most puzzled and annoyed at how the elves had disappeared without a trace.

Hibu was careful with his answer. 'I have never been here before,' he said slowly, 'I only knew of this castle and of the elves and the wizard through what I have read.' This was not true, he had stayed at the castle for many days just a few years back during a visit to the south, but Cacodyl could never know that. He and Elestyal had spent happy hours in the kitchen garden talking about the growing of healing herbs. He continued, 'It is written that the reindeer grow wings on the eve of Christmas, but it did not say how long the magic lasts. Maybe the elves flew away on the deer.' Even he was amazed as to how everyone at the castle had managed to disappear in such a short space of time.

'Lies!' growled Cacodyl, 'It must be lies. Whoever heard of reindeer with wings!' But then he remembered the clearing by the big pine when they had arrived. The tracks of many reindeer, leading nowhere. He still had no answer for that. 'The wizard had a hand in it,' he muttered.

'From what I read the wizard is old,' said Hibu, deliberately playing down Elestyal's powers, 'His spells are faded. I don't believe he could do very much.' He knew this might be partly true. Elestyal's wizardry probably was somewhat rusty, but he was sure it could be called up if necessary. Either way it was pleasing to see Cacodyl so frustrated by the puzzle.

'We'll find them one day,' grunted the leader, 'They can't have gone too far. Then we'll see how clever he is.'

As Hibu wandered back to the kitchen he pondered where Elestyal would have taken the elves. Some distance to the south, over the Crags, was Castle Iffi, the home of Panglossian, another even more elderly wizard who had preceded Elestyal in the role of St Nicholas. He was sure Elestyal would have gone to him for shelter. It would be the obvious place to go. He also found himself thinking about young Iceace. So much had rested on the shoulders of that young snowbun. He hoped with all his heart that the elves had taken him with them. If he'd stayed around the castle without doubt one of the Zorils' odious snow-vultures would have picked him off by now. The thought made him look up. As usual, there they were, perched on the towers, bald necks outstretched, squabbling and squawking. As he watched, one of them sidled to the end of the rampart, head on one side, and eyed him with a cold green eye, *Quark!* it screeched, as though it knew his thoughts. 'Feathered freaks!' muttered Hibu. You couldn't move a muscle without their beady eyes spotting you. What hope was there of ever escaping. He sighed and headed back to the kitchen. No doubt his scrawny little snaggle-toothed boss had a number of jobs awaiting him.

Before he even got to the door he could hear all hell breaking loose. Pots were obviously flying and trolls were fighting. Ear-splitting screeches filled the air followed by a loud crash. He cautiously pushed the door open to find Emlock on top of an exceptionally large and fat troll. He had his hands around the fat one's neck and was screaming blue-murder. The dispute appeared to be over some apples which were now rolling around the floor.

'We all gets an equal share!' screamed Emlock.

'I needs extra!' The voice of the fat one rose to a high-pitched furious screech.

'We'll ask the chief about that then! See what he says about some thinkin' they deserves more 'en others!'

'Eeeeeeeeee-Ahhhhhhhhhh!' was the reply.

The scream was ear-splitting. It brought half a dozen trolls including Codweb and Lirtob. They bounced past Hibu into the kitchen to see what all the fuss was about. Lirtob took one look at the spectacle in front of him and leaped into the fray. He yanked Emlock off the squealing troll and threw him across the room.

'You lay off her!' he bellowed. 'She's near her time! She needs to eat! You lay another finger on her and you're dead meat!' He helped the fat one up. As he did so the skins she wore fell apart and Hibu noticed the round taught belly. She scooped up the apples and hissed at Emlock. Lirtob, in an unusually gentle manner, helped her up the stairs, glowering at Emlock as he left.

'Boss of the kitchen eh!' smirked Codweb as Emlock licked at a deep cut on his arm where he'd collided with the corner of the cooker. Then he noticed Hibu looking at him. He stared deliberately down at the Erudite's boots and then back up to his face. 'One day you'll be barefoot again,' he said with menace. Hibu dropped his gaze. As much as he hated it he had to appear cowed. Let the enemy think it has the upper hand. Satisfied, Codweb loafed off after Lirtob.

'Are you okay?' Emlock was a pitiful sight. His arm was bleeding badly and he had a lump on his head. A puffy bruise was starting to appear on his cheek and one of his two front teeth was now missing. Lirtob had thrown him hard.

'Yeah,' Emlock sniffed, 'That stinkin' Lirtob thinks he's the dam chief!' He rubbed at his cheek and groaned slightly.

'Why was Lirtob defending that big fat troll?' asked Hibu quietly.

'Because she's Lirtob's she-troll. Big Urkha we call her. She's about to produce another like him. As if one isn't enough.'

'I had no idea that was a female.' Hibu was amazed, 'She looks just like the males.' Mind you it was quite often hard to tell the sexes apart.

'Yeah, she's an ugly scrag ain't she. Like the back-end of a weasel-dog.' For all his injuries he started to cackle with laughter at the thought of Hibu thinking Lirtob's she-troll was a he. Hibu suddenly found himself chuckling too. Who would ever have thought he'd share a joke with a Zoril troll. Life was very strange at times. He went to the sink and got a cloth soaked in cold water.

'Put this on your face,' he said, 'It'll help the swelling.' Emlock took it suspiciously, unused to gestures of kindness. Hibu fetched a broom. 'I'll start cleaning up.' Emlock pressed the cloth to his cheek. It felt good. He watched Hibu sweeping, and picking up fallen stools. Something stirred in him. A liking for this strange gangly prisoner. It was an alien feeling for a troll, a little disorienting, but good ... warm. He sort of liked it.

II
Castle Iffi

A storm had blown in and the wind was howling and bitter. Snow had started to fall heavily as the four reindeer and their riders circled Castle Iffi, the home of the wizard Panglossian. Iffi's many beautiful rounded turrets rose up sharply beneath them, peeking through the swirling flakes, the turret roofs like slate-grey pointy wizard's hats, encrusted with snow. Skyler guided the lead deer down. Visibility was difficult. He peered below, wiping at the stinging snowflakes that battered his eyes, eventually making out small waving figures in the courtyard. The others followed. They alighted in driving wind and a huge flurry of snow and cheers from the elves who had come out to meet them.

'I'll take the deer, you people go and warm up,' called Zeb over the howl of the wind. The eight shivering travellers didn't need to be asked twice. They headed up the steps to the main hall where Archy and Wingo were waiting for them.

'Where's Panglossian?' asked Elestyal as he stomped the snow from his boots and pulled off his dripping hat and beard.

'He's gone,' said Wingo, his words sounding as disbelieving as the expression on Elestyal's face.

'Gone! Gone where?'

'On holiday, is what he said.' Wingo threw his hands in the air.

'*Holiday?*'

'Come down to the kitchen and I'll tell you while you warm up.'

A fast change of clothes later and they were seated around Panglossian's ancient old table with steaming mugs of sweet hot chocolate. The kitchen gradually filled with elves as everyone heard of Elestyal's arrival.

'So what happened?' asked Elestyal.

'Well,' said Wingo, 'When we got here it took ages for him to answer the bell, and when he did he was wearing some strange clothes. A Mexican poncho and a big black sombrero. And there was Mariachi music blasting somewhere in the background which is probably why he couldn't hear us.'

'We told him about the trolls at Christmas Castle,' broke in Archy, 'And we asked him if we could take shelter here, and that you were on your way.'

'He slapped me on the back and said it was a wonderful idea!' exclaimed Wingo, 'Said we'd arrived exactly at the right time and that he'd been dying for some sun and sea, and a few exotic cocktails!'

'He ran off up the stairs and left us standing in the hall,' continued Archy, 'Two minutes later he came tearing back down in a ghastly psychedelic floral shirt, baggy shorts, sandals, and odd socks, one green one and one red one.'

'Still wearing the hat!' put in Wingo.

'And mirrored sunglasses,' added Archy.

'And carrying a suitcase and a deckchair,' called someone in the crowd around the table.

'Extraordinary!' said Elestyal shaking his head.

'And,' said Wingo, 'He said he couldn't have wished for a better castle-sitter than you.'

Elestyal nearly choked on his chocolate, '*Castle-sitter!*'

'He said we could stay for as long as we liked and were welcome to open up the old workshop, use all his tools and ... oh ... could we feed the deer and the ponies, do the garden, and look after Crumb.'

'Look after ... Crumb?' repeated Elestyal faintly, his face a question mark, as he wondered how much more bizarre the situation could get.

A tap on his arm made him look round. Petal was standing beside him grinning. She thrust out cupped hands. 'He's a wood mouse,' she said.

Elestyal stared at the tiny creature with the shiny black eyes, large ears and white chest. It stretched up in Petal's hands as though to greet him.

'Wonderful. We've lost our home and gained a castle-sitting job and a mouse! Is there anything else I should know?'

'Well,' said Wingo carefully, 'Just before Mr Panglossian disappeared - in a puff of orange and blue smoke on the doorstep, he did say ... 'See you in a few years'.'

Elestyal groaned, 'Years! Heavens above the silly old fart's gone bonkers at last.' He shook his head in disbelief.

'Look on the bright side,' said Perks, who had dug his sleighrider's hat out of his pocket and perched it back on his head, 'It's a fantastic second home and it's got a huge garden.'

'You would say that, being a gardener,' muttered Jake.

There was silence in the old kitchen. Elestyal hung his head and tugged thoughtfully at his beard. Crumb, who was now on the table, ran around the edge in short bursts, whiskers twitching, as he paused to check out the newcomers.

'I hope that mouse is clean!' called someone.

'Mr Panglossian said he's very old, very wise, and very ... castle-trained,' said Petal, who was delighted that Crumb seemed to have adopted her, and chosen her shirt pocket as his new residence. She scooped him up as he came past. He wriggled straight out of her hand and ran up her arm. From his new vantage point he watched the elves with intelligent black eyes.

'Perks is absolutely right,' said Elestyal, suddenly coming back from wherever his thoughts had taken him, 'I have been so obsessed with the Zorils and the loss of our home that I hadn't seen how much worse it could have been. If it wasn't for Panglossian we could be sitting in the middle of the forest with nothing but our jackets. And if the trolls had arrived a day earlier there wouldn't have been a Christmas delivery. We should actually be feeling mighty lucky. Castle Iffi is nearly twice the size of Christmas Castle, and when Panglossian was in charge of the delivery here all those years ago it ran like clockwork. There's no reason why it can't again.'

Skyler, who had been moving around in the back of the kitchen, suddenly pushed through the crowd carrying a huge wooden tray. On it were lots of small freshly washed glasses containing a pale amber liquid. A large dusty black bottle with a faded unreadable label stood in the centre.

'Mr P obviously enjoyed a little tipple. There's a cellar full of this,' he said, putting the tray down and pushing it towards Elestyal.

Elestyal got a gleam in his eye. 'The old devil brews his own mead, from honey from his own bees. It's delicious. Come on, we'll celebrate.' He picked up a glass and raised it defiantly, 'To Castle Iffi!'

Shouts of agreement came from around the table as elves reached for a tot of mead. Skyler had returned again with home-made apple juice for the elflings. When everyone had a drink Elestyal raised his glass again. 'Here's to a new challenge. You may feel that the happenings of this past day are a calamity, but remember, an optimist sees an opportunity in every calamity, while a pessimist sees a calamity in every opportunity. We are optimists are we not?'

Cries of assent came from around the room, 'We'll be up and running in a day!' 'No one stops the Christmas delivery!' 'Castle Iffi is perfect!' 'Great garden!' (Perks again), 'Further south, better weather!' And then Zeb came clumping through the door in snowy boots and red plaid stable jacket. His ancient woolly hat, covered with bits of hay and a sprinkling of snow was jammed down over his ears.

'Wonderful stables too, spacious and well organised!' he shouted as he caught the tail end of the conversation. He threw a soggy rolled-up ball of clothes onto the table. Then he picked up a glass of warm mead and downed it in one. 'And Panglossian has left us twelve deer and three ponies.'

'Ponies?' cried Petal, jumping up and almost dislodging Crumb.

'Yes Miss Petal. Reckon you're in for some extra work, if you can handle it.'

'Can I ever, how brilliant. Three ponies! I think I love Castle Iffi already.' She didn't see the disapproving look from Aleron. Loyal and steadfast to the end he couldn't understand her apparent ability to forget Christmas Castle at the drop of a hat, in order to gain some ponies. He thought her selfish, which at the same time conflicted with the closeness he'd come to feel for her recently. She disappointed him.

'Tomorrow,' said Elestyal, 'we open up the old workshop, dust off the cobwebs and set up shop.'

'A new start must call for a new suit ... '

Elestyal found himself looking straight across the table at Bizz. She was eyeing him wickedly. A second glass of mead in one hand, a piece of soggy red material in the other, one eyebrow raised, and a smug look on her face. He got the message and raised both hands in submission. He knew when he was beaten. She'd been nagging him for years. 'It uh ... had a little accident en-route,' he said, shoulders shrugged, going for the innocent look. 'Can you save those new buttons though? I really like them.'

'I can save the buttons,' she said, her round face beaming.

The next day everyone was up early. There was much to do. Castle Iffi had had little attention paid to it by its elderly owner for many years. Rooms were thick with dust and cobwebs, windows were grimy, hinges squeaked and the whole place smelled musty. Elestyal and the elves went to war with dusters, mops, brooms and brushes. Battle ensued with disgruntled spiders who were forced to look for alternative lodgings while a couple of sleepy bats, complaining bitterly and muttering darkly about 'castle-squatters', vacated to the stables. They hung themselves up in the roof over the stalls of the ponies.

'Bit niffy in here!' said one, wrinkling her nose.
'Horses,' said the other.
'Yeah, but it's warm,' said her friend. And with that they wrapped their wings around them and went back to sleep.

Down below in the stall belonging to a pretty chocolate coloured pony with a silver mane and tail, was Petal. The pony was fourteen and a half hands tall and Petal was short for her age. She had had to find a box to stand on in order to groom the creature's back. She was brushing determinedly at the soft coat with long sweeping strokes when Zeb came by to check on her.

'No leaping on and riding off into the sunset,' he warned, wagging a finger. 'Ponies are different from reindeer.'

'As if I would,' retorted Petal, 'But I would if I could.'

'Don't I know it. You need some riding lessons first.'

'When will you teach me?' Petal went into wheedling mode.

'When all the work's done.' He ignored the doe eyes and pleading smile.

'When will *that* be?'

'When the stables are cleaned, the straw and feed brought over from the barn, the water working properly, the tack cleaned ... '

'Okay! Okay!' broke in Petal, 'I get the message. Probably a couple of months!'

Zeb looked at her. Grubby and straw covered but startlingly pretty and unaware of it. The usual dirt streaks on her face and a cheeky grin on her lips. She seemed completely un-fazed by the sudden move and their flight from Christmas Castle. In fact she seemed almost excited by it, by the challenge. She was certainly different. A totally tomboy Elfrachaun with a double helping of energy, who shared his deep love of all the animals. As if hearing his thoughts Crumb appeared from her shirt pocket, nibbling on some small grain in his paws.

'I see that mouse is scoffing all the animal feed,' he said, looking severe.

Petal giggled, 'Only one sack full today.'

'He'll be a fat little fart if he keeps that up.'

Crumb dropped the grain and ran up to Petal's shoulder, then he stood up on his back legs and made himself as slim as possible, displaying his snow-white chest, and making little bows to Zeb.

'You understand us don't you?' Zeb looked at him curiously. Crumb waggled his seriously long whiskers, 'Well I'll be darned, *he* is one smart mouse.'

'Well he *was* Mr Panglossian's,' said Petal, stroking Crumb's delicate ears.

'You're right. He's a wizard's mouse,' said Zeb thoughtfully, 'You take good care of him Miss Petal.' He turned to go back to his work.

'Why can we talk to some animals and not to others?' asked Petal thoughtfully.

Zeb stopped and turned back. 'It's up to the nature of the animals. First they have to trust us. Some will sense immediately that we are their friends. Young Iceace for instance, he knew from his parents.'

'But what about Crumb?'

Zeb looked at Crumb, 'Some choose not to converse by way of words,' he said slowly, 'although they understand what we're saying. Do you not feel that Crumb understands you?'

Petal thought for a minute. 'Yes ... yes I think he does. I'm sure he does.'

'There you are,' said Zeb, 'For some reason he prefers to 'speak' to you in a more subtle way. One day he might use words, and when he does you'll hear them.'

'Do you understand all animal talk?' Petal was intrigued.

'I don't understand all their languages, but I somehow just know what they're saying. It's something you become tuned-in to. You just have to open your ears.'

Petal thought it a strange comment. She always had her ears open, or how could she hear Iceace, or Zeb. Zeb read her thoughts in a flash. He switched his glance to Crumb who was looking straight at him. They studied each other for a few long seconds. Petal watched the exchange.

'Crumb says you're young, but in time, and with patience, you'll master the art exceptionally well.'

'What! ... How did you do that?'

'I opened my ears,' laughed Zeb.

Petal picked the little mouse off her shoulder and held him in front of her, studying his face with an intense frown. Crumb washed his whiskers and stared back. She could read nothing. 'What's he saying?' she whispered.

Zeb leaned in closer and stared at Crumb, then he whispered back to Petal, 'He says this pony needs grooming or you won't get any lunch.'

Petal aimed a kick at Zeb's shin, but he was too quick and danced away chuckling.

'I love this pony,' she said, picking up the brush.

'He's called Seasurf.' Zeb pointed to a small nameplate above the manger, 'He's an Icelandic.'

'I shall call him Surf, I wish he was mine.' Petal lay her head on Surf's soft chocolate flank and inhaled the sweet smell of horse.

'I thought you loved the reindeer best?' teased Zeb.

'That was before I found Surf. I still love the deer though,' she added quickly, as though guilt had tweaked her.

'Well it's nearly lunch time. Finish brushing him and do Owl and Swallow this afternoon. I must try to get the water fixed.' The two ponies in the neighbouring stalls raised their heads at the mention of their names.

'Yes boss,' Petal gave him a cheeky salute.

Zeb left and Petal stood on tiptoe on her box. She leaned across Surf's warm back. He didn't seem to mind. She felt a little rush of excitement. She'd never sat on a horse. It was too inviting. She grabbed a big handful of silvery Seasurf mane and in seconds had pulled herself up and slid a leg over. Surf blew through his nostrils and swung his head around to inspect Petal's boot. He nibbled at it. Petal leaned down and put her arms around his neck as far as she could. This was heaven. She lay there for some minutes absorbing the scent and the warmth of him while he pulled at his hay net. The clang of a shovel at the other end of the stable made her jump and she hastily slid off, missing her footing on the box and landing in a heap in the straw. She scrambled to her feet and cursed. Crumb's head wiggled its way out of her shirt pocket. She could have sworn he gave her a dirty look. 'Sorry little friend,' she muttered. She quickly went back to her grooming job and was soon lost in thought, and dreams of riding Surf in the spring. She would take Iceace and Crumb and they would gallop through the forest paths. Her reverie was interrupted by Zeb calling to say lunch was ready.

Mealtimes were always an event with the elves. Not just because they loved their food, it was also when they shared information about work and everything else that was going on in the castle. Castle Iffi had a huge parlour off the kitchen and Skyler had butted up the two long oak tables so they could all sit round together. To one side he had set up a buffet with steaming tureens of home-made leek and potato soup, next to which was bread, cheeses, fruit and cured hams. Panglossian's larders and cold-store had been full. Petal helped herself to soup and bread and squeezed in beside Aleron.

'How was your morning?' she asked, slightly wary. He had been different towards her since they had arrived at Iffi. Kind of distant.

'Good,' he said, swallowing the mouthful of bread he'd been chewing, 'We've been cleaning the workshop and checking the machines. They haven't been used for years, but they're all oiled now and they run perfectly.

'That's great. I guess Elestyal was right, we should think ourselves really lucky that we were able to come here.

Where else would we have had everything we needed?'

'The first thing I'm going to make when we're fully set up is a dagger.'

'A dagger? Whatever for?'

'For killing trolls.'

Petal was about to laugh when she realised he was serious. She tried to swallow the grin but she wasn't quick enough. Aleron frowned.

'One day we'll go and get Christmas Castle back, and when we do I'll be there. Fighting!'

'From what I heard,' said Petal, spooning soup over a bit of floating bread, trolls are huge and strong and could kill a grown elf with one hand. And there's fifty or so of them.'

'We just need to be more clever than them.'

'How?'

'Surprise them.'

'If we had a chance of fighting them Elestyal wouldn't have made us leave.'

'He'll think of something,' insisted Aleron.

Petal shook her head and sighed.

Aleron looked at her sharply. 'You were the one who said 'We'll just have to get it back'. You said it when we were leaving.' He sounding frustrated.

'Yes, I know, but what's wrong with Iffi? I like it here, and we have everything we need. And it's bigger than Christmas Castle ... and ... '

'There are ponies,' muttered Aleron sullenly.

'That's not the reason,' said Petal a little too quickly, 'I just think why would we risk our lives if there's no necessity?'

'Because eventually those stinking trolls may decide they'd like this castle too. And then we'll have nowhere but the forest to live in and then there will be no more Christmas delivery. Think how the humans will feel if that happens. You need to think about other people too sometimes Petal.' Anger had coloured his face a shade darker.

Petal was tired of arguing. 'What sort of dagger are you going to make?' she asked quietly.

'A pointy one,' grumbled Aleron peevishly, irked at her quick dismissal of his plan to fight the trolls.

Petal took a sideways glance at his unhappy face and felt bad. 'I'm sorry about Christmas Castle,' she said gently, 'I think it meant more to you because you were there longer than I was.'

'It was my home,' Aleron sighed, 'It was bad enough losing my parents. And it was trolls that took them too.'

They were silent for a while, eating their fruit and cheese.

'Zeb has asked me to look after the ponies,' said Petal cautiously.

'That's nice, I'm glad for you.' It was said without enthusiasm.

'He's going to teach me how to ride when he has time.'

Aleron was quiet, watching Petal feed Crumb a small piece of apple. The bright-eyed wood mouse sat beside her plate twirling the apple in his tiny hands, nibbling and watching her.

'I must go back to work,' said Aleron sliding off his stool, 'Lots still to do. Enjoy your ponies.'

Petal watched him go. She thought about the fun they had had on Christmas eve, hiding in the loft and watching the loading of the sleigh. She decided when he got used to Castle Iffi he'd be fine. Maybe he'd even come riding with her.

Elestyal had chosen a small cosy room for himself just below the kitchen, similar to his old one at Christmas Castle. He enjoyed hearing the homely clank of pots and pans and catching the waft of baking bread and other tantalising aromas. There were signs that Bizz, who was currently in charge of domestic duties, had been by. The bed was made and sported a brightly coloured blanket with an eagle in the centre, and there was a nice fat feather pillow. Clean dungarees hung over a chair, and his favourite old red cardigan with odd buttons, darned at the elbows, was folded on the bed. How on earth had she got hold of that? He hadn't had time to pack his few things before they fled the castle. He picked up the cardigan. It took him back to days in spring and autumn when he and Perks would sit in the kitchen garden smoking their pipes and talking horticulture. He wondered if they would see those days again. If the spell he had left in the round-room worked then they had a good chance. He contemplated the troll leader, Cacodyl. He knew him well, knew his penchant for gold and silver and his greedy nature. Elestyal would have bet his cardigan and a whole lot more that Cacodyl would lock up the Christmas Castle silver for himself. But he wouldn't be able to stop himself bringing it out once in a while to show it off and lord it over the underlings. He would almost certainly use it on feast days. Cacodyl had always aspired to being something better than he was born to be, and he had just plundered his way up many rungs of the ladder. From cave to castle. He would be ecstatic, attempting to emulate civilized folk. You can take the troll out of the cave, said Elestyal to himself, but you'll never take the cave-nature out of the troll.

The old wizard felt tired. He stretched out on the bed and wondered if Panglossian was sitting on some beach with a fancy drink. I rather wish I was with him he thought as he drifted off to sleep.

Upstairs in the kitchen Skyler was busy. He and the kitchen elves had decided to try and put on a Christmas Day feast as best they could with whatever was in the larder. The parlour was already decorated with holly and ivy and small cedar boughs. Someone had found a stash of candles and set them in holders on the tables, and the aroma of mince-pies and baking shortbread was filling the air.

Skyler had decided he needed to do an inventory of the food. He and Perks, clipboard and oil lamp in hand, were moving through Panglossian's three enormous larders listing tinned goods, jars of preserves, canned fruits, smoked hams, baking ingredients, spices and much more.

'Why has one old wizard got so much grub?' whispered Skyler, as though Panglossian might be lurking nearby and able to hear him.

'Eccentric,' said Perks.

'Eccentric?'

'Whimsical ... a bit mad.'

'How do you know?'

'Been here on visits with Elestyal years ago. He always said old Mr P didn't like to follow the rules. Apparently got himself in hot water with illegal spells when he was young.'

'Never!'

'True enough. But Elestyal said when they threatened to chuck him out of the Wizards' Circle he smartened up a bit and kept his head down. He still hates conforming though. You see it in the socks thing.'

'The socks?'

'Yes. D'you remember Archy saying when they arrived how he nipped upstairs and come down in crazy clothes, including one green and one red sock?' Skyler nodded. 'Well he never wears two the same. Whenever I came here he always had different ones on. Sometimes even one long one and one short one. Stripes and spots, pigs and stars, check and plain. One on one foot, one on the other.'

'Weird,' whistled Skyler shaking his head, 'A shame he couldn't stay and help us get rid of the Zorils.' He was quiet for a few moments, then he sidled up close to Perks and lowered his voice to a barely audible whisper. 'D'you think that ... spell we did, will get rid of them?'

Perks looked around quickly, double-checking the

shadows, 'I don't think we should talk about it,' he said hastily.

'Did you understand *anything* Elestyal said when he was doing it?' persisted Skyler.

'Not a word,' whispered Perks, 'It was total gobbledegook to me. We mustn't discuss it.'

'That ... presence ... at the end ... Something came through that room in a big rush. It nearly knocked me over. And ... it *whispered* something!'

Perks moved close to Skyler and cupped his hands around the other elf's ear. '*Sassilvashakalim!*'

'Yes! Yes! That was it, but what does it mean?'

'How would I know? I'm a gardener, not a blinkin' wizard. Ask me one on parsnips.'

A noise in the corner of the larder brought them both upright. Skyler held up the lamp with beating heart, only to see a mouse scurry towards the door.

'No more discussion on the subject, to *anyone*,' hissed Perks, 'Elestyal said it's vital no word of what we were part of gets back to the Zorils.'

Skyler nodded, 'Yeah, you're right. Our lips must be sealed.'

Later that evening everyone took their places around

the table for supper. It wasn't the same as the hall would have been at Christmas Castle with all the gleaming silver and special decorations, but it was still special. Candles glowed and light danced on red holly berries, and the sweet scent of cedar mixed with a plethora of tantalizing spicy cooking smells filled the room. Panglossian's larder had done them proud. A massive oak log in the parlour hearth crackled and rolled slightly, sending up a shower of sparks. Some of them caught on the back of the blackened chimney wall and made pretty changing patterns, while new eager flames rose up and licked greedily, sending new fingers of light to dance around the room. The elves sang songs late into the evening and drank a toast of mead to absent friends. Panglossian was the first to be included, followed by Iceace's family.

Petal sat in a cosy corner with pad and pencil, sketching a picture of Crumb, her face full of concentration. Her subject watched the pencil strokes from her shoulder. She loved drawing animals. She had done a great one of the Christmas delivery and Ru with his nose in full glow but unfortunately it, and all her others had been left behind in her old bedroom. She was looking forward to her new subjects, the three gorgeous ponies. She already loved Iffi, and she knew Aleron would too in the end. Crumb suddenly ran down her arm, appeared to look at the picture, and then turned and stared at her.

'Don't tell me,' sighed Petal, 'I've made your ears too big.'

12

A Mission for a Spy – or Two

In the stables Petal had nearly finished grooming. She stood back and inspected Owl, the pretty skewbald mare, with a critical eye. Owl was the same height as Surf and a few years older. The patched coat shone. Petal had done a good job. Zeb would be pleased, and maybe give her another riding lesson. She was already getting pretty good and now the better weather was here she may get to go out on her own. Iceace joined her by the stall and stole a carrot out of a nearby bucket.

'Little bounder!' scolded Petal, feigning disapproval. But Iceace knew her too well and just sat and nibbled contentedly.

'You've really grown recently Ice,' said Petal, 'Must be all the carrots you steal.'

He certainly was a grand snowbun, a perfect specimen of his kind. With the care from the elves he had filled out and was no longer a baby. He stretched out a long lean back leg and cleaned a snowy foot, splaying the toes and licking carefully between them. He had the longest ears Petal had ever seen.

'I can run *super*-fast now,' he said between licks.

'When Zeb lets me ride Surf on my own we'll have a race,' said Petal.

Iceace stopped licking, 'That would be 'topsy-turvy and fantabitastic.'

'You mean fantastic,' said Petal, 'And topsy-turvy means upside down.' She loved the way he was constantly trying to learn new words and sayings, and mispronouncing them for a while before getting them right.

'Oh, right,' Iceace was thoughtful, 'My Ma used to tell me when I got my words wrong. Miss Petal, d'you think my family got away?'

Petal was sad for him. She knew what it was like to be left alone at a tender age. 'I'm sure, from what you told me about your father, that he would have taken your mother and sisters away from that place as soon as it was safe.'

'I just keep hoping they didn't wait for me to come back and then get … ' He didn't carry on. In his mind he kept seeing trolls with shovels, and weasels. He shivered at the thought.

'So this is where I find you!' The voice made them both jump and look up. Elestyal was in the next stall, peering over the partition.

'Mr Elestyal, you've got your hat back,' cried Petal.

Elestyal took off his cap and turned it around in his hands. 'It's a new one,' he said, 'Bizz ran it up for me from some old pair of jeans she found. My old one got left at Christmas Castle.'

'It's got a leek and a carrot on it.' Petal eyed the embroidery on the front.

'Clever elf-woman, that Bizz,' said Elestyal.

'I'd like a cap with a great big orange carrot on it,' put in Iceace enthusiastically.

'Well now,' said Elestyal thoughtfully tugging at his beard, 'Maybe you could earn a cap ... just like this one, with whatever you like on the front. What would you think to that?'

'Jeeples-creeples! I'd love to!'

'It's jeepers-creepers Ice,' giggled Petal.

'Oh ... right ... but what can I do to earn it?' Iceace was ready to burst with eagerness.

'Come to the garden with me and I'll tell you.'

'Now? Can we go now?' Iceace bounced up and down barely able to contain himself.

'Come on then,' said Elestyal, 'Now is as good a time as any.'

'Don't give him a job near the carrots!' called Petal as the wizard and the snowbun headed for the door. But they were talking and didn't hear her.

Outside in the courtyard the warm spring sunshine enveloped them. All around the castle grounds there were signs of new life as snow gradually melted and plants and bulbs pushed up through the earth. Trees and bushes were popping buds, and spring flowers peeped from everywhere. Elestyal took Iceace to the old walled kitchen garden and into the potting shed under the fig tree. At the other end of the garden Perks looked up as he cleared a vegetable patch. Elestyal closed the door firmly behind them and sat down on a small stool next to a box of seed packets. Sun slanted across his face through the small window. Iceace looked surprised as the wizard's expression turned suddenly serious and his whole tone had changed.

'Iceace, I have a task for you. But it is no simple task. I want you to listen and consider carefully. This is no gardening job ... no menial thing. I have been thinking about it for some time, wondering if it was right to ask you. I have watched you grow over the last four months. You are strong and intelligent, and I think you would be the best person to carry out this mission.'

Mission? Iceace was dumbfounded. Elestyal wanted *him* for a *mission*. He felt a thrill of pride shoot through him. He held his breath as Elestyal continued.

'It will be dangerous, but it's of great importance.' The old wizard drew in his breath. 'On the night of April thirtieth, in three days time, something is going to happen at Christmas Castle. I cannot tell you exactly what, suffice to say I'm hoping a little plan of mine will come to fruition. I need an observer, someone to go there and be my eyes and ears. Someone quick and careful who could slip through the night swiftly and unobserved.'

'I can run twice as fast now as when we first met,' broke in Iceace in a determined voice, 'And I'm ten times as strong.'

Elestyal looked even more serious. 'This is no game Iceace. You are well aware that there are fifty trolls in that castle. They would kill you as soon as look at you if they caught you. Your job is purely to watch, to stay out of sight, and to look and listen. And take no risks. It's a long way there, probably a day's travel at a good pace, and your way will take you through Bearban forest. Bearban is home to many enemies of a snowbun. If I could I would send one of the elves, but it would mean them taking a pony, and they would be too easy to ... '

Iceace interrupted. 'I want to go, I want to do this for you and the elves. You are my friends, and you have given me a home. I can move quickly, like a ghost in the shadows. They will not see me. Tell me when I have to go.' He sat round-eyed and hopelessly earnest, staring imploringly at the wizard.

Elestyal stroked his beard and nodded slowly. 'All right. But promise me you won't take any risks.'

'I promise. When must I go?'

'Three days from now. You must leave early in the morning and travel all day. The night you arrive at Christmas Castle will be Walpurgis night. It's a feast, a festival celebrated by pagans, and the Zorils always celebrate it. It's the biggest night of their year. It will start at midnight. Now, we must discuss the route you should take.' The wizard picked up a stick and started to draw in the dust on the potting shed floor. 'We are here, at Christmas Castle,' he said, drawing a circle, 'From here follow the edge of the lake until you reach the Meanda river. Where the river and the lake join take the path – there's only one - it runs north through Bearban forest. Eventually you will arrive here, at Kokanee Crags, a small mountain range running east-west and bisecting the Meanda. There is a path that follows the route of the river right through the mountains. It's very steep at times and you must take great care especially when you come to the gorge, Keeper's Gorge, where the bluffs fall hundreds of feet into the river.' Elestyal's stick drew a narrow channel between two mountains. 'After the gorge you will come down into a sparsely forested flat area known as Snaggle Plain. From there it's just a few miles north-east to Christmas Castle. My advice would be to make for Tall Pine Wood behind the castle ... the clearing where we all met that morning before we left to come here. Skirt around the wall from there when you go to the gate.'

Iceace studied the map in the dust on the potting shed floor and fixed it into his mind. Then he looked searchingly at the wizard. 'What will I be looking for?' he asked, mystified.

'Wait and see,' said Elestyal. 'If my assumption has been wrong then you will simply hear a great deal of revelry. Be close to the castle gate at midnight. If it happens you will know.'

Iceace wondered what on earth 'it' could be. More than that he couldn't believe that he, Iceace, had been chosen for such a special mission. He felt proud enough to burst.

'Iceace,' said Elestyal, 'No one else must know about this. Do not tell anyone. If word was to somehow get to the trolls then my plan will fail.'

Iceace nodded.

As they left the potting shed Perks was just coming to put his spade away. He looked at them curiously for a moment, pondering their length of time in the shed with the door shut.

'Just explaining how to grow the best carrots,' smiled Elestyal.

'Of course,' said Perks. But the expression on Iceace's face didn't convince him. Not even a rabbit looked that enthused about growing carrots.

The night before Iceace was due to leave he was late going to bed. Perks had been quizzing him in the kitchen on his knowledge of carrot growing. Iceace had been evasive. Perks was suspicious. Eventually he had slipped away to his bed, a basket in the corner of Petal's room, trying to be ultra-quiet so he didn't wake her. But Petal wasn't asleep and heard the small creak of the basket as Iceace lay down. She sat up and peered across the room.

'What's going on?' she said in a low voice.

Iceace jumped. 'What?' he whispered.

'Come on Ice. Ever since your little meeting with Elestyal you've been acting strangely. Even Perks has noticed it. What are you two cooking up?'

'We're not cooking anything,' replied Iceace trying to sound innocent. He hated not being able to tell her. Petal had become his best friend and had looked after him ever since that awful day at Christmas Castle. It seemed wrong to lie to her.

'I thought you were my friend,' said Petal, feigning hurt. Nothing like a little guilt trip to try and tease it out of him.

'I can't tell you.'

'So there *is* something going on, you just can't tell me about it?'

Iceace coughed and changed position in his basket. 'Well ... kind of ... '

'Kind of?' She sensed he was close to cracking. Just another little push. 'True friends trust one another with their secrets,' she said, sounding as sad as possible, and then leaving a pregnant pause.

Iceace squirmed. If he told Petal then he was going against his promise to Elestyal. On the other hand he knew he could trust Petal not to say anything. And Elestyal would never know he'd told her. Besides he wanted to share it with her. He'd been dying to tell someone about his special mission two seconds after he'd left the potting shed.

Decision made. He leapt onto Petal's bed. 'You must not breathe a word of this to anyone!' he whispered. And for the next few minutes he related what Elestyal had asked him to do.

'I'll come with you!'

'What?'

Petal was insistent. 'I'll come with you. I'll ride Surf and we'll go together. Two heads are better than one, and if anything happened to you I could help.'

Iceace was unsure. 'Elestyal said it wasn't safe for an elf. He said a pony would be spotted more easily.'

'Don't be silly Ice, Surf is mostly chocolate coloured anyway so he can't be seen at night – which is when we arrive at the castle.'

Iceace scratched an ear with a back foot and said nothing. His gut told him this was not a good idea, and his Ma had always said to listen to his gut. Or his instinct, as she had called it.

'And,' continued Petal having another thought, 'If I came with you it would show Aleron that I really do care about Christmas Castle, and about his feelings.'

'I see,' said Iceace, not seeing at all and wondering just how much trouble he was heading for.

'What time do we have to leave?'

'Elestyal said if I left at five o'clock it would give me time to spare.'

'Okay, I'll get up at half past four and feed Surf, and saddle him up.' She sounded so excited that Iceace didn't have the heart to argue. But his heart sank as he hopped back to his bed. All of a sudden he was getting a very bad feeling about this mission.

'Zeb will be very angry if he finds you've taken Surf out by yourself,' he said suddenly, trying one last attempt to deter her.

'No he won't. This afternoon he told me I was ready to go on my own and I could take him out tomorrow. It'll be a fantastic first ride. We'd better get some sleep if we're having such an early start.'

Iceace lay down in his basket. He was worried. Very worried. What if something happened to Petal. What if she fell off Surf and was injured? He would be to blame. But he knew she wouldn't be swayed now. He really shouldn't have told her.

13
Walpurgis Preparations - April 30th

In the kitchen at Christmas Castle Hibu was trying to help Emlock and two other trolls organise some sort of civilized banquet. During the four months they had been there Cacodyl had become more and more obsessed with 'living civilized' as he put it and 'educating' the stupid rabble. He was on a crusade to turn his motley band of savages into something better. To raise them from their lowly state. Hibu had become his chief advisor as to the ways of 'respectable folk' and if trolls didn't 'act respectable' as Cacodyl put it, they got a thrashing. Hibu refrained from trying to explain that thrashings were not the way of respectable folk.

If nothing else Hibu's new elevated position was definitely prolonging his existence. Sometimes he just could not believe he was living side by side with a bunch of Zorils who actually seemed to accept him. It was utterly bizarre. Having said that, not quite all of them accepted him. Lirtob, Lirtob's she-troll Urkha, and Codweb appeared to have taken a distinct dislike to him since the fight over the apples in the kitchen. They had somehow sensed Hibu's support for Emlock. Hibu wasn't too worried. His new position as advisor to the chief afforded him a certain protection.

The kitchen was manic as they prepared for the feast. Trolls scuttled hither and thither with platters. Steam rose from enormous pots of boiling potatoes and cabbage, and the smell of roasting meat wafted in from the courtyard through the open door. Hibu left the frantic atmosphere of the kitchen and went to the banquet hall. The doorway was being guarded by the friendly Codweb who raised a snarled lip as Hibu walked in.

'I'm guardin' the silver, so don't be tryin' ter steal it!'

Hibu didn't bother reminding him that the precious dinnerware was still locked in the two massive oak chests where Cacodyl had stored it, and that he, Hibu, had the key. It was his job to set up the table for the banquet. He unlocked the chests and stared at the beautiful pieces, lovingly cared for, for so many years. It was criminal that they should have fallen into the hands of these animals. He sighed and started with the platters, laying fifty around the table, polishing each till it shone before putting it in place.

Codweb sidled further into the room, eyeing them covetously. Hibu watched him out of the corner of his eye. The fat little troll was actually drooling with excitement. He wouldn't have put it past Codweb to steal something and blame him. He decided for the time being to only put out items of a size that Codweb was unable to secrete up his manky rabbit-fur waistcoat.

    The banquet room windows looked out onto the main courtyard where there was frenetic activity. In the centre trolls were building a monstrous bonfire. Walpurgis night said Hibu to himself. They would be feasting from midnight on and probably all day tomorrow. He watched six spits turning over fires, each skewering either venison or wild pig. Hibu was vegetarian and the sight of the roasting carcasses disgusted him. He turned back to his work, there was much to do. It was going to be a long job. There was a heck of a lot of silver to clean.

    It did in fact take so long that the unfortunate Codweb, bored with ogling the dishes, squatted down in the doorway and went to sleep. Late that afternoon Hibu was just putting the final touches to his handiwork when Cacodyl announced his arrival by way of a savage kick to Codweb's fat back-side. The shocked little troll screamed bloody-murder as Cacodyl dragged him upright and pinned him to the wall. One giant hairy hand around Codweb's throat. The smaller troll's yellow eyes bulged as he gurgled helplessly, limbs flailing as he tried to get his feet on the ground.

'It seems Lirtob has a poor choice of guards,' hissed Cacodyl. 'Whaddya mean by going to sleep?'

'Kkkkksh-shshKK,' wheezed Codweb through his flattened windpipe.

'What? Speak up!'

'Yyyyshshhkkkkkkk!'

Cacodyl squeezed a little longer. He enjoyed watching Codweb's face gradually turn purple as he struggled for life. Then he suddenly dropped him like a stone. Codweb fell forward hacking and gulping air, scrabbling away on all-fours in terror. Hibu fitted the last red candle into position in the candelabra as he watched the drama unfold. He hoped he never got on the wrong side of the chief. Hibu was a lot taller than Cacodyl, but Cacodyl outweighed him by at least fifty or sixty pounds. A bit like comparing a willow with an oak. The boss troll was pure muscle.

'Get out!' thundered Cacodyl. Codweb didn't need asking twice. He made for the tower rooms where he could skulk out of sight for the rest of the day.

Hibu stepped to one side as the chief swaggered into

the hall, hands on hips, chest out, white rabbit skins swinging from each shoulder. He stood for a few seconds, narrow yellow eyes taking in the display before him, and his face gradually broke into a leer of pure pleasure. The table was set to perfection, the glorious collection of elfin silver glittering on a deep red cloth. Matching red napkins crowned gleaming goblets. Tapered red and white candles adorned candelabras. Hibu had even made small table decorations of spring flowers from the kitchen garden.

Cacodyl seemed lost for words. He strode up and down the table shaking his head, eventually stopping and carefully picking up a goblet. He held it up to the light and turned it slowly. The leer broadened. Then he replaced the goblet and made a beeline for Hibu. Hibu backed up nervously as the big troll advanced. To his astonishment Cacodyl grabbed him roughly and then clapped on the back, the power of the slap nearly knocking him over.

'Good!' grunted Cacodyl, 'Good! Just like respectable folk. Very respectable.'

'Thank you,' said Hibu with a little bow, trying to hide his shock. Never had he been slapped on the back by a troll before. He wondered what Elestyal would think of him for doing such a fine job with their beautiful silver. For a troll's banquet.

'You join the party tonight,' Cacodyl was saying.

'Thank you,' said Hibu again, having no intention of going anywhere near it.

They left the hall. Reluctant to trust another lackey with guard duty Cacodyl locked the door. Hibu headed back to help Emlock in the kitchen. It was five o'clock.

It was still pitch dark when Iceace and Petal had sneaked away from Christmas Castle at five in the morning. The journey had gone well. Extremely well. Petal quickly felt completely confident on Surf and Iceace felt less worried about her. By eight that evening they had come over the top of Kokanee Crags and were starting their descent down the river path. They had made excellent time. Even the narrow path through Keeper's gorge hadn't been as bad as expected. Petal was a natural rider and the pony responded to her light hands and kind words. Surf was lively but dependable, fast, and sure-footed as a goat. Petal thought he was perfect. Iceace loped along in front, his long ears an antenna for every sound, his keen nose picking up every scent from fox to flowers. The snow had still been quite deep and hard-going high up, but as they descended there was less and less. They were at the bottom of the river path by ten.

'This must be the Snaggle Plains,' said Iceace quietly, looking around at the vast flat lands, as they stopped to get their bearings.

'Which way from here?' whispered Petal. It was so still. She found it a bit eerie being out this late at night in the middle of nowhere. Surf pulled on his bit and she let him nibble on a clump of spiky plains grass.

'Elestyal said north-east on Snaggle Plains.'

'Which way's that?'

Iceace checked his inbuilt compass and inclined his head. 'This way.'

He set off at a fast lope. Snaggle Plains was flat and littered with rocks, dead wood and small copses of scrub pine. Petal ducked branches and hung on as Surf jumped the smaller logs and weaved around the larger ones. An hour later they found themselves coming up behind Tall Pine Wood which clung to the rocky outcrop behind the castle. They stopped under cover of the trees and Petal dismounted. She loosened Surf's girth and gave him his nosebag of oats that she'd brought for him. Surf munched appreciatively.

'What now?' she whispered.

Iceace sat up on his haunches and snuffed the air, then

he looked at the sky for some minutes.

'What are you doing?' asked Petal more impatiently than she meant to sound.

Iceace immediately knew she was nervous. 'I'm just checking the time. Everything's fine,' he added, trying to reassure her.

Petal squatted down beside him. 'How can you tell what time it is?'

'I just sort of concentrate and I know.'

Petal shook her head in disbelief, 'Okay Mr clever buns, what *is* the time?'

'About eleven o'clock.'

'Damn, that means we have a whole hour to wait.'

'You shouldn't curse Miss Petal.'

Petal was just about to reply when an owl hooted loudly in a nearby pine. Iceace dived straight underneath Surf. 'Buggle Me!' he quavered.

'Buggle?' Petal raised an eyebrow.

'Perks says it when things go wrong.' Iceace peered at her from beneath Surf's belly.

'I see.' Maybe best not correct him on this occasion, she thought.

The owl called again, this time further off. Iceace crept out cautiously and scanned the overhead branches.

'Don't worry Ice, he won't come after you with me here.'

Iceace was snuffing the air again, 'I smell fire,' he whispered, 'Wood smoke, and roasting meat!'

'Hell's teeth!' muttered Petal, amazed at the distance at which Iceace could detect smells, and wondering what victims were being roasted.

'I can hear them too,' he whispered again, waggling an ear back and forth.

They kept absolutely still and in the distance Petal too could just catch the faint sounds of shouting and merrymaking.

'The feast of Waplurgis must have started,' said Iceace.

'Walpurgis,' corrected Petal, 'A feast for devilry and witches.'

The next hour seemed endless.

Petal asked for the fifteenth time, 'What's the time now?'

'Probably about time to go,' said Iceace at last.

When they arrived under the tall pine the moon came out from behind a cloud and Petal peered across the clearing. She knew that just through the trees in the deep shadow was the secret door to the long passage to the round-room. Even Surf seemed to sense the tense atmosphere and stood like a statue.

'I must go to the gate,' whispered Iceace.

'Are you sure you don't want me to come with you?'

'Definitely not. You must stay here and wait. If I'm not back in fifteen minutes then you must go. Go back to Iffi as fast as you can. Promise me you will?'

'Okay, but be careful!' Petal felt greatly relieved to be staying in the shadows. The idea of bumping into a troll terrified her, 'Good luck Ice!'

In a second he was gone, a flash of white streaking across the ground under the moon. Petal huddled against Surf's warm neck suddenly not feeling quite so brave. It had seemed a great idea at the time, this Christmas Castle mission, but standing here now, knowing fifty elf-eating trolls were just round the corner had caused all her courage to evaporate. She wished Aleron was here, with his troll-dagger. He always seemed so strong. She shifted uneasily from one foot to the other, peering in the direction of the castle. There was light, a distant orange glow from a bonfire. And she smelled the sweetness of the wood smoke as the wind changed. She moved deeper into the shadows with a nervous shiver praying Iceace wouldn't be too long. Praying he'd come back.

It was ten minutes to twelve. In the banquet hall inside Christmas Castle Emlock was doing his best to get the food on the table. Hibu had reluctantly been roped in to help. He sighed as he ferried yet another tureen of cabbage soup into the hall. Troll-sized chunks of venison and pork from the roasted carcasses in the courtyard had been piled high on silver platters, while other dishes sported small mountains of boiled potatoes. The table was heaving with food. The candles were lit. Trolls clamoured around the door sniffing the tantalising aroma of roast meat, waiting for the signal from Cacodyl that they were allowed in. The master strutted around the table, deliberately keeping them waiting. At five minutes to midnight he walked over to them.

'Civilized!' he shouted, 'Remember ... civilized! Walk in and wait for my signal before you start. Anyone who disobeys forfeits their dinner.'

They entered, scuttling as fast as they dared, going for the nearest seats and looking over their shoulders for Cacodyl. Hoping he'd sit down quickly. They were ravenous for the meat. He kept them waiting while he made one full circuit of the table before taking his place at the head. They muttered and growled and drooled, wishing they could get on with it and stop the ridiculous charade. They were trolls and wanted to act like trolls, and throw their dam bones all over the floor.

Each place was set with a goblet of Emlock's best potato wine. Cacodyl raised his glass just as the elves' old grandfather clock chimed the first note of twelve.

'To Walpurgis!' he shouted, 'Now we will celebrate!' And he downed the wine in one. It was the signal to start and the Zorils grabbed for the food. 'Emlock!' yelled Cacodyl. 'You didn't get enough wine! Get some more!' Emlock, who had only just sat down, stuffed as much meat into his mouth as possible, and with a furious glare at Cacodyl's back he hurried off to the cellar. Hibu slipped into the kitchen and found himself an apple and a hunk of bread. He decided he would escape to his room. He had little doubt that these 'civilized' creatures would shortly be completely intoxicated on the dreaded potato wine and chaos would follow. But first, he thought, I'll take my friend Greole a little treat. There was plenty of meat left on the spits. He pulled of a large piece of pork and walked quickly towards the stables.

Just before midnight at Castle Iffi Elestyal had called

together the sleighriders who had been with him in the round-room four months previously. They gathered in Elestyal's room. The door was locked. They sat in a circle. In the centre of the circle was a small round cushion made of black velvet. Eight silver tassels adorned the edge. Elestyal leaned forward and placed a silver spoon on the cushion, the very same he had used for the round-room spell. 'Thank you all for coming,' he said, 'Once again I need your help because tonight with the help of Megar we must activate the spell which we created in the round-room before we left Christmas Castle.'

The elves exchanged glances.

Elestyal continued: 'The spell we created four months ago was absorbed into every single piece of silver in Christmas Castle. Any Zoril troll who gazes upon so much as a teaspoon will be captivated, bewitched and ensnared. And will die. The magic will live on in the silver forever and will never lose its potency. It has been growing in power and strength now for four months. Tonight we release it. Tonight we bring down the power of Megar on the heads of our enemies. On those who stole our home. Its force will be mighty.'

There were murmurs of approval from around the circle.

'Please,' said Elestyal, 'All lean into the circle and put your right hand on top of mine.' He stretched out his arm and gently placed his right hand over the spoon, then he closed his eyes. Perks put his hand on top of Elestyal's, Skyler's slipped on top of Perks', and so on until all the hands rested together. The elves felt an immediate tension growing. It built and built, swirling amongst them. Now they could hear something too. A low vibration, as though the room was full of hummingbirds. As though fine currents of electricity charged the air between them. They closed their eyes and the energy increased, growing and growing and filling their heads and capturing their minds.

Suddenly Elestyal started to speak in the same trance-like tones he had used in the round-room. The elves were drawn into the power of his voice, the magic and mystery of the strange wizard-tongue.

'Mee-gar! ... Mee-gar! ... Icalyon euh agnin se noo
Jonwiszu. U'ten yepre wsus
Dispeville onveli
Leptoweskin -tath si ver
Wen t'enam si ownre felexion se's
Le bei magfeeden a thound
A-ver refleeten bach!
Le ta val-Zorrelle dizzarv ater belin owren – eyen.

Uni a u fer l sayke o seeouls oo bohn'

The strange words finished, and then he spoke to the seven:

'All of you! Repeat after me, *Sassilvashakalim!*'

'Sassilvashakalim!' they chorused together.

'Again!'

'Sassilvashakalim!'

'Again!'

'Sassilvashakalim!'

Eight times they repeated it, by which time the vibration had reached a crescendo. Things in the room had started to rattle. On the table Elestyal's cup and saucer was oscillating closer and closer to the edge. The elves felt pushed and pulled this way and that as though gripped by some unseen force. And then it ceased. The humming died away as quickly as it had started and they sat for a few seconds, recovering.

'It's done,' said Elestyal softly, 'The spell is released. Every piece of silver in Christmas Castle is now imbued with it. What I would give to be a fly on the wall there tonight. But no matter, I have eyes there on my behalf.' He nodded and smiled around at the elves, a knowing smile. And then he dived across the room to catch his cup and saucer before they hit the floor.

As the grandfather clock in the banquet hall struck midnight Iceace was squeezing under the heavily chained castle gates. Not a guard in sight, and at this time of night the snow-vultures would all be roosting. Security was lax on Walpurgis night. The young snowbun skirted the edge of the first courtyard, keeping deep in the shadows. As he passed the stables a familiar smell drove fear into his gut and set his heart pounding. The wolverine! It was close by. He loped quickly past and followed the wall around to the big archway into the main courtyard. Keeping low he slipped under the arch and stayed in the shadows. Now he could see the main building. Flames from an enormous bonfire lit every nook and cranny in the yard. 'Buggles!' he cursed. There was no hope of getting closer. He noticed the spits with the remains of the carcasses over by the kitchen door. But no trolls. He waggled an ear towards the banquet room windows, one of which was open. Between the pop and crackle of the fire he caught the sound of harsh screeches and growls, and the faint clink of cutlery. They were there, and they were eating. He would just have to wait. Elestyal said something would happen. He hoped it would be soon.

It was only seconds later and something did happen. A

most unexpected thing. The kitchen door opened and out came Hibu. Iceace couldn't believe his eyes. The lanky Erudite had stopped at one of the spits and was pulling off a chunk of meat. Now he was walking straight towards Iceace. The snowbun drew back against the wall and watched him come closer. Hibu came into the shadows under the old arch. He seemed lost in thought.

'Pssssssssssssssst!' went Iceace when Hibu was a couple of feet away. Hibu stopped and looked around in surprise. 'Down here!' whispered Iceace.

Hibu peered into the shadow and immediately made out the white form of the snowbun.

'Iceace?' He sounded astonished.

Iceace was equally astonished at seeing his friend. 'I'm so glad you're alive!'

'What on earth are you doing here?'

Iceace spoke quickly, falling over his words. 'A mission for Elestyal. Something is going to happen tonight ... to the trolls. Come with me when I go Hibu, there's no guard on the gate!'

'I ... ' But Hibu never finished. A screech from the kitchen doorway made him turn round.

'OY! Git back 'ere and help me with this frowsty wine!' yelled Emlock.

rsed. 'Stay out of sight,' he breathed, 'I'll try to
 a minute. Iceace watched him hurry back to
 loor where a skinny looking troll was waiting
 for him. A few minutes later all hell broke loose.

14
Lethal Reflections

At exactly eight minutes past twelve the trolls in the banquet room were, much to their master's irritation, licking their silver platters clean. Within seconds the elaborate knives and forks had been abandoned for grimy fingers. Meat was being scoffed in handfuls, but gravy needed tongues. Cacodyl, who had drained his large goblet of potato wine in one, and was feeling somewhat warm and expansive, decided not to chastise their ill-manners on this occasion. Civility was going to take time, but mark his words, one day the Zorils would be as good as everyone else. Elves, Erudites, humans, the whole snot-ridden lot!

He tested a little gravy on his fork. It sent his saliva glands into overdrive. It was *so* good he decided even he would relent tonight. With his neighbours engrossed in grabbing more meat he quickly bent his head and slurped the gravy from around the edge of the dish. He had never tasted anything quite as good. The Erudite had made it. That creature really had been quite a find. Hell with it! He picked his platter up with both hands and dragged his tongue from top to bottom, relishing the rich dark sauce, working up and down until every drop was gone. When he'd licked it almost to its original shine he held it up in front of him and stared into it dreamily ... *his silver*. He became mesmerized by his reflection, twisting the platter first one way and then the other like a mirror. His lopsided grin leered back at him. He was still hungry. He wanted more venison. He went to put the platter down. But the platter wouldn't go down. His hands were locked on to it like a magnet. His arms taut, out in front of him like some sort of statue. He tried to look away but his reflection had caught and captured him. What was happening? Why wouldn't his hands work? Now he couldn't move his head! Those eyes staring back at him, his own eyes, wouldn't let him go. Someone further down the table called for a toast to Hibu's gravy-making skills. It was greeted with raucous cheers of agreement and the entire company raised their gleaming, wine-filled goblets. 'To the Erudite!' they shouted. They didn't notice the candlelight suddenly flare more greedily and dance on the goblets.

A weird vibration had started around Cacodyl. A strange noise like the beating of moth wings. Like humming-birds diving among flowers. It darted and whirred around him, faint at first but increasing in volume. Louder and louder it rose. It filled his head. It seeped into his mind. He couldn't shut it out. Desperately, again he tried to force the platter away but failed, and then terror reared like a snake inside him. Fingers of strange white light, brilliant and blinding, were curling out of it. Curling towards him. Caressing him. He suddenly felt a searing pain in his head. He screamed and used every ounce of his brute-strength to try to push himself away, but it was useless. An unseen power gripped him. Other blood-curdling cries were joining his from around the table, but he hardly heard them. The platter started to move closer, and closer. He watched it, mouth open in horror as his own hands pulled it towards his face. His reflection leered at him in close-up, a misshapen gargoyle of terror. And then it was gone. Erased. A white mist in its place. And out of the mist something else was manifesting. Unclear at first, indistinct, but then it formed and he saw to his horror it was the face of a wizard. An ancient sorcerer. The chief troll's blood ran cold. He was under a spell. Immobilised and powerless.

The wizard spoke, his voice a harsh, ragged whisper.
'Zoril trolls!
Beings without souls...
'Meet Megar!

Your Nemesis.
I am the face in your stolen silver.
You came here to kill,
But your prey slipped away.
Barbarians!
You murder and defile
But no longer will you smile.
Pillagers and thieves!
You stole Christmas Castle
And now you must leave.
Megar has a gift for you
Sassilvashakalim!
Sassilvashakalim!
Sassilvashakalim!
Now you die!
Good-bye!

Hibu was still getting over the shock of finding Iceace in the courtyard. He hurried back into the kitchen, his mind racing. Emlock was just disappearing down the cellar steps en-route for yet more wine. He had left a flagon on the kitchen table.

'Take that one into them!' he called up.

Hibu Picked up the stone flagon, wrinkled his nose at

the sour odour, and headed for the banquet hall. Maybe Iceace was right? Maybe he could escape. No guards on the gate, apparently. But it would still be chained and padlocked. Could he climb over it? He doubted he could. And what else had the snowbun said? Something about a mission for Elestyal ... and something would happen to the trolls. He walked into the hall. They looked quite fine at the moment, gorging themselves on venison and guzzling their rot-gut wine. He planted the flagon in the middle of the table and started back to the kitchen.

'A toast to the tall one!' cackled one of them. 'Here's to the gravy-king!' roared another. Hibu kept walking, but was stopped in his tracks by a blood-curdling scream. He swung round. At the head of the table Cacodyl was in some sort of trance, his arms outstretched rigidly in front of him, hands gripped to his platter. Eyes wide, staring, transfixed on the dish.

'What in heaven ... ?' muttered Hibu. And then the whirring started. A weird vibration, as though the hall was full of moths. The hum of beating wings was everywhere, subtle at first, then it started to build. Now other trolls were screaming. Hibu stared around in confusion. There was light! Strange coiling fingers of light flowing from every piece of the elfin silver. Even from the candelabras. It snaked out in long tentacles and entwined the Zorils. Cacodyl sat stiff as a manikin, eyes bulging, teeth bared in a wild grimace. Unnerved, Hibu backed up in a hurry towards the door, just in time to avoid the body of the master troll as it was flung across the room like a rag doll, by some unseen force.

'Sassilvashakalim!' whispered something ... someone ...

'Sorcery!' whispered Hibu. This must be what Iceace had been talking about. Elestyal had left a spell in the silver! The white light was killing the trolls. He drew back into the doorway and watched in dreadful fascination as troll bodies were flung indiscriminately around the hall.

'OY! What the 'ell's goin' on?' came Emlock's voice behind him.

'Nothing!'

'Whaddya mean nothin'?' said the skinny troll as he collided with Hibu who was hurriedly pulling the hall door shut.

Hibu turned around, 'Don't go in there!'

'Don't go in there?' repeated Emlock, confused.

Bangs and crashes mingled with ghastly screams rocked the banquet hall. There was a tremendous thud as something heavy hit the door.

Emlock rolled his eyes and shook his head. 'Don't be

stupid! They're just fightin' that's all. It don't take too much of my good wine to set them off.'

'They're not fighting,' said Hibu.

'What the 'ell's goin' on then?' He made a lunge for the door but Hibu barred his way.'

'They're dying!'

'*What?*' Emlock's voice was a high-pitched squeak, 'Let me see!'

'Listen to me Emlock. Trust me. You don't want to go in there! I think there was a spell in the silver. I've no idea how it happened but somehow it was let loose tonight. Your mates were being hurled around in there like puppets. They were dying. I *saw* them!'

Emlock swallowed and sidled away from the door. He dodged past Hibu and scuttled to the other side of the hallway. At the same moment something growled loud and long in the shadows of the nearby stairwell. Hibu and Emlock both jumped and turned. A second later Big Urkha swung down the steps with the fat Codweb waddling in her wake.

Hibu cursed under his breath. He had assumed all the trolls except Emlock had been in the hall. So much for wishful thinking. Codweb must have been lurking upstairs, scared of another tangle with Cacodyl. And he'd completely forgotten the she-troll, Lirtob's mate, who had been spending a lot of time in one of the tower rooms. Big Urkha was no longer the fat turnip she had been a week ago. She must have given birth. The belly was gone, and now there was a new confident presence about her. She was a solid-looking beast, taller than Codweb by a head with a shock of wild black hair and piercing yellow eyes.

'What's going on?' she spat, 'What's all the screaming?'

'Somethin's murderin' them all!' quavered Emlock, waving a finger towards the door of the great hall, 'Wiv a magic spell! There's a spell in that silver of Cacodyl's wot he had locked up!'

As if to back up Emlock's words more deafening crashes and gurgling death cries emanated from the other side of the door. Urkha glanced quickly from Emlock to Hibu. She wasn't as stupid as she had been made out to be. Ever since the fight over the apples in the kitchen she had picked up on some vague, unnatural connection between these two. She had just seen Hibu stop the skinny kitchen troll from trying to get into the hall. The Erudite had saved his life. There was death in the hall. She could smell it. It was then that it suddenly seemed to hit her. Lirtob! Her mate, the father of her newborn son was in there, either dead or dying!

Urkha pulled herself up to her full height and roared, a raucous wail of rage and grief. Hibu froze. What sort of hell was about to be unleashed? He didn't wait to find out. He ran. He flew through the kitchen, heaved open the door and bolted across the courtyard. The wrath of the big she-troll fell hard on his heels. She pounded after him, screaming like a banshee. He made it halfway across the courtyard before she fell on him, slamming into him like a charging bull and taking him down. Knocking the wind out of him.

Iceace watched in horror from the shadows as Urkha rained down a hail of blows on Hibu's head and body, knocking him this way and that. The Erudites had never been warriors. They were gentle, thoughtful folk, given to learning not fighting. If this wild-looking black-haired monster decided to kill him nothing could stop it now. Iceace closed his eyes. He couldn't watch, couldn't bear it.

Hibu was curled in a ball, arms protecting his head, cursing his lanky lack of physical strength. Urkha suddenly gave up with fists and went in with feet. It was like being bludgeoned with a small tree trunk. After half a dozen well-aimed assaults she dragged him, beaten and winded into a sitting position.

'What did you see? What happened in there?' she

shrieked.

'I ... I ...' wheezed Hibu, unable to think clearly.

Urkha bent down and clamped a hand around his throat. She squeezed, and kept squeezing. Hibu's world gradually became a kaleidoscope of stars and red splodges. Sound faded and blood pulsed in his ears. Then she shook him until his teeth rattled.

'Speak or die!' she roared.

'Ah ... uh ... *spell* ...' he gurgled, gasping for air.

She released her grip slightly. 'Who did it? *Who*?'

The red splodges were clearing and Urkha's ugly face swam six inches from his.

'Don't know ... think it was ... in ... in the silver ... I was taking more wine ... and it all started ... hap ... happening,' said Hibu between gasps.

'What? What happened?'

'Strange noise ... humming ... white light. Came from the silver ... threw Cacodyl across the room.'

Urkha released her grip and Hibu fell forwards, chest heaving. The she-troll cursed. Emlock, standing a few feet away, gulped and tried to stop shaking.

'I want to know who did it?' she growled with curled lip. 'Who is this murderer? Who got in here and did this thing?'

Hibu lifted his head and looked her straight in the eye, 'I'm not a wizard,' he whispered, 'How would I know? The spell didn't have a damn signature!'

Urkha was taken aback at the edge in his voice. She believed him. Besides she knew well enough that Hibu had had no contact with the outside world since they had moved in. He must be telling the truth. In sheer fury she smashed a punch into his face. Someone had to pay. It was a brutal blow. Hibu fell backwards groaning and clutching his nose. Blood streamed down his shirt. The she-troll stepped back, winding up for more kicks, when a sudden noise from behind them made her stop and turn. Codweb heard it too. *Thump!* it went. *Thump-thump!* It was coming from the big archway.

'See what it is!' growled Urkha.

Codweb thought about his dead mates in the hall. 'Wh ... What if ... ?'

'Check it out!' It was a statement. She wasn't arguing.

The fat little troll scuttled forwards until he got to the archway, then he peered cautiously through in the darkness. Too many shadows. He crept in slowly, scanning ahead towards the castle gate, moonlit in the distance. *THUMP!* The sudden noise echoed loudly under the arch. Codweb nearly jumped out of his skin. And then he squealed as a large rabbit dived threw his legs, tripping him, and sending him sprawling onto the cobbles. He panicked, arms and legs wheeling as he scrambled to get up. Then he ran full tilt back to Urkha.

"T'was a rabbit!' he spluttered, 'A monstrous thing with eyes like fire! D'you think it did the spell?'

'Numb brain!' Urkha whacked him round the ear, 'Rabbit's don't cast spells you brainless lump of blubber.' Even so, it was most odd that a rabbit should have actually come into the castle grounds. 'It must have come looking for food,' she growled. Codweb cowered as she turned her attention back to Hibu. 'You!' she said, poking him in the chest, 'Get in that hall and get *every* piece of that silver packed away, locked up and out of sight! I mean *every* piece. And when it's done,' her gaze fell on Emlock, '*you* go in there and check.'

Emlock looked quickly from Urkha to Hibu and back again. There was fear in his eyes but he didn't argue. Clever, thought Hibu, covertly watching what appeared to be a new leader emerging. She's picked up on the connection I have with Emlock. She knows I'll not leave a piece lying around to ambush him. He was astonished and puzzled at how the situation was suddenly unfolding. She-trolls were usually under-dogs but this one was quite the opposite.

Maybe this take-over was born of protection for her new offspring. Maybe her instinct told her that the two males left were weak characters. She had immediately sensed that she could control them. Either way his gut told him she was both extremely clever, and extremely dangerous.

'What about the rabbit?' Codweb was looking nervously at the dark archway. Urkha glared at him in disgust and ignored the question.

'Cacodyl and Lirtob are both dead,' she announced in icy tones, '*I* will be in charge from now on. You will all take orders from me. Do you understand?'

Codweb and Emlock, exchanging cautious furtive glances, nodded in unison. Hibu stared at the ground and wiped the blood from his dripping nose. Urkha continued, 'It will please you to know that although Lirtob is dead, he has a son. In time he will be the master of this castle. In the meantime, should any harm come to him you will have me to answer to, and believe me, death will be preferable.'

There was stony silence. A half-burned branch fell somewhere in the bonfire and crackled. Hibu dabbed at his nose with a corner of his shirt.

'Codweb!'

The fat troll jumped to attention.

'When he's finished getting rid of the silver,' she hiked a

thumb towards Hibu, 'You and Emlock lock him in his room, then get rid of the bodies. Get a wheelbarrow and sling them on the bonfire. We might as well make use of it. I'll be back to check on progress.'

Hibu trudged painfully back behind Emlock and Codweb. Just before stepping into the kitchen he glanced quickly over his shoulder. Movement under the arch! A flash of white in the orange glow of the fire. Iceace!

Urkha headed for the tower, her mind churning, excitement rising within her like lava in a volcano. When had a she-troll ever been in command? Of *anything*? Never in history! How simple it had been to take control. To stamp on those two clod-brained males. A euphoria hit her like she had never known. For too long the she-trolls had been crushed and subservient. Never in her wildest dreams had she imagined it could be any other way. That was about to change.

In the tower room Urkha eyed her sleeping baby. He was ugly as sin. A wizened little bag of loose brownish skin covered with patches of spiky black hair. He had a pushed-in face, a heavy jaw, big ears, and the classic yellow slit eyes of the Zoril. But like any mother she thought he was beautiful. He had been born just after midnight. A

Walpurgis brat. A lucky day to be born on it was thought, if you were a troll. She picked him out of the old rabbit skin he was wrapped in and clasped him to her, still slightly damp and sticky from the birth. His hair was as black as his mother's. She stroked a patch on his back. He had all his toes, and fingers and was a healthy troll infant. The only imperfection was a rash of yellow pustules scattered across his belly. She had had the same affliction as a youngster.

'Still beautiful,' she crooned, 'A little bit of plague won't hurt you. In fact that shall be your name. Plague! It suits you, you hairy little scrap. D'you think yer father would approve?' Then she smiled, 'He can't do much about it now, can he? Not about that, or anything else!'

15

A Hidden Key and a Bear in Bearban

Petal waited for about two minutes after Iceace had headed for the castle gate, then she crept back into the deeper shadows. Her mind was doing overtime. What if Iceace was caught? They would torture him and he'd be forced to tell them she was waiting in the wood. They'd come for her ... fifty big hairy brutes ... and they'd eat Surf and ...! She decided to move around to the other side of the clearing and find a better place to hide. Not far from the secret door to the round-room passage she found a massive old oak, long dead and strewn with ivy. On closer inspection she discovered it was hollow. She tied Surf up nearby, pushed apart the ivy fronds and crept inside, shivering, and wishing for the thousandth time that she was back in her warm bed at Iffi. It was pitch dark inside the trunk and smelled of woodlice. Once again she found herself wishing Aleron was here. After a few minutes her eyes adjusted and she noticed a large and convenient creeper-covered hole right in front of her. With the ivy removed it provided a perfect view across the clearing. Where was Ice? She reminded herself that he'd only just gone. Every minute was seeming more like twenty.

She was still standing in concentrated anticipation, eye glued to the hole, when a movement inside her jacket made her squeak with fright. Her first thought was that something had crawled inside her clothing in the dark. Then she breathed a sigh of relief. It was Crumb. He must have popped into her inside pocket before they left, and slept all the way. Now, in the dim light, the little wood mouse peeped out and stared up at her. She was *so* pleased to see him. Even if he was just a mouse he still seemed like a great comfort. 'We're in a frowsty old tree trunk at Christmas Castle,' she told him, 'And I'm dead scared, and Ice hasn't come back, and we may get eaten by trolls!' Crumb waggled his whiskers, and then ran straight down her arm and dropped onto the ground. 'Come back!' whispered Petal urgently, 'This is no time to go looking for nuts. We may have to run for our lives at any moment!' She bent down to find him but he'd disappeared. 'Crumb?' she whispered, 'Crumb come back!' There was a rustle to her right. It was pitch dark in the base of the tree. She felt around gently in the direction of the noise. 'Pleeeese come back!' Another rustle. And then her fingers slipped into a cavity in the thick bark and Crumb ran across her hand.

'Stop being bad and come here,' she said crossly, pushing her hand further in. And then, instead of mouse, she felt metal. Something lying among the dead leaves and nut shells. As her fingers closed over it she felt Crumb run up her arm.

Petal inspected her find in a shaft of moonlight. It was a key. What was it doing here? What door did it unlock? Who put it here? Why was it hidden? She turned it over. It was old and smooth. She had seen a key like this somewhere before. Not long ago. She searched her memory. Not at Iffi. No, before that. And then she saw it in her mind's eye. It was the same as the one Skyler had taken from behind the stone when they were at the end of the round-room passage. It must be the key to the hidden door! With fear stuffed behind her and intrigue pulling her on she crept out of her hidey-hole and wove her way to the edge of the clearing. Almost on cue a cloud drifted across the moon and smothered everything in a cloak of darkness. She grabbed the moment and was over to the door in a flash, feverishly searching amongst the creepers and vines for the keyhole. It was spring and everything had gone wild, new shoots and leaves were bursting forth, covering the door in a tangle of foliage. 'Come *on!*' she said to herself, as she pushed aside more stems and leaves. A few minutes later she found it.

Relief. She slipped the key in. It fitted. She turned it. *Clunk* went the lock. Her heart thumped. She turned it back, making sure the door was locked, then she dashed back to the old oak. Her mind was in a whirl. What should she do with it? Should she keep it? What if someone needed to get into the passage? Who would want to with trolls in the castle? She turned it over in her hands. She could feel the initials CC etched on one side. If she left it in the tree the trolls might find it. She was still agonising over her decision when she saw Iceace racing towards the tall pine.

Five minutes later they were making off across Snaggle Plains and working their way quickly and quietly to the foot of the crags, both glad to put distance between themselves and the trolls. Only when they started up the river path did they talk of the events of the evening. Iceace told Petal what he had seen, and how overjoyed he was to find Hibu still alive. But also how sick he had felt when the she-troll with the wild black hair had beaten him.

'I did a couple of my biggest *thumps,*' he said, 'and it worked. It took her attention from Hibu.'

'It was a brave thing to do,' said Petal, 'And I can't believe you tripped up that fat troll!'

Iceace felt a huge bubble of pride swell inside him, 'It

was nothing really,' he said modestly, 'D'you know what he called me?'

'What?'

'He said I was a monstrous thing with eyes like fire!'

Petal giggled, 'You obviously impressed him.'

'What a bunch of boobrarb, he was scared of his own shadow.'

'Rhubarb Iceace, not boobrarb.'

'Oh,' said Iceace.

They were making excellent time. Surf, as sure-footed as a goat, picked his way quickly and nimbly through Keeper's Gorge. Petal peered over the edge with a shiver at the white water hundred's of feet below. After the gorge it was an easy descent all the way down to Bearban Forest. The sun was up and the forest was warm and buzzing with insects. The two young travellers breathed in the sweet smell of pine and oak, and marvelled at the blaze of bluebells splashed across the forest floor. The loud rat-tat-tat of a spotted woodpecker sounded in the distance and overhead in the canopy of branches, great-tits, nuthatches and other small birds peeped, and pecked in search of food.

They were nearly at the end of the forest path, passing through an area of thick undergrowth when they heard it, the sound of something snuffling and digging. Iceace stopped dead and sat bolt upright, snuffing the breeze.

'Bear!' he whispered to Petal.

Surf's head had come up too and his ears were pricked. He didn't like bear. He started side-stepping. Petal felt all his muscles tense beneath her. It was like sitting on a coiled spring. She whispered to him and patted his neck, trying to calm him. More grunting from the undergrowth. Surf snorted and blew and crabbed along the path. They kept going, hoping the creature would move away. And then a few yards further on Petal spied the source of the noise, a baby bear rooting for beetles and tasty morsels amongst the ferns.

'It's just a baby one,' she whispered to Iceace, feeling somewhat relieved. But relief was short-lived. A deep bellowing growl greeted them from the bushes on the other side of the path, and mama bear stood up to her full furry height. She was enormous, all teeth and claws and protective mother. It was too much for Surf. He was off, bolting down the path at full gallop with Petal clinging on for dear life. Considering her brief riding experience she did well to stay in the saddle. Reindeer weren't prone to taking off with you at top speed. But a few hundred yards later the path crossed a ditch. Surf spotted it at the last minute, slid almost to a stop, and then took off like a cat. Petal, who wasn't anticipating the sudden stop, flew straight over his shoulder and landed in the bottom of the ditch.

'Petal!' Iceace was there in a flash, peering down at her. 'Are you okay?'

Petal groaned, then cursed, 'Yuck and damn I'm all wet!' She crawled up the bank and stood up. She was plastered from head to toe in greenish-black mud. 'Blinking stinking stuff.' She wrinkled her nose, 'Oh my goodness! Crumb!' She undid the top of her jacket in a panic. At least the water hadn't penetrated right through. What if she'd squashed him? She pulled open the inner pocket and a sleepy head peered out. 'How on earth did you sleep through that?' she said, laughing with relief. Crumb eyed her for a second and then snuggled back down to continue his sleep. Petal zipped up her jacket. 'Well Ice,' she said, 'It looks like we're both on foot from here.

A few hours later they arrived at Castle Iffi and found half the castle waiting for them. Had Iceace gone on his mission alone no one would have been any the wiser, but the disappearance of Surf and Petal, followed by the reappearance of the sweaty riderless pony, had caused huge concern. Elestyal, Zeb and Aleron surrounded them, and they did not look happy. Elestyal was frowning, Zeb looked furious, and Aleron looked alternately puzzled and relieved. Petal had felt a funny little thrill when she had seen him running towards them. They were all staring at her, a fine spectacle covered in dried mud, hair caked, and a bloody scratch on her cheek from brambles in the ditch.

'Is Surf okay?' she asked quickly, 'Did he come home?'

'He did,' said Zeb with an angry glare, 'and not in the sort of shape he should have. He was filthy and completely sweated up. He'd obviously been ridden far too hard.'

'There was a bear,' said Petal helplessly, 'It spooked him and he bolted, and ... I fell off.'

'Where the devil have you been?' Zeb sounded incredulous. 'That pony has been gone since I got up yesterday morning! Were you crazy?'

Petal looked at her feet.

Elestyal spoke, 'Zeb, I think I can guess what's happened. Give me some time with these two and we'll talk later.'

Zeb nodded curtly, 'Whatever it is she's banned from riding for at least a month.' He turned on his heel and walked away. Petal looked devastated. Elestyal ushered them off to the kitchen.

'You two look like you could do with a drink and a bite,'

he said, 'after Miss Petal has removed some of her mud.'
Petal nodded humbly.

A little later the two weary travellers sat in front of Elestyal in the quiet of his room. He observed them sternly for a few minutes. Petal moved uncomfortably on her chair.

'Okay you two,' he said, after they had sweated for a minute, 'We need to have a little talk. First you, young Iceace. When I tell you something, and ask that you tell no one, I expect you to keep to your word.'

Petal immediately jumped in. 'It was my fault Elestyal, he didn't want to tell me. I tried to make him feel guilty and ... ' she tapered off.

'You succeeded,' said Elestyal with a wry smile.

Petal found an interesting spot to study on the floor.

'You used Iceace's soft-hearted nature to get what you wanted,' he continued. 'And in doing so you could have endangered his mission. Iceace could have been there and back much faster without you and Surf. And because of his size and speed he could have escaped all sorts of dangers which you and Surf could not. Fortunately you only ran into a bear, and that was bad enough. What you did was foolish and impetuous.'

Petal was close to tears, 'I'm really sorry,' she said,

hanging her head.

Iceace looked at Petal then up at Elestyal, 'She was a fantastic help, and I don't think I could have done it without her,' he said earnestly.

Elestyal loved his loyalty. He sat back in his chair and looked at the tousle-haired Elfrachaun in front of him, still with dirt smudges on her nose. 'Miss Petal,' he said, shaking his head, 'What am I going to do with you?'

Petal looked sheepish, 'I wanted to help,' she said quietly, 'To get Christmas Castle back. Aleron is so miserable since we left.'

Elestyal raised an eyebrow, 'You did it for him?' Surprise sounded in his voice.

'No ... well, not exactly. I did it for ... for you and for all the elves. And ... I thought it would be exciting,' she ended quietly.

'Exciting. Is that so? And was it?'

She couldn't hide the gleam in her eye, 'It was a bit scary at times.'

Elestyal couldn't help but admire her wild spirit. He turned to Iceace, 'So, now we've sorted out the rights and wrongs, tell me, what did you see at Christmas Castle?'

Iceace carefully related every detail.

'So from what you overheard in the courtyard it would

seem we've reduced their strength from fifty to just three, plus a new brat. This is good news indeed, but I had so hoped we would rid ourselves of the entire clan. How unfortunate that three missed the feast.' He rubbed his chin thoughtfully. 'This thing you tell me about the she-troll is most unusual. *Most* unusual. Never have I ever heard of a she-troll trying to take command. But it would appear she has. And the two males have accepted her role. She must be quite clever to have turned the situation to her advantage so quickly. She-trolls have always been subservient. This new power could make her extremely dangerous.'

'But it's good news about Hibu,' said Iceace eagerly.

'Yes, yes it is, very good,' agreed the wizard, 'One wonders how on earth he has survived four months living with Zorils. What troubles me is how he will fare now this vicious female is in control.' He trailed off into his own thoughts and sat quietly for a few minutes looking worried. Suddenly he looked up. 'Shame on me! I have not thanked you young Iceace. Once again you have accomplished a vitally important mission. I speak for everyone when I tell you how proud we all are of you. And once again we are in your debt.'

If Iceace hadn't been a rabbit he would have positively blushed with pride, 'It was really nothing,' he said, growing to about ten feet tall.

'You two had better run along now and get some sleep, you must be worn out.' They had turned to go when Elestyal spoke again, 'One minute Iceace, I think you've earned this.' He went over to his desk drawer, opened it, and drew out a denim cap. He presented it to the snowbun. 'Bizz has made special holes for rabbit ears.'

Iceace gazed at his prize. Embroidered on the front were a pair of bright orange carrots. 'Oh my! Just like yours but with carrots,' he squeaked, 'Thanks Elestyal!' He pulled it on, carefully tucking an ear through each hole. 'I must go and show Perks.'

Elestyal burst out laughing. Petal giggled. She turned to go. The wizard called her back. 'One last thing,' he said, 'What you did was both brave and irresponsible. Quite a feat for someone of only thirteen years. It took great fortitude. You are a remarkable young Elfrachaun Miss Petal, but *don't* do it again.'

Petal looked up, a small smile sprouting across her lips, 'Thank you.'

'Now go and apologise to Zeb,' said the wizard.

Petal shot out of the door and made a beeline for the stables, passing Aleron on the way.

'Hey ... ' he yelled.

'Back in a minute,' she called, 'Gotta see Zeb.' After she had made her apologies she would sit down with Aleron and tell him the whole story. He'd been funny and off with her for weeks. Surely he'd be pleased when she told him where she had been and why? Okay, so she hadn't exactly spied on the trolls herself, but she'd been pretty close. And then she suddenly remembered what was stuffed in her pocket. Guilt grabbed her. She hadn't mentioned it to anyone, not even Iceace. Something told her it might be best if she didn't. What if someone did need it? Elestyal had obviously returned it to its hiding place when they all escaped at Christmas. He must have wanted it left there. She kicked herself for once again being so impulsive.

In the stable all was quiet. Zeb wasn't about. Surf was pulling at his hay net. Petal pulled out her grooming box and opened the lid. It was full of brushes, curry-combs, mane-combs, hoof-picks and other odds and ends. She slipped the key into the very bottom. No one else used her grooming box. It would be safe here.

16

Little Plague

In the wee hours of the morning smoke from the Walpurgis bonfire drifted through the open kitchen door. Codweb grinned delightedly as he pulled on Hibu's boots. He was second in command now. No way *she* was going to choose the snotty Emlock over him, was she? Not when he was pals with the stupid Erudite. He had already taken it upon himself to order Hibu into the banquet room to remove the silver. Now he was sprawled in a chair at the kitchen table, head on one side, ogling his footwear. Emlock swept up remnants of the party and covertly eyed him with undisguised loathing. What a disaster. All the trolls dead, apart from the raving Urkha, Codweb, and Lirtob's new brat. The future suddenly looked very grim.

Hibu stepped into the banquet hall, closed the door behind him and surveyed the scene. A battlefield by candlelight. Trolls were scattered in grotesque misshaped poses around the room. The smell nearly made him sick.

He picked his way to a window in his socked feet, stepping gingerly over bodies, bits of food, and pieces of silver. He needed air. He threw open all the windows and inhaled deeply. After a few minutes he forced himself to turn around. Immediately behind him a troll lay on its back across the table, head lolling over the edge, mouth agape, its face still set in a death-mask of surprise and pain. The flesh was blackened and peeling, as though burned. The creature still gripped a gravy-streaked platter to its chest. Another lay to his left on the floor with the same charred and blackened face. It clasped a silver goblet with both hands. They lay everywhere, staring into goblets, spoons, bowls, and even a gravy-boat. Hibu suspected that death had been neither swift nor pleasant. He closed his eyes for a minute, dreading the revolting task before him. Then, drawing strength from some deep part of himself he leaned down and prized the goblet from the stiff, clawed hands of the troll on the floor.

For over an hour he made his way around the hall forcing the silver from the death-grips of the dead Zorils and carrying every piece back to the oak chests. He packed it in, complete with food and wine stains. Then he locked both chests and called Emlock. There was no reply. He opened the door and shouted, 'Emlock! The silver is packed away. It's safe to go in.' It was a few minutes before the skinny troll appeared, sidling down the passage looking terrified.

'Don't worry,' said Hibu. 'I've moved it all. Every single piece is packed in the chests. Here are the keys.'

Emlock squinted past him, bobbing this way and that, 'You sure?' he asked, hoarsely, wiping his nose nervously on the back of his hand.

'Absolutely sure.'

Hibu stepped to one side and Emlock sidled cautiously into the doorway. One brief look at the remains of his fellow Zorils was enough. His mouth dropped open in horror. Clutching his stomach with both hands he turned and raced to the courtyard where he threw up for some moments. The noise brought Codweb.

'Wor wrong with you?' he screeched

Emlock threw up some more.

'Get back in there and make sure he's got rid of it all! And if he 'as we 'ave to get a barrow and hike them bodies onto the bonfire.'

'*You* go in there,' gasped Emlock, still holding his stomach, 'I never smelled nothin' like it.'

'Oh no y'don't! Urkha said you 'ad to do it. Besides, yer lanky friend 'as probably left a nice shiny goblet out t'murder us with. You first!'

Emlock screwed up his face and spat. He took a step towards Codweb, eyes narrowed, 'Who put you in charge?' he sneered.

'She did! And if y'don't believe me I'll 'ave to go and get 'er!'

Emlock knew he would too. There was no choice. He turned his back on Codweb's smug smirk and shambled back to the hall, still looking decidedly green around the gills. Hibu stood in the kitchen doorway.

'Get in yer room Mr Bare Feet!' Quite intoxicated with his new power, Codweb followed Hibu down to his room and locked him in.

Hibu sat on his bed in despair, head in hands for a long time. What had Iceace said to him tonight ... something about a mission for Elestyal. *Something will happen tonight ... to the trolls!* It certainly had. Somehow the old wizard had created a spell here, before he left last Christmas day. It had been well-planned. If only all of the trolls had been around the table. Maybe with the exception of his skinny little 'friend' Emlock. But what now? This new situation looked no better than the old one, certainly not for him anyway, in fact it looked worse. Cacodyl, although a tough Zoril, had not treated him badly. In fact Cacodyl's rule had afforded him a certain protection, thanks to the chief's determination to rise up and learn. As an Erudite, Hibu had been a mine of information for the ignorant, ambitious troll. His knowledge had been his life-line. Now the she-troll had risen. Would he be as useful to her? Or would he be the next meal for the wolverine? Either way he couldn't do much about it unless he could escape, and that possibility looked as hopeless as ever. He laid down and pulled his blanket over himself. He was cold, desperately tired, and stank of charred troll. He wondered how long Urkha would let him live.

It was daylight when Emlock came to let him out of his room.

'Watch yer step,' he breathed hurriedly, 'She's evil!' Hibu saw the fear in his eyes and nodded. 'Can't help you much,' continued Emlock in a low whisper, 'I'll have to shout at you.'

'I understand.'

They headed up to the kitchen with Emlock screaming 'Get up those stairs!'

Urkha heard him as she stood in the banquet hall looking out at the remains of the bonfire in the courtyard, sniffing the pungent aroma of charcoaled troll as it drifted in through the open window on wisps of sweet, clinging smoke. A charred skull rolled down the pile of blackened bones and resettled with a little puff of grey ash as she watched. It seemed to look directly at her. Maybe it was Lirtob. She cocked her head on one side and grimaced at it. She had little use for him now. Her new infant was strapped to her chest in a rabbit skin pouch. She took one of its little fists and waved bye-bye to the macabre spectacle in the ashes. Then she turned and headed for the kitchen.

Emlock was hacking the remains from one of last night's carcasses. He didn't look up when she came in. Hibu continued peeling potatoes. She roared for Codweb. He came shooting through the door, dipping his head up and down in submissive little nods, having run at top-speed from wherever he'd been. Urkha ignored his posturing and lined the three of them up with their backs to the wall. Then she told them the way things would be under her rule. She seemed to have grown in stature overnight along with her new sense of power. She was an awesome sight as she strode up and down, black mane bristling, yellow eyes watching their every reaction. Others would eventually join them, she said, but they would be females, or males who agreed to her command. She suddenly advanced towards Hibu who stood his ground but dropped his head in a gesture of obedience.

'I will let you live, because you're useful,' she said softly. She was so close he could feel her hot breath on his ear. 'But one wrong move and you will be dinner for the gulo.'

Hibu nodded. His thoughts racing. Once again he should be dead. It would have been quite normal for the surviving trolls to have killed him off in a vengeful rage after what had happened. But it had worked differently because of the unusual take-over by the she-troll. His knowledge had yet again been the reason his life had been spared. He was more useful to her alive than dead. He sensed a new and terrible power about this beast in front of him and an unusually shrewd intelligence. But there was instability too. A lethal concoction thought Hibu. She was a child with a new toy, and a new and intoxicating power. Woe betide anyone or anything that got in her way.

And so a new era started at Christmas Castle under the eagle eye of Urkha. Her underlings did everything they could not to displease her. Hibu moved as silently as possible from job to job, almost an impossibility now that he was in chains. Urkha had had him shackled. She had also permanently chained and padlocked the main gate since she didn't have enough troll-power to post guards. A shadow fell over the castle. It had been bad enough living with Cacodyl and his clan, but Urkha was a menace of a whole different ilk.

Little Plague grew fast, as troll infants do, and picked up very quickly on the fact that he only answered to his mother. No one else challenged him. No one else dared. On the other hand if he injured himself doing something stupid everyone else got the blame. He quickly learned how to manipulate situations and make their lives hell. Troll-brats were normally brought up by the pack. Discipline was meted out by all. Without this input the little creature became an uncontrollable terror. Like any youngster, there was a whole new world to explore, and he wanted to investigate it. Taste it, touch it or play with it. And if possible tease it.

One morning Hibu found him in the kitchen standing on a chair staring with avid interest out of the window. Once in a while he would grasp the chair-back and bounce up and down in excitement, letting out ear-piercing shrieks. Over his shoulder Hibu saw he was watching a snow-vulture which had descended into the courtyard to scavenge on a rabbit carcass in the rubbish heap. Hibu had never seen him so agitated. He suddenly leapt off the chair and tore over to the kitchen door. He was still too short to reach the latch. He turned to Hibu and let out a ferocious squeal.

'Iboo!' he screeched, still unable to pronounce Hibu's name.

'Your mother says you can't go out till you're older,' said Hibu patiently.

'*Creeeee – eeech!*' squealed Plague. He started to kick the door.

Hibu ignored him.

'*Creeeee – eeeee – eeeee – eeeeech!*' Now he was throwing things. Anything he could get his hands on was flung at the object that prevented him from getting what he wanted. A tin plate sailed past Hibu's head and smacked Emlock on the nose as he came up from the larder.

'Arrgh!' yelled Emlock.

'Em' out!' screamed Plague, suddenly catching sight of the skinny troll. He pointed up to the latch.

Emlock looked nervously at Hibu and back again to Plague, 'Can't let you out. Yer Ma says no.'

They were both rewarded with a barrage of screaming and flying missiles, which, as usual, prompted the arrival of Urkha.

'What are you doing to him?' she growled.

'Ma-aa!' Plague drummed up his best 'they're being mean to me' whine.

Urkha picked up the tin plate suspiciously and glared at Emlock who reversed rapidly back towards the larder. She took his retreat as some sort of admission of guilt and bore down on him. Hibu, sick to death of the unmanageable, obnoxious, sneaky infant, found himself for once daring to speak up.

'He wanted to go into the courtyard to see the snow-vulture,' he said firmly and loudly. Urkha stopped, surprised at the decisive tone in the Erudite's voice'. She turned and walked slowly towards him. Hibu didn't budge. 'We thought it too dangerous,' he continued boldly, 'The birds are very big and unpredictable, and Plague would be vulnerable without your protection. He threw the plates because we refused to let him out.'

He had got it just right, and it worked. He hadn't defied her, he was showing concern for her offspring, but at the same time handing her the power to protect him. She stopped and looked across at her son, who had switched from wheedling to defiant. He bared his teeth and glared at her from under jutting brows, fixing her with a murderous little stare. God help them when he got bigger thought Hibu.

'You're right,' she said, 'Plague, you cannot go out. I've told you before. We'll see the birds later.'

As if it heard her words there was a noisy '*Quark*' in the distance from the vulture. Plague, now completely thwarted, promptly had a mega troll-tantrum, the focus of his aggression being his mother. He launched himself across the kitchen, head down, going for her legs. A ferocious snarling bundle of teeth, claws and spiky black hair. Urkha let out a bellowing laugh and grabbed him by the scruff. Holding him at arm's length she took him off upstairs, wailing in impotent fury.

Emlock let out a huge breath and slumped into a chair. He rubbed a hand across his brow and looked up at Hibu, 'Thanks,' he muttered.

'Someone had to try it sooner or later,' said Hibu.

'She'd 'ave had my 'ead if I'd said it,' said Emlock, keeping his voice low.

Hibu sat down next to him. 'That's one mean little bag of trouble she's produced. We have to be clever Emlock. Let her think we're concerned for the little beast. The best thing to do is to go to her whenever he gets heading for trouble. Make out we're concerned. I don't think she'll get too aggressive if we do it that way. Plus she may get sick of us asking, and knock some sense into him.'

Hibu got up and made himself a cup of herb tea while Emlock thought over his words. Codweb emerged from somewhere and slouched into the kitchen. Since Urkha's take-over he had somehow managed to perfect the art of quiet skulking, even in his clunky over-sized boots. He looked suspiciously at the two in the kitchen, detecting a sudden silence for his benefit.

'Wassup?' he growled.

'Nothin',' growled Emlock back at him.

'Who's screechin'?'

'Who d'you flamin' think!'

'Where is he?'

'She took him upstairs. He wanted to go play with the scavengers. He wouldn't let him out.' Emlock nodded towards Hibu, 'Then he told her the scavengers wos too big and dangerous and may eat the little weasel, and he needed her protection to go out.'

'Very brave!' sneered Codweb.

'It worked,' grunted Emlock.

Codweb studied Hibu. He would have liked to have strangled him with his bare hands, or maybe thrown him across the kitchen table and taken a knife to his throat. But he couldn't. Urkha would kill him. For some reason she wanted to keep the pathetic creature alive. He sat down at the table with Emlock and continued to glower. Hibu sighed, Codweb was in the mood for a fight. He wanted no part of it. Picking up his tea he set off down to his room with his ankle chains clank-clanking as he descended each stair.

'Don't forget to feed yer friendly gulo,' yelled Codweb at his departing back.

Hibu shut the door and put his tea on the table. Heavens his feet were cold. It seemed to seep right up through from the flagstones however many pairs of socks he wore. And the metal rings around his ankles made it a thousand times worse. He lifted down Elestyal's box of medicines and found one that said 'foot balm'. Then he removed his socks and took the lid off the little pot of cream. It smelled wonderful. Ginger and mint, with maybe a hint of eucalyptus. He rubbed a little onto his foot and felt a burst of warmth. Ah! Lovely! In his mind's eye the old wizard smiled at him. 'You always had a way with medicines,' said Hibu. He continued to rub the balm into both feet and then he pulled the socks back on. Then he had a brain-wave and wondered why he'd never thought of it before.

17

Vulture Attack

Single-parenthood was not Urkha's bag. She had started to see herself more as a warrior now, a new leader for what would eventually be a she-troll uprising. Her offspring, although she loved him, was a nuisance and a constant drain on her attention. She decided to go hunting and sharpen her skills.

Plague, after his severe scolding was sulking in one of the upstairs rooms, contenting himself with looking for spiders which he might terrorize and eventually squash, but there weren't any to be found. Bored, he poked around in the little cupboards and drawers in the elfin furniture. Nothing of interest. There were two small single beds in the room. He decided to have a look under the mattresses, there was bound to be a bug under there. The first one produced a beetle which wasn't much fun, especially when it escaped through a crack in the floor boards. He pushed the second mattress up and over. No bugs. But what was this? A pile of papers! He leaned over and picked them up. They were pictures. He was intrigued. He took them over to the window into the light and sat down.

Every one of the pictures was a childlike, but life-like sketch of reindeer. There were some depicted in a barn and some in a field in summer. Some were even in colour. It was the last one that Plague liked best, eight reindeer flying, pulling a sleigh through a dark and murky sky. The lead deer had a brightly shining nose which cast a beam of light ahead. Underneath it said *'Ru', by Petal.'* Plague rubbed his own nose thoughtfully, then he picked up the pictures and left the room. He hadn't gone far when he heard a tap-tapping noise coming from somewhere down one of the corridors. He padded quietly along following the sound and eventually came to a door with a sign on it that said *'Workshop'*. The door was ajar so he pushed it open. Inside, Hibu looked up from one of the old work benches. He had a large piece of leather in one hand, a small hammer in the other and some tacks held between his lips. He took the tacks out and put them back in a jar.

'What y'doin' Iboo?'

'Making shoes for cold feet,' replied Hibu, groaning inwardly. He really didn't want this little pain disturbing his peace and quiet and causing havoc in the old workshop. Plague made a beeline for the bench. He appeared to be trying to hide some pieces of paper behind his back.

'Wanna see!' he said in his demanding tone, pointing up at the bench. Hibu helped him onto a stool. Plague leaned forward and felt the leather, waved the hammer in the air, rattled the tacks in the jar and said, 'Shoes for Iboo!'

'Yes,' replied Hibu, 'I need shoes because I don't have hair to protect my feet like you do.' He pointed at Plague's furry feet.

'Hair good, feet warm,' said Plague eyeing his wriggling toes. Then, quickly bored with the foot subject he brought the papers from behind his back and put them on the bench. 'See!' he said, sounding excited. Hibu accepted the pictures and leafed through them.

'Very nice,' he said, noting the name Petal written neatly in the bottom right-hand corner of each one, 'Where did you find them?'

Plague smirked. He wasn't telling. 'An ... ee ... mal,' he said, pointing to the pictures.

'Yes, a reindeer animal,' said Hibu.

Plague looked intrigued, 'Rein-dee-a,' he repeated. He shuffled the papers till he got to the one of Rudolph. 'Nose,' he said, pressing at his own and going cross-eyed trying to look at it.

'Yours won't light up,' laughed Hibu. He pointed at the

drawing, 'He has a magic nose.' Plague looked puzzled. Hibu pressed his own nose. 'See, mine isn't magic either. That reindeer has the only magic nose in the whole world. And it only lights up at Christmas.'

'Ma-gic at Chris-mass.' He seemed to be giving it serious thought. Then he suddenly looked hard at Hibu, 'Mine!' he said sharply, and he picked up the papers and held them behind his back. As though suddenly wishing he hadn't shared them. 'Mine see-cret!' he growled. And then like the wind he changed, his tone suddenly becoming soft and pliant. He gave Hibu a pleading, doe-eyed stare. 'Not tell pleeeze?' he wheedled, with a crooked little smile.

Hibu shook his head in disbelief at the mercurial transformation, at the deliberate change in character. As slippery as a bag of eels he thought to himself. He nodded at Plague. 'Your secret, Plague's secret,' he said.

'Mmm!' Plague nodded happily.

'Okay, I won't tell anyone.'

Apparently satisfied, the little beast clambered down from the stool and headed out of the door. Hibu looked after him for some moments, pondering how such a young creature could learn to be so secretive and sneaky at such a tender age. Must be in the blood he decided. He picked up his hammer and continued with his project. One shoe was finished. It had been quite an easy task with all the materials he had found in the workshop. He would finish shoe number two and then walk over and feed his friend, Greole.

Half an hour later he was re-shod. The shoes were more like moccasins, lined with a warm fluffy fabric he'd found in a drawer in Bizz's old sewing room. Mostly they were warm and comfortable, and came well up the leg. He had managed to fit his shackles over the top of them. No more cold chafing metal on his legs. He felt a little thrill of pleasure as he clanked around the room. Then he suddenly remembered Greole, and hurried off down to the kitchen. After filling a bucket with scraps and bones he went off to the stable, being careful to latch the kitchen door after him.

The courtyard was full of spring sunshine. A pair of snow-vultures *quarked* at him from the rubbish pile in the far corner, arching their necks and eye-balling him. He kept a fast eye on them. He had named these two Syke, and Maldo, they were an old and particularly aggressive pair of hardened males. He wouldn't have put it past them to come after him for the scraps. The Zorils didn't seem bothered by them and seemed to have come to some sort of unspoken agreement over the years. The birds acted as watchdogs and the trolls let them feed on carcasses and food scraps. A good trade-off. If there weren't enough scraps then the vultures simply went hunting, usually in small groups. One would land and distract the prey while the others made a swift attack from above. Hibu watched Syke and Maldo out of the corner of his eye as they pecked at the dried bones of an old deer carcass. Syke suddenly stopped and eyed the bucket intently. Hibu hurried on, wishing he'd brought a stick with him.

He arrived, puffing slightly, in the stable. It was hard work trying to move quickly in chains. He opened the door to Greole's cage and put down the bucket. The gulo was lying against the far wall. It raised its head and stared at him mournfully. In all the time he had been looking after Greole he never seemed to have gained his trust, although in some deep part of him he sensed that the animal knew he meant it no harm. Its nature in the wild was to be solitary. That, combined with the ill-treatment by the Zorils seemed to have dissuaded any attempt at friendship. And since the take-over by Urkha, Greole's life had become even more miserable.

Last winter, she and a petrified Codweb had managed to somehow get a muzzle on the beast so he couldn't bite. Urkha had then found old pieces of reindeer harness which she had converted to fit the animal, and then she had hitched him up to a small sleigh. She had spent hours forcing him to pull it, and beaten him into submission when he resisted. Hibu sensed Greole's spirit was just about broken.

'Well my friend, how are you today?' he said softly as he put down the bucket. Greole didn't move. He dropped his head and licked his lips. His coat looked dull. The yellow-brown hair was spiky and matted. Hibu wanted to groom him but he didn't think Greole would allow it. He supposed that the animal's lack of looking after itself was due to being caged, and depressed. He poured the contents of the bucket into a large feeding tray. Greole looked at it.

'I have a treat for you today,' said Hibu. The wolverine raised his head and looked at him searchingly. 'Would you come and take it from my hand?' Hibu put his hand in his pocket and brought out an egg. He laid it on his palm and squatted down. 'Come,' he said softly. Greole looked at the egg and then up at Hibu. Hibu kept coaxing, talking quietly, reassuring. After five minutes or so he was about to give up when suddenly Greole stretched, stood up and inched forwards. Hibu stayed where he was, thrilled at the sudden response. 'You love eggs,' he said. Greole inched closer, neck outstretched, nose snuffing the treat. He was about a yard from Hibu when an almighty din suddenly started up in the courtyard. Screeching, squealing and quarking were followed by a loud clattering bang. Hibu, annoyed at the sudden interruption, placed the egg gently on the straw in front of Greole, locked the cage door and hurried out. On the far side of the courtyard beside the archway into the kitchen garden Syke and Maldo were attacking the wheelbarrow, which was upside down. On the kitchen doorstep Emlock and Codweb were screeching their lungs out. Now the wheelbarrow appeared to be joining in with terrified high-pitched squeals.

'Plague!' cursed Hibu. He knew that ear-piercing wail a mile off. Hell's teeth he was under the barrow! How had he got out? What if Urkha came back! Syke and Maldo were getting more and more frustrated, hopping and quarking all over the barrow, tugging at the wheel and the legs with their beaks, angry at being foiled. They weren't used to prey with a carapace.

Hibu looked around desperately for some sort of weapon. The long-handled pitch fork! It might be a good equalizer. He had to try. If he didn't rescue Plague they were all dead. Urkha would kill them. He went to the door. It was all or nothing. Holding the fork in front of him he said a quick prayer, took a huge breath and charged like a knight with a lance. Shackles clanking, he did the fastest stiff-legged shuffle in the world. letting out a blood-curdling roar as he went.

Syke and Maldo looked up in surprise at this lanky jangling apparition speeding towards them. It looked aggressive. They weren't sure. They hopped off the barrow and side-stepped around it, bald necks stretched forth, wings lifted warningly.

'GERRRRRRRR-CHA!' hollered Hibu. The birds spotted the pitch-fork. Hibu stabbed the air viciously. They weren't used to this sort of challenge. Intimidated, they took off screaming vulture-obscenities, hanging in the air some distance above Hibu's head. He grabbed one of the barrow handles and lifted it up. A terrified squealing Plague cowered underneath.

It was at that moment that Urkha came back from her hunting trip. She was just in time to see Hibu fend off the birds and grab Plague from under the barrow with one hand, while he continued threatening the vultures with the fork. Syke and Maldo were hungry. They had their taste buds set for baby troll. They were not being denied. Syke dropped to the ground for a frontal attack while Maldo sneaked in from the rear. Hibu knew their tricks and spun in a circle, flailing with the fork and catching Syke across his bald neck with one of the tines. The vulture screamed in pain and fury and dropped back. Maldo suddenly seemed to have second thoughts about tangling with the pitch-fork. It was the opportunity that Hibu needed. With Plague tucked tightly under his arm he scrambled for the kitchen door and threw himself inside. The bellow of a furious she-troll followed him in.

Pandemonium broke loose in the kitchen. Emlock and Codweb dived for cover, knocking over chairs as they went. Hibu tripped over one of the fallen chairs and fell heavily on his side as he attempted to protect Plague. Plague bawled blue murder. And then suddenly everything went quiet. Hibu suddenly realised with surprise that Plague was trembling like a leaf and clinging to him. The troll-child had had a huge fright, and was now obviously scared of imminent punishment for disobeying his mother. He knew he wasn't supposed to go outside without her. Codweb and Emlock were shaking almost as much as Plague and casting around for escape routes.

'None of you move!' bellowed Urkha, yellow eyes flashing, darting from one to the other.

'He did it!' screeched Codweb, pointing at Hibu who was still lying against the chair.

'Did what?' bawled Urkha.

'Let 'im out,' Codweb's voice had changed to a nasal

whine. 'He did it on purpose ... left the door open!'

Emlock stared at Codweb in amazement. He had seen Hibu go out with the wolverine's bucket and knew he had carefully latched the door. Plague had been in the kitchen at the time, bugging Codweb, teasing him and calling him Pig-Fat, and trying to prod the portly little troll in the belly. Everywhere Codweb went the troll-brat followed, thinking it a great game to wind him up. Codweb had become more and more angry. Emlock had stepped down to the larder for just a couple of minutes to get something and had emerged to find the fat troll standing in the doorway, sniggering. Curious as to what was pleasing him so much, he had gone to the window and immediately seen Plague heading for the rubbish heap, towards Syke and Maldo. He had shoved Codweb out of the way and screamed at Plague to come back. Codweb had screamed at him to shut up. Plague, picking up on the fear in Emlock's voice, had stopped, suddenly unsure. Syke had already risen into the air, quarking, powerful wings spread wide, green eyes fixed on the little troll. Plague's boldness abandoned him. He had turned tail and run for cover straight under the barrow which was leaning against the wall; accidentally and fortuitously toppling it over on top of him as he did so.

Emlock began to stutter. To side with Hibu against

another troll was deeply against his own nature. He would be going against his own kind. And yet at the same time some part of him felt he should speak out, but words wouldn't come. Codweb was staring straight at him, his expression pleading. Hibu sat up. Codweb had just tried to sign his death warrant. He was furious. If he had to die then he would go down fighting. If nothing else by way of words.

'You snivelling little sack of rat-droppings!' he thundered at Codweb, 'I know I latched the door. Why are you lying?'

'I'm not lying!' shouted Codweb, 'You did it ... I saw you! You wanted the old vultures to kill 'im!'

Urkha suddenly marched forwards and grabbed Hibu. She hauled him up off the ground as though he weighed nothing at all and pushed him backwards against the wall with a crash. Plague dropped to the ground and ran under the table. Urkha's nose was an inch from Hibu's, her hands around his throat like a vice. 'I let you *live*. I let you *live* and you try to murder my son!' she roared.

There was ringing in Hibu's ears. The world was fading. 'Ask ... Plague ... ' he wheezed with one last gasp. And then everything went black.

PART TWO

18

Seven Years Later

It was autumn and the woods around Castle Iffi were a kaleidoscope of colour. Bottle-green evergreens rubbed shoulders with the splash and splodge of auburn oak and soft yellow larch. Petal and Surf made their way along one of the many woodland paths. Iceace loped behind, stopping now and then to nibble at a plant, or sometimes a bit of bark which he found particularly tasty. They were making for Primrose Hill, a grassy area on the edge of a copse of oak some miles away. They were going to visit Iceace's family.

It had been a wondrous occasion some years back when one spring day Iceace and Petal, out on one of their almost daily explorations, had discovered the warren. Iceace had gone down one of the burrows to investigate and to his joy and utter amazement had found his mother. It had been a wonderful moment. All the family, now a considerable number, had been called together. Iceace told of his dramatic journey. Told how he had left their old home through the disused run, and landed on the sleeping wolverine after plucking up the courage to launch himself out of the tree. And how he now lived with the elves and helped Elestyal. Moonbeam and Frisk told of how they had been broken-hearted when they felt forced to leave without him, thinking him dead. Petal had sat in the sun on the bank amongst the primroses and was glad for all of them.

On this particular autumn day when they arrived at the hill Moonbeam took Iceace straight down into the burrow in a flurry of excitement.

'Come and see what Pa found!' she said.

Soon they were back with Iceace carrying something in his mouth. He hopped over to Petal and gave it to her.

She frowned as she turned the item around in her hands, 'We'll take it to Elestyal,' she said, 'He may know something about it.'

Later that afternoon, back at the castle, Petal eventually found Elestyal in the kitchen garden, picking Brussels sprouts.

'Come and see this wonderful crop,' he called to Petal, 'Prize-winners every one. I swear they're as big as apples!'

There was snort from further down the garden, 'No bigger than mine last year,' shouted Perks from his potato patch.

Petal laughed at the banter between the gardeners, and walked over to the wizard. 'Elestyal, I have something to show you, Iceace's father found it in the woods. We wondered if you would know anything about it. I think it's been there for a long time.'

'Of course, of course,' The wizard put down his basket and Petal handed him the object. It was clogged with dirt. He rubbed at it for a few minutes, then pulled out his handkerchief and wiped it more thoroughly. He let out a little gasp. 'I don't believe it. I *don't* believe it!' He shook his head in disbelief, 'This is my comb!'

It was Petal's turn to look amazed, 'Yours? But how ... ?'

Elestyal was turning it over in his hands. 'Perks!' he shouted, 'Come and look at this!' Perks put down his fork and came across. 'When you and I made that flight from Christmas Castle ten years ago,' said Elestyal, 'This must have fallen out of the pocket of my old suit. It had a mirror that went with it. Frisk found it in the forest.'

Perks shook his head, 'A million to one chance,' he said, 'Who would have thought it. A shame the mirror didn't land in the same place.'

Elestyal nodded ruefully, 'It was a presentation set given to me when I took on the role of St Nicholas. Can't ever be replaced. Bizz was furious when she found out I'd lost it. She polished it every Christmas and put it in my suit pocket. Ideal for combing the beard. Never mind, I must go and thank Iceace immediately.' He hurried off, still excited.

Petal suddenly eyed Perks with a look of complete mischief. 'Hey Perks,' she said.

'Yes Miss Petal?'

'Your sprouts were definitely only the size of *walnuts* last year!' And then she fled, laughing all the way to the stable.

After thanking Iceace Elestyal had gone to his room to clean the old comb properly. He washed it and dried it and then went up to the metalwork room for some silver polish. Aleron was absorbed in the finish on an elaborate dagger. Fynn had recently promoted him to assistant workshop manager, and he was very proud of his new position.

'Hey now young Aleron, what are you so engrossed in?' asked Elestyal. Aleron chuckled at the term young. He was twenty-five, and considered himself more in the realms of mature. But Elestyal had known him since he was a baby, and been like a father to him. He would always be young Aleron to the wizard. He looked up, 'Actually a personal project, I've been working on it for a while.'

'A fine-looking piece too.'

'I started it some years ago, it's my troll-dagger, I always swore I'd go back to Christmas Castle one day and bag myself a few Zoril, and get our castle back.'

Elestyal pulled a stool over to the bench and perched on it. He took off his cap and scratched his head. 'Yes,' he said, 'I always hoped we'd go back too, but fate hasn't gone our way. The she-troll was the first fly in the ointment. Then Panglossian, the crazy old fool, cons us into castle-sitting for him. Ten years we've been here and the old so and so is still travelling.'

Panglossian's post cards were a great source of amusement to the folk at Iffi. Magically at intervals they would appear, pinned to a large board in the hall. They told of a varied and colourful sojourn in many exotic countries. He had recently sent a letter instead, with a photograph attached. The picture showed Mr P posing on a sun-drenched beach with two beautiful dark-haired young ladies in bikinis. The trio were paddling in very blue water with white-capped waves curling up behind them, splashing Mr 'P's baggy Bermuda shorts. In this case a particularly colourful pair covered in red hearts, over which he wore a daffodil-yellow tank top. His ensemble was topped off with a floppy straw hat and mirrored shades.

Great debate was had as to whether he had removed his odd socks to go paddling.

'You still never know,' said Aleron, working at the dagger-blade with the finest of sand-papers.

'Never know what?'

'When I may need this. Seriously, you know how Iceace keeps hearing rumours from forest folk about troll sightings this side of the Crags.'

Elestyal shook his head, 'I doubt Urkha would bother to come hunting this far. She has no need, there's always been plenty around Christmas Castle.

'Maybe she has other plans.'

'Like ... ?'

Aleron shrugged, 'Just a feeling. While we're on the subject, would you have a word with Petal?'

'About what?' Elestyal looked surprised.

'About riding out too far. It could be dangerous, you know, if these rumours were true.'

Elestyal sighed, 'Have you spoken to her?'

'Humph,' she won't listen to me,' he said shortly, 'Stubborn should be her second name.'

Beneath the apparent anger the wizard picked up worry. 'She's a very capable young elf-woman and a skilled rider,' he said.

Another harrumph from Aleron. 'She's too confident for her own good,' he snapped. Then, annoyed with himself for taking his feelings out on Elestyal, he apologised. 'I just think one day she'll come up against something she can't handle. If you spoke to her she might listen. She doesn't give a jot for my opinion.'

Elestyal stood up and put a hand on Aleron's shoulder, 'I wish you two would be friends. I'll speak to her. Now, where is that good silver polish you keep hidden away? My old comb has come back to me, and it needs bringing back to life.'

Aleron took the comb from his hand, 'A favour for a favour,' he said, 'You speak to Petal and I'll have this like new in no time.'

Elestyal thanked him and decided to do a quick tour of the workshop to see how the elves were getting on with Christmas preparations. It was October 30th, less than two months to go to the delivery.

Aleron put down his dagger and picked up Elestyal's silver comb. He thought about Petal. He wanted to speak to her himself about his worries. About how she rode out too far, alone. About sightings of trolls. But he knew it would develop into a full-fledged argument. He knew a lot of it was his fault, his pathetic niggling jealousy. He still hadn't quite let go of it. And all because of her mission to Christmas Castle years ago with Iceace. She had come to him afterwards bubbling with enthusiasm, thinking he would be pleased with her. Pleased that she had done something to try to help. Instead he'd been furious, thinking it should have been him that had gone, not a slip of a girl-elf. Even more annoying was that she had managed to do it. Ridden there and back, lord knew how many miles, hidden just yards from a castle full of Zorils, escaped a mother bear, got dumped off her horse, and walked miles home. And it hadn't seemed to faze her. He hadn't had one good word to say to her. But he couldn't get around it, it had taken some strength and guts to have made that trip, and she'd only been thirteen at the time. He had reacted like a spoiled kid, joining with a few others who had criticized her soundly for being impetuous and foolish, and endangering Iceace's mission.

He remembered how hurt she had looked. He saw it in her eyes, those incredible violet eyes that a boy-elf could get lost in. She had seemed to shrink at his words, and pull into herself. And then she had rounded on him, eyes flashing, pain and fire in her voice. He could still hear her words: 'I *was* going to tell you what I found! I was going to share a secret with you, but not now. Not *ever!*' She had stormed off and they had barely spoken for months.

Over the years they had re-formed a cautious friendship. Neither spoke of the past. Aleron had never apologized. The little knot of resentment that stuck in his gut just wouldn't seem to dissolve, and alongside it was a larger knot, of guilt. They both loved being at Iffi, although Aleron would always consider Christmas Castle his real home. He had his ideal job working with his beloved metals, engineering all sorts of toys and other gifts. Petal had made her dream come true and had taken over the position of stable manager when Zeb semi-retired.

Aleron suddenly heaved a huge sigh. Dammit he would go and speak to her. Why not? She could only bite his head off. At least he could let her know that he worried about her. Surely that shouldn't upset her too much? He put down the comb, swung off his stool and headed for the courtyard. It was cold. An autumn chill was in the air, bringing with it hints of mushrooms, berries and the smell of damp earth.

'Have you seen Petal?' he asked Perks who was coming towards the kitchen.

'She's just gone back to the barn,' Perks narrowed his eyes, 'Hey, you tell her that she needs to get herself some spectacles!'

'Spectacles ... Why?' Aleron looked puzzled.

'Because,' said the gardener, 'She can't tell an apple from a walnut.' And then he walked off. Baffled, Aleron headed for the barn.

Petal was mucking out a loose box. She had her back to Aleron as he leaned over the door, chin on hands, watching her. Her snug-fitting, dark blue tank-top had a streak of sweat down the middle of the back. She worked quickly and methodically with the fork, separating clean straw from muck, her body lithe and fit from hours of physical work. Damp tendrils of dark hair had escaped from the knot on top of her head and fallen in disarray. After a couple of minutes Aleron felt as though he was spying on her, so he gave a cautious cough. Petal had been miles away, in a world of her own. She whirled around, letting out a little squeak.

'Sorry,' said Aleron, pretending to brush at an imaginary fly on the top of the door.

'You really shouldn't creep up on people,' said Petal, turning a delicate shade of pink, and not knowing whether to be annoyed or pleased that he'd obviously been watching her.

'I ... er ... I wasn't creeping up. You were so busy you didn't hear me.'

Petal brought her fork over to the door and leaned on it. 'I'm always busy,' she said, pushing damp hair off her forehead, and thinking she must look a right mess, 'I guess it's the nature of the work when you look after animals.'

'At least you get your riding.'

'That's the best reward.'

He noticed that when she smiled she had little tiny crinkles around her eyes – those very violet eyes. He suddenly felt slightly short of breath and noticed his mouth had gone dry. He coughed and rubbed the back of his neck. 'It was actually the riding, I mean you riding ... as far as you do ... um, that I came to talk to you about.'

Petal looked puzzled. 'What about my riding?'

'Well it's not about you riding so much as, well, the thing is it may be dangerous to go too far on your own.'

'Dangerous? What do you mean?'

Aleron's chewed at his bottom lip, 'The fact is Petal we're hearing rumours, although nothing has been confirmed. They say trolls have been sighted this side of the crags.'

Petal let out a small sigh, 'I've heard about them too.' There was a time when she would have got immediately exasperated with what he'd just said, and seen his concern as an attempt to curtail her freedom. But she was older now. Her promotion to stable manager had strengthened her confidence, and she no longer found the need to defend herself so vigorously. 'I really appreciate your worrying about me, but I'm sure there's no need. Iceace has told me about these supposed sightings, but even he's not sure they're real.'

'But what if they are Petal? What if those murdering, thieving savages that took Christmas Castle, the same species that murdered my parents, are sniffing around in this direction?'

'Why would they?' shrugged Petal casually, 'And why now? It's ten years since that she-troll took over. Besides, they must have loads of game in their own area. And they surely don't need another castle. There was only about four of them left.'

Just the same argument as Elestyal had come up with thought Aleron. And maybe they were both right. But something nagged at him. Petal looked at the darkness growing in his face, the strong jaw working, dark eyes intense as he turned it over in his mind.

'What would you think about maybe just keeping your rides to the west or the south and avoiding the direction of the crags?' His eyes were pleading.

'No,' said Petal.

Aleron scowled. He knew it would go this way.

'But what I would do,' she continued, 'is to go up north and have a scout around, with you if you'll come. We'll look for tracks. See if we can find any signs of anything that shouldn't be there. If we find nothing then I continue riding where I want. What would you say to that?'

Aleron couldn't believe his ears. She was asking him to go with her. That was a first. In the past she would have scoffed at him, given him an ear-bashing, and continued doing what she wanted. 'Of course I'll come,' he said quickly. 'When shall we go?'

'Tomorrow? While the weather's good? You could ride Owl.'

'Okay. We'd better take some lunch.'

'Good idea, I'll talk nicely to Skyler.'

Aleron figured she wouldn't need to worry about talking nicely. All the elf-guys fell over themselves to do things for her.

'What time then?'

'See you at the stable at seven sharp,' she said.

'Okay.'

And off he went, whistling. Petal felt her heart

thumping a little too fast. The last time they had done anything together was ten years ago, that night they had spied on the loading of the sleigh on Christmas Eve. They had been so much younger then and it had been such fun. And then shortly afterwards it had all gone wrong. She could never understand why she'd upset him so badly. If only they could be friends again. Good friends.

Aleron, head down and deep in thought, whistled his way across the main courtyard, nearly bumping into Elestyal on the way. He apologised and grinned, not his usual serious self the wizard noticed.

'I was just on my way to have a word with Miss Petal,' said Elestyal, 'About not riding north.'

'Oh ... oh don't worry. It's all taken care of. We're going to ride up there tomorrow and have a look around, see if there are any tracks. I'm amazed she suggested it. At least it will put my mind to rest.'

'Good, good! A grand idea. See if there is any foundation to these rumours. Just take care.' He patted Aleron on the shoulder, 'Let me know what you find.'

19

An Excursion North

At seven sharp the next morning Aleron arrived at the stable. It was cold and still dark, but cloudless. In the stable he found both ponies tacked up and ready to go, the light elfin saddles sporting pouches packed with food and other odds and ends. Nose bags of oats for the ponies were tied on with leather thongs. Petal came in from the feed room where she also kept the tack. She was carrying two halters. She waved them at Aleron.

'Morning,' she said cheerfully.

'Morning. You look like you're all ready to go.' He patted Owl's neck. The pretty skewbald mare nuzzled him and blew gently on his hand.

'Bad Owl,' said Petal pretending to scold her, 'Always looking for treats.' She passed Aleron a chunk of carrot. Aleron put it on the palm of his hand and Owl snaffled it up. 'Lunch is packed,' she added, 'Skyler has made us a real feast.'

'Weather's turning cold,' said Aleron.

'Yep, winter's on the way,' She patted her bright red padded jacket, 'Need to dress warm.' She noticed he was wearing a similar jacket to hers only it was black. Like so many of the elves he was converting to human styles, and lived in jeans. His hair, wavy and dark, was pulled back and tied with the usual green scarf. As they spoke he pulled on his hat; an old wide-brimmed thing, black felt, that had seen better days. Petal couldn't decide whether it made him look macho or mysterious. She decided both.

'We better get going,' she said, 'It's quite a way to the Crags.'

They set off around the edge of the lake. Mist rose off the water and all was quiet except for the distant haunting call of a loon and the soft thud of hoof beats on packed earth. The sun came up, wrapping the landscape in warm gold and painting the lake with a thousand gilded ripples. The two riders were both quiet, wrapped in their own thoughts, both wondering how this day together would go. It was nearly ten by the time they reached the path through Bearban forest.

'I love autumn,' said Petal, thinking small-talk may ease the tense atmosphere, 'There are so many colours. All the different leaves and berries. And the weather is so misty and cool.'

'I should get out more,' said Aleron, 'I don't see enough of it. I'm too cooped up in the workshop.'

'But you love what you do?'

'Oh yes, but I miss out on all this.' He waved an arm towards the overhead branches, thick with coloured leaves. 'A person needs a balance,' he said thoughtfully.

'What are you working on, in the workshop?'

'Lots of Christmas orders, but I'm also just finishing my dagger.'

'Dagger?'

'The one I said I wanted to make to kill trolls with, when we were young.'

Petal chuckled, 'You actually made one?'

'Yes, and it's a beauty. I even brought it with me today.' He pulled up his jacket and Petal saw a leather scabbard with the hilt of the dagger sticking out.

'I hope we won't need it,' she said, trying to keep her voice neutral and repress a laugh. She thought all these rumours about trolls were rubbish, but she didn't want to upset Aleron by flippantly dismissing his concerns for her safety. Especially when they suddenly seemed to be getting along again.

'So do I. I've never seen a troll. But the pictures of the ones I've seen in books look pretty scary. They're ghastly looking creatures. All muscles and claws and wrinkly skin.'

'The ones Iceace has seen, the Zorils, apparently have spiky black hair and really mean yellow eyes,' said Petal, 'Elestyal says none of them are very intelligent.'

'No but he thinks the she-troll at Christmas Castle might be a bit of a worry. He says it's unheard of for a she-troll to take command of a pack.'

'Girl-power!' said Petal, deliberately deepening her voice and shaking a fist in the air, 'We'll take over the world!'

'As long as you don't end up with yellow eyes, a hairy chest and wrinkly skin.' said Aleron wickedly.

Petal scrunched up her face and made her eyes as small as she could. Then she bared her teeth and snarled, 'Show us yer dagger!'

'I'll run you through, oh hairy chested one!'

'You'll have to catch me first!' And with that she kicked Surf into a canter and shot off up the path. Aleron let out a hoot and followed. They raced on through the forest, jumping small logs here and there under a canopy of copper leaves and autumn sunshine. Aleron suddenly felt a great happiness flow through him. As though he'd arrived in a good place, although he wasn't quite sure where that place was. It didn't matter, he was determined to just enjoy the day. Eventually they slowed. They were getting further north, into the area where suspicions had been raised about trolls.

'Maybe we should head straight to where the river path comes down from the crags into Bearban,' said Petal, 'If the Zorils are paying visits over to this side we'd be bound to see tracks there. They'd have to be using that route.'

Aleron agreed, 'Sounds sensible to me. We'll check that path first and
then check the surrounding forest. We'll criss-cross back and forth, east to west.'

It took them another hour to reach the start of the River Path, by which time both they and the ponies were tired and hungry. They decided to rest, and found a grassy spot by the river for Owl and Surf. Petal took off their bridles and put on halters so they could eat, then she loosened the girths. Aleron took the lunches out of the saddle bags and put them on a large flat rock, then he started wandering around carefully scanning the ground. Petal sat down on the rock and unpacked their picnic. She was starving. She took a man-sized bite from a hunk of fresh bread and stuffed a piece of cheese in along side it.

'Mm ... found anything?' she mumbled.

'Not yet,' said Aleron.

And you won't, thought Petal, but didn't say it.

'I guess they ... or it, doesn't come to this spot for water,' said Aleron, 'Good idea to check though. It would be the obvious place, after coming down from the crags.' He inched his way to the water's edge studying the ground closely, then he walked back and sat down, frowning. 'There are some strange marks in the sand, all the way along that bit of beach,' he said.

'Have some lunch,' said Petal, poised to demolish an enormous wedge of Skyler's special fruit cake.

'They're very odd, sort of ripple-shaped.'

'Mmm ... mmmaybe waves!'

Aleron looked at her sideways. One cheek was bulging like a hamster, 'But they're only in one place. If the river made them they'd be all the way along.'

Petal swallowed. 'Birds, with long tails?' she suggested helpfully.

Aleron got the sudden feeling she was humouring him. 'What birds have tails that are wide enough and heavy enough to make marks spanning at least six feet?' he said, studying her suspiciously from under his brows.

Petal screwed up her mouth, frowned, and thought for a moment. 'Peacocks!' She tried to keep a straight face.

'Now I know you're having a laugh.' He grabbed some

bread and cheese and refused to get annoyed. Instead he rolled his eyes and gave her a 'what am I going to do with you' look. Petal kicked herself. She just couldn't help the comment slipping out. Damn her quick tongue. She regrouped, coughed, and tried to look as serious as possible.

'Well, whatever they are they obviously aren't troll tracks. And that's the main thing.'

Aleron conceded the point and picked a large red apple out of the bag. He studied it for a second. 'By the way,' he said, 'Perks says you need spectacles.'

'What?'

'He says you can't tell the difference between a walnut and an apple.'

Petal giggled, 'Oh the sprouts! Those two and their darned vegetable contests. They're so funny.' She lay back on the rock and watched a skein of geese fly over in a huge V form in the very blue, cloudless sky.

Aleron leaned on an elbow and looked down at her, thoughtfully, 'That was a great lunch. You must have spoken *very* nicely to Skyler.'

'I only told him he made the best bread in the entire world.'

'You just wind them all around your little finger.'

'All?' she looked puzzled.

'All the elf-guys.'

'I don't.'

'You do. They all fall under your charms.'

'Well I don't know why.'

'Because you're different.'

'Different?'

'You're just ... not a normal little elf-chick.'

'Oh thanks!'

'No, I didn't mean it like that. It's just that you're not all demure and ... domesticated.'

'I could sew if I decided to!' she looked reproachful.

'What I mean is you have fire in you. You're so full of life, and you're vibrant and ... ' he stopped suddenly and squinted at Petal, deciding to keep whatever he'd been about to say to himself.

Petal gave him one of her dazzling smiles and yanked his old felt hat down over his eyes. Whatever it was that used to be between them was still there.

'Come on,' she said, leaping off the rock, 'You pack up the bags and I'll sort out the ponies. We have to go hunt troll tracks.'

Aleron re-adjusted his hat, donated an apple core each to Surf and Owl, and loaded the saddle-bags.

An hour later, after checking the path down from the crags and then methodically criss-crossing the forest, they had found the tracks of deer, rabbit, wild pig, wolverine and bear, but nothing that might have resembled a troll footprint. Then, in a dusty treeless glade Aleron had found more of the same strange swirling pattern that he'd seen by the river. They had come into the glade via a narrow path in heavy undergrowth. The path continued on in the same fashion on the other side of the clearing. He was fascinated and got off Owl for a closer look.

'Well *this* wasn't made by river water!' he said, almost triumphantly, bending down and tracing the lines with his fingers.

'True,' said Petal, 'Maybe it's from flying fish!' She dodged a handful of acorns flung in her direction as Aleron walked over to where the path exited the glade between a young pine and a blackthorn. The blackthorn was encroaching across the path. He looked at it for a few minutes. Petal groaned to herself. Then he switched his attention to the pine. He started prizing something off the trunk.

'What is it?' she asked, feigning interest.

He walked back to her, leaned on Surf's saddle and held up two or three strands of long, course, black hair. 'Troll,' he whispered.

'Rubbish,' said Petal, 'It's black bear.'

'No,' Aleron was insistent, 'One, there are no bear tracks, and two, if it had been a bear it would undoubtedly have left hair on the bush *and* on the tree when it pushed through. Whatever it was deliberately squeezed to the left to avoid the thorns. Bears don't avoid thorns.'

'Okay,' said Petal, 'I agree there are no bear tracks, but equally there are no *troll* tracks.'

'It's covered them up.'

'What?'

'It's covered them up. It must have backed through the clearing and wiped out its tracks with a branch.

'Oh come *on* Aleron. Elestyal said they're all stupid. D'you think one has suddenly grown a brain or something?'

'Elestyal also said the idea of a she-troll taking over disturbed him. He said it was unheard of. This one is different I tell you. For some reason it must be smarter than average.'

Petal shook her head.

'Come on,' said Aleron, 'Let's go, I'm starting to get a bad feeling about this place.'

A few yards further along the path after they had squeezed between the pine and the blackthorn Aleron pulled up. He leaned off Owl and reached into a hazel bush. He pulled out a short cedar bough. 'Look,' he said, turning in his saddle to Petal, 'Tell me how this got here? We haven't passed a cedar for ages.' Petal shrugged, she had no explanation, but she refused to believe it was anything to do with an intelligent troll. There had to be another explanation. Aleron had quickened the pace. He was nervous. If they were attacked he only had a dagger and he didn't know if he alone was strong enough to defend Petal. He glanced quickly over his shoulder. 'Let's get out of here!'

The journey back was quiet. Neither of them spoke very much, both feeling it would end in disagreement. Eventually, as they came in sight of Iffi the tension eased. They found themselves talking about the past again. It was getting dark as they skirted the lake.

'Can I ask you something?' asked Aleron suddenly.
'Of course.'
'What did you find that night, when you went to Christmas Castle with Iceace? I know you said you'd never tell me, but I guess I've always been curious.'

Petal thought about the key. The one she felt so guilty for having taken. The one still lying in the bottom of her grooming box. She laughed lightly. 'I didn't really find anything. I guess I was just trying to get back at you in the heat of the moment, when you got so angry. So I made it up.' Aleron looked across at her, but she kept her gaze on Iffi.

20

In the Kitchen Garden

Iceace awoke in a cold sweat with his heart thumping. He had been napping in a shady corner of the garden and he'd had a dreadful dream. In the dream Urkha had killed Hibu and was cutting him up into chunks. She was throwing the pieces into a cauldron of boiling water set on the Walpurgis night bonfire. The cauldron was boiling over, but instead of water overflowing it was blood. Dark red steam billowed upwards, staining the stars and painting the moon, and filling the air with a swirling red mist. Then Urkha picked up the last piece of Hibu, his head. She held it up by the hair and let out a ghastly, murderous laugh. The head swung back and forth, staring towards Iceace. The eyes pleading. And then the lips began to move, mouthing a single word over and over again - *help!* That was when Iceace woke up. He sat for some minutes, shaking. I must see him, he whispered to himself.

It was ten years since the night he had witnessed the aftermath of Elestyal's spell at Christmas Castle. Ten years since the she-troll menace had taken over. He had never been back. What was the point? No one was even sure if Hibu was still alive. Besides, how could he help his friend even if he was? Stories reached him via his family, carried to them by birds and beasts from the other side of the crags. Stories of a savage she-troll that hunted not just for meat but for pleasure, and who now came with another, younger version of herself. Her offspring he supposed, now grown up.

Iceace went to find Elestyal who was in the potting shed storing seeds in jars ready for next spring. He told him about the dream. 'I have to try and see him,' he said.

'I understand,' said the wizard, nodding, but looking worried. After a minute he said, 'If you're determined to go you must be extremely careful. My intuition tells me the she-troll is dangerous. Possibly more dangerous than Cacodyl ever was. To have taken over a pack as she did, albeit a small one, was unnatural. A freak of nature. You must be doubly careful this time Iceace.'

'I'll be fine. I have a plan. But first I need to know a little more about the layout of the castle. My previous visits were very short. Mostly I need to know where the kitchen garden is?'

Elestyal found a stub of a pencil and started drawing on

the back of an old seed packet. Iceace jumped up and sat on the bench.

'Here's the main gate,' said Elestyal, 'You know where that is. It's on the north wall. The kitchen garden is on the south side, on the other side of the castle, exactly in line with the big pine in Tall Pine Wood. The stables are off the main courtyard to the east.'

'That's good. Very good,' Iceace looked pleased. 'I can remember that. I will leave tomorrow.' He jumped down off the bench without saying any more about his plan.

'Thanks Elestyal.'

'Iceace ... '

'Yes?'

'This time ... don't tell Petal.'

'No,' said the snowbun, 'And this time I'll keep my promise.'

Elestyal watched him go. Although ten years older he never seemed to age. Maybe it had something to do with living with the elves. Maybe the Christmas magic. He didn't know. Either way he sensed that Iceace had many more years in him yet. He didn't like the idea of him going to Christmas Castle, but he was confident that if anyone could get there and back safely he could.

Iceace left the next morning. He told no one of his plan. Petal assumed he was going to visit his family at Primrose Hill. His recent dream still haunted him as he loped at a fast clip around the lake and took the path through Bearban forest. Autumn was parading her finest colours, flaunting shades of amber, yellow and gold, but Iceace could only see what was in his mind, Hibu mouthing *help*, over and over again. The forest was easy running. He flew over the dry leaf-strewn paths, faster and faster. Over the stream where Petal had fallen off Surf on their first trip. On and on until he was soon heading up the river path into the Crags, then he slowed a little. At Keeper's Gorge he stopped and looked down for a few minutes at the foaming white water hundreds of feet below. He could do with a drink. There was a small stream further on, he would stop there.

It was dusk when he reached Tall Pine Wood. Darkness came early at this time of year. He found a hollow log and hopped inside for a short rest, not fancying the thought of an owl dropping on him silently from above. He decided to wait until full dark before going to the wall. He would go to the big pine and then take a straight line north which would bring him this side of the kitchen garden. More darkness fell. Time to go.

When he arrived at the wall he immediately started

checking the ground. It was rocky, but there was one place where it appeared much softer, and a few plants were growing. He started digging. He could have gone to the gate and slipped underneath and not bothered with tunnelling, but he wanted a back door. An escape route if he had to make a quick exit. The trolls, if they discovered him, would assume that he couldn't escape via the kitchen garden. His big strong paws, designed for digging, shifted the earth in no time. His need to see his friend, to know that he was alive and well, drove him on. It was a long hard dig to go deep under the wall. Earth had to be moved all the way back down the tunnel. Sometime in the early hours of the morning he came to the roots of plants, dandelions according to the taste, and ivy. Dandelion roots didn't go that deep. He must be close to the surface. He decided not to break through tonight, instead he dug out a small hollow, curled up, and went to sleep.

The occupants of Christmas Castle didn't get up very early. Of recent they had started partaking of a little too much of Emlock's home-made wine with their supper. This autumn he had made a particularly potent batch from the pears in the kitchen garden. It was well after sunrise when Emlock appeared in the castle kitchen.

'You're up early,' he said to the figure at the table.
'Yes,' said Hibu without turning around.

Emlock, against all the rules of his race, had discovered that he had a heart. He had become aware of it on the day that Codweb had lied about letting Plague out to see the vultures, and Urkha had nearly killed Hibu. She had only stopped because Plague had suddenly flung himself at her leg like something possessed, and bitten her. The shock had made her release her grip on Hibu's throat. Hibu had fainted. Urkha, shocked by her son's attack, realised immediately that Plague was simply trying to protect Hibu. Why? Now, slightly calmer, she also recalled that it had been Hibu who was fending off the vultures when she had arrived. Hardly the action of someone trying to kill her offspring. On top of that the Erudite had shown an unnatural fury, completely alien to his nature, and called Codweb a liar. Emlock had seen the flash of recognition cross her face, and then she had cast a knowing look at Codweb. She should kill him. Maybe she would one day. Right now with still only three in the pack she needed him. Codweb caught the glance and knew instinctively that she knew. He wouldn't dare mess with Plague again.

Urkha had ordered them to carry Hibu down to his

room. She had followed them down. After they had laid him on his bed she had unlocked and removed his shackles. Then she turned and threw them with full force at Codweb. The heavy chain caught him on the side of the head with a dull thunk and sent him flying backwards. He collapsed in a quivering heap with blood streaming down his face. Urkha stood over him. She pointed a gnarled claw at his boots. 'Leave them here,' she had said, ever so softly.

Since that day Hibu had never been the same. Emlock, in his bumbling way, tried to show concern when they were on their own, but Hibu had withdrawn into a place deep within himself. He said little and would sit for hours just staring into space. The only thing he took any interest in was the miserable gulo. Emlock had found him talking to it on a number of occasions. The skinny troll didn't like it. He wanted the old Hibu back. They had had many little jokes at Codweb's expense, and he missed the friendship that at one time he would have sneered at.

'Want a drop of my nice pear wine?' he asked.
'I'd rather have a pear,' said Hibu quietly.
'Still a few on the tree.'
'Yes, maybe I'll get one.' He got up and walked out.

Emlock stared out of the window and shook his head. It was a bad thing indeed, this thing that had come over the Erudite. And it seemed to have got worse and worse. It was seven years since the incident. Plague was fully grown now, physically nearly as big as his mother, but shorter on intelligence and lazy as sin. Urkha was teaching him to hunt and to fight but was rarely pleased with his performance.

'Wot you starin' at?' came the dulcet tones of Codweb from behind him.

Emlock turned on him and gave him a hard stare. Then he grabbed a hunk of bread off the table and turned his back. Codweb hissed at him. The fat troll had been subtly cast out since the incident with Plague. He was only tolerated, and he knew it. He grabbed bread and a huge hunk of meat, and glared at Emlock's back. He had never been able to figure Emlock and Hibu. There had never been any open acknowledgement of friendship between them, and yet he sensed that the skinny troll preferred the lanky creature to himself. It was out-of-order. It wasn't troll-like. At least Emlock had not exposed him to Urkha the day he had let Plague out to play with the vultures. He had some loyalty to his tribe. Codweb thought about Urkha. She treated him like the lowest lackey. She despised him. He knew that she knew what he'd done, and he'd paid for it for the last seven years. He hadn't dared put a single toe out of place in Plague's direction. He had loathed it, seven years of serious sucking-up to the rotten little beast. Pandering to his every whim, and enduring endless teasing and name calling along the way. To compensate for his miserable exile he ate, drank, and skulked for hours in his room.

Hibu sat in the kitchen garden under the pear tree that climbed and spread over the old stone wall like a fan. Emlock had been right, there were a few fruits left. He turned over the one in his hands. It was golden, imperfect where a bird had briefly pecked at it. He had always loved fruit. It had been while he was gathering berries that the Zorils had come along and thrown a net over him. Eleven years of his life wasted. Eleven years living a fragile existence with a savage alien race, wondering each day if this one may be his last. And yet he had survived. There must be a lesson in it all somewhere, although he was darned if he could see it. He had to admit he didn't much care now. Since the day that Urkha had nearly killed him he had lost interest in life. He could see no end to this miserable existence. That was all it had become, an existence. He and Greole were the same, both robbed of life and freedom. Their spirits broken.

Hibu sat in the autumn sun in the walled garden, staring into space. In the distance he heard orders barked by Urkha to Plague as they went off on another hunting trip. A normal castle routine. They would hunt, Codweb would lurk in his room and eat, and Emlock would busy himself making wine or cooking up stew or something. Hibu stroked his fingers through his beard. It was long and entangled. He couldn't remember when he had last combed it. He felt tired. He always seemed to feel tired. His head nodded forwards and he closed his eyes. And then he heard a dull thump. His mind noted vaguely that it was a different sort of noise to the usual ones he heard in the garden. The sun was warm on his head. He relaxed. A few late wasps buzzed around the over-ripe fruit fallen under the tree. It was peaceful. *Thump!* It came again only this time it was louder. His brain started searching his memory's archives. That sound was in there somewhere. The wheels churned. A second later - *Rabbit!*

Hibu sat bolt upright and looked around the garden. It couldn't be. His eyes probed every bush. Back and forth he scanned, this way and that. And then, a movement on the other side of the garden in the flowerbed by the wall. The bed was weed-ridden and overhung with trailing ivy. He stood up cautiously and rubbed his eyes.

Iceace had woken before sunrise and started the short dig to the surface. He'd had quite a tough time breaking through. The ivy roots were thick and tangled, and bitter. When he first looked across Christmas Castle kitchen garden it was just starting to get light. Birds were still roosting and all was quiet. He hunkered back into the hole and waited. Some time later he heard the faint squeak of hinges as the door to the kitchen garden was pushed open. He peeped out. Hibu! It was Hibu! He was walking towards the pear tree. It was him, his friend, he was alive. But he moved so slowly. He seemed bent, older, and thinner. He had a defeated look. Iceace's heart went out to him. He watched Hibu pull a pear off the tree and sit down on the bench. He seemed to look at the pear for a long time, and then his head nodded forwards. He was going to sleep. Iceace squeezed out of the hole into the undergrowth of ivy and did a small *thump*. Nothing. He tried another and upped the volume. So intent was he on catching Hibu's attention that he didn't notice the two snow-vultures peering down from the ramparts way above the pear tree. They had heard the thump and knew quite well what made that particular noise. They craned their necks eagerly and put their heads on one side, eye-balling the ivy where Iceace was hiding, on stand-by at the prospect of rabbit for breakfast.

Iceace couldn't stand it, there wasn't a troll in sight and he had his bolt-hole if necessary. Unable to contain himself for a minute longer he squeezed out of the ivy and started a cautious lope across the garden. 'Hibu!' he called.

The sight of Iceace coming towards him was the most wonderful thing that Hibu had seen in years. Tears of joy sprang instantly to his eyes. 'Iceace ... ?' he whispered, 'Can it really be you?'

And then Syke dropped like a stone off the rampart. Iceace saw the big bird's dark shadow float in front of him on the light flagstones, and he recognised instant peril. In a split second he stopped, leapt, twisted, and was running for his life back to the bolt-hole. Hibu cried out as Syke changed his angle and dived. Iceace was fast but not fast enough. Syke had momentum. One of the vulture's taloned claws closed on the snowbun's back paw just as he was disappearing into the ivy. He yanked the rabbit out and took off.

Iceace was suddenly seeing the world from a whole new perspective as he left the ground and swung precariously from Syke's talons. Wild with panic and pain he squealed and let out an enormous driving kick with his free leg. The power in it was quite phenomenal. It connected just above the talons of the foot that held him and smashed the vulture's leg almost in two. Release was instant. Syke screamed in agony as his left leg dangled uselessly. Iceace started to fall.

Hibu ran. He hadn't run as fast in his whole life. Across the courtyard and over the vegetable patch he flew. He was almost directly under Syke when Iceace started heading earthwards. Down, down, he came, over and over, waiting for the moment when death would inevitably greet him on the courtyard floor.

'AHHH!' cried Hibu as the large descending snowbun landed in his open arms and slammed into his chest. The force of Iceace's landing knocked every ounce of wind out of him and knocked him over backwards into the cabbage patch. The two of them lay in a heap for a few minutes with heads spinning. Hibu regained his breath and was just sitting up when he heard a loud *quark*. A short distance away Maldo had landed and was advancing towards them. With a limp Iceace under one arm Hibu jumped to his feet and looked around frantically for some sort of weapon. He spied a rake which had been left among the cabbages. Maldo kept coming, but Hibu had the rake. He waved it and shook it and stabbed the air with the tines. Maldo stopped and eyed the tool with caution. Without his buddy he was suddenly wary of making an attack. A rabbit was one thing, but this armed and angry creature was a different story. He thought better of the idea and flapped off back up to the ramparts where Syke was still yelping.

Hibu made a fast check of the garden. The noise apparently hadn't alerted Emlock or Codweb. He was a few yards from the old potting shed. Pushing Iceace gently inside his jacket he made for the door.

21

Desperate Measures

Inside the shed Hibu laid the panting snowbun on a pile of old sacks.

'Iceace!' he whispered frantically, 'Iceace! Speak to me!'

It was a few minutes before Iceace started to come round. Slowly one blue eye opened, then the other. His world was swimming. His collision with Hibu had knocked the breath out of him. He shook his head and looked around. 'Phew!' he whispered, 'That was close!'

'Far too close for comfort,' said Hibu, 'Let's check you out.'

Iceace tried to stand but sank back in pain, 'It's my foot,' he said.

Hibu gently examined it. Thankfully it wasn't broken, but there were deep gashes where the vulture's talons had dug in. It was caked with blood and already starting to swell. Hibu's heart sank and his mind raced. What was he to do? Trolls could smell a rabbit a mile off. Iceace was in no state to even walk, let alone attempt to run back to Iffi. He wanted to get him to his room where he had medicine, but how? Suddenly he had an idea.

'I'm leaving you here for a few minutes,' he whispered urgently, 'Don't try to go anywhere.' Iceace nodded. His leg hurt far too much to even think about it. Hibu headed to his room. No sign of Codweb. That was good. No Emlock. He was probably in the cellar.

In his room Hibu took down Elestyal's box of medicines. He had started to make various potions for himself too, for minor ailments. He grabbed his own home-made pot of 'soothing balm' as he called it. A cure for aching muscles and colds. Next he took off his jacket and shirt. He started to rub a quantity of the balm all over himself. It had a powerful aromatic pong of camphor, mint and various other herbs. It would kill any other scent within range, including rabbit. After dressing again he looked for something to make into a bandage. An old shirt ripped up did the trick. He wrapped it around his ankle and rubbed some balm into it. The stronger the smell the better. An injured ankle would give him an excuse to stay in his room - and look after Iceace.

Iceace was in pain. He winced when Hibu moved him. His foot was puffed to twice its normal size. What if it became infected? Hibu swore silently. The stinking vultures probably carried all sorts of vile diseases in their talons. He swiftly made-up a sling from an old seed sack and secured it around his chest, then as gently as he could he lifted up the snowbun and set him inside.

'Do not make a sound until I tell you!' he whispered, 'I'm taking you into the castle and down to my room.' Iceace nodded. Hibu buttoned his jacket. Fortunately he had lost weight over the last few years so there was plenty of room inside. He looked around for a stick and found a sturdy piece of hazel about the right length. Using it to lean on he pretended to hobble back to the kitchen. Emlock was chopping up a cabbage at the table. He looked up in surprise and immediately wrinkled his nose.

'Phew!' he said, 'You stink!' and then, 'What's happened?'

Hibu coughed a little. 'My chest has been hurting for a few days,' he said. 'Think I'm getting an infection. Rubbed it with a bit of my special balm. And then this morning,' he pointed to his ankle, 'I tripped over a rake in the cabbage patch. I think I need to rest.'

Emlock nodded. 'Sure. Best thing to do. Want some help down the stairs?'

'Got a stick.'

Emlock sighed. 'Be careful then.'

After an appropriate amount of hobbling and groaning down each step Hibu reached his door and slipped inside. He jammed his chair under the door handle, whipped off his jacket and laid Iceace on the bed. He didn't look good. He was shivering. Probably shock. He asked for water. Hibu had a jug in his room. He poured some into a cup and Iceace took small sips. Hibu covered him with his blanket. The situation was not good. He needed to treat the wound now, but his experience with medicines was limited. There must be something in Elestyal's *Wizardopaedia*. He pulled the Wiz-P, as he called it, down off the shelf and flicked through to the part he wanted. It listed ailments in alphabetical order, and underneath each there was a recommended remedy. He went straight to *Cuts* and then to *Infections.* He must clean the wound using some alcohol, and then apply *anti-infection-salve*. He rummaged through the medicine box. Almost immediately he found a small bottle labelled *Wound Cleanse Alc'* which was next to a little pack of cleansing pads.

'Iceace,' he whispered, 'You have to be brave and don't cry out. We're in my room in the castle.' Iceace nodded weakly. He would be brave. Hibu started to work gently with the cleanser and the pads. Iceace gritted his teeth and scrunched his face in pain.

'You did well,' whispered Hibu when he'd finished. Then he went to look for the salve. Elestyal had acquired an amazing conglomeration of medicines. It took some minutes to find the right one. But when he unscrewed the lid dismay flooded through him, combined with a rising feeling of panic. It was empty! He quickly searched through the box again, hoping for a second pot. Nothing. His mind whirled. It was far too dangerous to keep Iceace in his room long enough to give the wound time to heal, and more than that he felt it was almost sure to become poisoned. If it did there was little doubt that the snowbun would die. He needed Elestyal. Somehow Hibu had to get him to Elestyal. But how? His mind ran back and forth like a rat in a trap, seeking a way of escape, but no answers came.

Hibu sat for many minutes deep in thought. Iceace had willingly risked his life for the elves and Elestyal. He'd come to Hibu on that first meeting, just a slip of a snowbun, wanting to chew through his ropes. Then on Walpurgis night he had returned on his mission, and tried to coax Hibu to escape. Now he'd come back again. Hibu owed him so much. They all owed him.

Sighing heavily he wrapped the snowbun warmly and slipped him out of sight under his bed. Normally none of the trolls ever came to his room, but he couldn't risk it. Iceace seemed to be dozing fitfully but he was still shivering. Hibu sat, head in hands and racked his brain for a plan. How could he get himself and Iceace out of the castle?

Until this moment he had never seriously considered escaping. He wasn't the brave and daring sort. He wasn't made of the stuff heroes were made of. His race had never been fighters, they wielded pens not swords. His mind scrambled this way and that as he fought for a solution. There was no ladder to try to scale one of the walls, and even if he did how did he get down the other side without a rope? What about other exits ... secret ones? He had always suspected that the elves had escaped via some sort of secret passage. Maybe he could find it. And maybe he'd get hopelessly lost in what he knew to be a maze of deep passageways in the bowels of the castle. His thoughts flashed this way and that, each time coming to a dead-end. He was still thinking an hour later when Emlock called down the stairs.

'Ay! Hibu ... grub if y'want some?'

'Thank you,' called Hibu, 'Up in a minute.' He thought it a good idea to show his face again and keep up the charade. He rubbed a bit more of his smelly salve on for good measure, checked Iceace, and did a stiff hobble up to the kitchen.

'Phew!' sniffed Emlock, 'D'you think that stuff works?'

'It was a recipe of my father's,' said Hibu, falling into a chair and rubbing his ankle. It's an aid to many ailments.'

'Hmm,' Emlock looked dubious. Then, glad that Hibu had come to eat, he told of his morning's wine-making effort. 'As you suggested,' he finished, 'I'm storing it in order, so we drink the oldest first.'

'Good,' nodded Hibu, 'I'm sure you'll be pleased with the result.'

'I already am.' The skinny troll was beaming, 'I tried a sip of this today and it's the best ever.' He pointed to a large stone flagon on the floor by the table. 'Pear and potato. Found it in the very back of the cellar. It'll knock their heads off at supper tonight. Wanna try a glass?'

'Oh no, no. I'd like something hot. A herb tea will be good for the chest.' He got up and hopped around, made the tea and then took an apple and a piece of bread.

'No cheese?' frowned Emlock.

'Not terribly hungry.' Hibu rubbed his chest. 'Maybe later.' He drank his tea and then excused himself on the pretence that he needed to put his foot up and rest it. He took the apple and bread and went back down to his room.

Iceace was getting worse. He was soaked with sweat and

his entire back leg was now swollen. A cold dread hit Hibu in the stomach. He stroked Iceace's head and told him it would all be okay, but he felt helpless. He sat for an hour watching over his friend.

Eventually he got up and put the box of medicines away. Then he went to pick up the Wiz-P which seemed to have fallen open at a page headed *Dangerous Soporifics,* underlined in red. That was funny, he hadn't been reading that section. He frowned and cast an eye down the page. It was all about sleeping potions. Listed in order of strength. Different potions were prescribed for different uses. Hibu's eye fell on the last entry which had a warning attached to it. A drug called *Narkbark*. It appeared to be used in extreme situations in order to knock someone out for a long period of time. For example, to perform some sort of operation. It gave a small table of dosage, drops in relation to body-weight.

It was then that the seed of an idea sprang forth in Hibu's mind, and grew. Bursting with excitement he rushed to get the medicine box down again, his fingers trembling as he searched desperately through the bottles and jars. There! There it was! Three vials of golden liquid labelled *Narkbark - Use with Extreme Caution.* He took them out and laid them on the table. According to the dosage tables there was enough here to knock out a herd of reindeer for a week. He only needed enough for four trolls.

His thoughts fell over themselves. If he was going to escape he must prepare for the journey. He needed something warm to wrap Iceace in. A sling secured around his waist would be the best way to keep the snowbun stable. He could make it from the material in the cupboard upstairs, the same stuff he'd used for his shoe-linings. He'd give Iceace one of the light sleeping draughts to sedate him and help with any pain on the long trip. It was October, cold and autumnal. His old coat would have to do. He felt around under the bed and pulled out his boots; unworn since Codweb had his filthy feet in them. He dusted them off. It was a long walk to Castle Iffi.

Ten minutes later he was upstairs in the elves old workshops. He found the items he needed. He also found a large leather satchel which he hid in the middle of the bundle of material. He was hobbling back through the kitchen when he bumped into Codweb.

'Wass that?' demanded the fat troll.

Hibu rounded on him, '*That* my friend is an extra blanket for my bed. Because I'm cold and I'm old, and I have a *bad chest*! Okay!'

Codweb was quite taken aback at the sharp retort. The lanky creature had hardly said a word for months. He looked sickly, all hunched and coughing. And he stank of some home-made remedy. The troll took a step back. He despised the gangly figure with its silent ways. He hoped he would die and do it quickly. Hibu hobbled off down the stairs muttering under his breath.

Once in his room he went to work making the sling. The material was wonderful, a sort of fake fur. He made straps and ties to keep it in place, and a separate protective sheath to put around Iceace's leg. In the satchel he placed the Wiz-P and some extra sleeping draught for Iceace, mixed in a small flask of water. Then he waited for the right time to go upstairs. He wanted to time it so he got into the kitchen before Urkha and Plague came back from hunting. He just prayed that Codweb wouldn't be there.

It was time. He slipped the vials of *Narkbark* into his pocket and made his way upstairs. Codweb was nowhere in sight. Emlock was stirring some stew-like concoction on the stove. He turned around and grinned as Hibu eased himself into a chair. The table was set for supper. The stone flagon of pear and potato wine took pride of place in the centre.

'Can I have a sniff of this fine brew?' asked Hibu.

'Of course,' said Emlock, pleased as punch that he was interested. He rushed over and forced the cork out. Hibu almost felt guilty for the deceit. He took a long slow sniff.

'Superb,' he exclaimed.

'Want some?'

'Oh, well, I don't think tonight. But maybe tomorrow.'

'Tomorrow,' chuckled Emlock, 'there won't be any left!'

'Actually,' said Hibu, 'I was going to ask you a small favour. I wondered if you might get me a little cheese. It's in the downstairs larder, and my ankle ... '

'Of course,' said Emlock, cutting him off, 'I keep saying you should eat more.' He went straight off to get it. As quick as a flash Hibu had the three vials out of his pocket, uncorked, and the contents poured carefully into the neck of the flagon. He re-corked it and gave it a good shake.

'Sleep well,' he whispered under his breath.

A few minutes later Emlock appeared with the cheese. He cut a huge wedge and handed it to Hibu along with a doorstep sized piece of bread. Hibu nibbled on it and sat for a while. Emlock thought he was even more thoughtful than usual. Then outside came distant shouts as Urkha and Plague returned. Hibu picked up his food.

'I'll be off,' he said. Emlock didn't blame him.

In his room Hibu paced back and forth in nervous anticipation. He'd done it! Now he just had to wait for them to have their supper. He sat on the bed for a minute, stroking Iceace's head. The snowbun was very hot and breathing rapidly. 'Hang on my friend,' he said quietly, 'Hang on.' He couldn't sit for too long. Restless with anticipation he got up and checked that everything was ready for departure. After years of lethargy he suddenly had energy to burn.

A while later upstairs he heard the sound of chairs banging and scraping across flagstones. Raucous screeches as Urkha and Plague related their hunting achievements. Supper had started. Within thirty minutes there was dead silence. He gave them an hour, and then crept up the stairs. All four were sprawled face-down in their supper dishes. He tiptoed around the table, prodding each one gently, then a bit harder. Not a muscle moved. He picked up the wine flagon. Empty! They had been thirsty. He needed the keys to the padlock on the castle gate. Urkha kept them around her neck on a chain. He moved back to her, repulsed at the thought of lifting the great head. It had to be done. Grimacing, he grasped a handful of matted black hair and pulled. Her head flopped back with a clunk against the chair and a few pieces of onion from the stew slid off her chin. He could see the chain. In a second it was over her head and in his hands. The keys to freedom.

22

Escape

Hibu's hands trembled as he slid the key into the lock. What if the sleeping draught only worked temporarily for some reason? He glanced over his shoulder, half expecting to see Urkha dashing towards him. Nothing. He removed the padlock, loosened the chain and opened the huge gate just far enough to squeeze through. Then he took his first step out of the castle grounds in ten years. As he looked up at the stars he thought he would never forget this moment. But no time to star-gaze. He must make tracks, and quickly. There was no telling how long the trolls would sleep. It was possible that the *Narkbark* solution was old and had lost its potency. He had only gone a few yards when he had a sudden thought and walked straight back to the gate. He could buy himself some extra time. It was easy enough to reverse the chain so that the padlock was now connected on the outside. He smiled as he put the keys in his pocket and headed south.

Hibu strode across the Snaggle Plains. The moon was

full and bathed his path in milky white as he followed a well-worn trail through the scattered rocks and scrub pines. He suspected this well-used path had been made by Urkha and Plague on their hunting trips. They talked regularly of going over the Crags and down into Bearban. The night was silent but for the distant call of an owl. Hibu was full of emotions. It had been too long since he had walked free. It had been too long since he had actually walked any distance at all. He had always loved hiking, journeying to visit friends and relatives. And sometimes taking long pilgrimages to foreign parts. It allowed him to learn and gave him time to think. He hoped his legs would cope with the long journey to Iffi.

It was cold, his breath puffed out in clouds of misty white in the night air. Soon there would be snow, maybe even in the next day or so. He felt the chill air through his thin trousers. The warmest part of him was where Iceace slept, strapped snugly to his chest. God how he loved the crazy snowbun. How could one small creature have so much courage and determination? If he had half of Iceace's spirit and fortitude he would have tried to escape long ago. He sighed and decided that it took all kinds. Right now he must just think of getting to Elestyal as quickly as possible.

The new energy that his freedom had bestowed gave a

spring to his step and it wasn't long before he was at the bottom of the Crags. The jagged outline of the peaks towered above him. Snow had already dusted them, and now the moonshine polished them with a pale luminous glow. Hibu's nose was cold and his legs ached a little. He wished he had gloves. At least he had the old knitted hat that he had found in the stable. He had read that a lot of heat was lost through the head. He tugged it further down over his ears and spied a comfortable looking log. He must sit down and check Iceace.

Iceace hadn't changed position. The sleeping draught had worked, and maybe even eased the pain. Hibu stroked the snowbun's long ears. He wouldn't give him any more medicine unless he woke up. He drew his jacket back around him and buttoned it up. He must start the steep climb up to Keepers Gorge, but before he left he stood up on the log and scanned back the way he had come. No movements. No bulky figures galloping towards him. No noise except for the slight breeze attempting to dislodge the last reluctant leaves from the branches of a gnarled oak. Relieved, he stepped down off the log, careful not to jar Iceace, and set off up the River Path.

It wasn't long before Hibu suddenly felt immensely

tired. The steep climb was strenuous and his initial energy burst, supplied by the euphoria of escape, was failing, as were his leg muscles. His back ached and he found himself having to stop every few yards to catch his breath. He talked to himself as his father used to talk to him when he was small. When he'd wanted to give up - *'Come on Hibu! You can do it! Don't rush, just take your time. One foot in front of the other. Think positive. Stay in the now and don't think about getting to the end, just think about the next step.'* The words helped, and before he knew it he had gained ground. He started picking small goals up ahead. He would walk to that boulder, or to the next tree, stop, take some deep breaths, a small rest, and then a new goal. Hours passed as he trudged on.

Dawn hinted its approach by painting a few streaks of pink across the eastern skies. Birds called. But it was another hour before Hibu reached the gorge and the narrow path through the cut. He had to rest. He sank, weak and worried, onto a nearby rock, heart thumping and chest wheezing. Suddenly he was furious. 'Damn! Damn! Damn!' he yelled at the sky. 'Damn you Zoril philistines for stealing my good health! For stealing my life! Damn you all to hell!' His words echoed through the stillness and seemed to mock as they bounced off the mountain sides - *Hell! ... hell! ... hell! ...* they mimicked. He was disappointed with himself for losing his temper, he didn't usually. But these were not usual circumstances.

An early-morning red squirrel had come to see what all the noise was about. It chattered at him from a nearby tree. Hibu gazed up at the dark-eyed little creature as it batted its tail back and forth and told him off. He managed a smile. Then it hit him. Greole! He'd forgotten Greole! How could he have? He'd been so totally focused on Iceace and his escape plan, his need to fly as fast as he could, that he hadn't given his friend a thought. He felt sick. He could have given Greole his freedom, the same as he had grasped his own. He shook his head and agonized over his lack of forethought again and again. It was all too late now, and little point in beating himself up. He couldn't change it, but a great sadness gripped him and weighed him down. Somewhere in his mind a pair of eyes stared sadly at him from the dark corner of a stable.

Iceace stirred. Hibu came back to the present in a flash and opened his jacket. Iceace was soaking wet with sweat in his sling. He whimpered in his sleep. There was nothing Hibu could do except to administer a few drops of the sleeping potion. It was Elestyal's skills that he needed. On the River Path, now levelled out, Hibu pushed on faster. His short rest had revived him. He could hear the water roaring hundreds of feet below. Soon the way would start down towards Bearban Forest and walking would be easier.

23
A Surprise Meeting

Petal packed the remains of her picnic in her saddle bag and tightened Owl's girth. She noticed she had to use a looser notch these days. 'You're getting a bit porky!' she said to the pony, 'I should ride you more often.' She had deliberately chosen Owl for the long ride today for that very reason. Owl was so reliable and placid compared to the often feisty and excitable Surf. Petal preferred excitable.

Today she had come all the way up to the Crags, to the spot by the river where she and Aleron had had their picnic. Such a good day that had been. A new start to their friendship. He'd be furious if he knew she was back here. She had agreed not to ride north in order to keep the peace between them, and had kept her word, until today. Then her love of riding up through Bearban in the Autumn had won out. She still considered the troll stories to be rubbish. Besides, he'd never know she'd been here. They were getting along so well again she didn't want to spoil it with a big argument and him getting all protective.

'Ok Miss Owl, home we go,' she said, swinging up into the saddle. She gave the pony a little kick, but Owl ignored her and stood stock-still. Her ears were pricked and she was staring with interest up the River Path. 'Come along lazybones,' said Petal, kicking again. Owl wouldn't budge. She just side-stepped, head up, staring intently. It was unusual for her to ignore a command. 'What's so interesting?' Petal followed the pony's intense gaze, and then she saw it. High up where the path disappeared around the rocks was a figure, an odd figure. Even at this distance Petal could tell it wasn't an elf. It was far too tall. It certainly wasn't a troll either. It was moving slowly, carefully, picking its way down the steep path. Owl whinnied, a deep squeal which shook her whole body. The figure on the path stopped and looked up, immediately catching sight of them. Then faintly Petal heard a call, a male voice that sounded urgent and desperate. 'Help! Don't go!' She waited, whoever it was was obviously in some sort of trouble. He came faster now, stumbling at times, and eventually arrived breathless at Owl's side.

'Thank you! Thank you! I am in great need of your help.'

Petal looked at him curiously. He was stick-thin and very tall. He wore an old green jacket, thin trousers, and an old pair of boots that had seen better days. He had a black woollen hat pulled down over his ears that reminded her of Zeb's. His beard was long and unkempt, and he had a leather satchel slung across his shoulders. Mostly what caught her attention was his eyes, full of intelligence and urgency. She felt no fear of him. 'How may I help you stranger?' she asked.

'My name is Hibu, I ... '

'*Hibu?*' broke in Petal, astonished, 'You're the Erudite from Christmas Castle! Iceace has talked of you many times.'

'It is Iceace who needs your help,' said Hibu, almost falling over his words in his urgency, 'He came to find me and was attacked by a snow-vulture. He is injured and very, very sick. The wound is poisoned. I have to get him to Elestyal. He's the only one who can save him. I have been walking since yesterday evening.'

He opened his coat and showed Petal the white bundle in the sling strapped to his chest. Petal's heart dropped like a stone and she felt a cold shadow pass over her. Tears welled up as she looked at him. 'He will die without Elestyal's help,' said Hibu.

'Quickly!' she said, leaping off Owl, 'Take the pony! She will take you to Iffi. She knows the way. You're too tall for her but I don't think you're very heavy.'

'You could take him ... ' said Hibu.

'No,' said Petal firmly, 'You must go. You can tell Elestyal what has happened. When you get to Iffi ask someone to ask Zeb to come, and bring me a pony.' Hibu looked slightly doubtful. It was years since he'd been on a horse. 'Don't worry,' urged Petal, 'Owl is very reliable and she knows the way, she will carry you safely.' Hibu slid a leg over the pony's stout back. He gathered up the reins. Petal spoke to Owl, 'Steady to Iffi Owl, swift and gentle!' And then to Hibu, 'Go! Go quickly!'

In a minute they were gone, Hibu's feet dangling not far from the ground as they cantered off through the forest. Petal watched them until they disappeared from view. She wondered how Hibu had managed to escape. What had happened? And then she wondered if he was being followed. What if the trolls were tracking him? She looked nervously up to the top of the River Path. Nothing. Then she turned and started jogging towards home as fast as she could.

Owl cantered gently through the gates of Castle Iffi and came to a stop in the middle of the courtyard. She was puffing and sweating. Shouts of surprise came at this strange lanky figure arriving on the elves' pony. Hibu slid off. He was immediately surrounded by excited voices and a dozen curious faces. The commotion brought Elestyal out of the garden. He looked across the courtyard at the tall figure and couldn't believe what his eyes were telling him. *Surely ... it was Hibu!* But it couldn't possibly be. And if it was him, where was Iceace? A sudden chill crawled over the wizard. Something had happened. He broke into a run.

'Hibu! Is it truly you!' He stood in front of the thin and dishevelled figure, looking up at him with a mixture of amazement and caution.

'Yes, dear Elestyal, it is, and I'm sorry to say I bring great sorrow with me. I will tell you my story later. But first, Iceace is wounded, maybe mortally. He was caught by a snow-vulture and the wound is infected. He needs your help. I think you are the only one who can save him.'

Murmurs of shock rippled through the crowd as Hibu opened his jacket and showed Elestyal Iceace in his sling.

'Quickly!' said the wizard, 'Bring him.'

Aleron suddenly pushed in beside Hibu, his face serious, 'You came on Owl,' he said quickly, 'Where's Petal?'

Hibu pulled off his hat and wiped his forehead. 'I nearly forgot,' he said, 'She said to ask for Zeb to take her a pony. I left her at the start of the River Path, at the base of the Crags.'

'Thanks,' said Aleron, his face turning grim and angry. He grabbed Owl's bridle. Zeb, who had been standing nearby, came up to him.

'I'll saddle Swallow and Surf,' he said, 'and go fetch her.'

'No,' replied Aleron bluntly, 'I'll go.' He dropped Owl's reins and ran towards the stable. A short while later he rode off on Swallow with Surf behind on a lead rein. Zeb shook his head. There was going to be trouble. Why did Petal always have to ignore advice and be so darned headstrong. Aleron was going to be really hurt over this.

Hibu laid Iceace on a blanket on the kitchen table while Elestyal ran for his medicines. When he came back he unwrapped the injured paw and quickly assessed the snowbun's condition. It looked serious.

'It's going to be touch and go,' muttered the wizard, 'The poison has spread through his body. See how shallow his breathing is. His heart ... the beat is so faint, like the wings of a butterfly.' He didn't say that Iceace may not make it through the night. He cleansed the wound and applied special medicines, then he made a poultice to draw the infection.

'Why did he come back to Christmas Castle?' whispered

Hibu, shaking his head in despair.

'He didn't tell you?' Elestyal frowned.

'There was no time.'

'He had a dream ... that Urkha killed you.'

Hibu slumped into a chair and covered his face with his hands. 'He came back just to see that I was all right. And now he may die.'

'Don't feel bad,' said Elestyal softly, 'Nothing would have stopped him.' The wizard picked up a vial of rose-coloured liquid and poured it into a dropper. 'Here ... hold his mouth open a little so I can give him a few drops of this.'

Perks had come to the table. He stroked Iceace's ears. 'You can save him ... can't you?' he said very quietly.

Elestyal didn't look at him. 'I can only do my best.' His voice was gruff, and caught in his throat. He spread both his hands wide then and laid them across the snowbun's body. The elves who had gathered around the table fell silent. Elestyal started to speak. The words he uttered were strange and sing-song, a wizard's language. A combination of magic and prayer, and healing. Afterwards he bent his head and there was silence in the old kitchen for a few minutes.

'There is nothing more I can do,' he said, 'We will have to wait now. Make up a bed for him by the fire. Somebody should sit with him at all times.'

Perks was first to volunteer. Then Bizz produced a large basket which she lined with soft bedding. Iceace was laid in it and set by the hearth while Skyler and Perks and half a dozen other elves hung around staring at the small still figure.

Elestyal looked at Hibu, 'You are very tired and must also be very hungry, can I get you some food?'

'That would be wonderful, but first a favour if I may. I would just love a proper wash. I have lived with trolls for nearly eleven years. I would give my right arm for a bath, with hot water.'

'And you shall have it,' said the wizard.

Hibu luxuriated in the steamy, lavender-scented water. It was, without doubt, pure luxury. He soaked in the tub, eyes closed, drifting, and afterwards he washed with a rose-scented soap made by the elves. Sore and aching muscles were soothed and relaxed and he gradually felt like a new person. Bizz had managed to run him up some new clothes. No one knew quite how she managed it so quickly. She had even produced a pair of soft red leather slippers. Hibu shook his head in amazement as he slipped them on to go down to supper. Before he went though, he decided he would cut his beard. A round of applause greeted him as he walked into the kitchen. He nodded shyly, unused to so much attention, and took his place next to Elestyal.

It was a good supper. Afterwards they all stayed in the parlour. They wanted to hear Hibu's story, and stay close to Iceace. Someone had hung a carrot on the handle of his basket, someone else had tied on a ribbon. One of the elflings sat on a small stool beside him and sang a get-well song.

Hibu told his story. He described how he had been captured in the forest when the Zorils had thrown a net over him, and how he had expected to be killed and eaten. Instead Cacodyl had wanted him for his knowledge. He told of Iceace coming to him the night before Christmas Castle was invaded, intending to chew through his ropes which had been swapped for chains. And then he had been taken and thrown into Elestyal's old room. He had discovered pies, and bread and cheese, and a lovely drink, and medicine for his feet. And then three months later, on Walpurgis night, the spell in the silver had killed all but four of the trolls.

'What was it like?'
'What happened?'

'Did you see it?'

Questions popped up all around the table. Elestyal noticed they were all from the sleighriders who had a hand in creating the spell.

'It was a terrible sight,' said Hibu soberly. As glad as he had been to see the back of the trolls he had still found the death scene particularly ghastly. 'Urkha made me collect all the silver still stuck to the bodies.'

There was silence in the parlour. They sensed he didn't want to describe it further.

'Urkha's brat was born on Walpurgis night,' continued Hibu, 'That's why she survived. She was giving birth. There were two others who escaped as well, Codweb, who was in trouble with Cacodyl and who was hiding upstairs, and Emlock, who worked in the kitchen. He was getting more wine when it all happened.' Hibu laughed a little, 'I stopped him from going into the banquet hall.' Eyebrows were raised around the table. 'You will all think I'm quite mad, but he became a kind of friend. He's a skinny little chap, rather despised by the others. I was very fond of him.'

'It would take something special to convert a Zoril,' laughed Elestyal. 'But there is good in all of us somewhere.'

'What about Iceace?' piped up Perks' 'How did he get caught?'

'He'd dug a tunnel underneath the wall of the kitchen garden,' said Hibu, 'I was sitting on a bench on the far side, half asleep under the pear tree, and I heard him do a couple of his thumps. I couldn't believe what I was hearing. The next minute he was running across to me. Then Syke, one of the snow-vultures, he must have been up above me on the turret and he just dropped out of the sky. Iceace tried to make it back to the hole but Syke caught him by the back foot and took off with him. He was up in the air, dangling from Syke's talons, and then I think he must have kicked out and injured the bird. It screamed blue-murder and dropped him and I managed to run across the garden and catch him. We fell into the cabbages!'

A second round of applause that evening greeted Hibu's ears. He gave a small smile, 'It was nothing,' he said, 'In fact it's me who needs to thank Iceace. If it hadn't been for him I would still be there. I never have had the courage to try and escape. Ten years I was imprisoned, and I had never even considered it a real possibility. I suppose you don't know what you're capable of until someone else depends on you. I had fallen into a deep depression in these last few years and my life had become ... well ... just a worthless existence. When Iceace was injured I was forced to look for a way out.' He told them how he had found the

Wiz-P strangely fallen open at the page marked *Dangerous Soporifics*. And then he'd had the idea to add the *Narkbark* to the troll's wine.

Everyone laughed and clapped again. Skyler stood up. 'Talking of wine, how about a glass of Panglossian's best mead?' Heads nodded. Skyler went for the mead while Perks and Jake put out the glasses.

'I have just remembered something,' said Hibu. He left the table and went over to the leather satchel that he had brought with him. He took out the *Wizardopaedia* and handed it to Elestyal. 'Neither Iceace or I would be here if it wasn't for this.'

Elestyal beamed and ran his hand over the cover of the ancient book. 'Well, well, I never thought I would see this old tome again,' then he looked at Hibu and winked. 'I knew there must be a reason I forgot it.'

Petal jogged gently along the forest path looking back over her shoulder once in a while. She was optimistic. The trolls would surely not come this far to try to re-capture Hibu. The afternoon sun sparkled through the trees, now nearly naked of leaves which had fallen into a wonderful copper carpet across the forest floor. A pair of jays called their sharp warning cry as she passed by. She barely heard them, her mind was so fixed on Iceace. Surely Elestyal would be able to heal him. He had skills that no one else had. Iceace *had* to be okay. She refused to think of the alternative. She jogged on harder, wanting to get back to Iffi and sit with Ice. Dumb rabbit! How had he managed to get caught? And how had Hibu managed to get free after all these years? She was still deep in thought when she heard the sound of hoof beats up ahead where the path curved. Good! That would be Zeb. And then towards her at full gallop came Aleron. Her heart sank. How was she going to explain this.

He pulled up hard beside her flinging leaves in all directions as Swallow lunged and snorted, and Surf, wild-eyed, bucked and threw his head.

'What in hell were you doing out here?' he shouted, his face all accusatory anger.

Petal quickly grabbed Surf's lead rein and tried to calm the excited pony. 'What do you mean by running the ponies this hard?' she flared back, instantly riled by his attitude.

'Believe it or not, it just happened that I was worried about you. I came to possibly save your silly neck!'

'From what? A dangerous squirrel?'

'You know damn well from what!'

'I know what's in your imagination,' she muttered, quickly mounting Surf who danced in circles.

'Petal, we had this all out weeks ago! You promised me you wouldn't ride up here, not after I found those tracks.'

'But you didn't *find* tracks,' said Petal, exasperated, 'You just think you found something covered up. Lets face it, the trolls at Christmas Castle have never, and will never come this far. Trolls just want meat and they have plenty of game on the other side of the Crags.'

Aleron glowered at her. 'You really don't care do you? My opinion counts for nothing with you. It never has and it never will. You will always do things your way. All you think about is yourself.'

'That's just not true!'

'Oh yes it is! It goes right back to when we were forced to leave Christmas Castle. Everyone else was gutted at having to leave. But you ... you were actually excited. And you were pleased to bits to stay at Iffi because of the ponies. Then you went off on that insane venture with Iceace – which you had no right to do. And which could have put *his* life in danger. Now I find that your promise to me, to not ride up here, meant absolutely nothing, and you were simply humouring me and laughing behind my back!'

'I was not laughing. I just don't appreciate having my freedom curtailed. I admit I didn't agree with you over the troll thing, I just didn't want to argue about it. I didn't want to lose your friendship ... again.' She trailed off looking miserable.

'Friendship has rules,' snapped Aleron, 'One of them being honesty.'

'If I'd been honest I would have disagreed with you over the supposed troll tracks. And you, being your immovable, obstinate self, would have just got angry and hurt because I disagreed. It's hard to be honest with you when you take offence just because my opinion differs from yours!'

'It wasn't a case of an *opinion*!' shouted Aleron angrily, hauling on Swallow's reins and causing her to reverse into Surf who squealed, 'It was a darned fact!'

Petal swung Surf around and came up beside him. His dark eyes fixed hers, his mouth was set in a grim line. He hadn't bothered with a hat and he seemed to have lost his scarf. Locks of wind-whipped black hair fell across his face.

'Rubbish!' she shot at him.

'You know what,' he growled, angrily brushing hair from his eyes, 'One day you may have to eat those words. And one day your foolhardy determination to ignore good advice will land you in big trouble.'

Petal kicked Surf and cut in front of Swallow, 'My foolhardiness today may have helped save Iceace's life.' Her tone was icy. 'If I hadn't been here I wouldn't have met Hibu.'

Aleron had no answer for that so he just muttered, 'You're impossible,' and said no more. They rode hard back to Iffi without another word, both cloaked in their own dark emotions.

Petal put the ponies away as quickly as she could. Aleron had stormed off and left her to unsaddle Swallow, for which he was called a few choice names. Supper had finished by the time she got into the kitchen.

'Where's Ice?' she said, rushing over to Elestyal who was still talking to Hibu. Elestyal pointed to the basket by the fire by which sat various elves. 'How is he? Will he be okay? What's wrong with him?' Before the wizard could answer Petal had shot over to the basket and was on her knees beside Iceace.

Elestyal got up and went over to her. He bent down and put a hand on her arm. 'He's very poorly Petal. We can only wait and see if he finds the strength to pull through. The wound from the vulture became infected and the poison has spread. If Hibu hadn't arrived when he did ... if he hadn't met you, it would have been too late. Another hour and we would have lost him.'

'Tell that to Aleron,' said Petal, her voice cracking.

'Pardon?'

'Nothing.' Iceace was near death and Aleron wasn't speaking to her. How much worse could things be? She rubbed angrily at her eyes. 'He *will* live,' she said stubbornly, staring at the still white form in the basket.

It seemed Elestyal's request for volunteers to sit with Iceace had caused a problem. No one was prepared to go to bed. Arguments ensued as to how long people had kept watch, and who should be next. In the end everyone slept in the kitchen, either on chairs or the floor. Somehow, around midnight, Petal used her usual charms and acquired the ringside seat from which she flatly refused to budge. Candles glowed and elves nodded off to the sound of the crackling fire. Petal's head drooped as she leant against the warm hearth. She dozed, one hand slipping into the basket and gently encircling one of Iceace's forepaws.

About two o'clock in the morning she was woken by a dream, a dream that something furry was rubbing itself on her hand. She drew herself up sleepily and looked at the elves slumped in various states of repose all around the kitchen. Snores and whistles of varying pitches emanated from the inert figures. She vaguely wondered why she was sleeping in the kitchen, and then it all flooded back. It was also at that moment that she realised the furry sensation wasn't a dream. With a start she peered into the basket. In the flickering light of the low fire she saw Iceace's cheek nuzzling her hand. He was looking up at her. Petal burst into tears.

24

A Locked Gate

Urkha's head hurt like someone had kicked it for a whole hour. She raised it up heavily and squinted across the table at Codweb. The idiot had his head in his dish. Then she realised hers had been in a similar position. She snarled and shook bits of cold cooked cabbage off her face. Some of them spattered onto Emlock's head. She focused on him for a minute. The wine. The damn wine had knocked them all senseless. She dragged herself to the window. The sun was going down! How could that be? They must have been out of it a night and another whole day! What in the name of the devil had that stupid troll put in the wine? She went to Emlock and shook him. Nothing. She tried Codweb, the same. Plague too. All with their stupid heads in their dinner plates. She decided to go and get some air.

By eight o'clock they had all come round and were sitting groggily in the kitchen. Urkha had joined them. 'What in hell was it made of?' she growled, riveting her yellow eyes on Emlock.

'P-p-pear and p-potato,' said Emlock, looking helpless.

'A bit p-p-potent don't you think,' she mimicked, 'What else?'

'Nothing! Nothing different to what I always put in ... sugar, spices ...!'

'Then why did we all sleep for twenty-four hours?'

Emlock shook his head in complete bewilderment. He had no idea. It had never happened before. 'Maybe I brewed it a bit longer,' he said, raising his arms in a helpless gesture. I swear it had nothing special in it.'

'It tasted like fox pee,' said Codweb scowling.

'You know what fox pee tastes like?' Plague stared at him contemptuously.

'Like his wine!' cackled Codweb.

'If it was that bad why did you drink it?' challenged Emlock.

'Cos there was nothin' else!'

'Well you certainly had your fill according to how long you slept,' said Urkha softly.

Codweb dropped his gaze to the table which still had the remains of last night's meal cast around it. Emlock got up and started clearing the dirty plates. He shook the wine flagon. Empty. They had all drunk their fill rather quickly he recalled.

'Where's Hibu?' grunted Urkha looking around at all of them.

'Dodgin' his duties as usual probably,' muttered Codweb.

'He was sick yesterday,' said Emlock, 'Coughing and wheezing.'

Codweb curled his lip, 'Covered 'imself in some stinkin' balm. Enough to choke a bear.'

'Probably made from fox pee?' sneered Plague sarcastically. Codweb looked at him briefly, barely able to keep the loathing out of his eyes. Plague continued, 'Maybe it was made of ... let me see ... potion of fox pee, oil of owl droppings, a spoon of squirrel dung, and a bowl of bat blood. That would cure anyone's chest problem. It may even cure your fat belly!'

'He makes the stuff from herbs from the garden,' said Emlock bluntly.

Codweb looked round at him, 'He probably drank some of your rancid wine after it knocked us out, and he's probably still snoring. And if he still pongs as bad as he did yesterday he can stay down there.'

Emlock ignored him and started putting clean dishes on the table. 'Anyone want supper? There's cold venison and bread.'

'Yeah,' said Urkha, 'But I'll pass on the wine tonight.'

'Codweb wants a glass of fox pee,' said Plague bursting into laughter. Codweb got up and stormed out of the room. The other three settled down to a quiet supper and an early night.

The next morning, still unbelievably bleary-eyed, the four trolls mooched around the kitchen feeling fractious and irritable. Urkha had had enough of it. She banged a fist on the table and said she was going hunting. Plague groaned inwardly. He couldn't be bothered.

'I've got a bad stomach Ma. I don't wanna go today.'

Urkha eyed him suspiciously and decided to give him the benefit of the doubt. 'You'll come tomorrow,' she said. It was a statement not a question.

'Yeah, yeah,' nodded Plague.

Urkha went off to the stable. The gulo was howling. She looked in on it and noticed it was out of food and water. 'Damn Hibu. Lazy ass,' she muttered. She grabbed her hunting knife, her net and her club and walked back to the kitchen. 'Oy! Emlock! Get that lazy ass Erudite to feed his pet. It's howling its head off.'

'Yeah,' called Emlock from the cellar.

Urkha stomped off towards the gate. On the way she

slid her hand up to her neck, feeling for her key chain. Funny, it wasn't there. Maybe it had broken and fallen into her clothes. She stopped and fished around in her animal skins to no avail, then shook her head in puzzlement and tried all over again. It was definitely missing. Could she have possibly left the keys in the padlock? Very unlikely, but she'd check anyway. She hurried to the gate and stared in disbelief at the heavy chain that secured it. There was no padlock! She grabbed the chain and pulled on it. It was tight. She stood there staring at it for some minutes before it dawned on her. Someone had padlocked it on the outside. Someone had stolen her keys while she was asleep and locked them in! There were two choices, an outsider who had somehow got into the castle, or, that wretch Hibu! Wheels started churning in her head. Why would an outsider come in and then leave and lock them in for the fun of it when he could have murdered them all where they slept? She turned and tore back to the kitchen, taking the stairs down to Hibu's room two at a time. She burst through his door. Empty! She leapt back up the steps and screamed for all of them to get in the kitchen. Emlock came shooting up from the cellar, Codweb from the larder, and then Plague ambled down from his hidey-hole upstairs.

'The Erudite!' she roared. 'Has anyone seen him since

we woke up yesterday evening?' She stood, legs apart, chest heaving, pulled up to her full height as she searched each of their faces. They all shook their heads. Emlock and Codweb shrank. They had never seen her like this. Not this mad.

Plague was scowling, 'What's the big problem?'

'The big problem my son, is that we are locked in our own castle!' Jaws dropped and faces fell. '*Someone* stole my keys while we slept with our heads in our stew, and they have chained the gate and padlocked it from the outside!'

Emlock was looking astonished, 'But Hibu wouldn't do that. He's never tried to escape. And he was sick and had a twisted ankle. He was limping.'

'Maybe he wasn't as sick as you thought he was,' Codweb sneered.

'Maybe he fixed the damn wine!' growled Urkha.

'What with?' Emlock looked mystified.

'Some of his weird herbs,' spat out Codweb.

'Maybe ... extract of fox pee!' Plague gave Codweb an evil grin.

Urkha flew at them. 'Enough! Bickering won't unlock the gate or find the damn creature! Plague, come with me. We have to break the chain on the gate somehow. Emlock, you and Codweb look around and see if you can find anything – any trace of what he was up to.'

She marched off with Plague in tow leaving the other two eyeing each other in the kitchen.

'You slimy Erudite-lover,' growled Codweb, his voice pure contempt. 'I wouldn't mind betting you helped him.'

'Oh yes! And of course I put myself to sleep as well. That's very smart Codweb. But then you always were a bit short in the old brains department. Do you really think I'd have risked the wrath of Urkha by helping anyone escape this place?'

Codweb thought about it. He was terrified of the she-troll, and had at times considered leaving. But he had nowhere to go. He was a pack animal, and used to the protection it gave him. Urkha was a curse and a blessing. She was fearful if you crossed her, but in the same way she offered immense protection. Although he hated Emlock he couldn't believe the skinny weasel would have risked his neck for the pathetic Erudite.

'If you run downstairs real quick,' whispered Emlock, in a theatrical whisper, 'you might get your boots back. Except if he has escaped, he's most likely wearing them!'

He was sick of being mocked. The fat troll lost his temper and started throwing anything he could get his hands on at Emlock. A barrage of plates, spoons, knives and anything within Codweb's reach rained down. Emlock ran for cover in the larder, slammed the door and sank onto the floor. Silence. Codweb didn't follow. No doubt he had gone to see if the boots actually had been left. Emlock sat in the dark with his back against the door. He felt a great sadness fall over him. He was unused to emotions. He didn't understand this sudden empty feeling, as though he'd lost something special. Not like a favourite knife, or a trinket. You could replace those sorts of things. It was more than that. Deeper. He thought about Hibu and how he had fixed-up the cut on Emlock's arm, that time Lirtob threw him across the kitchen. How he'd stopped him from going into the hall on the night of the spell, stopped him from getting killed. The little jokes they had shared about Codweb. How Hibu had taught him to make better wine. He had never really felt close to another creature before. Even in the pack he had felt odd, a bit of an outcast, always singled out by the bigger, stronger and bolder Zorils when they felt like a bit of bullying.

Half of him was glad for Hibu that he had managed to escape, and half of him was angry. The angry half felt deserted, and disturbed by the strange emotions. What had made Hibu suddenly find the need to leave? Emlock would never know. He just hoped his friend (if he dare use that word) had made good speed to wherever he was headed. He pondered the twisted ankle. Something told him that both the ankle and the chest infection were a sham, but he couldn't figure out why. He got up with a resigned sigh. Best he tidy up the kitchen before Urkha reappeared. He had just started to pick up some of the debris when he heard a mournful howl in the distance. The gulo. He must feed it. Hibu would want him to look after it.

Urkha and Plague were contemplating the heavy-duty chain. It was linked through two holes, one in each of the massive wooden gates. Urkha had tried prizing it off using an iron bar she had discovered behind the stables. Even with her and Plague's brute strength combined they couldn't break it.

'One of us will have to go over,' raged Urkha.

'Over?'

'Yes! Over the damn gate, idiot! We'll have to break the padlock off on the other side.'

'Oh ... ' said Plague, looking up at the towering obstacle. 'Looks a bit high.'

'Well what else would you suggest? Maybe we should just stay in here till we run out of food. And then, when we've eaten Emlock and Codweb, and the gulo, we can decide whose next!'

Plague frowned at her, 'That would only leave me and you Ma.'

'Exactly,' Urkha raised an eyebrow, 'How would you like to be cooked?'

Plague swallowed, 'I think there's some rope in the loft over the old stable.'

'Best get it then,' snapped his mother.

Half an hour later they were on the other side. Urkha had piled up a stack of old boxes and pushed Plague, carrying the rope, up the stack. He had wobbled precariously for some moments on the top box before eventually lassoing the gate post and pulling himself up. Then he swung down the other side and threw the rope back over to Urkha. She was quick to join him. They used the metal bar to smash the padlock and were soon pulling the gate open. As soon as they were back through the gate Plague stormed off.

'Get back here! We're going hunting ... for that damned creature!' yelled Urkha at his departing back.

Plague was having none of it. His mother had actually suggested cooking him. How dare she! He had little doubt she might have done it too. She could go to hell and hunt by her miserable self. He dodged through the kitchen, grabbed a couple of apples off the table and legged it up to his room. Urkha, livid at the whole morning's events, decided she'd rather go alone anyway. She wanted to track the creature. He was weak and slow. She would find him, bring him back, and teach him a lesson. Her rule was law and her minions, him included, would obey.

25
Death in the Round-Room

Plague was relieved to escape the hunting trip. He liked eating fresh meat but he would rather someone else spent their efforts tracking and killing it. He had not inherited his mother's passion for the kill. He decided he must be endowed with the gene of a less-enthusiastic ancestor. He laid on his bed biting chunks out of an apple and looking at Petal's old pictures which he kept hidden away in a drawer. He still found them fascinating, most especially the ones of the flying deer pulling the sleigh. He particularly liked the idea of the one with the shining nose. Of course it had to be imaginary. I mean this supposed thing called magic, like the story Hibu had told him about these pictures, when he was a troll-child, it couldn't possibly be true. But then again, how did you explain the trolls all dying on the night he was born? That had been to do with magic too, but his mother refused to tell him exactly what had happened. It was to do with the elves who had lived here before the trolls took the castle. Apparently they had all escaped, which had infuriated his father. His mother reckoned they had some sort of secret passage down in the dungeons, but no one wanted to go down there and look. Why didn't he go? Now there was an idea! Maybe for once he could impress his Ma, the old hag was never pleased with anything he did. While she was away Plague would play, in the dungeons. He jumped off the bed and hurriedly slipped the pictures under his mattress. Picking up his other apple he headed quietly down to the kitchen, grabbing a couple of new candles and some matches on the way through. Then an idea occurred to him and he came back and went to a box of odds and ends that Emlock used in the garden. He pulled out a large ball of twine. Emlock was just coming in from feeding the wolverine. He frowned as Plague disappeared down the back stairs.

'Oy!' he yelled, 'Bring my string back!' Plague ignored him and kept going. Emlock shook his head. The only places down there were Hibu's old room and the door to the rabbit warren of passages in the bowels of the castle. He shrugged to himself. The string wasn't worth a battle, and Plague was a big troll now. No longer a child, but in Emlock's opinion still far from mature. He had a lot to learn. If he was fiddling around down there in the passages where he shouldn't be it wasn't Emlock's problem.

The passageway was dark and smelled damp and musty. Plague's candle flickered and made grotesque moving shadows on the arched walls as he moved along allowing the string to unravel from the ball. It had been a brilliant idea. He had tied it to the door handle on the way in. That way he could always find his way back. He wandered here and there and up and down the maze of passages, unravelling as he went. At the end of one particularly deep and dark dead-end he had found three rooms. The doors all had little barred windows. Prisons! He wondered what fate had befallen the unlucky creatures who had been interred down here. Creepy he thought. There was a rusty key in one of the doors but it was solid, corroded from years of disuse. He held up the candle and peered in through the bars. No secret passages likely here.

Water drip-dripped in places as he wandered along. A mouse skittered across his path. He was, he had to admit, getting a bit bored. He had lit his second candle, and it seemed as though he'd been down here for ages. Twice he had ended up at the same place. He decided to give it another ten minutes, and set off again down a long straight stretch of passage, feeling sure he had been down it before. Half way along, the apple, which he had stuffed inside his rabbit-fur waistcoat, worked itself loose and fell out. It bounced along the dark passage. Plague cursed and plodded after it. It stopped rolling a few yards further on. When he bent down to pick it up he saw a narrow passage slipping off to the right. 'Hey!' he exclaimed as he raised the candle. 'I reckon I missed this one!' He hurriedly shoved the apple just inside his waistcoat again, picked up the twine and set off. It was a short passage and he was quickly at the end of it and disappointed. Another dead-end. He patted at the stone wall in front of him. Just solid rock. Still no secret passage. He swung round to go back and dislodged the apple again. There was a thud as it dropped and rolled away. Plague felt like kicking it. Where was the pesky thing? There, a few yards away. When he got to it he put down the ball of twine in order to grab the apple, accidentally tipping the candle as he did so. Molten wax splashed across his hand. 'OUCH!' he yelled. His cry echoed in the dark passage, made suddenly darker by the fact that he had dropped the candle.

He didn't like being in the pitch black. He dropped to his knees and felt around in a panic, casting across the floor for the candle. His hand knocked the apple. It rolled away. Then he knocked the twine. That rolled away too. He mustn't lose that! Where was the candle? He floundered around on all fours reaching out in all directions, then he heard the matches fall out of his waistcoat. Panic grasped his stomach and squeezed. Without light he couldn't find the twine, and without the twine he would never find his way back. He could die down here. Starve to death! He felt around more slowly, carefully, and eventually his fingers bumped into the match box. Lo and behold the candle was lying right beside it! Relief flooded through him. He set the candle upright on the floor in its little holder and relit it. Light flooded over the old flagstones where he'd been scrabbling around. He noticed that the stone he was kneeling on had a perfectly round crack in it. But what was odd was that when he put his weight on the crack, the circular piece flipped up. He pushed his knee down again and when the piece tipped he slipped his fingers under it. He was surprised to find it was thin, and it lifted out. It was a cover. Underneath, in a perfectly formed recess, was a key! Plague's heart missed a beat and excitement flooded through him. Where there was a hidden key there must be a hidden keyhole! Eagerly he started searching, going over every square inch of the floor, pushing the candle along as he did so, and brushing away every bit of dust that the years had laid down. His efforts were rewarded. Ten minutes later he found the keyhole hidden in the centre of the four flagstones. Four flagstones that were a cleverly camouflaged trap door.

Urkha was on her way home. She had tracked the Erudite to the foot of the Crags. It wasn't difficult. He had worn the old boots that Codweb had coveted so badly. They left a very specific pattern in the damp soil. He had also left a scent. A strange mixture of Erudite, medicinal potions, and a third scent which she was positive was rabbit. Why would he smell like rabbit? Urkha couldn't figure that one out at all. At the Crags she decided to return. It was too late to go over the top today. She and Plague would make an early start tomorrow and continue the tracking. It would be interesting to see where the creature was headed. If he did have an injured ankle, like he'd told Emlock, they may find him holed up somewhere nursing his wounds.

It was dark by the time she got back. She drew the chain around the castle gate and cursed Hibu for the thousandth time. She had to find another padlock. Maybe tomorrow she'd find *him,* and put the chain around *his* neck. It would be fun to squeeze the life out of him for the trouble he'd caused. She ambled into the kitchen. Emlock looked up from peeling potatoes.

'I'm worried about Plague,' he said cautiously, not wanting to set her off on a rampage.

'Why? What's he done now?'

'It's not what he's done ... it's where he's gone.'

'Where has he gone?'

'I tried to stop him but he wouldn't listen ... '

'*Where* did he *go?* She was getting annoyed.

Emlock looked scared, 'Down there,' he said, pointing to the back stairs, 'And he's not in Hibu's room because I checked. He must have gone down into the passages.'

'Dam him!' cursed Urkha, 'If he gets lost down there how in the hell do we find him?' Emlock assumed it was a question to herself. He sincerely hoped it would be *she* and not *we* going to find him. If anyone went to look for the rotten little beast in those tunnels he certainly didn't wish to be included. He was not inclined to go anywhere near the underground passages. The very thought terrified him.

'How long has he been gone?' asked Urkha sharply.

Emlock thought for a minute and scratched his head. 'Probably between three and four hours.'

'What in hell's name is he doing down there all this time?'

Emlock looked helpless. 'Don't know,' he said, 'But I've been working in here since he left and he hasn't come back up the stairs.'

'Where's Codweb?'

Emlock hooked a thumb towards the larder.

'Codweb get out here!' she bellowed.

The fat troll came shooting out of the larder door. He had a mouth full of something. 'Wha ... wha ... wot?' he spluttered.

'Grab a candle. You're coming with me!'

Emlock breathed a huge sigh of relief. He even handed Codweb a new candle. Codweb looked at them both blankly.

'My son,' said Urkha, 'has seen fit to go exploring down in the dungeons. We have to look for him.'

Codweb's eyes got very big and Emlock could have sworn his legs were shaking. 'I ... I ... I'm not much liking those passages,' he said, swallowing and looking from Emlock to the she-troll and back again. 'Emlock ... he's better in confined spaces!'

'Emlock stays here in case we miss him and he gets back first. Now get going!' She herded him down the stairs, took his candle from him at the door and handed him a lighted one. Codweb pushed the heavy door open and was hit by the smell of dank musty air. He gulped, held the candle aloft and started to edge forwards. Up ahead the long passageway disappeared into inky darkness. God, they were going into the bowels of the earth!

'Just a minute,' growled Urkha, 'What the ... ?' She had suddenly seen the twine dangling from the door handle and snaking off up the passage. 'Well, well, the clever little fox! He's tied a line on so he can find his way back.'

Codweb turned around. Urkha had the twine in her hand. Great!

'We don't have to go then,' he said happily.

'Oh yes we do, I want to find out what he's up to. Get going.'

Plague had opened the trap door and was peering down into the black hole that was the round-room. All he could see was the top of a spiral staircase. Wow! Weren't they all going to be annoyed that it was him that found the secret passage! Maybe the elves had even hidden treasure down here. He wondered how far down the staircase went. He would drop the apple down and see how long it took to hit the bottom. He dropped it and listened carefully. It took some seconds before he heard a distant plop. Must be deep. Now he realised he had a problem. How did he carry the candle and the twine and manoeuvre down the narrow stairs? He decided to leave the twine and do a quick check down below. If the passage continued, as he suspected it would, he would leave the candle at the bottom and come back up for the twine.

He started down the stairs. It was freezing in the room. Many degrees colder than above in the passage. He shivered. Must be because it was deeper he thought. He wound down and around and down and around. The candlelight seemed to get brighter as he descended. It lit the room which Plague could now see was completely round. How strange! Then he stopped dead. He was sure he had heard whispering. A word that sounded like *Meee-gar?* Then above, way in the distance he heard his mother calling his name. 'Damn, damn, damn!' he cursed, why was she following him down here. He was furious. This was *his* discovery. He stepped off the bottom stair and started to walk slowly around the room. His mother had stopped calling. Maybe she'd gone back. He saw the door in the far wall. The passage *did* continue! He ran over to it and tried the handle. It was locked. There must be a hidden key ... maybe like upstairs in the flagstones. Holding the candle low he started walking very slowly around the room scanning the floor intently with his sharp eyes. Step by step,

step by step, around and around he went. On his third circuit something glinted ever so slightly in the dust as he passed behind the spiral staircase ... something was lying just under the stairs. The key? He reached down and carefully pulled it out. It wasn't a key. The candlelight in the room suddenly flickered and dimmed. What was going on? The thing was the wrong shape for a key. It was thick with dust and hard to distinguish. He rubbed it briefly against his waistcoat. It was round and made of some sort of metal. It had a small handle. He needed more light so he could see it better. He put the candle on one of the stairs at eye-level. Then he heard the whispering again ... *Megar ... Meee - gar!* It floated around the cold round room as though carried on a breeze. Weird! he thought. His mother's voice suddenly called again, this time from above.

'Plague? Are you down there?'

Damn her! With both hands now free he started cleaning the thing with a corner of his waistcoat. He rubbed at it for some seconds, and then brought it up into the light of the candle which immediately flared, brightly. He blinked hard. He was staring into a small silver mirror, with letters inscribed around the edge, but Plague couldn't read. He turned the piece over. The back was highly polished silver with a filigree border of suns and moons and elves, strangely unmarked by its years in the damp darkness. It was beautiful, thought Plague ... entrancing. He couldn't pull his eyes away from it. It was like a magnet drawing him into its centre with a strange beckoning power. He suddenly didn't like the feeling and an uneasiness gripped him. He tried to put the mirror down but he found he couldn't move his hands. Fascinated and fearful, he watched fingers of brilliant white light start to radiate towards him. They curled towards him gently, coiling and twisting like snakes, encircling him and then reaching *into* him ... deep into his head. Burning pain exploded in his brain. White-hot. He gagged and gurgled in agony as the molten heat raced through his body, searing bone and melting flesh. In a far off place he heard his mother calling. He didn't see her come half-way down the staircase, or hear her howl for him to drop the thing. He didn't see her turn tail and lunge back to the top, because something picked him up and threw him backwards with unbelievable force.

Urkha came up through the trap door like a raging bull, screaming for Codweb to get out of the way. 'They've killed him!' she howled, 'Dead! He's dead! They left a piece of silver! The foul elves and the vile wizard. He's burned! They've murdered my son!' She was tearing at her hair and beating on the walls. Rage pouring from her like a river.

Codweb was poorly equipped to deal with this sort of situation. 'W... wot shall I do?'

'Get down there,' shrieked Urkha, 'Get down there and bring it up. Bring it up and throw it down the well.'

'The ... the ... *silver?*'

'Of course the stinking silver!'

'But what if ... ?'

'Wrap it in something!' she screamed.

Codweb thought about arguing the point. He thought about it for exactly a second. Then he decided on balance the silver was less likely to kill him than the apoplectic she-troll. He grabbed a candle and slid down the stairs as Urkha sank into a wailing heap. A few minutes later he re-appeared hugging his waistcoat.

'Better get it down the well quick-like!' he said, arms in a death-grip around his chest and panic scrawled across his face.

Urkha didn't answer. She sat on the floor of the passage, numb. Codweb grabbed the twine and his candle and trotted towards the kitchen as fast as his fat little legs would carry him. Emlock was sitting at the table when a white-faced Codweb shot past him muttering something about going to the well. He rushed back in a few seconds later.

'You won't believe this,' he whispered, collapsing onto a chair.

'What?' Emlock had never seen him in such a state.

'Plague's dead!'

'What!'

'Killed in a secret room down in the bowels of those passageways!'

'Killed ... how?'

'Silver! There was a piece, must have been left by those stinkin' elves, and that stinkin' wizard, and he found it!'

'No!' Emlock couldn't believe it.

'Sure as I'm sitting here. And *she* saw it happen, and so did I! And she's gone mad.'

'Where's the silver now?'

'She told me to go and get it and throw it down the well ... so I did.'

'You picked up the silver?' said Emlock, astonished and disbelieving.

'No choice, she made me. I shut me eyes and shoved it inside me waistcoat.'

'Hell,' said Emlock.

The sound of footsteps made them both sit up. Urkha came up the back stairs and into the kitchen. She walked slowly past them, staring straight ahead.

'I won't be wanting supper,' she said hoarsely.

26

Drawn and Denied

Iceace, now completely recovered from his injuries, was nibbling a large carrot and relaxing on top of a wheelbarrow load of hay which was about to be distributed to the eight chosen reindeer who would pull the sleigh this year.

'You look tired,' he said.

The object of his comment was Petal, who was going hammer and tongs with a broom as she swept out a loose-box. She stopped sweeping and stood up, wiping a strand of damp hair from her face. She let out a big breath.

'It's always the same,' she sighed, 'The last few days before the delivery is always manic however hard I try to get ahead. And I'm not complaining, I've had lots of help.'

'I've helped a lot haven't I?' said a small voice from inside the loose box. Iceace waggled an ear and tried to peer around the stable door.

'You certainly have!' said Petal, grinning.

The owner of the voice appeared in the doorway. She was a tiny elfling with a mass of dark curls and big brown eyes. She looked up at Petal and then proceeded to lean on her miniature broom exactly the way Petal was leaning on hers.

'Flower here has been working all week,' said Petal, 'Don't know what I'd have done without her.'

'One day I'm going to run the stables aren't I?' said Flower, 'And if I work very hard Petal is going to teach me how to ride a pony.'

'Wow!' said Iceace, 'D'you know, you remind me of somebody.'

Flower chewed her lip and frowned, wondering who Iceace was talking about. 'Not Bizz?' she queried, 'She's my Aunt.'

'Nope,' chuckled Iceace, 'You remind me of Petal when she was a lot younger. And she had exactly the same dream. And come to think of it, you two even look alike.'

Flower visibly puffed with happiness. She looked up at her idol and said in a serious voice, 'I must get back to work.'

'Absolutely,' said Petal trying to sound deadly serious while smothering a smile, 'Riding lessons don't come cheap.' A few seconds later they heard Flower's small broom being worked hard in the loose box. 'You're right Ice, she's exactly like I was. Single-minded and determined.'

'Stubborn too?'

Petal grinned, 'Whatever do you mean?'

'I'm only repeating what I heard Aleron say yesterday.'

'Humph. He can talk!'

'Maybe you two should have a talk,' said Iceace nibbling more carrot and watching Petal out of the corner of his eye. She was scowling, and her chin had taken on that stubborn tilt.

'What's there to talk about? He's always right. He can never see my point of view.'

'Can you see his?'

'Hey, whose side are you on?'

Iceace chewed thoughtfully for a minute. 'I don't take sides, because I can see both sides. I understand you wanting to ride where you want to ride, and you don't want to be restricted. But from what Hibu has told us Urkha and Plague have definitely been paying visits to this side of the Crags. Which means Aleron was right to worry. Urkha probably *is* clever enough to have been wiping out her tracks.'

'But he didn't have to get so angry.' Petal was wearing her defensive look. 'He just about bit my head and my shoulders off when he came to get me that day. He can't speak to me like that and expect me to just forget it!'

'He was angry because he cares.'

Petal pouted, 'Then he should come to me and say he's sorry. Besides, if I hadn't come up to the Crags that day I wouldn't have met Hibu and ... '

'I know, I know,' put in Iceace quickly, 'I wouldn't be here. That's what makes the whole thing so difficult.'

Petal looked at him. They had been best friends for ten years, since they were both young. She loved the snowbun to bits. 'The most important thing is that you recovered.' Leaning forward she gently brushed a few hayseeds off the pure white fur on his back, 'I'd have killed you if you'd died!'

Iceace looked puzzled for a second. Once in a while he still had a little problem with words and expressions. Then he realised it was a joke. 'I'm as fit as a fish!' he said, and he did a huge hop off the barrow to prove it.

'I think you mean as fit as a flea!'

'Go talk to Aleron,' said Iceace, and he loped off out of the stable before she could answer. Petal leaned on her broom. She wondered, slightly grudgingly, if maybe he was right. Then she straightened up. If she had time she'd go and look for him later and test the water, see what sort of mood he was in. In the meantime she had eight reindeer, her flyers as she called them, to groom. They and Ru had been brought in early for pre-flying preparations. It included the oiling of antlers which took ages but she liked them to look absolutely perfect for the delivery.

All the help she had started out with seemed to have dwindled. Zeb, who still worked part-time, had come down with a heavy cold, another elf had twisted his ankle badly when he fell off a hay bale, and a third had asked if he could help in packing for a change, so she had let him go. She wandered over to the stable door and eyed the snow falling thick and fast in the courtyard. It had started in earnest a couple of weeks ago. Now everything was blanketed in white. It was beautiful, but as usual it added to Petal's workload. All the deer had been brought into the yards and required haying-up every day, and it all took longer when one was hampered by deep snow. The deer didn't mind it. Their long slender legs coped with it easily. They made wonderful mounts in winter and were nimble and fast, a time when the ponies struggled.

'You have a far-away look in your eyes Miss Petal.' Perks was coming towards her with his usual cheeky grin, wearing his snow-covered sleigh- rider's hat from ten years ago. He wore it every Christmas with enormous pride.

'Just looking at that sky,' said Petal, 'It's getting darker and darker.'

'Yep, funnily enough I was just talking to Elestyal and he said we'll be needing Ru this year. Apparently this front is here to stay for a while and there's a pea-souper of a fog down south.'

'I guessed that. I brought him in a couple of days ago. He's been driving the others nuts with his glow already. Quite amazing how he picks up on the energy and senses the bad weather. And judging by how brightly he's shining the magic's already high and the weather's going to be particularly foul.'

'Wonderful creature,' laughed Perks.

'Trouble is he glows away merrily in his stall and no one else can get any sleep. I had to move him into the loose-box at the far end. And I got Bizz to run me up a special nose-bag. She did a great job. It's double-thickness black velvet, with his name on it in red letters. Works a treat!'

Perks had other things on his mind. 'You coming to the draw this afternoon? Remember Elestyal has brought it forward this year, to give Bizz a bit more time to get sleigh-rider suits fitted.'

'I'd like to, but then again ... well I guess it still bugs me ...'

'That girls are still banned,' finished Perks.

'Yeah,' Petal suddenly grinned evilly, 'But I put my

name in that damn box again anyway. And one of these years they'll pull it out!'

'They still won't let you go,' laughed Perks, shaking his head.

'No but I'll get on that stage and give them hell about their old-fashioned rules.'

'Have you seen Aleron recently?' Perks slipped the question in casually, a little too casually for Petal. She narrowed her eyes and gave him a short sharp look.

'Why do you ask?'

Perks shrugged and looked the picture of innocence. 'Oh ... no reason,' he said airily, 'It's just that he did ask after you the other day.'

'Well he never asks *me*,' said Petal. She could see the old gardener was trying to choose his words carefully.

'He um ... I think he's a bit nervous'

'Nervous! What's he got to be nervous about? He chewed my head off that day I met Hibu, weeks ago, and he hasn't spoken to me since.'

Perks concentrated on flattening a circle of fluffy snow with the toe of his boot. 'All the same, he does ... I mean, well ... well why don't you come along to the draw this afternoon anyway,' he finished in a rush.

Petal smelled a conspiracy. First Ice and now Perks.

Something was going on. She was about to launch into why she shouldn't bother with Aleron or the darned Riders' draw when Flower's voice interrupted them.

'Miss Petal, I've finished Ru's box, what's next?' The elfling appeared and propped her broom up beside Petal.

'Well, well, peas in a pod,' said Perks looking at the two of them.

'Ice said I look like Petal too, when she was young,' said Flower, pleased as punch that someone else had noticed the likeness.

'I just hope you're not as stubborn,' whispered Perks.

'Iceace said that as well,' giggled Flower.

'OY you two! Enough!' Petal found herself trying not to smile. Then she looked a bit resigned, 'Ok, Flower and I will nip over to the draw if we get caught up. I've lost all my help for various reasons.'

'I'll see you there,' said Perks, doffing his hat to Flower, 'You make sure to bring her.'

Flower saluted him.

It was nearly two o'clock and Iffi banquet hall was crammed with elves. The atmosphere as usual was electric and a buzz of anticipation filled the old hall as the time of the draw drew closer. The stage had been set up at one end as usual, and residing in the centre, on a small table, was the famous carved wooden box, the only thing rescued from Christmas Castle ten years ago. As always it was filled with the names of the hopeful. They had scribbled their names on slips of paper and posted them through the slit in the top, praying that theirs would be one of the ones pulled out.

Petal had slipped into the hall at the last minute with Flower, who had immediately dashed to the front of the crowd and squeezed between the other elflings to get a better view. A more fastidious little girl elfling, standing next to her, wrinkled her nose, 'You smell,' she whispered.

'Reindeer dung,' replied Flower matter-of-factly.

The girl moved back a few paces along with a few others. Flower was too excited about the draw to notice.

A sudden cheer announced the arrival of Elestyal. He came through the door with Hibu, who had become a permanent fixture at Iffi. Everyone loved him. Elestyal mounted the stage. The roar increased. Elestyal raised his hands for silence.

'Thank you all,' he called. 'Thank you. As usual I would like to check on how preparations are going, and then we'll move straight on to the draw.' The check took about fifteen minutes, and everyone appeared to be up to speed. 'Now,' said Elestyal, 'Since we had no young trainees this year I thought I might ask one of our elflings to help me with the draw. Is there anyone who would like to come up and pull out some names?' He scanned the huddle of young ones a short distance from the stage. Flower, who had by now been distanced by all of them, due to the overly-ripe aroma of eau-de-reindeer-dung, stood alone just below him. Barely had his request left his lips and her short arm was up and waving. The others never had a chance.

'Come along then Miss Flower,' called Elestyal, thinking how much she looked like a young version of Petal.

A proud Flower pulled name after name from the box and read them out clearly and carefully. The hall was a riot. Nine elves were going insane with excitement, dancing and shouting. There was one place left. You could have heard a pin drop as Flower dipped her hand in again and pulled out a folded paper. Breaths were held. She opened it and immediately put her hand over her mouth, stifled a giggle, and cast a mischievous glance up at Elestyal. Her face was a picture.

'Well, go on, call out the lucky name,' laughed Elestyal.

Flower faced the hall. They waited, each one willing it to be them. She hung on, grinning like a Cheshire cat.

'Come on Flower!' yelled somebody.

'Read it!' called another.

Flower took a breath. 'The last name is ... *PETAL!*'

There was immediate uproar in the hall.

'*Petal?*' repeated Elestyal, 'Let me see that!' he grabbed the paper and adjusted his spectacles. It clearly said *Petal*, and underneath, written in bold handwriting it said: 'EQUAL RIGHTS FOR ELF CHICKS!' The pandemonium in the hall increased as the elf-guys cat-called and whistled and made thumbs-down signs. A few of the girls were nodding and saying it was only fair.

Elestyal cast an eagle-eye around the hall and spotted Petal lurking by the door. He inclined his head and motioned her up on to the stage. She clambered up leaving a small trail of mud in her wake. He waved the paper at her. 'What's the meaning of this?' he asked with a raised eyebrow.

Petal turned to the crowd, 'It's as I've said for years,' she shouted, over the barrage of whistles and jibes, 'Females should have a right to ride the sleigh if they want to and if they're able. You lot,' she shouted, pointing at the laughing elf-guys, 'Are living in the past. You need to move on. The barring of female riders is unfair, and unreasonable. It's quite simply discrimination!'

'It wouldn't be traditional!' called someone.

'You'd only fall off!' yelled someone else.

'Girls should stick to sewing!' came a shout from the back.

'I hate sewing and I think Petal is right and you should listen to her!' Flower had marched to the front of the stage and was glowering, hands on hips, in the direction of the elf who had made the sewing comment. Her brown eyes blazed and she waved a small and furious finger. 'I want to be a sleighrider too one day!'

Elestyal groaned. Wasn't one Petal enough? It appeared they had a new miniature one ready to take up the torch for female rights. He tried to calm the audience who were relishing the banter. 'Okay! Okay! Settle down all of you. Petal and I ... ' He suddenly noticed a pair of brown eyes frowning in his direction. 'And er, Miss Flower here, will have a meeting in private and discuss the situation.'

Flower clapped her hands. Petal already knew what the outcome of any such meeting would be. Elestyal would apologise profusely, pretend to understand her feelings, and then feign helplessness for reasons of tradition and safety. It infuriated her. It was like banging your head on the stable wall.

'Guess you'd better pick out another name,' she said to

Flower.

Flower looked disappointed but did as Petal asked. She dug around in the box of papers, her face a picture of concentration. Then she suddenly stopped and pulled her hand out with nothing in it. She looked up at Elestyal. 'Elestyal I think Petal should draw this one.'

'Fine,' said the wizard, 'A good idea. Go on Petal, pick a replacement.'

Petal shook her head and tried not to grimace. Heaving a sigh she dug around most unenthusiastically in the box and drew out a folded paper. As she opened it her expression changed from resigned to livid. She screwed it into a ball, threw it across the stage and marched straight out of the hall.

Flower looked after her in surprise, then ran over and picked up the paper. She walked back to the front of the stage smoothing it out. 'The last rider is Aleron.' Then she tore off after Petal.

27
December 22nd

Urkha stood at the open window in her tower room in the pitch dark. Howling winds drove snow into her face, pelting her with fat stinging flakes. She felt nothing. She had been up since four, unable to sleep, unable to find any peace.

It was many weeks since Plague had died down in the underground room, but she couldn't get those last ghastly moments out of her mind. It drove her mad. Over and over again she was looking down the spiral staircase and seeing the piece of silver in his hand in the candlelight. Remembering how she had instantly sensed terrible danger. How she couldn't stop him looking into it, and then, his screams, his dying in that terrible manner. She shuddered, and cursed her mind for replaying the scene. Revenge. She knew it was the only thing to assuage the pain. Do unto others as they do unto you. She would take her revenge on those who had murdered her child. She knew where they were. All she needed was a plan.

She had tracked the Erudite to the base of the crags some days after he'd escaped. Days later she had gone back, this time taking the path over the top. At the bottom of the River Path she had found a place where his tracks joined with those of a pony and an elf. After that they vanished. She noticed that the pony's tracks suddenly deepened, probably from carrying extra weight, and it had also taken off in a hurry. The elf had walked back for some distance before being met by two ponies. The pony tracks had then returned back through the forest and out to the edge of a lake. On the far side of the lake was a big old castle. It had suddenly all made sense. This is where the elves and the damn wizard had fled to when they escaped the Zorils ten years ago. This was where the Erudite was hiding.

It was freezing. She came away from the window and lit a candle. Sometimes a light helped to chase away the demons in her mind. Then she wandered the corridors, as she so often did, ending up in the room that Plague had chosen for himself from the time he was small. She put the candle down on the table and felt the old emotions well up inside her, the anger and the loss. It rose inside her like a tide. 'DEVILS!' she screamed, and she picked up Plague's mattress and heaved it across the room. Beneath it a few pieces of paper floated about and came to rest again.

Urkha closed her eyes and tried to regain control. She waited until her breathing had slowed a little, then she slumped down onto the bare boards of the bed. After a while she looked up. Her son had always been a secretive little swine. She wondered half-heartedly what these treasures were that he'd stuffed under his mattress. She poked at one of the bits of paper, dragging it towards her absent-mindedly with a yellowed claw. It was a picture of some sort but she couldn't see it properly. She picked up the candle and set it on the bed. The picture became clear. She frowned and suddenly became more interested. It wasn't one of Plague's childhood scrawls. He must have found it somewhere in the castle, maybe in this very room. So it must have been drawn by an elf. She scanned through the rest of the pictures and her heart began to quicken

For many hours during the last weeks she had sat in deep thought and tried to remember all she could about the elves and the wizard. Her memory was keen. She had recalled conversations going back ten years, between Lirtob and Cacodyl. She had overheard the Erudite being forced to tell what he knew about the role of the elves. Snippets of information had gradually re-surfaced in her brain and allowed her to build up a picture. She ran it through her mind one more time. December the twenty-fourth,

Christmas Eve the elves called it, preceded the main human feast day on the twenty-fifth which they called Christmas Day. On the night of the twenty-fourth the elves and the wizard apparently made some kind of traditional delivery of gifts to all the human children in far off lands. They did this, so it was said, by way of a sleigh pulled by flying reindeer, and aided by magic.

She looked at the picture in her hand. What Hibu had described, an elf had drawn. It had to be true. She shuffled through the papers until she got to the coloured one. It would appear that in times of severe weather and poor visibility they were aided by a deer with a strange glowing nose. Under the picture of the deer was written 'Ru'.

It all sounded crazy, but she mustn't forget that there was a wizard involved. And apparently the night of Christmas Eve as they called it was also a night of the most powerful magic, generated by what the Erudite had called *positive human energy.* She had never heard of such a thing, but for now she must accept that it was true. Apparently the elves lived their lives entirely devoted to this annual task. If this was true then it was also how she could hurt them most. Mortal wounds would be bad but she could destroy them if she put paid to their sole purpose. The thing they called Christmas.

Emlock yawned, dragged himself from his bed and plodded down to the kitchen. Urkha was already there, sitting at the kitchen table with some pieces of paper in front of her. His heart sank. Since Plague's death Urkha had become completely unstable and would go into orbit over the most innocent remark. Emlock was worn down, always on edge, his gut a knot of continual fear. He was tired of it. He said nothing and put water on to heat. He had started drinking Hibu's tea. It seemed to help the gnawing pain in his stomach. He missed Hibu. He didn't understand why but something in him had changed over the last years. Maybe he'd just become soft? Whatever it was it had set off emotions and feelings in him that he never knew existed. Until he came to the castle life had been a simple case of killing, eating, fighting and surviving. But that had all changed when he was put in charge of the kitchen and started working with the gentle Erudite. He suddenly saw that there were other ways of being, and, reluctantly, he had to admit he liked them.

For a change Urkha didn't give him a bad time about drinking tea. She was somehow different this morning. More alert. Pre-occupied. Something had changed. He sat down cautiously and scooped two spoons of sugar into his mug.

'What d'you know about elves?' she suddenly asked.

Emlock looked up in surprise, 'Not a lot. There's various sorts and they live in various places, you know, woodland ... '

'No, I mean what do you know about the ones that lived here?'

'Only what we were told ten years ago, that they make gifts for humans and deliver them at some festival called Christmas.'

'Did Hibu ever speak of it?'

'I did ask 'im once but he said he only knew a little, what he'd read in a book. The same as what he told Cacodyl when they captured 'im.'

'I think it was true,' said Urkha, 'Look,' She pushed the pieces of paper enthusiastically across the table towards Emlock.

Emlock studied them carefully one by one. 'Drawn by an elf,' he murmured.

'Why do you say that?'

'They all have a word underneath them. Look,' he pointed to Petal's signature. 'We trolls can't write. So if you found them in the castle they were probably left by the elves.'

'Hmm, my thoughts exactly. They were under Plague's mattress.'

Emlock was studying the coloured one. 'Looks like they really do have flying reindeer. Can you believe it! Scary though.'

'Why?'

Emlock frowned and looked straight at Urkha, 'Imagine the sort of magical power it takes to make something like that happen.'

'Yeah, well,' She stood up, smiling for the first time in weeks. 'Magical powers or not,' she said, 'They still have a weakness. I'm going out later. I won't be back till tomorrow.'

Emlock swallowed some tea and waited until she had left the room. He looked at the pictures again and wondered if the word *Petal* was the name of the person who had drawn the pictures. Then he heard the clump of Codweb's feet on the stairs. He quickly put the pictures in a drawer. The fat troll lumbered down the last couple of steps.

'Stinkin' 'erb tea!' he growled, sniffing the air, 'Where's the wine?'

'None left,' said Emlock shortly, 'You finished it off last night.'

'Where's the she-troll?'

'Dunno. She was in here earlier. She's different today, I reckon she's planning something. Says she's going out later and won't be back till tomorrow.'

Codweb looked surprised, 'Good riddance to 'er,' he growled, 'Maybe she won't come back. I'm sick of 'er crazy moods.' Silence reigned. Codweb started on his usual routine of eating anything in sight and Emlock wondered what he could cook up for dinner.

Just before midday Urkha harnessed the gulo up to the sleigh. Greole had learned a long time ago that submission was less painful than resistance. He was fit and well-fed by Emlock and docile under Urkha's command. The she-troll threw a few items into the back of the sled, then she climbed into the driving seat. Once out of the castle gate she cracked the whip. The wolverine ran easily across the white world. More snow fell. The sky was as black as a bear's armpit, and it was getting worse.

Castle Iffi, Stables, 10pm

Petal had her head almost under Gigi's belly as she made long, smooth strokes with the brush. She just had Ru left to do after this and then she was going to call it a night.

She felt physically and emotionally shattered, and was still smarting from the shock of Aleron getting his damn name pulled for sleighrider. He must be revelling in it. It just seemed so unfair.

Footsteps approached the stall. Probably dear old Perks worrying about her working too hard.

'Hi Petal.'

She nearly dropped her brush. Her stomach scrunched into a knot. She stood up and looked at Aleron who was looking back at her uncertainly.

'I came to say that I'm sorry, for shouting at you and getting so angry. It was wrong of me. And I hate the thought of us not speaking all over Christmas.' He looked genuinely upset. Any thought that Petal might have had of giving him a piece of her mind died a quick death. She came out of the stall with shoulders slumped and leaned against the post.

'I suppose I'm just as much to blame,' she said catching his eye and then looking down at her boots, 'I shouldn't have taken it so badly, you trying to look out for me and everything.'

'Maybe we should both try and be a bit less ... '

'Sensitive?' said Petal, finishing his sentence, 'In which case I guess congratulations are in order,' She gave him the hint of a smile.

'Oh, yeah, I got picked this year. It's great, I can't really believe it.'

'Yes, well, enjoy every minute of the trip, and make sure you tell me how it was. I'll want a blow-by-blow account when you get back.'

'I'll do that,' he said, breaking into that wonderful grin which affected Petal's breathing. 'Hey, can I help? How much more have you got to do?'

'I'm finished with this old girl,' said Petal, patting Gigi's rump, 'Just need to run a brush over Ru. He's up in the loose-box.'

'I'll help you, and then we'll go and have a glass of old Panglossian's best mead.'

They wandered up to the loose box where a sign hung on the door. It had been made by Flower: *'Ru is shining very brightly! Please keep the door shut.'* Aleron chuckled.

'Actually,' said Petal, he's got a wonderful new double-thickness, black-velvet, tailor-made nose-bag, made by Bizz. So we only shut the top door when the bag's off and he's eating his hay. You just need your sunglasses if you're in there with him!'

Ru greeted them by throwing his head up and down and making funny little grunting noises inside his new nose-bag.

'Hello, oh brightly shining one,' said Petal, stroking his neck. Aleron looked around for a spare brush. Petal pointed to the corner, 'There's one in my grooming box down there.' She started brushing Ru's chest. Aleron lifted the lid of the box and nearly jumped out of his skin. Petal stifled a giggle.

'That darned mouse! What's he doing in here?' Crumb had been curled up in a duster. 'How come the little devil is still alive anyway? He must be a hundred years old by now.'

'Wizard's mouse!' said Petal.

Aleron put Crumb and the duster carefully to one side and rooted around for another brush. Petal must be mistaken, he couldn't find one. Just to be sure he tipped the entire contents of the box onto the straw. A strange looking key landed on his foot. He picked it up. It was smooth and heavy. At the top of the shaft were etched the letters *R.R.* He turned it over, frowning. At the top on the other side were the letters *C.C.* He could only think of one thing that those letters represented.

'What's this Petal?' he asked quietly.

Puzzled at his sudden change in tone she left Ru and came over to him. Her heart froze in her chest when she saw what he was holding. There was no way out of this. It seemed like an eternity before she was able to speak. Then the words came, faltering, stumbling over each other.

'*Please* Aleron, don't be angry, I was going to tell you but, well it's just that I've never found the right moment. And, also I felt, well I felt guilty for taking it ... but then it was too late!'

'It's from Christmas Castle?' He sounded puzzled.

'Yes.'

'When did you take it? Where did you get it?'

'It was what I found, that night Iceace and I went to Christmas Castle ten years ago. It's the special thing I found that I told you I'd never show you. After you got so angry.'

'But you told me just weeks ago that you made that whole story up at the time ... that you were just getting back at me for being angry with you! What the hell is it the key to?'

She faltered, 'The ... er ... door to the passage to the round-room, by the clearing in Tall Pine Wood.'

'You stole the key to the passage?' Aleron was looking at her as though she was mad, 'What if someone wants to get in? What if Elestyal wanted it for some reason. You had *no right* to take it! It's a key to a secret passage! What on earth were you thinking about? You get on your darned high horse about not being allowed to go on the delivery, but why should you when you don't have an ounce of common sense!' He threw the key back on the ground in front of her. 'I think *you* need to go and talk to Elestyal!' He turned on his heel, took a few steps then swung back, eyes blazing. 'And thanks for lying to me!'

'Aleron ... I was just a kid when I took it! I didn't think ...'

'That's the trouble with you Petal,' His words rang clearly as he walked away. 'You never do!'

Petal felt numb. Tears were flooding hotly down her cheeks. She hadn't cried for years, other than when Ice was on death's door, but that was different.
She had felt so positive tonight, after they had both apologised, thought that things could actually work out. She had planned to tell him how much she cared, and thought she'd picked up the same vibes from him. But now it had all come crashing down. There would be no hope of mending this rift.

Her nose was running. Miserably she wiped it down her sleeve, and picked up the key. Unfortunately not the one to Aleron's heart. She sniffed back more tears and shoved it into her jeans pocket. She would go to Elestyal tomorrow and confess. She felt bone-weary, and exhausted. To hell with it, she'd sleep with Ru tonight. She needed company.

First she lit a small lamp and hung it up on a hook outside the loose- box door, then she shut the bottom section of the door and pushed the bolt along. It resisted and squeaked. She really must oil it sometime. She curled up in the thick straw under Ru's manger, listening to him contentedly chewing crushed oats in his new nose-bag. She was asleep in seconds.

28

A Visitor in the Night

Petal was dreaming. She and Aleron were standing at the gate of Christmas Castle while she tried to unlock it, but for some reason the key didn't fit. 'You've brought the wrong one!' he was shouting angrily. 'How could you do that?' Petal was so agitated that she pushed the key in again and tried to force it but it just made a horrible squeaking noise. It was then that she woke up, but the squeaking noise continued.

Bleary-eyed and befuddled with sleep she poked her head up out of the straw and wondered what was going on. Then she remembered that she'd decided to sleep in Ru's stable. The squeak came again. Surely that was the bolt being drawn back on Ru's door? Drowsily she wondered who was coming to check on her, in what must be the middle of the night. She was just about to call out when the bolt went clunk, the door opened, and a foul odour hit her. She froze, and peered across the stall. In the soft amber light of the lamp, on the hook above the door, she saw a grotesque figure approaching. Ru was on his feet in a second, backing up and stamping his hooves.

Urkha was pleased with herself. She had made it to the castle by midnight, which was an achievement considering the weather. The castle gate had been open. Trusting little fools! All was quiet and not an elf in sight. Her nose had led her straight to the stable full of reindeer, none of which were emitting light from their noses. Obviously none of them were the one called Ru, that she'd seen in the picture. He must be separated, maybe in a special pen? But there was no bright light anywhere? She noticed the lamp hanging up at the other end of the stable and slipped up towards it. It was hanging outside a loose-box, and on the front of the door was a sign. Yes!One of the words was 'Ru'! But she was puzzled, there was still no light? She peered over the door. There was a reindeer lying down in the straw. Its eyes were closed and it was chewing … but its face was odd. It appeared to have a baggy, jet black nose … with … yes … tiny beams of light escaping from it! Urkha leaned closer. Now she could see that the deer's nose was covered with some sort of bag.

The bolt on the door was rusted, it squeaked when she pulled it back. She drew her hunting knife and crept in. The deer, suddenly becoming aware of her presence, leapt up and backed straight into the corner, stamping its feet. A cornered deer was easy meat for her, and in an instant she was beside it, grabbing Ru's head in an arm-lock and ripping off the nosebag. The stall was immediately lit with a most brilliant and powerful light. Then there was a flash as a knife-blade arced, and Ru was bellowing in pain. Urkha held up her prize, astonished that it was still shining. Expecting it to die when severed from its owner! She thought quickly. She must get out of here fast and take it with her. She dropped her knife and reached for the bag.

Petal, hiding under the manger, was nearly dumb with terror at what she was witnessing. It was a *huge* troll. The size of a mountain. It must be the one from Christmas Castle ... the black-haired beast they called Urkha. And it had just cut Ru's nose off! The filthy pig! No one did that to *her* reindeer! The stinking monster was reaching for the velvet bag. It had its back to her. She hiked her penknife out of her pocket, flicked out the biggest blade, and dove out from her corner. Urkha heard the movement, sensed an attack and pivoted. Petal ran straight into her muscular thigh, stabbing wildly.

Urkha was surprised. An elf had come from nowhere

and was attacking her. It was a female too, armed with a pathetic weapon. She dodged Petal's stabs easily, and lightening fast lashed out with a meaty fist which connected solidly with Petal's determined chin. Petal went down like a rag doll. The deer had thankfully stopped its bawling and was trembling in the corner. Urkha grabbed up the black bag and shoved Ru's nose into the bottom. It was like flipping a switch. The stall was immediately thrown back into darkness. She pushed the bag deep into her waistcoat and looked around for something to tie up the elf. Twine from hay bales hung on a hook outside the door. Perfect. It took a minute to securely tie Petal's wrists and ankles. She threw her prisoner over one shoulder as though she was a feather, and hastened back to the sleigh.

    The wind had increased. It howled through the trees like a lost child. Snow piled on snow. The wolverine shook itself as Urkha dumped Petal in the back of the sleigh. She had just wiped out any hope of the elves making their Christmas delivery - the thing they lived for! Plus she had a bonus, an elf to roast. Maybe she would have some fun with it first, a little revenge for what they did to Plague. She leapt into the driving seat and cracked the whip. In seconds the storm-filled night had swallowed them up.

Iceace woke with a start and a cold dread in his stomach, like the remnants of a nightmare only worse. He sat up, sweating, his heart going ten to the dozen. Something was horribly wrong. His inner clock told him it was the middle of the night, about two in the morning. He jumped out of his basket in the room he still shared with Petal. Was she okay? He hopped over to her bed. Empty! And it hadn't been slept in. Where was she? He filtered information rapidly. Something had happened at about ten o'clock yesterday evening. He had overheard Aleron telling Perks that he was going to talk to Petal, who was still working over at the stable. He had returned about twenty minutes later with a face like thunder, but he wouldn't tell anyone why, and then he had slumped off to bed. Considering he had just won a place on the sleigh this year it was very odd behaviour, and Iceace reckoned it could only be due to one thing, another fall-out with Petal. He guessed that Petal might have been so upset that she'd slept in the stable. She'd done it before. He knew she found comfort there. He must go and see. The bad feeling was still with him as he dashed across the windswept courtyard, leaping over the drifts.

As soon as he got to the stable door the bad feeling got a whole lot worse. He could smell troll. His heart lurched. He took a quick look at the deer in the stalls. They were fine. There was a lamp hanging outside Ru's loose-box. If Petal was sleeping here, that's where she would be. He tore down to the far end of the stable. The door to Ru's box was ajar and the smell of Zoril was everywhere. Iceace nosed his way in and was met by the grisly sight of Ru. The reindeer was a desperate figure, standing splay-legged, as though he may fall at any minute, shaking uncontrollably. Small droplets of bright red blood dripped from the place where once his nose had been.

In the amber light from the lamp Iceace saw splatters of blood in the straw, and half buried beside him a troll's hunting knife. A few feet away lay another knife, Petal's penknife! Iceace had seen her using it to cut the strings on the hay bales hundreds of times. Cold dread seeped through the snowbun's entire being. The she-troll had been here and it had taken Petal.

'I'm coming right back!' he called to Ru. In thirty seconds he was inside the castle and waking Aleron. 'The she-troll has been in the barn!' he gasped, 'She's done a terrible thing to Ru and she's taken Petal!'

'What!' Aleron, torn from a deep sleep, thought he was either dreaming, or else Iceace was playing some weird practical joke on him.

'Hurry!' cried Iceace, 'We must wake Elestyal!'

Aleron suddenly realised that Iceace was serious. He had never seen the snowbun in such a state. He came out of his bed like a rocket, throwing his clothes on and pulling on boots. Ice had to be wrong! He couldn't believe it ... a troll in their stable. He *must* be wrong. And how could it take Petal? She would be in bed ... wouldn't she? Then he recalled the events of yesterday evening with the key. She had looked devastated when he had stormed off. She might well have slept in the stable. Something terrible twisted inside him.

Arriving in Ru's stall he stared in disbelief at the wounded animal. Ru was in shock. He needed Elestyal. Aleron picked the big hunting knife out of the straw. There was blood on it. Was it only Ru's? He didn't dare think any further. Petal's penknife lay, blade open, nearby. He saw the straw flattened in a corner under the manger. She had slept there! She had seen the troll come in and she'd attempted to fight it. In God's name what possessed her to do it?' She could have stayed hidden. And how had the troll known about Ru? About the light he carried for them ... for the delivery. It suddenly hit him. There would be no delivery without Ru's light. It would be the first time in history that there was no Santa Claus. It was unthinkable.

Iceace came galloping in covered in snow, 'She came on a sleigh!' he cried, 'Pulled by the wolverine ... I found what was left of the tracks, heading round the lake towards Bearban!'

Aleron had already made a decision. 'I'm going after them,' he said, 'I have to find Petal, and the she-troll must have taken Ru's light. He was wearing a black velvet cover over it last night. It's missing. I have to go! Wake Elestyal! Ru needs him!'

By the time Iceace had woken Elestyal and told him of the disaster in the stable Aleron was heading around the lake on Petal's favourite reindeer, Smooch. The snow was deep. In front of him in more sheltered spots there was the faintest outline of sleigh tracks. He reckoned Urkha had at least two hours start. He pulled his cape more snugly around him and his hat down more firmly. He'd left in an awful hurry and was now thinking of the things he could do with that he didn't have, like his dagger. His only weapon against Urkha was her own hunting knife which he'd picked out of the straw. Petal's penknife was hardly going to do much damage. He wondered again what had been going through her mind when she'd gone into attack mode. No doubt she couldn't bear to see Ru being hurt. He shook his head. She certainly had fire in her. Dammit! It was that fire he loved,- that passion! But it was that same side of her that rubbed him right up the wrong way at times. His mouth set in a grim line when he thought about what the she-troll might do to her, then he cursed himself. He had to believe he could find her, and bring her back safely. The snow was falling faster again as he entered the path through Bearban. The forest was beautiful, its bushes and trees sculpted in soft white. The snow on the path was thinner, protected by groves of thick pine and fir, and less arduous for Smooch. Aleron patted his neck. They had a long way to go. He prayed he would be in time.

In Ru's stable Elestyal barked orders. He was devastated at the state of his beloved Ru who was sinking fast. They would lose him if they didn't do something, and do it quickly. 'Blankets and ropes!' cried the wizard. 'And bring the big toboggan!'

Minutes later, Hibu, Zeb and Perks, and a dozen other elves pulled Ru across the yard. It took even more of them to get the toboggan with the heavy reindeer up the steps and into the banquet hall. Bizz had a roaring fire going and Ru was placed gently in front of it on a heap of blankets. Elestyal ran for his medicines. He came flying back a few seconds later.

'Hell of a wound,' he gasped to Zeb, who was holding Ru's head, 'But a clean cut. And the cold has helped stem some of the bleeding.' He fished in his box of potions and pulled out a bottle of bright blue liquid, 'This should help to anaesthetize and disinfect it, then we'll bandage it very lightly. I'll give him a draught of sedative to make him sleep too. We must keep the fire going and keep him warm to help with the shock.'

'I'll sit with him,' said Zeb.

Elestyal nodded, 'The bandage is only thin, and quite loose, so he can breathe. If he wakes and becomes too stressed give him some more of the sedative.

Zeb looked at him sideways, 'Where are you going?'

Elestyal had a hard look in his eyes, 'To Christmas Castle,' he said softly, 'Aleron will need our help. I just pray that Petal is ... ' He didn't finish the sentence.   Zeb didn't want to think of the other option either.

Another equally inconceivable thought was in everyone's mind. No one had dared voice it, but sooner or later it would have to be faced. In the end it was Zeb. He turned to face Elestyal. 'The delivery ... without Ru ... '

'Impossible.' Elestyal's voice was barely a whisper.

Elves stood dumbly, unwilling to comprehend the true

implication of what was happening. No delivery? It just wasn't possible. It *must* go on ... somehow. They gazed at Ru in despair. Their precious light, so still in front of the fire.

'I want to come with you!' growled Zeb.

'No, I need you to care for Ru.'

'I'll come!' said Perks.

'Me too!' came Skyler's voice, which was quickly followed by Jake, Sid, Hugo, and a chorus of others.

'You're not going without me!' said Hibu firmly.

Elestyal turned to them, 'Okay,' he said, 'Bring the deer in from the big yard and get them ready. Dress warmly and arm yourselves as best you can.'

'The snow will be deep over the crags,' said Hibu, 'It's going to be a devil of a journey.'

Elestyal was already making for the door. He cast a quick glance back over his shoulder. 'I have a little something that may aid us.'

29

All Tied Up

Petal regained consciousness by degrees. Things kept fading in and out. Her head hurt like hell, so did her jaw, she was freezing cold and for some reason couldn't seem to move her hands or feet. Their was a swaying sensation. She thought vaguely she should be in bed, but beds didn't sway. She dug through her mind, trying to shake off the groggy feeling. The woolliness cleared slightly. Hang on ... she'd slept in the stable ... with Ru ... *Oh my God!* It suddenly started to flood back ... *the troll ... Ru ... the knife!* Vivid pictures slammed into her mind. She had charged at the she-troll in a fury, that was the last thing she remembered. Her head started to clear more and she opened her eyes. It was daylight. She must have been out of it for a long time. In a few seconds she realised that the swaying sensation was being caused by a sleigh ... and she was in the back of it! Her wrists were bound behind her back and her ankles tied equally tight. She could barely feel her fingers, and she was covered in snow. The storm was still in full swing as Urkha whipped the gulo faster.

There was now no doubt in Petal's mind as to who her captor was and where they were headed. Two things, she told herself, don't panic and escape as quick as possible. She felt escape may be rather optimistic. She was lying on her side and could see the terrain quite well as it passed. It was flat country, strewn with rock and scraggy clumps of bush. Scattered with little groves of stunted trees. She had seen it before. They were heading across the Snaggle Plains. It was the same route that she and Ice had taken many years ago, only last time it hadn't been in a snowstorm.

Petal closed her eyes and racked her brains for a plan, but came up with nothing. She was bound far too tightly to do anything. Even if she could have got to her pocket her penknife was lying somewhere in Ru's stall. Too bad it wasn't embedded in Urkha's gut she thought viciously. One of Aleron's comments suddenly echoed through her mind, something about *'Foolhardy determination landing her in trouble one day!* Damn, he'd been right this time. So what should she have done? Let the damn troll do as it pleased? God, she was arguing with him and he wasn't even here! She wished he was. Oh how she wished he was.

She wondered if anyone had noticed her missing. They must have found Ru by now. Ru horribly injured, with no light. Urkha had been about to put it in the black nosebag when Petal had gone for her. She must have meant to steal it. Why? What on earth could she want it for. And then the obviousness of it hit her like a brick, the Christmas delivery! It couldn't happen without Ru, not in this weather. Her heart plummeted. It was unthinkable that Christmas wouldn't happen. The whole world waited for St Nicholas every year. She desperately fought her bound wrists again. It was hopeless. The circulation in her hands was all but cut off. She couldn't even feel her fingers. Her head fell back as she fought the feeling of defeat, and she heard Urkha curse the gulo for slowing, heard the whip crack. The animal was all but done-in but the she-troll paid no heed. She would extract every last ounce of its energy.

The sleigh continued on. Petal lay shivering, legs drawn up to chest, her head on an old sack. Eyes closed. Snow swirled down on top of her, the fat flakes melting on her face and tickling her nose. Really tickling her nose. Unnaturally so in fact. She opened one eye. It wasn't snow … it was whiskers! Crumb's whiskers! Her other eye shot open and she stared at him in astonishment. He must have been in her pocket and slept through this entire event. He was sitting absolutely still now, staring at her with those bright black eyes. 'Oh Crumb,' she whispered sadly, 'We're really in the reindeer poo! The stinking beast of a troll knocked me senseless and tied me up. And she's stolen Ru's nose, and there won't be a Christmas delivery.'

Crumb gave a quick whisker-waggle and ran straight over her shoulder. If things weren't bad enough. Now she had to worry about Crumb. What if he fell off the sleigh? He'd freeze to death. She was about to call him when she felt something on her hands. There was just enough sensation left to feel the little claws. She knew immediately what he was doing. Minutes later her hands were free and the twine fell away. She eased her arms in front of her and rubbed her hands fiercely to regain circulation. Crumb was chewing away at the string around her ankles. Job done he scampered back up to her shirt pocket and disappeared inside. 'Stay safe you fantastic magic mouse,' she whispered. With feeling pouring back into her fingers she lay down and pretended she was still tied up, in case Urkha turned round.

Urkha was getting angry. She didn't care if the stinking gulo was tired. She didn't care if its legs were worn down to stumps. She wanted to be back at the castle now. The elf in the back was trussed up like a wild turkey, and she knew it was going to taste better than any bird. Mostly she wanted to sit and gloat over her trophy in the black bag ... the light of the elves! Their passport to Christmas! Revenge was feeling sweet.

They were coming to a small copse of about twenty stunted pines. The path meandered through the middle, narrowing in places where it passed between large rocks, or where trees grew close on either side. It took all of Urkha's attention to keep the gulo up to speed and navigate the narrow path. She cursed and ducked the low branches which were even lower than usual with their dump of snow. After the copse the going would be easy.

It was late morning when she pulled up outside the castle gate. The gulo hung its head and shook with exhaustion as she got out to undo the padlock. She glanced into the back of the sleigh and stopped dead. It was empty! The twine lay in the bottom but the elf was gone. She let out a scream of pure rage. How could it have undone the string? She leapt back into her seat, livid at losing her prisoner, and whipped the wolverine back the way they had come. After four miles or so she gave up. There was nothing. Absolutely nothing. If the creep of an elf had jumped off she would have found tracks, but there wasn't a single footprint. It was her own fault, she had been so sure of the creature not being able to escape that she hadn't bothered to check it since the Crags. She wasn't going back that far. Anyway she still had a far greater prize to savour.

Petal hugged the trunk of the pine like it was her best friend and watched Urkha pass underneath for the second time, this time on her way home, empty-handed! She had been expecting the she-troll to come back and look for her. As soon as the sleigh was out of sight she clambered back down through the branches and dropped to the ground, brushing fallen snow off her head and shoulders. Thank heavens for the little copse, and those heavily laden boughs over the path. She had just managed to grab one and swing herself up as the sleigh slowed to navigate between two trees.

Now she stood in the middle of the path wondering what to do. Her hands were freezing from grabbing snowy branches. She shoved them deep in her jeans pockets, and felt the key. The key to the round-room! She'd completely forgotten it. If she hadn't had the row with Aleron it wouldn't be there. Mind you, nor would she have slept in the stable and be in this situation now. No time to think about that. Now she had the key she could get into the castle. The thought hit her like a flash. She could look for

Ru's light, maybe get it back, and save Christmas! Then she thought about having to creep through those long dark passages, that rabbit-warren of tunnels in the bowels of Christmas Castle. The idea didn't fill her with enthusiasm, in fact it scared her to death. But there was no one else to do it.

She set off, walking in the tracks that the gulo had made. Well before the castle walls she veered off through deep snow and struggled across to Tall Pine Wood, hoping that the falling snow would quickly cover her tracks. She skirted around the clearing and arrived at the secret door, now under deep snow.

Aleron dismounted and dropped Smooch's reins. They had come up and over the top of the Crags and it hadn't been easy. The snow was particularly deep and almost up to the reindeer's belly in some places. He had to give him a rest. Smooch nibbled disinterestedly at a clump of hazel while Aleron took shelter from the wind and snow under a big old fir tree. He kept wondering what was happening to Petal. Dark images crowded his mind. He pushed them roughly away, determined that he would find her safe and well. He was still a long way from Christmas Castle, but at least it was all down hill from here, and then flat across the

Snaggle Plains. It would take him a few more hours for sure.

Urkha barged into the kitchen dripping melted snow from her wild black mane and stood looking at Emlock with an evil grin. For some reason she had one arm tucked behind her back. Emlock returned her stare nervously. What was she up to? Had he done something wrong? She was about as stable as the weather these days. He was sure she'd gone a bit mad since Plague had got killed. He wondered where she had been for the last twenty-four hours.

'I have a little trophy!' she trilled.

Emlock looked even more nervous. A raging, ranting Urkha was reasonably normal, but a trilling one was positively macabre and a thousand times more scary. Had she gone completely over the edge? He tried to sound interested. 'Trophy? ... That's good. What is it?' He expected her to throw a severed bear's head or some other grotesque body part onto the table. Instead she leaned forward and gently set down a black bag with something inside it. A shaft of light seemed to be streaming from the loosely tied end. Emlock looked down at it and back up at her and frowned. Whatever was in there wasn't going to feed three of them. He decided she had completely flipped.

'You, have never seen anything like this in your life!' she crowed. She drew up a chair and sat down with the bag in front of her. 'Got any of that good wine you make?'

Emlock nodded and went down to the cellar. 'Good wine', she called it. She had changed! She never praised anything or anyone. He had recently been forced to hide the wine, to prevent Codweb from becoming permanently intoxicated. Back in the kitchen he put the stone jar on the table and pushed it and a mug towards Urkha. 'Good stuff, it's pear,' he said.

Urkha poured herself a mug full, 'It's celebration time!' she cried, and took a huge swallow. Then she poked a hairy finger towards the bag. 'This is a light! Not just *any* light. *This* is the light that those stinking elves and that murdering wizard use to light their way on their famous delivery to the humans! They need it in foul weather. And they'll need it tomorrow night!' She started to roar with uncontrolled laughter.

The sound brought Codweb out of his hole. He sidled into the kitchen and stared at Urkha in amazement.

'I've stolen their light!' she chortled, and refilled her mug. Then she gently stroked the black bag. Codweb looked at Emlock, Emlock shrugged and rolled his eyes. 'Food!' she suddenly shouted, slapping her hands down on the kitchen table with a bang, 'Get us some food, I'm starving!' Emlock went for venison steaks. He came back, heated a pan and threw them in. 'While you're at it the gulo needs a spot of grub too. I think it's on its last legs.' Emlock's heart sank. He'd promised himself to look after the creature for Hibu.

'I'll take him the scraps,' he said, 'Keep an eye on the steaks.' A while later he returned to find the kitchen full of black smoke. Urkha, now definitely the worse for wear after two large mugs of pear wine, was giggling uncontrollably and caressing her prize. Codweb was watching Urkha with fascination and pouring his second mug. Emlock cursed them. The kitchen stank. The gulo had looked half-dead. He was fed up. The steaks were burnt but Urkha ate them and didn't even seem to notice. She was playing with the bag, opening the end and letting a flash of brilliant light out, then closing it again, and cackling 'ON! OFF! ON! OFF!' as she did so.

The light! Emlock's memory was suddenly jolted back to the pictures Urkha had shown him just before she went off on her little expedition, the reindeer at the front of the sleigh with the brightly shining nose. He looked at the lump in the bag, and suddenly felt sick.

30

Lost

The entrance to the hidden passage was blocked by drifted snow. Petal had to dig down to it with bare hands. She was freezing by the time she reached the door, which was rampant with ivy, the stems thick and resistant, hugging it for all they were worth. She pulled and tore and swore, once again wishing she had her penknife. Eventually it was free and unhindered and she was able to push it open until there was enough room to squeeze through. She crept in and promptly tripped over something. 'Dam!' she cursed as she sprawled headlong into the passage. She got up and turned around. A shaft of light from outside was falling on a number of candles that were rolling round the floor. She looked at them and frowned. There were eight. She thought back. Seven elves and Elestyal! They must have left them here all those years ago before they flew to Iffi. What a bonus. She thanked her lucky stars. She still had matches in her pocket from lighting the oil lamp in the stable. Now she wouldn't have to feel her way along the tunnel in the pitch dark. What a relief. Should she lock the door behind her? No, she decided she may need a hasty exit.

With one candle lit and two spares in her pocket she started along the musty passageway. She walked softly, slowly, her thoughts all over the place. Ten years ago they had all rushed along here to escape the Zorils. She and Aleron had fallen out over something that she'd said. That trend had continued she thought wryly. She looked up and around at the old passage carved through the rock and wondered how long ago it had been built, and who had used it to escape, and from what. She remembered that it went straight to the round-room, that cold eerie underground place that had once given her a chill as she passed through it. Perks had told her that it was there that they had created the silver spell, and that it used to be a magician's room.

She had come to some steps, and vaguely recalled that they went down to the round-room door. She wound her way carefully down holding the candle aloft. She couldn't afford to slip and fall and end up with a twisted ankle. Suddenly the door was in front of her, strung with cobwebs; unopened for ten years. Now she had to find the key. It had to be behind a loose stone, like the one she and Skyler had found at the entrance. She scanned the walls and noticed a pinkish one lower down. It looked loose. It was the right place. She pulled out the key and pushed it into the lock. Strangely, after years of disuse, it turned smoothly. Gingerly, holding her breath, she turned the handle and pushed on the door. The hinges gave a small groan. The sound, in the otherwise deathly quiet, made her shudder. And then the smell hit her. A stale rank odour, of something burned. Petal wrinkled her nose and put her hand over her mouth. The place was as cold as a grave. She edged nervously across the room, glancing quickly this way and that, half expecting something to leap out of the shadows. The candlelight picked out the tall spiral staircase winding its way up into darkness. She was about to mount the first step when she noticed a stub of a candle in a small holder sitting on the edge of a stair a bit higher up. Maybe left by one of the elves?

On the way up the stairs Petal's mind had started racing. She had no idea where the key to the trap door was hidden. She could be down here for days searching for it, in this stink! And when she got up into the passage, if she ever did, then how on earth would she find her way to the main part of the castle? And then there were the trolls! Panic could so easily set in. She must take it one step at a time. When she got to the top of the stairs, just for the hell of it, she put down her candle and reached up to the trap. She gave a push, expecting resistance. Astonishingly there was none. Her mind whirled. Someone must have been down here since the elves left. She knew they would have locked everything very carefully behind them to keep the passage secret. Who could have found the secret room? And what about the smell? She shook her head. No point in wondering, she must just keep going.

The trap door pushed up and open easily on silent hinges. Petal stepped up into the narrow passage with her candle held aloft, left the trap open and looked around. It was warmer up here and nice to get away from that smell. She tried to get her bearings, and felt sure they had come from the right when they came down here. She walked quietly on and quickly came to a junction where the narrow passage joined a much wider one. Her heart sank. She didn't have a clue which way to go. It was a fifty-fifty choice. She chose right and followed the wider tunnel for ages. Eventually it came to a place where it split three ways. This was crazy. It was a lottery. She decided to bear sharp left. Her candle had burned to a stub so she lit another and carried on. Another junction further along forced another choice and so on until she was hopelessly lost. Panic gripped her. She could die down here.

An hour later the last candle was nearly gone and she was no nearer finding the entrance to the main part of the castle. She had arrived in a dank passage where there were three little rooms that looked like prison cells. They had an ominous air about them. Each had a small barred window set in the top of a solid door. She half expected a face to appear, a fleshless zombie pleading to be freed, with its skeletal hands groping through the bars. She shuddered. One door still had a rusty key in the lock. Her heart thumped. She wasn't locked in a cell but she felt just as much a prisoner down here. She was still staring at one of the cell windows in morbid fascination when the candle flickered and died, throwing her into inky blackness. She squealed in terror and backed up against the wall, hardly able to breathe. She was never going to get out. She was going to die down here, in the dark. Her world closed in and she sank to the floor and sobbed. It would have been better to have stayed in the sleigh and died quickly at the hands of Urkha. Anything would be better than slow, wandering starvation, down here in the bowels of the earth. In the dark.

A small movement against her chest made her jump. *Crumb!* What would happen to him now? He would die of starvation too and it would be her fault. She put her hand up to her pocket and he ran onto her palm. He felt warm and soft. She held him gently against her cheek. 'I'm sorry,' she whispered, 'I've made a right mess of things.' He nuzzled her cheek for a second and then he slipped off her hand and was gone. 'Crumb! Come back!' she squealed, 'Please don't leave me ... stupid mouse ... where are you? Crumb! *Crummy?* She laid down flat on the floor hoping he would climb onto her. Nothing. 'Crumb!' She must feel for him. She spread out her arms and did very slow swimming motions, at the same time thinking how ridiculous she must look, lying here in the dark 'swimming' after a mouse. Then she felt him touch her hand, and run off again. 'Not the time for games Crumb,' she called frantically. Again, he was on her right hand and then gone. She slid further to the right and gently fanned her hand. There he was! She scooped him up. But as she did so her fingers caught in something ... some sort of fine twine! In an instant she knew he meant her to find it. What was it for? What was it attached to? She popped Crumb back in her pocket and stood up holding it loosely in her hand, then, with it running gently through her fingers she started walking. Ten minutes later she was back at the trap door to the round-room. She knew this because she walked straight into the edge of the lid and bashed her shin, at the same time thanking her lucky stars that she hadn't fallen down the hole. Relief flooded through her. She wasn't going to die after all. She followed the twine to its end and picked up the ball, then she tied it securely to the handrail at the top of the staircase. She started thinking. If it ended here, where did it begin? Only one way to find out. After twenty minutes following it back she saw light up ahead, a thin stream peeping under a doorway. The string was attached to the door-handle. Whoever had laid this trail had saved her life.

Urkha had had enough wine, and enough of Codweb and Emlock's company. She was dog tired from her expedition and more than a little pleased with the results of her labours. Too bad she'd lost the elf. Maybe she'd go back and bag another one in a few days. She got up, pushed her chair back, and headed to her room in the tower. It was cold. A few snowflakes blew in through the open window. She wandered over and watched the storm for a while, then lay down on her old mattress, hugging the black nosebag close to her chest. It was only a few minutes before wine and tiredness overtook her and she was snoring.

Codweb got up from the table and staggered to the

larder. He needed something to snack on. Grabbing an armful of meat, bread and apples he waddled off to his room before Emlock could catch him. Hopefully the skinny troll was down in the cellars, making more wine. He'd told Codweb only yesterday that they'd run out, and then produced a jar for Urkha today. Little liar! He yawned and lay down on his bed. Should he nibble on the raw steak or an apple? Before he could decide he'd nodded off.

Petal looked at the door in front of her. It was no good standing here forever. Sooner or later she had to go through it. She remembered that on the other side was a small hall where Elestyal's room had been, and then stairs that went up to the kitchen. With her heart in her mouth she grabbed the door handle, twisted, and pushed. It opened easily, scraping a flagstone lightly as it went. The hall was empty and there were no sounds from above.

She decided to slip into Elestyal's old room and see what was in there. Hibu had told them it had also been his room while he was imprisoned. She left the door ajar and went to the tall cupboard. Unlikely she'd find any sort of weapon to defend herself with in here. She was right. There were a few pots of Hibu's home-made medicines, a pair of socks and not much else.

She was just stretching up and feeling around on the shelf above when she heard a movement behind her. She turned, fear filling her, and found herself looking straight at a troll. It was a much smaller and skinnier one than Urkha, and it was looking at her with an expression of amazement. They stared at one another for some seconds, then the troll eased the door shut behind him and said, 'Who are you?' in a raspy sort of whisper.

Petal swallowed. 'I'm ... I'm an elf!' she said, flattening herself against the cupboard and wondering why he'd shut the door so softly.

'Where are you from? How did you get in?' The tone wasn't aggressive; more curious.

'I live at Castle Iffi, over the Crags, and I came through the secret passageway.' Might as well tell the truth now she was cornered.

'You walked here?' he sounded disbelieving.

'No ... the big troll ... she caught me in our barn, and tied me up. She came after one of our reindeer. She brought me back on the sleigh but I escaped about a mile from the castle.' Why wasn't he calling his mates?

Emlock stared at her. He hadn't seen many elves. Certainly never a female. She was cute, in an elvish sort of way, with those big violet eyes. What on earth was he going to do? Where had all his troll instincts gone? He should have throttled her by now. But somehow he was rooted to the spot. 'Do you know Hibu?' he asked gruffly.

'Hibu? Yes! He lives with us. Are you ... are you by any chance his friend Emlock?'

'He said I was his friend?'

It *was* Emlock! Maybe he would help her and not hand her over to Urkha. 'Yes,' said Petal, 'He spoke well of you. He felt very bad about the way he had to leave without saying goodbye.'

A warm feeling crept through the skinny troll. Then he looked at Petal again and his expression changed. 'You have to get out of here!' he whispered, 'Urkha will kill you. I can't help you very much, or she'll kill me too.'

'She has something I have to get back,' whispered Petal.

'The reindeer's light.' The troll nodded slowly.

'You saw it?' Petal tried to stop her excitement.

'I saw a black bag with a beam of light coming from it,' said Emlock, 'And Urkha was crowing about how she's sabotaged your delivery to the humans.'

'I have to get it back. Not for me, or for the elves. It's for people all over the world, for the children.'

Emlock was shaking his head. 'It's impossible! You'll never get it back from Urkha. Save your own life and leave now, while you still can!'

'Where is she?' asked Petal stubbornly, 'Where would she take it?'

Emlock sighed, 'The tower room, in the north tower, the one overlooking the main courtyard. She sleeps up there.'

'My room was up there when we lived here. I'll find my way. What about the other trolls?'

'There's only one and he's probably sleeping, he has a room below Urkha's.'

'Hibu said there were four of you. What about the other one?'

'Urkha's son?' Emlock shook his head, 'He won't be bothering you, he came to a sticky end the day after Hibu left.'

Before he could say more Petal had slipped past him and was heading silently up the stairs.

'Please come back! She'll kill you!' hissed Emlock.

It was ten years since Petal, as a young elf girl, had run up the stairs of the north tower of Christmas Castle. Ten years, but the memories flooded back. She remembered every room, every inch of the place. Light-footed, silent and fast she headed for the top, to the tower room. Silently she slipped up the last few steps. The door was open and she could hear gentle snoring.

Urkha lay on her side on the grungy mattress still clasping the velvet bag to her chest with both hands, as though someone in a dream was trying to prize it away from her. Petal peered around the door at the sparsely furnished room. The troll's bed was just a few yards away with the head against the wall. Also against the wall and this side of the bed was a big old chest heaped with animal skins. A blue and white enamel water pitcher was perched on the corner. Petal checked the floor, no rug. Nothing to trip over. I just need Aleron's troll dagger she thought, and I could finish her off right here, but I don't even have a damn penknife! If Urkha woke up she would have to depend on her speed and agility. She watched the velvet bag gently rise and fall with the troll's breathing. Suddenly there was a grunt as Urkha cleared her throat and changed position, letting one hand drop limply away from the bag. Petal jumped at the sudden noise, and then waited five long minutes hoping the other hand would relax too, but it didn't. She couldn't wait any longer.

 Holding her breath she tiptoed across the room to the bed. Urkha stank of wine, and smoke from burned venison. She was drooling as she slept, her mouth half-open, one fang-like incisor hooked over her bottom lip. Petal's heart thumped as she looked down on the beast. Taking the bag in one hand she gently opened each of Urkha's fingers until it pulled free, then she started to back carefully out of the room. She'd got it! All she had to do now was to get to the passage and escape and Urkha would be none the wiser. She was giving a little mental cheer at the exact moment that she caught her elbow on the handle of the enamel water pitcher. The thing went flying, crashing and clanging as it hit bare floorboards and rolled. It was followed by a grunt as Urkha was jerked out of her slumber. She shook her head, befuddled and surprised, and stared straight at Petal. The she-elf? Here in her room! What the ... ? Then she saw the bag in Petal's hand, and she roared.

Petal ran. She was as fleet as a deer and almost as agile. She tore down the spiral steps in the tower, through the great hall, down the steps to the kitchen, and on down towards the door to the tunnels.

Urkha's howls of rage woke Codweb. He leapt off his bed in a panic and threw open the door just in time to see a strange elf-like figure pass by. A few seconds later Urkha hurtled after it. Excited by the chase he joined in and tore after them.

Emlock, who had been pacing the kitchen and chewing

his nails, saw Petal fly through. He heard Urkha's murderous roars coming closer as the she-troll gave chase. He could slow her! He quickly slipped a couple of chairs into the gangway and then nipped into the larder. Urkha came around the corner like a charging bull, fell straight over the first chair and head-butted the second. She let out a wild bellow, accentuated when Codweb, who had no time to stop, joined her and they both ended in a tangled heap on the floor.

'FOOL!' shrieked Urkha. Then, 'FOLLOW ME!' as she picked herself up. They tore off down the back stairs. Urkha threw open the door to Hibu's old room. Nothing! Then the door to the tunnels. She was just in time to glimpse Petal disappearing into the dark further up.

'There she is!'

Codweb was beginning to wish he'd stayed in bed. Emlock let them go then picked up a couple of candles and followed at a cautious distance.

As Petal dived through the door into the tunnels she pushed Ru's light deep into her shirt underneath her jacket. She couldn't risk dropping it. Then she grabbed the twine and headed into the darkness as fast as she dared. Damn, if only she'd had time she'd have untied it from the door handle so no one else could follow it. She felt it guiding her around a corner at the same moment as she heard a shout. Light shot up the passage for a second through the open door. The she-troll was coming.

31

The Last Battle

Aleron left Smooch in Tall Pine Wood next to the clearing and stumbled through the deep drifts towards the secret door. He had decided he would try to break it down somehow, kick it in, or maybe pick the lock with the troll's knife. If he was going to get Petal back he needed an element of surprise. No good going to the main gates, which according to Hibu were padlocked anyway. When he arrived he couldn't believe his eyes. It was open! Just a couple of inches, but it *was* open! How could it be? Who would use it? Especially when the key was missing. Who had another key? He must be careful.

As soon as he stepped into the old passage he saw the small pile of candles lying by the wall. They must have been left by the elves all that time ago, or maybe by the person who had left the door open? He grabbed up three, put two in his pocket and lit one. Then he set off down the silent tunnel into the bowels of the castle, thinking as Petal had, about how they'd walked here ten years ago. It was an eerie journey in the candlelight, musty and dank, the only sound, his own breathing. Eventually he reached the stone steps that wound down to the entrance to the round-room. Then it would be the spiral staircase up to the long section of twisting passages to the main body of the castle. How on earth was he going to navigate that? As he started down the steps he thought he heard a distant howl. A troll!

Petal's lungs were burning as she stumbled to the corner where the string did a sharp right into the narrow passage where the trap door was. She could hear the footfalls of more than one troll behind her and they were catching up. Like her, they'd had no time to grab candles. She jogged along the passage, hugging the wall and flailing in front of her with her left arm to feel for the lid of the trap which she had left open. Clunk! Her hand hit it. She let go of the string and slipped down onto the top step, then down and around as fast as she could go. She heard Urkha above her. God it was SO dark! How would she find the door before Urkha caught her up. She could use Ru's light, but then she'd give her position away. Jumping off the last step in a panic she slipped left and dodged around behind the stairs. There she sat petrified, not even breathing.

The she-troll didn't like this room. She had never been down here, and she didn't want to be here now. It still smelled of her dead son, and gave her a very bad feeling, but not as bad as the thought of the vile little elf escaping with her trophy. No! That could not happen. She wanted the elf. She wanted its neck in her powerful fingers. She wanted to squeeze, squeeze, squeeze! More than that she wanted that light back. She swung down to the ground in the pitch black silence. The room was freezing cold. She was sure some evil lurked down here. Where was her prey?

'Come here foul creature!' she hissed. 'Come here and die!' It was then that Aleron opened the door.

The last thing he expected to be greeted by when he stepped into the round-room was the incensed and menacing figure of Urkha. The she-troll, on the hunt for Petal, swung round sharply as she heard the door open, and saw the light from Aleron's candle. She was equally surprised, having never known about the passage that led off from this room. It was a big room and Urkha was a good distance from the door. Aleron's jaw dropped as he stared at the beast. Petal had tried to fight *this?* In an instant he was backing round the room, the she-troll's own hunting knife in his hand.

Petal, peering from behind the staircase, was astonished

at the sight of him. Her heart flipped at the thought that he'd come to find her. She was about to scream out for him to be careful but stopped herself. Instead she dodged further round the staircase. Urkha was growling and hissing as she advanced towards this new intruder. Two in one day! This one must have come looking for the female. A fine dinner the trolls would be having tonight! Aleron backed up step by step, brandishing the knife. He had never been in a serious fight in his life, and this was not the best one to be cutting his teeth on. He thought of his troll-dagger and wished he was as good at wielding weapons as he was at making them. Nothing like a challenge he thought, girding himself with his own anger. 'Stinking troll!' he cursed. 'What have you done with her?

Urkha shrieked and then hissed at him, 'Eaten her! I've eaten her! And you're going to be my next course!'

Petal wanted to shout that she was fine, but something told her to stay hidden. Then she stood on something. There was a small crunching sound. She bent down and felt around her. *Bones!* Something ... someone ... had died down here! She thought about the strange smell hanging around in the room and cringed. Who was it? How had it happened? Maybe she could use a bone to club Urkha with? A big one preferably. It was better than nothing. She started groping around in the dark, recoiling as her fingers bumped into more of the grim remains. The skull! Ugh! Aleron's candle was moving closer and closer as Urkha stalked him. The she-troll suddenly dodged sideways and he stumbled as he tried to swing the candle and keep her in the light. For a second the candle flared in Petal's direction and glinted on something beside her foot. Something metallic. Could it be a knife? Please let it be a knife. Desperately she felt for whatever it was. Her fingers flew from bone to bone. Large ones and small ones, short ones and long ones. A skeletal hand! She could tell by the shape. And clenched in the fingers was the metal thing. She pulled it free.

Aleron was backing up fast towards her around the staircase when Urkha lunged. Now the she-troll spied her too.

'Ah!' she screamed, 'The *thief*. No good hiding, miserable she-elf, I'm going to wring your little neck when I get hold of it!'

The light from Aleron's candle now fell on the object in Petal's hand. Not a knife. A hand mirror of all things! Maybe silver judging by the weight? She peered closer and in the amber light she could just make out the elves engraved around one edge. Instantly it made sense. The dead creature and the piece of silver. It must be the other troll, the one that Emlock said came to a sticky end.

Aleron, wondering who on earth Urkha was talking to, cast a quick glance over his shoulder and was amazed to see Petal crouching under the stairs.

'Petal!' he yelled, 'RUN! Get out of here! Get to the door!'

'Not without you!' she yelled back.

Urkha charged. She came at Aleron head down intending to knock this new elf straight into his little friend and take them both out. She reckoned he couldn't use the knife against her and hold onto the candle at the same time. If he dropped the knife he was unarmed, and if he dropped the candle she'd stalk him in the dark. But she wasn't expecting him to be so fast. He leapt sideways and she ran straight past and had to turn back. Now her temper was up. She growled and spat and bristled as she started another foray. This time Aleron went for the stairs, leaping up the first four in one go. She was after him in a flash, but being higher up gave him an advantage. His feet were level with her face as she came at him. He kicked out, catching her on her nose and sending her reeling backwards, only to pick herself up and come in for another assault. Still on the step, Aleron waited till the right moment and let out a second vicious kick. But she was cunning, expected it, threw her head sideways and grabbed his ankle. She hauled him off the stairs effortlessly and threw him half way across the room. The knife skittered across the floor and the candle bounced, rolled, and snuffed itself out.

In the sudden pitch dark all Petal could hear was struggling, then Aleron screaming. Then he was wheezing and gasping. Urkha was killing him! Petal dug desperately in her shirt for the velvet bag, found it, and pulled it out. Ru's light streamed from the open end. It drowned the round-room in its brilliance. Urkha hardly seemed to notice. She was far too intent upon throttling Aleron. When she'd finished with this one she'd murder the thieving she-elf. She leaned harder on Aleron, thumbs dug into his windpipe for all she was worth.

The sudden intense pain in her side surprised her, stopped her, made her gasp and sit up. There was a puzzled look in her yellow eyes as she swung her powerful head and looked down at her own hunting knife embedded in her side, then back up at Petal. Petal rubbed the dust off the silver mirror. Elestyal's mirror. She shoved it in front of Urkha's face and held it steady.

Freezing air exploded through the half-open door, slamming it back against the wall, and engulfing the round-room in an icy vortex. Fine sand and dust were sucked up, and spun on the current. It gathered Plague's bones and scattered them, hurling his skull at the staircase.

Petal hung on to the mirror.

And now a voice, riding on the air-currents. A powerful, whispering voice.

'Megar! ... ' it called.
Meee -gar! ...
Sassilvashakalim! ...
Sassilvashakalim! ...
SASSILVASHAKALIM! ... '

The ghostly whisper filled the room, rising and falling, echoing and caressing as the icy blast whipped Petal's hair into her face. She clung to the mirror. She hung on until Urkha stopped screaming. Until the air was full of smoke. And the acrid stench of burning troll made her eyes water.

Aleron was coughing and spluttering and trying to push the heavy she-troll off him when another uproar started at the top of the staircase. Petal looked up, wondering what could possibly happen next, only to see a figure flip over the handrail and tumble headlong towards them. It let out a blood-curdling wail before crashing onto the floor with a sickening dull thud.

'Oh please, not Emlock!' she whispered. She slipped the mirror into her pocket and helped Aleron out from under the dead weight of Urkha.

'That was a bit close!' he said shakily, looking down at the grisly and blackened remains, still smouldering beside them.

Petal hugged him hard, 'You saved my life,' she mumbled as shock and tears overtook her.

'Actually,' said Aleron, 'I think *you* saved *mine*!'

'Wanna argue about it?'

'No! I'm finished arguing with you.' He pulled her close and kissed her. 'How did you do it?'

'Do what?'

'Kill the damn beast?'

'With this,' Petal showed him the mirror she had found amongst the charred bones behind the staircase. 'I can't believe it, it's Elestyal's. Look at the engraving. It's the one he lost the day we all left here, it's the partner to the silver comb that Frisk found in the forest. Elestyal thought both must have fallen out of his suit at the same time, but they didn't, the mirror must have fallen when he was carrying his suit down the stairs. It killed Urkha's son. I found the bones under the staircase. I was only guessing when I thought it might have enough of the old spell left in it to kill Urkha.'

Aleron narrowed his eyes and pulled her closer to him, 'What if it hadn't worked?'

Petal shrugged, 'I'd have left you in her murderous clutches and made a quick escape. Couldn't hang about, I have to get Ru's nose back to Iffi!' She held up the velvet bag.

Aleron nodded knowingly, 'I always knew I meant less to you than a reindeer's nose.'

'Not just *any* reindeer,' said Petal in mock surprise, 'It's Ru's.'

'I'll hear how you managed to get that back later, in the meantime ... ' A cough from above stopped him. 'Not more of them,' he whispered, casting anxious eyes up to the trap door.

The cough came cautiously again, but no one appeared. A raspy voice asked 'Are you elves okay?'

'Emlock!' cried Petal, 'Thank goodness it's you!'

'Yes, it is me,' continued the voice, 'I'm afraid my friend Codweb was coming down to join the fight and he ... er ... tripped. I'm rather glad he didn't fall on anyone. I just wanted to say that if you would like some tea in the kitchen please come up. But could you please keep that piece of silver out of sight. I just knew Codweb never had the guts to take it to the well.'

'We would love tea,' called Petal, 'And the mirror will be stowed away in a safe place. You're safe Emlock.'

'Tea with a troll?' Aleron raised an eyebrow.

'He's Hibu's friend. He helped me tonight. Come on.'

They shut the round-room door and picking up Urkha's keys they took a last glance around at the grisly remains of Urkha, Codweb, and the bones of Plague lying next to his mother.

'Mother and son together,' murmured Petal as she slipped the mirror into her deepest pocket. Then they allowed Ru's light to guide their way back to the kitchen.

Emlock placed two steaming mugs of sweet tea in front of them as they sat down. 'I am very glad you're okay,' he said. Then to Aleron, 'She's a very brave female if you don't mind me saying so.'

Aleron groaned and rolled his eyes, 'She's too damn brave, that's the trouble with her.' He turned to Petal, 'So, how on earth did you manage to escape Urkha? And get Ru's light back?'

Petal briefly told him her story, describing how Crumb had saved her life twice, once by chewing through her bonds, and then by helping her find the string in the passages. On hearing his name he woke up and squeezed his head out of her buttoned pocket.

Aleron shook his head, 'Still sleeping just as much then.'

'Magic mice need extra rest don't they Crumb?' Petal gently caressed one of his ears.

Aleron suddenly remembered Smooch, 'I must go and get him,' he said, 'He'll need feed and water before we leave. We have to get Ru's light back as soon as we can.'

The three of them trudged across the courtyard through deep snow to the castle gate while high above them the snow-vultures circled in the storm, screeching and *quarking*.

Emlock looked up, 'They've seen something.'

Aleron used Urkha's keys to unlock the gate. Drifts were piled against it. It took a few minutes to clear them and then Aleron stepped through. 'I'll go round to the wood and get Smooch,' he shouted against the driving snow and wind. Seconds later they heard him shout again, 'Elestyal! Elestyal's here!'

32

The Sleighrider Girl

Elestyal, Hibu, and a dozen elves sat around the table in Christmas Castle kitchen. Emlock was trying to find more mugs for tea. He was both amazed and thrilled at how they had all accepted him. Hibu had given him the biggest smile and shaken his hand. He didn't ever remember feeling so ... happy. So proud. Strange feelings for a troll he thought to himself.

Aleron and Petal were fielding questions.

'Tell us what happened!' said Perks eagerly.

'How in the world did you manage to escape ... *and* kill the she-troll?' asked Skyler wide-eyed.

'How did Aleron manage to find you?' put in Jake.

Aleron and Petal gave potted editions of their stories amidst gasps of wonder and the shaking of heads.

'So what piece of silver was it that was lying around in the round-room?' asked Elestyal, puzzled.

'Well I'd show you,' said Petal, 'But I've promised Emlock I'll keep it well out of sight until we're away from the castle. I do have this though. Very carefully she eased the black velvet bag from inside her shirt, and handed over Ru's light. 'It's amazing. I thought it would die if it wasn't part of Ru any more.'

'It's the energy,' said Elestyal with a sense of wonder, 'The Christmas energy is still flowing to it because it's part of Ru. It's quite incredible! I really didn't know if it would survive. We must get it back to him as quickly as we can. We'll rest a while here. The deer need to rest too, and finish their food.'

'Can someone give me a lift back?' asked Petal.

Emlock put three more mugs of tea on the table and wondered what life would be like completely on his own. He had no home, no companions, nothing. He somehow didn't feel he wanted to join a new pack of Zorils even if he had the opportunity. He was much changed since he had come here. But this castle belonged to the elves. The Zorils had taken it from them. There was no place for him here now.

Hibu noticed the shadow pass across the troll's lined face. He turned to Petal. 'You can take the deer that I rode,' he said, 'I won't be needing it. I'm going to stay here and give Emlock a hand to clear up a bit.'

'Good idea and much appreciated,' said Elestyal, 'It

would be nice' to know the old place is being looked after.'

'I can stay?' Emlock drew a stool up between the wizard and the Erudite and looked from one to the other in astonishment.

'We'll be most upset if you don't,' said Elestyal.

'I could teach you how to make some good remedies … for chest colds and the like,' said Hibu, 'And some new wines.'

Emlock's face cracked into an enormous grin. He pulled a mug of tea towards him. 'Oh I would like that *very* much!'

After a lengthy rest and a simple meal of bread and cheese and apples, which was all Emlock could offer them, the little company mounted up and were ready to start the long journey back to Iffi. It was already late in the afternoon. They would be travelling in the dark.

Aleron came over to Hibu, 'I don't like to think of you here without a mount of any sort,' he said, 'You keep Cedar, the deer you came on. Who knows, you may want to pop over the Crags and visit us in the New Year.'

'What about you?'

'I'll double-up with Petal, we'll ride Smooch back. He can easily carry both of us.' Perks overheard him, and with a gleam in his eye nudged Skyler.

Wrapped snugly for the journey in warm clothes, capes and hoods, and each carrying a lantern, the elves set off, waving a last farewell to Hibu and Emlock who were standing by the gate. They were soon enveloped by the dark, snow-filled night.

Petal had never felt so safe. She rode in front of Aleron who had both arms around her as he guided Smooch's reins. She leaned her head back on his chest and sighed. 'I certainly hope I never have another adventure like that again.'

Aleron hugged her a little closer, 'So do I, I don't think I'm very good at fighting large she-trolls.'

'You were amazing.'

'No, it was you who killed her remember, while she was choking the life out of me.'

'Rubbish,' muttered Petal, 'I just waved the mirror at her. It was Elestyal's spell that finished her off.' She thought back to the moment, to the strange whispering voice and the power of the energy in the round-room. A shiver ran through her. 'Magic is a scary thing,' she said softly.

The wind blew a gale across the Snaggle Plains, driving the snow into a flat white world and sculpting the stunted trees into weird statue-like shapes. At the Crags it had drifted badly, filling the narrow path up the mountain. Perks who was on the lead reindeer stopped and called Elestyal.

'I think we may need a bit of help here!'

Elestyal moved into the lead and suddenly there was a tremendous roaring-whoosh! Snow cascaded in towering plumes on either side of the path. Aleron and Petal, riding behind Perks, both jumped.

'What's he doing?' shouted Petal.

'Blowing the snow away,' yelled Perks over the din, 'He's remembered one of his old spells.'

Aleron was shaking his head in amusement, 'I wondered how he made such good time getting here.'

With the wizard clearing the deep snow as they went it made travelling easy. The reindeer trotted along an almost bare path as they rode on, up and over the Crags and down the River Path to Bearban. A while later, tired and weary, they arrived in the courtyard at Castle Iffi. It was Christmas Eve.

Christmas Eve supper time at Iffi was as usual taken in the enormous old parlour. Holly, pine and fir decorated the walls and fireplace, and framed the old slit windows, where tall white candles burned. Tinsel glittered amongst the red berries of the holly and the white of the mistletoe. In the centre of the room the ancient tables were set. Everything sparkled: glasses, dishes and cutlery on the red cloths. An enormous oak log burned steadily on the hearth, scenting the room now and then with little puffs of sweet wood smoke.

At six o'clock Skyler rang the supper bell and folk started to wander in. Soon the gathering was complete. Petal and Aleron found they had been placed either side of Elestyal. Flower had bagged the chair next to Petal, and Iceace, who had joined them (for salad only) sat on a tall stool next to her. There was a double sense of anticipation tonight in the buzz of conversation. Not only was it delivery night, but there was also a fabulous story to be heard. Only snippets and rumours had met their ears so far. They had already heard that Ru was fully recovered and had been successfully reunited with his stolen nose. Elestyal had told them that his light had fused with him instantly, and that he had never seen such rapid healing.

The first course on the supper menu was soup, but before they started Elestyal stood up and called for quiet.

'There is a long and quite extraordinary tale to be told this evening,' he said, 'but first we'll eat. Petal and Aleron can tell their tale afterwards. Save your curiosity until after pudding!'

There were groans of disappointment as he sat down. They wanted it now! A blow-by-blow account from Petal. How had she dared to attack the she-troll with a penknife? How had she escaped and got into the secret passage? Where did she find the nerve to try to steal Ru's light back - right out of Urkha's hands they'd heard! And how had she and Aleron won the battle to the death in the round-room? There was so much to hear that they could barely contain themselves. Petal was their heroine. Without her there would have been no Christmas this year. She had shrugged off the compliments so far, saying that it wasn't just her doing, and that she couldn't have done it without the help of Aleron and Emlock, not to mention Crumb.

There was a buzz of excited anticipation in the old parlour as the pudding came round. Skyler's mince pies with succulent home-made mincemeat in delicate warm pastry, and the option of cream or custard. For some reason everyone except Petal seemed to finish extremely quickly, then they sat and watched her in silence. Sensing all eyes upon her she looked up. Then she laughed and crammed the remains of her second pie in, in one go. Perks stifled a chuckle. Some things would never change. Petal did hamster impressions, chewed and swallowed.

'Okay,' she said at last, 'First of all there is something you all have to know. I had help escaping from Urkha.' No one said a word. They waited, all ears, wondering who on earth the person was. Petal dropped her head and started undoing the button on her shirt pocket. A sleepy head appeared, and then Crumb slipped onto her palm. He sat up and looked around, chest immaculately white and whiskers quivering. She lifted him up for all to see. 'This is the guy you really need to thank,' she said quietly, 'When I was trussed up like a Christmas parcel in Urkha's sleigh he chewed through the twine and set me free. And when I was lost, with no light, in the maze of dark passages under the castle, he took me to the string that led me back.' The room went quiet as everyone stared at Crumb, the wizard's mouse. Crumb washed his face and then his long whiskers, and then they could all have sworn he bowed. Either way he got a huge round of applause.

'Come on Petal,' shouted someone, 'Tell us what happened. From beginning to end!'

And so the story of the she-troll was told until they ran out of questions.

Time crept on. The delivery drew closer, and talk turned to the sleighriders who as usual were brimming with anticipation. Perks was sporting his ancient green hat which he dragged out every year to remind people that he had once had the honour. Aleron had already donned his brand new one. Petal felt seriously envious and ever so slightly jealous, but was determined to button her lip and not spoil the closeness that their recent adventure had brought them. Then Elestyal stood up and the room fell silent.

'I have a special announcement tonight,' he said. 'It is one I never thought I would make, that I never ever intended to make, but sometimes in life one has to accept change. I have been wrong about certain things. In some ways I suppose I haven't wanted to keep up with the times. But recent events have forced me to review my ... let's say, rather old-fashioned ideas.' Everyone around the table, with the exception of Aleron, was looking at him curiously as he continued. 'I have decided it's time to propose a review, a review of a tradition. And that the tradition is that only elf-guys ride the sleigh.'

Gasps of astonishment rippled around the table. Elestyal held up a hand and carried on. 'I have no choice,' he said, 'After what Petal has done. After what she has overcome during this dreadful attack on Ru, on us, ... on Christmas! Can any of you really say she's not worthy?'

Silence.

Petal stared up at Elestyal in amazement.

Jake, who had always been ardently against elf-chicks ever being considered, and had spoken up against Petal at every opportunity stood up. He looked straight at her. 'Take back all I said Petal. Anyone, male or female, who has had the courage to do what you've done, has every right to ride the sleigh. You have my vote any day!'

'Seconded!' cried Perks.

And then the whole room joined in.

'I'll take it that the motion is carried then!' shouted Elestyal over the cheers. Then he called for quiet again. 'I have one final announcement,' he said, putting his hand on Aleron's shoulder and looking down at him. 'As you all know Petal's name was drawn this year before she was actually allowed to take part in the draw. Aleron's name was then drawn afterwards.'

Silence fell.

'Aleron has asked me to tell you all that he wishes to give up his place on the sleigh this year, and that he would like Petal to have it.'

You could have heard a pin drop in the old parlour.

Petal looked absolutely stunned. She stared at Aleron open-mouthed. He promptly removed his sleighrider hat, leaned around Elestyal and set it on her head. 'Trouble is I don't think you'll fit my uniform,' he said with a grin.

'I can't believe you!' she whispered.

'Just *part* repayment for saving my life.'

'You mean there's more payment?' she whispered.

'Maybe when you get back,' He shrugged carelessly, but there was a gleam in his eye.

Hoots and whistles filled the old parlour, followed by cries of 'speech!'

'No speeches,' said Petal, 'I just want to say that if fighting a monster she-troll was what it took, at long last, to get elf-girls a place on the sleigh then it was worth it.'

'Girl-Power!' shouted Flower, shaking a fist in the air.

Petal leaned down and whispered in her ear, 'Always remember, if you really want something in life, never give up!'

At ten minutes to ten Elestyal was almost ready to walk over to the barn for the loading of the sleigh. He patted his large red-suited belly, tightened his belt a fraction, and adjusted his beard. Just a quick check on the old whiskers he said to himself. He pulled the red leather case from his pocket and took out the mirror. Bizz had polished it until it shimmered, just as she had ten years ago. He had missed it every Christmas since. Had it not fallen from his pocket when it did, what a different outcome it could have been for Petal and Aleron, and Christmas. He smiled and nodded slowly. Things always happened for a reason. He was sure of that.

Just before midnight, togged up in warm clothes, Hibu and Emlock stood expectantly in the courtyard at Christmas Castle, each holding a glass of Emlock's best pear wine, and staring around in the blizzard above. It wasn't long before the object of their anticipation appeared. A wonderful sleigh lit with tiny Christmas lights and pulled by eight reindeer swooped low over the castle. Ru's powerful light shone down and illuminated them for a few seconds as it passed overhead, then there was a tremendous '*WHOOSH*' and the magical jingling of a hundred silver bells as it climbed heavenwards. And on the wind the elves' cries of *Merry Christmas* was carried back to them.

'Merry Christmas!' cried Hibu and Emlock together as they raised their glasses.

'D'you know what,' said Emlock, his eyes still on the

point where the sleigh had disappeared.

'What?' said Hibu.

'I've got a picture of that.'

'You have?'

'Yes, Petal painted it a long time ago, come on I'll show you!'

Many miles away to the north a wolverine called Greole looked up at the strange light in the sky as it passed overhead. Then he turned and disappeared into the forest.

Website

judethompsonbooks.wordpress.com

Facebook

www.facebook.com/thewriterinthewoods/

Printed in Great Britain
by Amazon